**LARGE PRINT EDITION**

**RANDOM HOUSE**

*Also available*
*in Random House Large Print*
SAINT MAYBE

# LADDER OF YEARS

## ANNE TYLER

Published by Random House Large Print
in association with Alfred A. Knopf, Inc.
New York      1995

LIBRARY OF CONGRESS CATALOGING-IN-PUBLICATION DATA
Tyler, Anne.
Ladder of years / Anne Tyler.—
1st large print ed.
p.   cm.
ISBN 0–679–76225–6 (PB)
1. Missing persons—United States—Fiction.
2. Identity (Psychology)—Fiction.
3. Women—United States—Fiction.
4. Large type books.   I. Title.
[PS3570.Y45L33   1995b]
813'.54—dc20        94–47564        CIP

*Manufactured in the United States of America*
FIRST LARGE PRINT EDITION

This Large Print Book carries the
Seal of Approval of N.A.V.H.

# LADDER
## OF YEARS

## BALTIMORE WOMAN DISAPPEARS
## DURING FAMILY VACATION

Delaware State Police announced early today that Cordelia F. Grinstead, 40, wife of a Roland Park physician, has been reported missing while on holiday with her family in Bethany Beach.

Mrs. Grinstead was last seen around noon this past Monday, walking south along the stretch of sand between Bethany and Sea Colony.

Witnesses of her departure—her husband, Dr. Samuel Grinstead, 55, and her three children, Susan, 21, Ramsay, 19, and Carroll, 15—were unable to recall any suspicious characters in the vicinity. They reported that to the best of their recollection she simply strolled away. Her failure to return was not remarked until late afternoon.

A slender, small-boned woman with curly fair or light-brown hair, Mrs. Grinstead stands 5'2" or possibly 5'5" and weighs either 90 or 110 pounds. Her eyes are blue or gray or perhaps green, and her nose is mildly sunburned in addition to being freckled.

Presumably she was carrying a large straw tote trimmed with a pink bow, but family members could not agree upon her clothing. In all probability it was something pink or blue, her husband suggested, either frilled or lacy or "looking kind of baby-doll."

Authorities do not suspect drowning, since Mrs. Grinstead avoided swimming whenever possible and professed a distinct aversion to water. In fact, her sister, Eliza Felson, 52, has alleged to reporters that the missing woman "may have been a cat in her most recent incarnation."

Anyone with knowledge of Mrs. Grinstead's whereabouts is urged to contact the Delaware State Police at once.

I

This all started on a Saturday morning in May, one of those warm spring days that smell like clean linen. Delia had gone to the supermarket to shop for the week's meals. She was standing in the produce section, languidly choosing a bunch of celery. Grocery stores always made her reflective. Why was it, she was wondering, that celery was not called "corduroy plant"? That would be much more colorful. And garlic bulbs should be "moneybags," because their shape reminded her of the sacks of gold coins in folktales.

A customer on her right was sorting through the green onions. It was early enough so the store was nearly empty, and yet this person seemed to be edging in on her a bit. Once or twice the fabric of his shirt sleeve brushed her dress sleeve. Also, he was really no more than stirring those onions around. He would lift one rubber-banded clump and then drop it and alight on another. His fingers were very long and agile, almost spidery. His cuffs were yellow oxford cloth.

He said, "Would you know if these are called scallions?"

"Well, sometimes," Delia said. She seized the

nearest bunch of celery and stepped toward the plastic bags.

"Or would they be shallots?"

"No, they're scallions," she told him.

Needlessly, he steadied the roll of bags overhead while she peeled one off. (He towered a good foot above her.) She dropped the celery into the bag and reached toward the cup of twist ties, but he had already plucked one out for her. "What are shallots, anyway?" he asked.

She would have feared that he was trying to pick her up, except that when she turned she saw he was surely ten years her junior, and very good-looking besides. He had straight, dark-yellow hair and milky blue eyes that made him seem dreamy and peaceful. He was smiling down at her, standing a little closer than strangers ordinarily stand.

"Um . . . ," she said, flustered.

"Shallots," he reminded her.

"Shallots are fatter," she said. She set the celery in her grocery cart. "I believe they're above the parsley," she called over her shoulder, but she found him next to her, keeping step with her as she wheeled her cart toward the citrus fruits. He wore blue jeans, very faded, and soft moccasins that couldn't be heard above "King of the Road" on the public sound system.

"I also need lemons," he told her.

She slid another glance at him.

"Look," he said suddenly. He lowered his voice. "Could I ask you a big favor?"

"Um . . ."

"My ex-wife is up ahead in potatoes. Or not ex I guess but . . . estranged, let's say, and she's got her boyfriend with her. Could you just pretend we're together? Just till I can duck out of here?"

"Well, of course," Delia said.

And without even taking a deep breath first, she plunged happily back into the old high-school atmosphere of romantic intrigue and deception. She narrowed her eyes and lifted her chin and said, "We'll show *her*!" and sailed past the fruits and made a U-turn into root vegetables. "Which one is she?" she murmured through ventriloquist lips.

"Tan shirt," he whispered. Then he startled her with a sudden burst of laughter. "Ha, ha!" he told her too loudly. "Aren't you clever to say so!"

But "tan shirt" was nowhere near an adequate description. The woman who turned at the sound of his voice wore an ecru raw-silk tunic over black silk trousers as slim as two pencils. Her hair was absolutely black, cut shorter on one side, and her face was a perfect oval. "Why, Adrian," she said. Whoever was with her—some man or other—turned too, still gripping a potato. A dark, thick man with rough skin like stucco and eyebrows that met in the middle. Not up to the woman's standard at all; but how many people were?

Delia's companion said, "Rosemary. I didn't see you. So don't forget," he told Delia, not breaking his stride. He set a hand on her cart to steer it into aisle 3. "You promised me you'd make your marvelous blancmange tonight."

"Oh, yes, my . . . blancmange," Delia echoed faintly. Whatever blancmange might be, it sounded the way she felt just then: pale and plain-faced and skinny, with her freckles and her frizzy brown curls and her ruffled pink round-collared dress.

They had bypassed the dairy case and the juice aisle, where Delia had planned to pick up several items, but she didn't point that out because this Adrian person was still talking. "Your blancmange and then your, uh, what, your meat and vegetables and da-da-da . . ."

The way he let his voice die reminded her of those popular songs that end with the singers just absentmindedly drifting away from the microphone. "Is she looking at us?" he whispered. "Check it out. Don't make it obvious."

Delia glanced over, pretending to be struck by a display of converted rice. Both the wife and the boyfriend had their backs to her, but there was something artificial in their posture. No one could find russet potatoes so mesmerizing.

"Well, she's *mentally* looking," Delia murmured. She turned to see her grocery cart rapidly filling with pasta. Egg noodles, rotini, linguine —Adrian flung in boxes at random. "Excuse me . . . ," she said.

"Oh, sorry," he told her. He stuffed his hands in his pockets and loped off. Delia followed, pushing her cart very slowly in case he meant for them to separate now. But at the end of the aisle, he paused and considered a row of tinned ravioli until she caught up with him. "The boyfriend's name is Skipper," he said. "He's her accountant."

"Accountant!" Delia said. He didn't fit the image.

"Half a dozen times, at least, he's come to our house. Sat in our actual living room, going over her taxes. Rosemary owns this catering firm. The Guilty Party, it's called. Ha. 'Sinfully Delicious Foods for Every Occasion.' Then next thing I know, she's moved in with him. She claimed she only needed a few weeks by herself, but when she phoned to say so, I could hear him coaching her in the background."

"Oh, that's terrible," Delia said.

A woman with a baby in her cart reached between them for a can of macaroni and cheese. Delia stepped back to give her room.

"If it's not too much trouble," Adrian said when the woman had moved away, "I'll just tag along while you finish your shopping. It would look sort of fishy if I left right now, all alone. I hope you don't mind."

Mind? This was the most interesting thing that had happened to her in years. "Not a bit," she told him. She wheeled her cart into aisle 4. Adrian strolled alongside her.

"I'm Adrian Bly-Brice, by the way," he said. "I guess I ought to know *your* name."

"I'm Delia Grinstead," she told him. She plucked a bottle of mint flakes from the spice rack.

"I don't believe I've ever run into a Delia before."

"Well, it's *Cor*delia, really. My father named me that."

"And are you one?"

"Am I one what?"

"Are you your father's Cordelia?"

"I don't know," she said. "He's dead."

"Oh, I'm sorry."

"He died this past winter," she said.

Ridiculously, tears filled her eyes. This whole conversation had taken a wrong turn somewhere. She squared her shoulders and pushed her cart on down the aisle, veering around an elderly couple conferring over salt substitutes. "Anyhow," she said, "it got shortened to Delia right away. Like in the song."

"What song?"

"Oh, the . . . you know, the one about Delia's gone, one more round . . . My father used to sing me to sleep with that."

"I never heard it," Adrian said.

The tune on the loudspeaker now was "By the Time I Get to Phoenix," competing with her father's gruff voice muttering "Delia's Gone" in her mind. "Anyhow!" she said again, more brightly.

They started up the next aisle: cereals on the left, popcorn and sweets on the right. Delia needed cornflakes, but cornflakes were such a *family* item, she decided against them. (What ingredients were required for blancmange?) Adrian gazed idly at sacks of butterscotch drops and rum balls. His skin had that slight tawniness that you occasionally see in fair-haired men, and it seemed almost without texture. He must not have to shave more than two or three times a week.

"I myself was named for an uncle," he said. "Rich Uncle Adrian Brice. Probably all for nothing, though. He's mad I changed my name when I married."

"You changed your name when you married?"

"I used to be Adrian Brice the Second, but then I married Rosemary Bly and we both became Bly-Brice."

"Oh, so there's a hyphen," Delia said. She hadn't realized.

"It was entirely her idea, believe me."

As if summoned up by his words, Rosemary appeared at the other end of the aisle. She tossed something into the red plastic tote basket hanging from Skipper's fist. Women like Rosemary never purchased their groceries by the cartload.

"If we went to the movie, though, we'd miss the concert," Adrian said instantly, "and you know how I've looked forward to the concert."

"I forgot," Delia said. "The concert! They'll be playing . . ."

But she couldn't think of a single composer. (And maybe he had meant some other kind of concert—a rock show, for instance. He was young enough.) Rosemary watched without a flicker of expression as Delia and Adrian approached. Delia was the first to lower her eyes. "We'll just save the movie for tomorrow," Adrian was saying. He guided her cart to the left a bit. All at once Delia felt woefully small—not dainty and petite, but squat, humble, insignificant. She didn't stand much taller than Adrian's armpit. She increased her speed, anxious to leave this image of herself behind. "They do have a Sunday matinee, don't they?" Adrian was asking.

"Of course they do," she told him, a little too emphatically. "We could go to the two o'clock showing, right after our champagne brunch."

By now she was tearing down the next aisle.

Adrian had to lengthen his stride to keep up. They narrowly missed hitting a man whose cart was stacked with gigantic Pampers boxes.

In aisle 7 they zipped through the gourmet section—anchovy paste, smoked oysters—and arrived at baby foods, where Delia collected herself enough to remember she needed strained spinach. She slowed to study the rows of little jars. "Not those!" Adrian hissed. They raced on, leaving behind aisle 7 and careening into 8. "Sorry," he said. "I just thought if Rosemary saw you buying baby food . . ."

If she saw her buying baby food, she'd think Delia was just a housewife with an infant waiting at home. Ironically, though, Delia had long passed the infant stage. To suspect her of having a child that young was to flatter her. All she needed the spinach for was her mint pea soup. But she didn't bother explaining that and instead selected a can of chicken broth. "Oh," Adrian said, traveling past her, "consommé! I meant to buy some."

He dropped a tin in her cart—a fancy brand with a sleek white label. Then he wandered on, hands jammed flat in his rear pockets. Come to think of it, he reminded Delia of her first real boyfriend—in fact, her only boyfriend, not counting her husband. Will Britt had possessed this same angularity, which had seemed graceful at some moments and ungainly at others; and he had cocked his elbows behind him in just this way, like knobby, sharp wings, and his ears had stuck out a bit too. It was a relief to find that Adrian's ears stuck out. She distrusted men who were too handsome.

At the end of the aisle they looked in both directions. No telling where Rosemary might pop up next, with that carefree, untrammeled tote basket. But the coast was clear, and Delia nosed her cart toward paper goods. "What," Adrian said, "you want to buy *more?*"

Yes, she did. She had barely passed the halfway mark. But she saw his point. The longer they hung around, the greater his chances of another confrontation. "We'll leave," she decided. She started for the nearest checkout counter, but Adrian, lacing his fingers through the grid of the cart, drew it toward the express lanes. "One, two, three . . ." She counted her purchases aloud. "We can't go there! I've got sixteen, seventeen . . ."

He pulled the cart into the fifteen-item lane, behind an old woman buying nothing but a sack of dog chow. He started dumping noodle boxes onto the counter. Ah, well. Delia rummaged through her bag for her checkbook. The old woman in front of them, meanwhile, was depositing bits of small change in the cashier's palm. She handed over a penny and then, after a search, another penny. A third penny had a

piece of lint stuck to it, and she plucked that
away painstakingly. Adrian gave an exasperated
sigh. "I forgot cat food," Delia told him. She
hadn't a hope in this world that he would volunteer to go back for it; she just thought a flow
of talk might settle him down some. "Seeing that
dog chow reminded me, we're almost out," she
said. "Oh, never mind. I'll send Ramsay for it
later."

The old woman was hunting a fourth penny.
She was positive, she said, that she had another
one somewhere.

"Ramsay!" Adrian repeated to himself. He
sighed again—or no, this time he was laughing.
"I bet you live in Roland Park," he told Delia.

"Well, yes, I do."

"I knew it! Everybody in Roland Park has a
last name for a first name."

"So?" she said, stung. "What's wrong with
that?"

"Oh, nothing."

"It isn't even true," she said. "Why, I know
lots of people who—"

"Don't take offense! I live in Roland Park
myself," he said. "It's just pure luck I wasn't
named . . . oh, Bennington, or McKinney;
McKinney was my mother's maiden name. I bet
your *husband's* mother's . . . and if we decide
against the blancmange tonight we can always
have it tomorrow night, don't you think?"

She felt dislocated for a second, until she understood that Rosemary must be in earshot again. Sure enough: a tote basket, still loaded, arrived on the counter behind her own groceries. By now the old woman had moved away, tottering under her burden of dog chow, and the cashier was asking them, "Plastic bags, or paper?"

"Plastic, please," Adrian said.

Delia opened her mouth to object (she generally chose paper, herself), but she didn't want to contradict Adrian in front of his wife.

Adrian said, "Delia, I don't believe you've met my . . ."

Delia turned around, already plastering a pleasantly surprised smile on her face.

"My, ah, Rosemary," Adrian said, "and her, ah, Skipper. This is Delia Grinstead."

Rosemary wasn't smiling at all, which made Delia feel foolish, but Skipper gave her an amiable nod. He kept his arms folded across his chest—short, muscular arms, heavily furred, bulging from the sleeves of his polo shirt. "Any relation to *Dr.* Grinstead?" he asked her.

"Yes! He's my . . . he was my . . . he's my husband," she said. How to explain the existence of a husband, in the present situation?

But Skipper seemed to take this in stride. He told Rosemary, "Dr. Grinstead's my mother's GP. Been treating her forever. Right?" he asked Delia.

"Right," she agreed, not having the faintest idea. Rosemary, meanwhile, went on studying her coolly. She carried her head at a deliberate tilt, accentuating the asymmetrical hairdo with its dramatic downward slant toward her chin. It was none of Delia's business, of course, but privately she thought Adrian deserved somebody more likable. She thought even Skipper deserved somebody more likable. She wished she had worn high heels this morning, and a dressier dress.

"Dr. Grinstead is just about the last man in Baltimore who makes house calls," Skipper was telling Rosemary.

"Well, only if it's absolutely essential," Delia said. A reflex: she never gave up trying to protect her husband from his patients.

Behind her, the scanner said *peep . . . peep . . . peep,* registering her groceries. The music had stopped playing several minutes back, as Delia just now noticed, and the murmuring of shoppers elsewhere in the store sounded hushed and ominous.

"That'll be thirty-three forty," the cashier announced.

Delia turned to fill in her check and found Adrian handing over the money. "Oh!" she said, preparing to argue. But then she grew conscious of Rosemary listening.

Adrian flashed her a wide, sweet smile and accepted his change. "Good seeing you," he told the other couple. He walked on out, pushing the cart, with Delia trailing behind.

It had been raining off and on for days, but this morning had dawned clear and the parking lot had a rinsed, fresh, soft look under a film of lemony sunlight. Adrian halted the cart at the curb and lifted out two of the grocery bags, leaving the third for Delia. Next came the problem of whose car to head for. He was already starting toward his own, which was evidently parked somewhere near the dry cleaner's, when she stopped him. "Wait," she said. "I'm right here."

"But what if they see us? We can't leave in two different cars!"

"Well, I do have a *life* to get back to," Delia snapped. This whole business had gone far enough, it occurred to her. She was missing her baby-food spinach and her cornflakes and untold other items on account of a total stranger. She flung open the trunk of her Plymouth.

"Oh, all right," Adrian said. "What we'll do is load these groceries very, very slowly, and by that time they'll have driven away. They didn't have so much to ring up: two steaks, two potatoes, a head of lettuce, and a box of after-dinner mints. That won't take long."

Delia was astonished at his powers of observation. She watched him arrange his bags in her trunk, after which he consumed a good half minute repositioning a small box of something.

Orzo, it was—a most peculiar, tiny-sized pasta that she'd often noticed on the shelf but never bought. She had thought it resembled rice, in which case why not serve rice instead, which was surely more nutritious? She handed him the bag she was holding, and he settled that with elaborate care between the first two. "Are they coming out yet?" he asked.

"No," she said, looking past him toward the store. "Listen, I owe you some money."

"My treat."

"No, really, I have to pay you back. Only I planned to write a check and I don't have any cash. Would you accept a check? I could show you my driver's license," she said.

He laughed.

"I'm serious," she told him. "If you don't mind taking a—"

Then she caught sight of Skipper and Rosemary emerging from the supermarket. Skipper hugged a single brown paper bag. Rosemary carried nothing but a purse the size of a sandwich, on a glittery golden chain.

"Is it them?" Adrian asked.

"It's them."

He bent inside her trunk and started rearranging groceries again. "Tell me when they're gone," he said.

The couple crossed to a low red sports car. Rosemary was at least Skipper's height if not taller, and she had the slouching, indifferent gait of a runway model. If she had walked into a wall, her hipbones would have hit first.

"Are they looking our way?" Adrian asked.

"I don't think they see us."

Skipper opened the passenger door, and Rosemary folded herself out of sight. He handed in the sack of groceries and shut the door, strode to the driver's side, slid in and started the engine. Only then did he shut his own door. With a tightly knit, snarling sound, the little car spun around and buzzed off.

"They're gone," Delia said.

Adrian closed the trunk lid. He seemed older now. For the first time, Delia saw the fragile lines etched at the corners of his mouth.

"Well," he said sadly.

It seemed crass to mention money again, but she had to say, "About the check . . ."

"Please. I owe *you*," he said. "I owe you more than that. Thanks for going along with me on this."

"It was nothing," she told him. "I just wish there'd been, oh, somebody really appropriate."

"Appropriate?"

"Somebody . . . *you* know," she said. "As glamorous as your wife."

"What are you talking about?" he asked. "Why, you're very pretty! You have such a little face, like a flower."

She felt herself blushing. He must have thought she was fishing for compliments. "Anyhow, I'm glad I could help out," she said. She backed away from him and opened her car door. "Bye, now!"

"Goodbye," he said. "Thanks again."

As if he had been her host, he went on standing there while she maneuvered out of the parking slot. Naturally she made a mess of it, knowing he was watching. She cut her wheel too sharply, and the power-steering belt gave an embarrassing screech. But finally the car was free and she rolled away. Her rearview mirror showed Adrian lifting a palm in farewell, holding it steady until she turned south at the light.

Halfway home, she had a sudden realization: she should have given him the groceries he had picked out. Good heavens—all that pasta, those little grains of orzo, and now she remembered his consommé too. Consommé madrilene: she wasn't even sure how to pronounce it. She was driving away with property that belonged to someone else, and it was shameful how pleased she felt, and how lucky, and how rich.

# 2

The trouble with plastic bags was, those convenient handles tempted you to carry too many
at once. Delia had forgotten that. She remembered halfway across her front yard, when the
crooks of her fingers began to ache. She hadn't
been able to bring the car around to the rear
because someone's station wagon was blocking
the driveway. Nailed to the trunk of the largest
oak was a rusty metal sign directing patients to
park on the street, but people tended to ignore
it.

She circled the front porch and picked her way
through the scribble of spent forsythia bushes at
the side. This was a large house but shabby, its
brown shingles streaked with mildew and its
shutters snaggletoothed where the louvers had
fallen out over the years. Delia had never lived
anywhere else. Neither had her father, for that
matter. Her mother, an import from the Eastern
Shore, had died of kidney failure before Delia
could remember, leaving her in the care of her
father and her two older sisters. Delia had played
hopscotch on the parquet squares in the hall
while her father doctored his patients in the

glassed-in porch off the kitchen, and she had married his assistant beneath the sprawling brass chandelier that reminded her to this day of a daddy longlegs. Even after the wedding she had not moved away but simply installed her husband among her sweet-sixteen bedroom furniture, and once her children were born it was not uncommon for a patient to wander out of the waiting room calling, "Delia? Where are you, darlin'? Just wanted to see how those precious little babies were getting along."

The cat was perched on the back stoop, meowing at her reproachfully. His short gray fur was flattened here and there by drops of water. "Didn't I tell you?" Delia scolded as she let him in. "Didn't I warn you the grass would still be wet?" Her shoes were soaked just from crossing the lawn, the thin soles cold and papery-feeling. She stepped out of them as soon as she entered the kitchen. "Well, hi there!" she said to her son. He sat slumped over the table in his pajamas, buttering a piece of toast. She placed her bags on the counter and said, "Fancy finding you awake so early!"

"It's not like I had any choice," he told her glumly.

He was her youngest child and the one who most resembled her, she had always thought (with his hair the light-brown color and frazzled texture of binder's twine, his freckled white face

shadowed violet beneath the eyes), but last
month he had turned fifteen, and all at once she
saw more of Sam in him. He had shot up to
nearly six feet, and his pointy chin had suddenly
squared, and his hands had grown muscular and
disconcertingly competent-looking. Even the
way he held his butter knife suggested some new
authority.

His voice was Sam's too: deep but fine-
grained, not subject to the cracks and creaks his
brother had gone through. "I hope you bought
cornflakes," he told her.

"Why, no, I—"

"Aw, Mom!"

"But wait till you hear why I didn't," she said.
"The funniest thing, Carroll! This real adventure. I was standing in the produce section, mind-
ing my own business—"

"There's not one decent thing in this house to
eat."

"Well, you don't usually want breakfast on a
Saturday."

He scowled at her. "Try telling Ramsay that,"
he said.

"Ramsay?"

"He's the one who woke me. Came stumbling
into the room in broad daylight, out all night
with his lady friend. No way could I get back to
sleep after that."

Delia turned her attention to the grocery bags.

(She knew where this conversation was headed.) She started rummaging through them as if the cornflakes might emerge after all. "But let me tell you my adventure," she said over her shoulder. "Out of the blue, this man is standing next to me. . . . Good-looking? He looked like my very first sweetheart, Will Britt. I don't believe I ever mentioned Will to you."

"Mom," Carroll said. "When are you going to let me move across the hall?"

"Oh, Carroll."

"Nobody else I know has to room with their brother."

"Now, now. Plenty of people in this world have to room with whole families," she told him.

"Not with their boozehead college-boy brother, though. Not when there's another room, perfectly empty, right across the hall."

Delia set down the box of orzo and faced him squarely. She noticed that he needed a haircut, but this was not the moment to point that out. "Carroll, I'm sorry," she said, "but I am just not ready."

"Aunt Eliza's ready! Why aren't you? Aunt Liza was Grandpa's daughter too, and she says of course I should have his room. She doesn't understand what's stopping me."

"Oh, listen to us!" Delia said gaily. "Spoiling such a pretty day with disagreements! Where's your father? Is he seeing a patient?"

Carroll didn't answer. He had dropped his toast to his plate, and now he sat tipping his chair back defiantly, no doubt adding more dents to the linoleum. Delia sighed.

"Sweetie," she said, "I do know how you feel. And pretty soon you can have the room, I promise. But not just yet! Not right now! Right now it still smells of his pipe tobacco."

"It won't once I'm living there," Carroll said.

"But that's what I'm afraid of."

"Shoot, I'll take up smoking, then."

She waved his words away with a dutiful laugh. "Anyhow," she said. "Is your father with a patient?"

"Naw."

"Where is he?"

"He's out running."

"He's what?"

Carroll picked up his toast again and chomped down on it noisily.

"He's doing *what*?"

"He's running, Mom."

"Well, didn't you at least offer to go with him?"

"He's only running around the Gilman track, for gosh sakes."

"I asked you children; I begged you not to let him go alone. What if something happens and no one's around to help?"

"Fat chance, on the Gilman track," Carroll said.

"He shouldn't be running anyway. He ought to be walking."

"Running's good for him," Carroll said. "Look. He's not worried. His doctor's not worried. So what's your problem, Mom?"

Delia could have come up with so many responses to that; all she did was press a hand to her forehead.

These were the facts she had neglected to tell that young man in the supermarket: She was a sad, tired, anxious, forty-year-old woman who hadn't had a champagne brunch in decades. And her husband was even older, by a good fifteen years, and just this past February he had suffered a bout of severe chest pain. Angina, they said in the emergency room. And now she was terrified any time he went anywhere alone, and she hated to let him drive, and she kept finding excuses not to make love for fear it would kill him, and at night while he slept she lay awake, tensing every muscle between each of his long, slow breaths.

And not only were her children past infancy; they were huge. They were great, galumphing, unmannerly, supercilious creatures—Susie a Goucher junior consumed by a baffling enthusiasm for various outdoor sports; Ramsay a Hopkins freshman on the brink of flunking out, thanks to the twenty-eight-year-old single-parent girlfriend he had somehow acquired. (And both of them, Susie and Ramsay both, were miffed beyond belief that the family finances forced them to live at home.) And Delia's baby, her sweet, winsome Carroll, had been replaced by this rude adolescent, flinching from his mother's hugs and criticizing her clothes and rolling his eyes disgustedly at every word she uttered.

Like now, for instance. Determined to start afresh, she perked all her features upward and asked, "Any calls while I was gone?" and he said, "Why would I answer the *grown-ups'* line," not bothering to add a question mark.

*Because the grown-ups buy the celery for your favorite mint pea soup,* she could have told him, but years of dealing with teenagers had turned her into a pacifist, and she merely padded out of the kitchen in her stocking feet and crossed the hall to the study, where Sam kept the answering machine.

The study was what they called it, and books did line the floor-to-ceiling shelves, but mainly this was a TV room now. The velvet draperies were kept permanently drawn, coloring the air the dusty dark red of an old-time movie house. Soft-drink cans and empty pretzel bags and stacks of rented videotapes littered the coffee table, and Susie lounged on the couch, watching Saturday-morning cartoons with her boyfriend, Driscoll Avery. The two of them had been dating so long that they looked like brother and sister, with their smooth beige coloring and stocky, waistless figures and identical baggy sweat suits. Driscoll barely blinked when Delia entered. Susie didn't even do that much; just flipped a channel on the remote control.

"Morning, you two," Delia said. "Any calls?"

Susie shrugged and flipped another channel. Driscoll yawned out loud. Just for that, Delia didn't excuse herself when she walked in front of them to the answering machine. She bent to press the Message button, but nothing happened. Electronic devices were always double-crossing her. "How do I—?" she said, and then an old man's splintery voice filled the room. "Dr. Grinstead, can you get back to me right away? It's Grayson Knowles, and I told the pharmacist about those pills, but he asked if—"

Whatever the pharmacist had asked was submerged by a flood of Bugs Bunny music. Susie must have raised the volume on the TV. *Beep,* the machine said, and then Delia's sister came on. "Dee, it's Eliza. I need an address. Could you please call me at work?"

"What's she doing at work on a Saturday?" Delia asked, but nobody answered.

*Beep.* "This is Myrtle Allingham," an old woman stated forthrightly.

"Oh, God," Susie told Driscoll.

"Marshall and I were wondering if you-all would like to take supper with us Sunday evening. Nothing fancy! Just us folks! And do tell

young Miss Susie she should bring that darlin'
Driscoll. Say seven o'clock?"

*Beep beep beep beep beep.* The end.

"We went *last* time," Susie said, slouching
lower on the couch. "Count us out."

"Well, I don't know," Driscoll said. "That
crab dip she served was not half bad."

"We aren't going, Driscoll, so forget it."

"She's lonesome, is all," Delia said. "Stuck at
home with her hip, no way to get around—"

Something banged overhead.

"What's that?" she asked.

More bangs. Or clanks, really. *Clank! Clank!*
at measured intervals, as if on purpose.

"Plumber?" Driscoll said tentatively.

"What plumber?"

"Plumber upstairs in the bathroom?"

"I never called for a plumber."

"Dr. Grinstead did, maybe?"

Delia gave Susie a look. Susie met it blandly.

"I don't know what's come over that man,"
Delia said. "He's been re—what's the word?—
rejuvenating, resuscitating . . ." Fully aware that
neither one of them was listening, she walked
on out of the room, still talking. ". . . renovating,
I mean: renovating this house to a fare-thee-well.
If it's about that place in the ceiling, then really
you'd think . . ."

She climbed the stairs, halfway up encounter-
ing the cat, who was hurrying down in a scat-

tered, ungraceful fashion. Vernon detested loud noises. "Hello?" Delia called. She poked her head into the bathroom off the hall. A ponytailed man in coveralls crouched beside the claw-footed tub, studying its pipes. "Well, hello," she said.

He twisted around to look at her. "Oh. Hey," he said.

"What seems to be the trouble?"

"Can't say just yet," he said. He turned back to the pipes.

She waited a moment, in case he wanted to add something, but she could tell he was one of those repairmen who think only the husband worth talking to.

In her bedroom, she sat down on Sam's side of the bed, picked up the telephone, and dialed Eliza's work number. "Pratt Library," a woman said.

"Eliza Felson, please."

"Just a minute."

Delia propped a pillow against the headboard, and then she swung her feet up onto the frilled pink spread. The plumber had progressed to the bathroom between her room and her father's. She couldn't see him, but she could hear him banging around. What information could you hope to gain from whacking pipes?

"I'm sorry," the woman said, "but we can't seem to locate Miss Felson. Are you sure she's working today?"

"She must be; she told me to call her there, and she isn't here at home."

"I'm sorry."

"Well, thanks anyway."

She hung up. The plumber was whistling "Clementine." While Delia was dialing Mrs. Allingham, he ambled into the bedroom, still whistling, and she demurely smoothed her skirt around her knees. He squatted in front of the miniature door that opened onto the pipes in the wall. *Thou art lost and gone forever,* he whistled; Delia mentally supplied the words. One tug at the door's wooden knob, and it came off in his hand. She could have told him it would. She watched with some satisfaction as he muttered a curse beneath his breath and fished a pair of pliers from his belt loop.

Seven rings. Eight. She wasn't discouraged. Mrs. Allingham walked with a limp, and it took her ages to get to the phone.

Nine rings. "Hello?"

"Mrs. Allingham, it's Delia."

"Delia, dear! How *are* you?"

"I'm fine, how are you?"

"Oh, we're fine, doing just fine. Enjoying this nice spring weather! Nearly forgot what sunshine looks like, till today."

"Yes, me too," Delia said. She was overtaken suddenly by a swell of something like homesickness; Mrs. Allingham's chipper, slightly rasping voice was so reminiscent of all the women on this street where she had grown up. "Mrs. Allingham," she said, "Sam and I would love to come for supper tomorrow night, but we can't bring the children, I'm afraid."

"Oh!" Mrs. Allingham said.

"It's just that they're so busy these days. You know how it is."

"Yes, of course," Mrs. Allingham said faintly.

"But another time, maybe! They always enjoy your company."

"Yes, well, and we enjoy theirs too."

"So we'll see you at seven tomorrow," Delia said briskly, for she could hear Sam downstairs and she had a million things to do. "Goodbye till then."

By now the plumber had the little door prized open and was peering into the bowels of the wall, but she knew better than to ask him what he'd found.

In the kitchen, Sam stood propped against a counter, taking off his mud-caked running shoes. He was telling Carroll, ". . . sort of a toboggan effect when you hit those cedar chips . . ."

"Sam, how could you go off alone like that?" Delia asked. "You knew I'd worry!"

"Hello, Dee," he said.

His T-shirt was translucent with sweat, his sharp-boned face glistened, and his glasses were fogged. His hair—that shade that could be either

blond or gray, it had faded so imperceptibly—
lay in damp spikes on his forehead. "Look at
you," Delia scolded. "You got overheated. You
went running all alone and got overheated to
boot when the doctor told you a dozen times—"

"Whose car is that in the driveway?"

"Car?"

"Station wagon parked in the driveway."

"Well, doesn't it belong to a patient? No, I
guess not."

"Plumber," Carroll said from behind a glass
of orange juice.

"Oh, good," Sam said. "The plumber's here."

He set his shoes on the doormat and started
out of the kitchen, no doubt happily anticipating
one of those laconic, man-to-man discussions of
valves and joints and gaskets. "Sam, wait," Delia said, for she had a pang of guilt nagging at
the back of her mind. "Before I forget—"

He turned, already wary.

"Mr. Knowles phoned—something to do with
his pills," she said.

"I thought he got that straightened out."

"And also, um, Mrs. Allingham. She wanted
to know if we could come for—"

He groaned. "No," he said, "we can't."

"But you haven't even heard yet! A light Sunday supper, she said, and I told her—"

"*I'm* sure not going," Carroll broke in.

"No, I told her that; I told her you kids were
tied up. But you and I, Sam, just for—"

"We can't make it," Sam said flatly.

"But I've already accepted."

He had been on the point of turning away again, but now he stopped and looked at her.

"I know I should have checked with you first, but by accident somehow I just went ahead and accepted."

"Well, then," he said, "you'll have to call her back and unaccept."

"But, Sam!"

He left.

She looked over at Carroll. "How can he be so mean?" she asked, but Carroll just raised one eyebrow in that urbane new way she suspected him of practicing in the mirror.

Sometimes she felt like a tiny gnat, whirring around her family's edges.

The linoleum was slick and chilly beneath her feet, and she would have gone back upstairs for her slippers except that Sam and the plumber were upstairs. Instead, she turned to her grocery bags and unpacked several more boxes of pasta. Maybe she could tell Mrs. Allingham that Sam had been taken ill. That was always risky, though, when you lived in the same block and could so easily be observed, hale and hearty, stepping out to collect your morning paper or whatever. She sighed and shut a cabinet door. "When did this start happening to me?" she asked Carroll.

"Huh?"

"When did sweet and cute turn into silly and inefficient?"

He didn't seem to have an opinion.

Her sister appeared in the doorway, rolling up her shirt sleeves. "Morning, all!" she announced.

"Eliza?"

There were days when Eliza seemed almost gnomish, and this was one of them. She wore her gardening clothes—a pith helmet that all but obscured her straight black Dutch-boy bob, a khaki shirt and stubby brown trousers, and boys' brown oxfords with thick, thick soles intended to make her seem taller. (She was the shortest of the three Felson sisters.) Her horn-rimmed glasses overwhelmed her small, blunt, sallow face. "I figured I'd transplant some of those herbs before the ground dried out," she told Delia.

"But I thought you were at work."

"Work? It's Saturday."

"You called from work, I thought."

Eliza looked over at Carroll. He raised that eyebrow again.

"You called and left a message on the machine," Delia said, "asking me to find an address."

"That was ten days ago, at least. I needed Jenny Coop's address, remember?"

"Then why did I just get it off the answering machine?"

"Mom," Carroll said. "You must have been playing back *old* calls."

"Well, how is that possible?"

"You didn't have the machine turned on in the first place, see, and then when you pressed the Message button—"

"Oh, Lord," Delia said. "Mrs. Allingham."

"Is there coffee?" Eliza asked her.

"Not that I know of. Oh, Lord . . ."

She went over to the wall phone and dialed Mrs. Allingham's number. "I'm snug in bed," Eliza was telling Carroll, "thinking, *Goody, Saturday morning, I can sleep till noon*—when who should come crawling through that door in the back of my closet but another one of your father's blasted repairmen."

"Mrs. Allingham?" Delia said into the phone. "This is Delia again. Mrs. Allingham, I feel like such a dummy but it seems I got my calls mixed up and it was *last* week you invited us for. And of course last week we went, and a lovely time we had too; did I write you a thank-you note? I meant to write you a thank-you note. But *this* week we're not coming; I mean I realize now that you didn't invite us for—"

"But, Delia, darlin', we'd be happy to have you this week! We'd be happy to have you any old time, and I've already sent Marshall off to the Gourmet To Go with a shopping list."

"Oh, I'm so sorry," Delia said, but then the coffee grinder started up—a deafening racket—

and she shouted, "Anyhow! We'll have to invite you to our place, very soon! Goodbye!"

She replaced the receiver and glared at Eliza.

"If only coffee tasted as good as it smells," Eliza said serenely when the grinder stopped.

Sam and the plumber were descending the stairs. Delia could hear the plumber's elasticized East Baltimore vowels; he was waxing lyrical about water. "It's the most amazing substance," he was saying. "It'll burst out one place and run twenty-five feet along the underside of a pipe and commence to dripping another place, where you least expect to see it. It'll lie in wait, it'll bide its time, it'll search out some little cranny you would never think to look."

Delia placed her hands on her hips and stood waiting. The instant the two men stepped through the door, she said, "I certainly hope you're satisfied, Sam Grinstead."

"Hmm?"

"I called back poor Mrs. Allingham and canceled supper."

"Oh, good," Sam said absently.

"I broke our promise. I ducked out of our commitment. I probably hurt her feelings for all time," Delia told him.

But Sam wasn't listening. He was following the plumber's forefinger as it pointed upward to a line of blistered plaster. And Eliza was measuring coffee, so the only one who paid any heed

was Carroll. He sent Delia a look of utter con-
tempt.

Delia turned sheepishly to her grocery bags.
From the depths of one she drew the celery, pale
green and pearly and precisely ribbed. She gazed
at it for a long, thoughtful moment. "Aren't you
clever to say so!" she heard Adrian exclaim once
again, and she held the words close; she hugged
them to her breast as she turned back to give
her son a beatific smile.

# 3

"Aren't you clever to say so," he had said, and, "Why, you're very pretty!" and, "You have such a little face, like a flower." Had he meant that she had such a flowerlike face, which incidentally was little? Or had its littleness been his sole point? She preferred the first interpretation, although the second, she supposed, was more likely.

Also, he had praised her marvelous blancmange. Of course the blancmange did not really exist, but still she felt a lilt of pride, remembering that he had found it marvelous.

She studied her face in the mirror when nobody else was around. Yes, maybe it did resemble a flower. If he had been referring to those flowers that seem freckled. She had always wanted to look more dramatic, more mysterious—more adult, in fact. It had struck her as unfair that she should be wrinkling around the eyes without ever losing the prim-featured, artless, triangular face of her childhood. But evidently Adrian had considered that attractive.

Unless he had been speaking out of kindness.

She checked for his name in the phone book,

but he must have had an unlisted number. She kept watch for him on the streets and in the local shops. Twice in the next three days she drove back to the supermarket, on both occasions wearing the dress with the smocked, gathered front that made her seem less flat-chested. But Adrian never appeared.

And if he had, what would she have done? It wasn't that she'd fallen in love with him or anything like that. Why, she didn't even know what kind of person he was! And she certainly didn't want (as she put it to herself) "something to start up." Ever since she was seventeen, she had centered her life on Sam Grinstead. She had not so much as glanced at any other man from the moment she first met him. Even in her daydreams, she wasn't the type to be unfaithful.

Still, whenever she imagined running into Adrian, she was conscious all at once of the light, quick way she naturally moved, and the outline of her body within the folds of her dress. She couldn't remember when she had last been so aware of herself from outside, from a distance.

At home, four workmen were installing air-conditioning—another of Sam's sudden renovations. They were slicing through floors and walls; they were running huge, roaring machines; they were lugging in metal ducts and bales of what looked like gray cotton candy. Delia could lie in bed at night and gaze straight upward through a new rectangle in the ceiling to the stark bones of the attic. She pictured bats and barn swallows swooping down on her while she slept. She fancied she could hear the house groaning in distress—such a modest, mild house, so unprepared for change.

But Sam was jubilant. Oh, he could hardly fit in his patients between visits from repairmen. Electricians, plasterers, and painters streamed through his office with estimates for the many improvements he planned. A carpenter arrived for the shutters, and a man with a spray for the mildewed shingles. Twenty-two years Sam had lived here; had he felt so critical of his surroundings all along?

He had first walked into her father's waiting room on a Monday morning in July, some three weeks after her high-school graduation. Delia had been sitting in her usual place at the desk, even though it was not her usual time (she worked afternoons, mostly), because she was so eager to meet him. She and her sisters had talked of nothing else since Dr. Felson had announced his hiring. Was this person married? they had asked, and how old was he? and what did he look like? (No, he was not married, their father said, and he was, oh, thirty-two, thirty-three, and he looked fine. Fine? Well, normal; perfectly all right, their father said impatiently, for to him what counted most was whether the man could ease his workload some—take over house calls and the morning office hours.) So Delia rose early that summer day and put on her prettiest sundress, the one with the sweetheart neckline. Then she seated herself behind the spinet desk, where she ostentatiously set to work transcribing her father's notes. At nine o'clock exactly, young Dr. Grinstead stepped through the outside door, carrying a starched white coat folded over his forearm. Sunlight flashed off his clear-rimmed, serious glasses and glazed his sifted-looking blond hair, and Delia could still recall the pang of pure desire that had caused her insides to lurch as if she had leaned out over a canyon.

Sam didn't even remember that meeting. He claimed he'd first seen her when he came to dinner. It was true there had been such a dinner, on the evening of that same day. Eliza had cooked a roast and Linda had baked a cake (both advertising their housewifely skills), while Delia, the baby, still two months short of her eighteenth birthday and supposedly not even in the running, sat across from Sam and her father in the living room and sipped a grown-up glass of sherry. The sherry had tasted like liquefied raisins and flowed directly to that powerful new root of longing that branched deeper minute by minute. But Sam claimed that when he first walked in, all three girls had been seated on the couch. Like the king's three daughters in a fairy tale, he said, they'd been lined up according to age, the oldest farthest left, and like the woodcutter's honest son, he had chosen the youngest and prettiest, the shy little one on the right who didn't think she stood a chance.

Well, let him believe what he wanted. In any case, it had *ended* like a fairy tale.

Except that real life continues past the end, and here they were with air-conditioning men destroying the attic, and the cat hiding under the bed, and Delia reading a paperback romance on the love seat in Sam's waiting room—the house's only refuge, since the office and the waiting room were air-conditioned already. Her head was propped on one arm of the love seat, and her feet, in fluffy pink slippers, rested on the other. Above her hung her father's framed Norman Rockwell print of the kindly old doctor setting his stethoscope to the chest of a little girl's doll. And behind the flimsy partition that rose not quite all the way to the ceiling, Sam was explaining Mrs. Harper's elbow trouble. Her joints were wearing out, he said. There was a stupefied silence; even the electric saw fell silent. Then, "Oh, no!" Mrs. Harper gasped. "Oh, my! Oh, my heavens above! This comes as such a shock!"

A shock? Mrs. Harper was ninety-two years old. What did she expect? Delia would have asked. But Sam said, gently, "Yes, well, I suppose . . ." and something else, which Delia couldn't catch, for the saw just then started up again as if all at once recalling its assignment.

She turned a page. The heroine was touring the hero's vast estate, admiring its magnificent grounds and its tasteful "appointments," whatever those might be. So many of these books had wealthy heroes, Delia had noticed. It didn't matter about the women; sometimes they were rich and sometimes they were poor, but the men came complete with castles and a staff of devoted servants. Never again would the women they married need to give a thought to the grinding gears of daily life—the leaky basement, the faulty oven, the missing car keys. It sounded wonderful.

"Delia, dear heart!" Mrs. Harper cried, staggering out of the office. She was a stylish, silk-clad skeleton of a woman with clawlike hands, which she stretched toward Delia beseechingly. "Your husband tells me my joints have just ground themselves down to nubbins!"

"Now, now," Sam protested behind her. "I didn't say that exactly, Mrs. Harper."

Delia sat up guiltily and smoothed her skirt. She grew aware of the bunny ears on her slippers and the temptress on the cover of her book. "I'm so sorry, Mrs. Harper," she said. "Should I schedule another appointment?"

"No, he says I have to go to a specialist. A man I don't know from Adam!"

"Get her Peterson's phone number, would you, Dee?" Sam asked.

She rose and went over to the desk, scuffing along in her slippers. (Mrs. Harper herself wore sharp-toed high heels, which she kept planted on the rug in a herringbone pattern to show off her trim ankles.) Delia flipped through Rolodex cards arranged not by name but by specialty— allergy, arthritis. . . . Nowadays, this office served most often as a sort of clearinghouse. Her father used to deliver babies and even performed the more elementary surgeries once upon a time, but now it was largely a matter of bee shots in the spring, flu shots in the fall; and as for child-birth, why, these patients were long past the age. They were hand-me-downs from her father, most of them. (Or even, Sam joked, from her grand-father, who had opened this office in 1902, when Roland Park was still country and no one batted an eye at running a practice out of a residence.)

She copied Dr. Peterson's number onto a card and passed it to Mrs. Harper, who examined it suspiciously before tucking it into her bag. "I trust this person is not some mere snip of a boy," she told Sam.

"He's thirty if he's a day," Sam assured her.

"Thirty! My grandson is older than that! Oh, please, can't I go on seeing you instead?" But already knowing his answer, she turned without a pause toward Delia. "This husband of yours is a saint," she said. "He's just too good to exist on this earth. I hope you realize that."

"Oh, yes."

"You make sure you appreciate him, hear?"

"Yes, Mrs. Harper."

Delia watched Sam escort the old woman to the door, and then she dropped back onto the love seat and picked up her book. "Beatrice," the hero was saying, "I want you more than life itself," and his voice was rough and desperate— uncontrolled, was the way the author put it: *uncontrolled, and it sent a thrill down her slender spine within the clinging ivory satin of her negligee.*

Maybe, instead of running into Adrian, she could just sit still and let him track her down. Maybe he was even now dwelling on his image of her and cruising the streets in search of her. Or he had looked up her address, perhaps; for he did know her last name. He was parked down the block at this very moment, hoping to catch a glimpse of her.

She took to stepping into the yard several times a day. She seized any excuse to arrange herself on the front-porch swing. Never an outdoor person, and most certainly not a gardener, she spent half an hour posed in goatskin gloves among Eliza's medicinal herbs. And after someone telephoned but merely breathed and said

nothing when she answered, she jumped up at
every new call like a teenager. "I'll get it! I'll get
it!" When there weren't any calls, she made a
teenager's bargains with Fate: *I won't think
about it, and then the phone will ring. I'll go out
of the room; I'll pretend I'm busy and the phone
will ring for sure.* Shepherding her family into
the car for a Sunday visit to Sam's mother, she
moved fluidly, sensuously, like an actress or a
dancer conscious every minute of being watched.

But if someone really had been watching,
think of what he would see: the ragged disarray
of Delia's home life. Ramsay, short and stone-
faced and sullen, kicking a tire in disgust; Carroll
and Susie bickering over who would get a window seat; Sam settling himself behind the wheel,
pushing his glasses higher on his nose, wearing
an unaccustomed knit shirt that made him look
weak-armed and fussy. And at the end of their
trip, the Iron Mama (as Delia called her)—
sturdy, plain Eleanor Grinstead, who patched
her own roof and mowed her own lawn and had
reared her one son single-handed in that spotless
Calvert Street row house where she waited now,
lips clamped tight, to hear what new piece of
tomfoolery her daughter-in-law had contrived.

No, not a one of them would bear up beneath
the celestial blue gaze of Adrian Bly-Brice.

The oldest of the air-conditioning men, the one
named Lysander, asked what those hay-bunch

things were doing, hanging from the attic rafters. "Those are my sister's herbs," Delia said. She hoped to let it rest at that, but her sister happened to be right there in the kitchen with her, stringing beans for supper, and she told him, "Yes, I burn them in little pots around the house."

"You set fire to them?" Lysander asked.

"Each one does something different," Eliza explained. "One prevents bad dreams and another promotes a focused mind and another clears the atmosphere after interpersonal strife."

Lysander looked over at Delia, raising his gray toothbrush eyebrows.

"So anyhow," Delia said hastily. "Is this job about wrapped up, do you think?"

"This one here? Oh, no," he said. He plodded toward the sink; he had come down to refill his thermos. Waiting for the water to run cold, he said, "We got several more days, at the least."

"Several days!" Delia squawked. She cleared her throat. "But the noisy part: will that be over soon? Even the cat is getting a headache."

"Now, how would you know that?" he asked.

"Oh, Delia can read a cat's mind," Eliza told him. "She's got all of us trained in cat etiquette: what kind of voice to use with them and how to do your eyes when you look at them and—"

"Eliza, I need those beans *now*," Delia broke in.

Too late, though: Lysander snorted as he set

his thermos under the faucet. "Me, I'll take a
dog any day," he said. "Cats are too sneaky for
my taste."

"Oh, well, I like dogs too, of course," Delia
said. (In fact, she was slightly afraid of dogs.)
"It's just that dogs are so . . . sudden. You
know?"

"But honest," Lysander said. It sounded like
an accusation. "Okay if I swipe a few ice cubes?"

"Go right ahead," Delia told him.

He stood there helplessly, clasping the neck
of his thermos, until she realized that he meant
for her to get them. He would be one of those
men who didn't know where their wives kept the
spoons. She dried her hands on her apron and
went to fetch the bin from the freezer.

"Last place we worked?" he said. "Putting in
a new heat pump? Guy next door owned one of
them attack dogs. Dog trained to attack. Lady
we was working for warned us all about him."

He kept a staunch grip on his thermos while
Delia tried to fit an ice cube in. It wouldn't go.
She hit it with the flat of her hand (Lysander not
even flinching) and, "Eek!" she cried, for the
ice cube flew up in the air and then skittered
across the floor. Lysander stared down at it
dolefully.

"Just let me at this little devil," Delia told him,
and she snatched the thermos from him and
slammed it into the sink. She ran water over a

second ice cube. "Aha!" she crowed, pounding it in. She started working on a third.

Lysander said, "So we're hauling in stuff from the truck one day, come to see the attack dog rounding the side of the house. Big old bristle-necked dog like a wolf, growling real deep in his throat. Lord, I thought I would die. Then out steps the lady we worked for like she had just been waiting for this. Says, '*Come* along,' and takes hold of his collar, calm-natured as you please. Walks him into the yard next door and, 'Mr. What's-it?' she calls. 'I'm about to shoot your dog dead unless you come out this minute and retrieve him.' With her voice just as clear, just as cool. That was some kind of woman, believe me."

Why was he telling this story? Was it meant to show Delia up? She dispatched the third ice cube with as little commotion as possible. For some reason, she imagined that the woman had resembled Rosemary Bly-Brice. Maybe she *was* Rosemary Bly-Brice. She wore an expression of tolerant detachment; she bent in a graceful S-curve; she hooked a single finger through the dog's spiked collar. Unexpectedly, Delia felt a rush of admiration, as if her entrancement with Adrian extended to his wife as well.

She turned off the faucet, picked up the thermos, and offered it to Lysander. "Why, looky there," Lysander said. Water was dripping rapidly from the bottom of the thermos. "Why, you've gone and broke it," he said.

Delia didn't apologize. She went on offering the thermos, wishing he would just take it and leave. In the supermarket, she recalled at that instant, she had made some reference to Ramsay, and Adrian had assumed she meant her husband. No wonder he hadn't come by yet! He'd been looking for Ramsay Grinstead, who wasn't in the phone book. Sooner or later, though, he would realize his mistake. She began smiling at the thought, and she continued holding the thermos out until Eliza, clucking, rose to fetch the mop.

In the dark the phone rang twice, and Delia woke with a start. She was reviewing her children's whereabouts even before her eyes were fully open. All three were safe in bed, she decided, but her heart went on racing anyhow.

"Hello?" Sam said. "Yes, this is Dr. Grinstead. Oh. Mr. Maxwell."

Delia sighed and rolled over. Mr. Maxwell was married to the Dowager Queen of Hypochondria.

"How long has she been experiencing this?" Sam asked. "I see. Well, that doesn't sound serious. Yes, I'm sure it *is* uncomfortable, but I doubt very much if—"

A miniature babbling sound issued from the receiver.

"Of course she does," Sam said. "I understand. All right, Mr. Maxwell—if you think it's
that important, I'll come take a look."

"Oh, Sam!" Delia hissed, sitting up.

He ignored her. "See you in a few minutes,
then," he was telling Mr. Maxwell.

As soon as he had replaced the receiver, Delia
said, "Sam Grinstead, you are such a patsy. You
know it's going to be nothing. Why can't he take
her to the emergency room, if she's so sick?"

"Well, neither one of them drives anymore,"
Sam said mildly. He swung his feet to the floor
and reached for his trousers, which lay folded
over the back of the rocker. As always, he'd
worn tomorrow's underwear to bed and placed
tomorrow's clothes conveniently at hand.

Delia pressed a palm to her heart, which was
only now settling down. Was this anything like
what Sam had felt with his chest pains? She kept
trying to imagine. Think of him operating a car
at such a time—humming along toward a meeting and then noticing his symptoms and
smoothly, composedly (she pictured) turning his
wheel toward Sinai Hospital. Arranging his own
admission and asking a nurse to phone Delia and
break the news by degrees. ("Your husband
wants you to know he'll be a tad bit later getting
home than planned.") And Delia, meanwhile,
had been reading *Lucinda's Lover* by the fire,
without a qualm.

She switched on her lamp and climbed out of

bed. Two-fifteen, the alarm clock said. Squinting
against the light, Sam reached for his glasses and
put them on to look at her. "Where are *you* off
to?" he asked. The glasses made his face seem
crisper, less vague around the eyes, as if they
had corrected Delia's vision rather than his.

She drew her ruffled housecoat over her nightgown and zipped the front before she answered.
"I'm coming with you," she said.

"Pardon?"

"I'll take you in my car."

"Why on earth would you do that?"

"I just want to, that's why," she said. She tied
her sash very tight, in hopes her housecoat would
pass for streetwear. As she stepped into her flats,
she could feel him staring at her, but all she said
was, "Ready?" She collected her keys from the
bureau.

"Delia, are you doubting my ability to drive
my own car anymore?" Sam asked.

"Oh, no! What a thought!" she told him. "But
I'm awake, why not come with you? Besides, it's
such a nice spring night."

He didn't look convinced, but he offered no
more arguments when she led the way downstairs.

It was not a nice spring night at all. It was cool
and breezy, and she wished for a sweater as soon
as they stepped out the back door. Towering,
luminous clouds scudded across an inky sky. But

she headed toward her car at a leisurely pace, resisting the urge to hunch her shoulders against the chill. The streetlights were so bright that she could see her shadow, elongated like a stick figure in a child's drawing.

"This makes me think of Daddy," she said. She had to speak up, since Sam had walked over to his Buick to retrieve his black bag. She hoped he didn't hear the shiver in her voice. "All the house calls I used to make with Daddy, just the two of us! Seems like old times."

She slid behind her steering wheel and reached across to unlock the passenger door. The air inside the car felt refrigerated. It even smelled refrigerated—dank and stale.

"Of course, Daddy never let me drive him," she said when Sam had got in. Then she worried this would give him second thoughts, and so she added, laughing slightly, "You know how prejudiced he was! Women drivers, he always said . . ." She started the engine and turned on her lights, illuminating the double doors of the garage and the tattered net of the basketball hoop overhead. "But whenever I was still up, he'd say I could come with him. Oh, I tagged along many a night! Eliza just never was interested, and Linda was so, you know, at odds with him all the time, but I was ready at a moment's notice. I just loved to go."

Sam had heard all this before, of course. He

merely settled his bag between his feet while she backed the car out of the driveway.

Once they were on Roland Avenue, she said, "In fact I ought to come with you more often, now the kids are growing up. Don't you think?" She was aware that she was chattering, but she said, "It might be kind of fun! And it's not as if you go out every night, or even every week anymore."

"Delia, I give you my word I am still capable of making the odd house call without a baby-sitter," Sam told her.

"Baby-sitter!"

"I'm strong as an ox. Stop fretting."

"I'm not fretting! I just thought it would be romantic, something the two of us could do to-gether!" she said.

This wasn't the whole truth, but as soon as she said it she started to believe it, and so she felt a bit hurt. Sam merely sat back and gazed out the side window.

There was almost no traffic at this hour, and the avenue seemed very flat and empty, shim-mering pallidly beneath the streetlights as if veiled by yellow chiffon. The newly leafed trees, lit from below, had a tumbled, upside-down look. Here and there a second-floor window glowed cozily, and Delia sent it a wistful glance as they passed.

In front of the Maxwells' house, she parked.

She turned off the headlights but left the engine and the heater on. "Aren't you coming in?" Sam asked.

"I'll wait in the car."

"You'll freeze!"

"I'm not dressed for company."

"Come in, Dee. The Maxwells don't care how you're dressed."

He was right, she supposed. (And the heater hadn't even started heating yet.) She took the keys from the ignition and slid out of the car to follow him up the front walk, toward the broad, columned house where those two lone Maxwells must rattle around like dice in a cup. All the windows were blazing, and the inner door stood open. Mr. Maxwell waited just inside, a stooped, bulky figure fumbling to unhook the screen as they crossed the porch.

"Dr. Grinstead!" he said. "Thank you so much for coming. And Delia too. Hello, dear."

He wore food-stained trousers belted just beneath his armpits, and a frayed gray cardigan over a T-shirt. (He used to be such a natty dresser.) Without a pause, he turned to lead Sam toward the carpeted stairs. "It breaks my heart to see her this way," he said as they started the climb. "I'd suffer in her stead, if I could."

Delia watched after them from the foyer, and when they were out of sight she sat down on one of the two antique chairs that flanked a highboy.

She sat cautiously; for all she knew, the chairs were purely for show.

Overhead the voices murmured—Mrs. Maxwell's thin and complaining, Sam's a rumble. The grandfather clock facing Delia ticked so slowly that it seemed each tick might be its last. For lack of anything better to do (she had thoughtlessly left her purse at home), she fanned her keys across her lap and sorted through them.

How many hours had she sat like this in her childhood? Perched on a chair or a bottom step, scratching at the insect bites on her bare knees or leafing through a magazine some grown-up had thrust upon her before leading her father up the stairs. And overhead that same murmur, the words never quite distinguishable. When her father spoke, all others fell silent, and she had felt proud and flattered to hear how people revered him.

The stairs creaked, and she looked up. It was Mr. Maxwell, descending by himself. "Dr. Grinstead's just examining her," he said. He inched down, clinging to the banister, and when he reached the foyer he settled with a wheeze onto the other antique chair. Because the highboy stood between them, all she saw of him was his outstretched trouser legs and his leather slippers, backless, exposing maroon silk socks with transparent heels. "He says he thinks it's a touch of indigestion, but I told him, I said, at our age . . . well, you can't be too careful, I told him."

"I'm sure she'll be all right," Delia said.

"I just thank heaven for Dr. Grinstead. A lot of those younger fellows wouldn't come out like this."

"None of them would," Delia couldn't resist saying.

"Oh, some, maybe."

"None. Believe me."

Mr. Maxwell sat forward to look at her. She found his veiny, florid face peering around the highboy.

"That Sam is just too nice for his own good," she told him. "Did you know he has angina? Angina, at age fifty-five! What could that mean for his future? If it were up to me, he'd be home in bed this very minute."

"Well, luckily it's *not* up to you," Mr. Maxwell said a bit peevishly. He sat back again and there was a pause, during which she heard Mrs. Maxwell say something opinionated that sounded like "Nee-nee. Nee-nee."

"We were Dr. Grinstead's first house call—did he ever mention that?" Mr. Maxwell asked. "Yessir: very first house call. Your dad said, 'Think you'll like this boy.' I admit we were a mite apprehensive, having relied on your dad all those years."

Sam was speaking more briskly now. He must be finishing up.

"I asked Dr. Grinstead when he came to us," Mr. Maxwell said dreamily. "I said, 'Well, young man?' He'd only been on the job a couple days by then. I said, 'Well?' Said, 'Which one of those Felson girls do you plan to set about marrying?' Pretty smart of me, eh?''

Delia laughed politely and rearranged her keys.

" 'Oh,' he said; said, 'I guess I've got my eye on the youngest.' Said, 'The oldest is too short and the middle one's too plump, but the youngest,' he said, 'is just right.' So. See there? I knew before you did."

"Yes, I guess you did," Delia said, and then Sam started down the stairs, the instruments in his black bag cheerily jingling. Mr. Maxwell rose at once, but Delia stayed seated and kept her gaze fixed on her keys. They seemed uncannily distinct—dull-finished, ill-assorted, incised with brand names as clipped and choppy as words from another language.

"Just what I . . . ," Sam was saying, and, "Nothing but a touch of . . . ," and, "Left some medication on the . . ." Then he and Mr. Maxwell were shaking hands, and he said, "Dee?" and she stood up without a word and stepped through the door that Mr. Maxwell held open.

Outside, the grass had grown white with dew and the air itself seemed white, as if dawn were not far off. Delia climbed into the car and started the engine before Sam was completely settled.

"You have to feel for those folks," he said, shutting his door. "Aging all alone like that, they must dwell on every symptom."

Delia swung out into the street and drove slightly above the speed limit, concentrating, not speaking. They were nearly home before she said, "Mr. Maxwell told me they were your very first house call."

"Really?"

"The second day you worked here."

"I'd forgotten."

"He said he asked which of the Felson girls you planned to marry and you said the youngest."

"Hmm," Sam said, unzipping his bag. He checked something inside and told her, "Delia, remind me tomorrow morning to pick up more—"

" 'The oldest is too short and the middle one's too plump,' you said, 'but the youngest one is just right.' "

Sam laughed.

"Did you say that?" she asked him.

"Oh, sweetie, how would I remember after all these years?"

She pulled into their driveway and turned the engine off. Sam opened his door, but then, noticing she had not moved, he looked over at her. The little ceiling bulb cast sharp hollows in his face.

"You did say it," she told him. "I recognize the fairy-tale sound of it."

"So? Maybe I did," he said. "Gosh, Dee, I wasn't weighing every word. I might have *said* 'too short' and 'too plump,' but what I probably meant was 'too unconventional' and 'too Francophile.' "

"That's not it," Delia said.

"Why, Linda spent half the evening speaking French, remember? And when your dad made her switch to English, she still had an accent."

"You don't even know what I'm objecting to, do you?" Delia asked.

"Well, no," Sam said. "I don't."

She got out of the car and walked toward the back steps. Sam went to replace his bag in the Buick; she heard the clunk of his trunk lid.

"And Eliza!" he said as he followed her to the house. "She kept asking my opinion of homeopathic medicine."

"You arrived here that very first day planning to marry one of the Felson girls," Delia told him.

She had unlocked the door now, but instead of entering she turned to face him. He was looking down at her, with his forehead creased.

"Why, I suppose it must naturally have crossed my mind," he said. "I'd completed all my training by then. I'd reached the marrying age, so to speak. The marrying stage of life."

"But then why not a nurse, or a fellow student, or some girl your mother knew?"

"My mother?" he said. He blinked.

"You had your eye on Daddy's practice, that's why," she told him. "You thought, 'I'll just marry one of Dr. Felson's daughters and inherit all his patients and his nice old comfortable house.' "

"Well, sweetheart, I probably did think that. Probably I did. But I never would have married someone I didn't love. Is that what you believe? You believe I didn't marry for love?"

"I don't know what to believe," she told him.

Then she spun around and walked back down the steps.

"Dee?" Sam called.

She passed her car without slowing. Most women would have *driven* away, but she preferred to walk. The soles of her flats gritted against the asphalt driveway in a purposeful rhythm, reminding her of some tune she could almost name but not quite. Part of her was listening for Sam (she had a sense of perking one ear backward, like a cat), but another part was glad to be rid of him and pleased to have her view of him confirmed. *Look at that, he won't even deign to come after me.* She reached the street, turned right, and kept going. Her frail-edged shadow preceded her and then drew back and then fell behind as she traveled from streetlight to streetlight. No longer did she feel the cold. She seemed warmed from inside by her anger.

Now she understood why Sam had forgotten his actual first glimpse of her. He had prepared to meet the Felson girls as a boxed set, that was why. It had not figured in his plans to encounter an isolated sample ahead of time. What *had* figured was the social occasion that evening, with marriageable maidens one, two, and three on display on the living-room couch. She could envision that scene herself now. All it took was the proper perspective to bring it back entire: the itchy red plush cushions, the clothlike texture of her frosted sherry glass, and the fidgeting, encroaching, irritating plumpness of the middle sister, next to her.

On a branch overhead, the neighborhood's silly mockingbird was imitating a burglar alarm. "Doy! Doy! Doy!" he sang in his most lyrical voice, until he was silenced by a billow of rock music approaching from the south. Teenagers, evidently—a whole carload. Delia heard their hoots and cheers growing steadily louder. It occurred to her that even Roland Park was not absolutely safe at this hour. Also, her housecoat wouldn't fool a soul. She was running around in her nightclothes, basically. She took a sudden right turn onto a smaller, darker street and walked close to a boxwood hedge, whose shadow swallowed hers.

Sam would be back in bed now, his trousers draped over the rocking chair. And the children didn't know she was missing. With their jumbled, separate schedules, they might not know for days.

What kind of a life was she leading, if every single one of last week's telephone messages could as easily be this week's?

She walked faster, hearing the carload of music fade away behind her. She reached Bouton Road, crossed over, and turned left, and one split second later, *whomp!* she collided with someone. She ran smack against a stretch of tall-ness and boniness, overlaid by warm flannel. "Oh!" she said, and she recoiled violently, heart pounding, while somehow a dog became in-volved as well, one of those shaggy hunting-type dogs shouting around her knees.

"Butch! Down!" the man commanded. "Are you all right?" he asked Delia.

Delia said, "Adrian?"

In the half-dark he had no color, but still she recognized his narrow, distinctly cheekboned face. She saw that his mouth was wider and fuller, more sculptured, than she had been imag-ining, and she wondered how she could have forgotten something so important. "Adrian, it's me. Delia," she said. The dog was still barking. She said, "Delia Grinstead? From the super-market?"

"Why, Delia," Adrian said. "My rescuer!" He laughed, and the dog grew quiet. "What are *you* doing here?"

She said, "Oh, just . . . ," and then she laughed

too, glancing down at her housecoat and smoothing it with her palms. "Just couldn't sleep," she
said.

She was relieved to find that he was not so
well dressed himself. He wore a dark-hued robe
of some kind and pale pajamas. On his feet were
jogging shoes, laces trailing, no socks. "Do you
live nearby?" she asked him.

"Right here," he said, and he waved toward
a matted screen of barberry bushes. Behind it
Delia glimpsed a porch light and a section of
white clapboard. "I got up to let Butch here take
a pee," he said. "It's his new hobby: waking me
in the dead of night and claiming he needs to go
out."

At the sound of his name, Butch sat down
on his haunches and grinned up at her. Delia
leaned over to give his muzzle a timid pat.
His breath warmed and dampened her fingers.
"I ran off with your groceries that day," she
said, ostensibly to the dog. "I felt terrible about
it."

"Groceries?" Adrian asked.

"Your orzo and your rotini . . ." She straightened and met his eyes. "I considered hunting up
your address and bringing them over."

"Oh. Well . . . orzo? Well, never mind," he
told her. "I'm just grateful you helped me out
like that. You must have thought I was kind of
weird, right?"

"No, not at all! I enjoyed it," she said.

"You know how sometimes you just want to, say, keep up appearances in front of someone."

"Certainly," she said. "I ought to start a business: Appearances, Incorporated."

"Rent-a-Date," Adrian suggested. "Impostors To Go."

"With blondes to pose as second wives, and football stars to take jilted girls to proms—"

"And beautiful women in black to weep at funerals," Adrian said.

"Oh, why *don't* they have such things?" Delia asked. "There's just nothing like that . . . what? Like that fury, that prideful sort of fury you feel when you've been hurt or insulted or taken for granted—"

Well. She stopped herself. Adrian was watching her with such peculiar intentness, she worried all at once that she had curlers in her hair. She nearly raised a hand to check, till she remembered she hadn't worn curlers since high school. "Goodness. I should get home," she said.

"Wait!" Adrian said. "Would you like . . . could I offer you some coffee?"

"Coffee?"

"Or tea? Or cocoa? Or a drink?"

"Well," she said, "I guess cocoa, maybe. Cocoa might be nice. I mean caffeine at this hour would probably . . . But are you sure it's not too much trouble?"

"No trouble at all," he told her. "Come on inside."

He led her to a gap in the barberry bushes. A flagstone path curved toward the house, which was one of those lace-trimmed Victorian cottages young couples nowadays found so charming. The front door was paned with lozenges of glass in sugared-almond colors impossible to see through. Delia felt a sudden pinch of uneasiness. Why, she didn't know a thing about this man! And no one else on earth had any inkling where she was.

"Usually if I'm up at this hour I'm up for good," Adrian was saying, "so I fix myself a pot of—"

"What a lovely porch!" Delia exclaimed. "Maybe we could have our cocoa out here."

"Here?"

He paused on the topmost step and looked around him. It was a depressing porch, really. The floorboards were battleship gray, and the furniture was painted a harsh bright shade of green. "Don't you think you'd be cold?" he asked.

"Not a bit," she told him, although now that she had stopped walking, it did seem cold. She stuffed both fists in the pockets of her housecoat.

He gazed down at her a moment. Then he said, "Ah. I see," and the corners of his mouth quirked upward with amusement.

"But if *you're* cold . . . ," she said, flushing.

"I understand," he said. "You can't be too careful."

"Oh, it's not that! Heavens!"

"I don't blame you in the least. We'll have our cocoa out here."

"Really," she said, "why don't I come in?"

"No, you wait here. I'll bring it out."

"Please," she said. "Please let me come in."

And because she saw that the argument would otherwise go on forever, she took one hand from her pocket and laid it on his wrist. "I want to," she said.

She wanted to come in, she meant. That was what she honestly meant, but the moment the words were out of her mouth she saw that they implied something more, and she dropped her hand and stepped back. "Or maybe . . . ," she said. "Yes, the . . . porch, why don't we have our cocoa on the . . ." And she felt behind her for a chair and sat down. The icy, uncushioned seat took her breath away for an instant, as if she had heard a piece of startling news, or glimpsed some possibility that had never crossed her mind before.

# 4

"I told Eliza when she picked us up at the airport," Linda said. "I told her, 'Well, one good thing: now that Dad's gone I won't have to share a room with you, Eliza.' Considering how she snores."

Delia said, "Yes, but—"

" 'And the twins won't have to bunk with Susie,' I said. I figured I could fit both of them in Dad's big bed with me. Then I get to the house, and guess what."

"I did plan at first for you to stay there," Delia said, "but it seemed so . . . when I walked in to put the sheets on, it seemed so . . ."

"Fine, I'll put the sheets on myself," Linda said. "I'll tell you this much: I am surely not sleeping with Eliza when there's a whole extra room going empty."

They were standing in the doorway of their father's room at that moment, gazing in on its heartbreaking neatness, the dim air laden with dust motes, the candlewick bedspread unnaturally straight on the mattress. Linda, still in her traveling clothes, had not yet lost that aura of focus and efficiency that travel gives some people. She surveyed the room without a trace of sentiment, as far as Delia could see. "You've certainly wasted no time making changes elsewhere," she said. "Air-conditioning vents every place you look, nursery men tearing out the shrubs, I don't know *what* all."

"Oh, well, that's—"

"I suppose it's what Sam Grinstead has been waiting for," Linda said. "He's finally got the house in his clutches."

Delia didn't argue. Linda sent her a quizzical glance before crossing to their father's bureau. Leaning into the mirror above it, she raked her fingers through her short brown pageboy. Then she removed her pocketbook, which she wore bandolier style, with the strap slanted over her chest—just one more of her European ways. You would never take her for American. (You would never guess she lived in Michigan, divorced from the French-literature professor who had not, after all, swooped her off to his native Paris as she'd hoped.) Her full, soft face was powdered white, her only other makeup a bloom of sticky scarlet on her lips, and although her clothes were unexceptional, she wore them with authority—those dowdy brown medium-heeled pumps, for instance, defiantly teamed with a navy suit. "But why are we standing around? No telling what Marie-Claire and Thérèse have got into," she said, and the *r*'s in her children's

names were very nearly gargled. When she
whisked past Delia toward the stairs, she smelled
of airplane.

In the kitchen, they found Eliza making lemonade for the twins. This fall the twins would be
nine years old—a long-limbed, sproutlike stage
—and although they had their mother's blocky
brown haircut, they resembled the professor in
every other way. Their eyes were almost black,
mournfully downturned; their mouths were the
color of plums. They were assisting each other
up a bank of glass-fronted cabinets, the first pulling the second after her once she'd reached the
counter, and for mobility's sake they had tucked
their old-fashioned, European-schoolgirl dresses
into their underpants, which made them look all
the leggier.

"As soon as your cousin Susie shows up, she'll
take you to the pool," Eliza was saying. She
stood at the drainboard, reaming lemons.
"She promised she'd do it first thing, but I guess
she must be off someplace with her boyfriend."

The mention of a boyfriend diverted them for
a second. "Driscoll?" Marie-Claire asked, pausing in her climb. "Does Susie still date Driscoll?"

"She does indeed."

"Do they go to dances together? Do they kiss
good night?"

"Now, that I wouldn't know," Eliza said
tartly, and she bent to take a pitcher from a
cupboard.

The twins had reached their goal: a jar of peppermints on the top shelf. Inch by inch, Thérèse maneuvered it through the partially opened door. (Thérèse was the uneven-featured twin, her face less balanced, less symmetrical, which made her appear slightly anxious. There was one in every set, Delia had noticed.) For a moment the jar seemed suspended, but then it arrived safely in Marie-Claire's outstretched hands. "Do Ramsay and Carroll have sweethearts too?" she asked.

"Well, Ramsay does, I'm sorry to say."

"How come you're sorry?" Thérèse asked, and Marie-Claire said, "What's wrong with her?"—the two of them so alert for scandal that Delia laughed aloud. Thérèse wheeled and said, "Are you sorry too, Aunt Delia? Do you forbid her to darken your door? Is she coming to the beach with us?"

"No, she's not," Delia said, answering only the easiest question. "The beach is just a family trip."

They were leaving for a week at the beach early the following morning, a Sunday. It had come to be an annual event. In mid-June, as soon as the schools closed, Linda arrived from Michigan and they all took off for a cottage they rented on the Delaware shore. Already the front porch was heaped with rubber rafts and badminton rackets; the freezer was stuffed with casseroles; and Sam's patients were thronging in for

last-minute consultations in hopes of avoiding
any contact with his backup.

"Delia, could you get the sugar?" Eliza asked.
She was running water into the pitcher. "And
girls, I'd like five tumblers from that cabinet to
your right."

While Delia was measuring sugar, she secretly
checked the clock on the wall above her. Ten
minutes till four. She glanced at the twins and
cleared her throat. "If Susie isn't back by the
time you finish your lemonade, maybe *I* could
take you to the pool," she said.

Linda said, "You?" and the twins said, in a
single voice, "You *hate* to swim!"

"Oh, well, I wouldn't actually go in. I'd just
drive you over, and then Susie could pick you
up later."

Eliza clinked ice into the tumblers. Linda took
a seat at the head of the table, and the twins
claimed the chairs on either side of her. When
Delia placed the pitcher of lemonade in front of
them, Marie-Claire cried, "Ick! It's full of
shreddy things!"

"Those are good for you," Linda said as she
started pouring.

"And big seeds besides!"

"They won't hurt you."

"That's what *she* says," Thérèse told Marie-
Claire in an ominous tone. "Really they'll take
root in your stomach and grow lemon trees out
your ears."

"Oh, honestly, Thérèse," Linda said.

Ignoring her, the twins gazed significantly across the table at each other. Finally Marie-Claire said, "I guess we're not thirsty after all."

"We'll just go change into our swimsuits," Thérèse added.

They scooted their chairs back and raced out of the kitchen.

"Ah, me," Linda sighed. "Sorry, Lize."

"That's all right," Eliza said stiffly.

There were times when Delia realized, for an instant, that Eliza was what they used to call an old maid. She looked so forlorn in her eccentric weekend outfit of safari suit and clunky shoes; she pulled out a chair with her head down, her chopped black hair falling forward to hide her expression, and she seated herself and folded her small hands resolutely on the table.

"Well, *I'm* thirsty!" Delia said loudly, and she sat down too and reached for one of the tumblers. From the hall she heard a series of thumps—the twins' suitcase, no doubt, being hauled up the stairs. Apparently they still planned to room with Susie, if the creaks that began overhead were any indication.

Outside the open window, a workman's bearded face popped into view. He looked at the women, blinked, and disappeared. Delia and Linda saw him, but Eliza, who had her back to him, did not. "What is he up to, anyhow?" Linda asked.

Eliza said, "He? Who?"

"The workman," Delia explained.

"No, not the workman," Linda said. "I meant Sam. Why is he having all the shrubs torn out?"

"Well, they're old and straggly, he says."

"Can't he just cut them back or something? And central air-conditioning! This house is not the type for air-conditioning."

"I'm sure we'll appreciate it once the weather heats up," Eliza said. "Have some lemonade, Linda."

Linda took a tumbler, but she didn't drink from it. "I'd just like to know where he found the money," she said darkly. "Plus: this house is in *our* three names, not his. We're the ones Dad left it to."

Delia glanced toward the window. (She suspected the workman of lurking beneath it, absorbed as all workmen seemed to be in other people's private lives.) "Goodness!" she said. "We'd better get to the pool. Anybody want anything from Eddie's?"

"Eddie's?" Eliza asked.

"I might stop for some fruit on my way home."

"Delia, have you forgotten Sam's mother is coming to dinner? And you still have the Medicare bills to see to! Why don't I take the twins, instead, and then go to Eddie's after."

"No! Please!" Delia said. "I mean, I have plenty of time. And besides, I need to choose the fruit myself because I'm not sure what I—"

She was offering too many explanations—always a mistake. Linda didn't notice, but Eliza could read her mind, Delia sometimes thought, and she was watching Delia consideringly. "Anyhow," Delia said. "I'll see you both in a while. Okay?" And she stood up. Already she heard the twins racketing down the stairs. "Hand me my purse, will you?" she asked. Eliza was still watching her, but she reached for Delia's purse on the counter and passed it over.

In the hall, the twins were quarreling over a pair of goggles they must have liberated from the beach equipment. They wore identical skinny knit swimsuits in different colors—one red, one blue—and a red-and-blue flip-flop apiece on their long, pale, knobby feet. Neither one had a towel, but the towels were upstairs and so Delia didn't remind them. "Let's go," she told them. "I'm parked out front." From the kitchen, Linda called, "You do what the lifeguard tells you, girls, hear?"

Delia followed them across the porch, avoiding the shaft of a beach umbrella. Beside the steps, a young man in a red bandanna was hacking at the roots of an azalea bush. He straightened, wiped his face on his forearm, and gave them a grin. "Wisht *I* was going swimming," he said.

"Come with us, then," Thérèse said, but

Marie-Claire told her, "Dope, you can see he's not wearing his bathing suit." They skipped ahead of Delia down the walk, chanting a routine that she remembered from her childhood:

"Well, that's life."

"*What's* life?"

"Fifteen cents a copy."

"But I only have a dime."

"Well, that's life."

"*What's* life?"

"Fifteen cents a . . ."

The weather was perfect, sunny and not too warm, but Delia's car had been sitting at the curb collecting heat all day. Both girls squealed as they slid across the back seat. "Could you turn on the air-conditioning?" they asked Delia.

"I don't have air-conditioning."

"Don't have air-conditioning!"

"Just open your windows," she told them, rolling down her own. She started the engine and pulled into the street. The steering wheel was almost too hot to touch.

You could tell it was a weekend, because so many joggers were out. And people were at work in their yards, running their mowers or their hedge trimmers, filling the air with a visible green dust that made Thérèse (the allergic one) sneeze. At Wyndhurst the traffic light changed to amber, but Delia didn't stop. She had a sense of time slipping away from her. She took the long downhill slope at a good ten miles above the speed limit, and screeched left on Lawndale and parked in the first available space. The twins were in a hurry themselves; they tore ahead of her to the gate, and even before she paid for them they had disappeared among the other swimmers.

Driving back up the hill, she kept plucking at the front of her blouse and blowing toward the damp frizz sticking to her forehead. If only she could stop by home and freshen up a bit! But she would never manage to escape her sisters a second time. She turned south, not so much as glancing northward to Eddie's. She traveled through a blessedly cool corridor of shade trees, and when she reached Bouton Road she parked beneath a maple. Before she got out, she blotted her face on a tissue from her purse. Then she walked through Adrian's front yard and climbed the porch steps and rang the doorbell.

By now the dog knew her well enough so he merely roused himself from the mat to nose her skirt. "Hi, Butch," she said. She dabbed at his muzzle ineptly, at the same time backing off a bit. The front door opened, and Adrian said, "Finally!"

"I'm sorry," she told him, stepping inside. "I couldn't get away till Linda came, and wouldn't you know her plane was late, and then of course I had to make sure that she and the children were . . ."

She was talking too much, but she couldn't

seem to stop herself. These first few minutes were always so awkward. Adrian took her purse from her and set it on a chair, and she fell silent. Then he bent and kissed her. She supposed she must taste of salt. They had not been kissing for very long—at least not like this, so seriously. They had started with the breeziest peck on the cheek, pretending to be just friends; then day by day more parts of them became involved—their lips, their open mouths, their arms around each other, their bodies pressing closer until Delia (it was always Delia) drew back with a little laugh and a "Well!" and some adjustment of her clothes. "Well! Did you get much work done?" she asked now. He was looking down at her, smiling. He wore khakis and a faded blue chambray shirt that matched his eyes. Over these past few weeks of sunshine his hair had turned almost golden, so that it seemed to give off a light of its own as he stood in the dark hallway—one more detail to make her spin away abruptly and walk on into the house as if she had some business to attend to.

Adrian's house always struck her as only marginally inhabited, which was odd because until three months ago his wife had lived here too. Why, then, did the rooms have this feeling of long-term indifference and neglect? The living room, viewed from the hall, never enticed her inside. Its walls were bare except for a single bland still life above the mantel, and instead of a couch, three chairs stood at offended-looking angles to each other. The tabletops bore only what was useful—a lamp, a telephone; none of the decorative this-and-thats that would have taken the chill off.

"I finished printing out the Adwater piece," Adrian was saying. "I thought you might look it over and tell me what you think."

He was leading her up the narrow stairway and across the hall, into an area that must once have been called the conservatory or the sunroom. Now it was his office. Cloudy windows lined three walls, their sills piled high with papers. Along the fourth wall ran a built-in desk that held various pieces of computer equipment. This was where Adrian produced his newsletter. Subscribers from thirty-four states paid actual money for *Hurry Up, Please*, a quarterly devoted to the subject of time travel. Its cover was a glossy sky blue, its logo an arched wooden mantel clock on spoked wheels. Each issue contained an assortment of science fiction and nonfiction, as well as reviews of time-machine novels and time-machine movies, and even an occasional cartoon or joke. In fact, was this whole publication a joke, or was it for real? Reading the letters to the editor, Delia often wondered. Many of the subscribers seemed to believe in earnest. At least a few claimed to speak from personal experience. And she detected an almost anthropological tone to the article Adrian handed her now—an essay by one Charles L. Adwater, Ph.D., proposing that the quality known as "charisma" was merely the superior grace and dash found in visitors from the future who are sojourning in the present. *Consider,* Dr. Adwater wrote, *how easily you and I would navigate the 1940s, which today seems a rather naive period, by and large, and one in which a denizen of our own decade could hope to make a considerable impact with relatively little effort.*

"Would you say the 1940s seems, or the 1940s seem?" Adrian asked. "Either one has arguments for and against it."

Delia didn't answer. She paced the room as she read, chewing her lower lip, squinting at draft-quality print as dotty and sparse as the scabs on an old brier scratch. "Well . . . ," she said, and pretending absentmindedness, she wandered out to the hall while she flipped to the second page.

Adrian followed. "In my opinion, Adwater's style is kind of stuffy," he was saying, "but I can't suggest too many changes because he's one of the biggest names in the field."

How would you make a name for yourself in the time-travel field? Delia was intrigued, but only briefly. Her visit to Adrian's office was a ruse, in fact, as even Adrian must know. It was being upstairs that mattered: roaming the second floor, the *bedroom* floor, and peeking through each doorway. Adrian slept in a drab little dressing room; he had moved there after Rosemary left him, so Delia felt free to stroll into the master bedroom while flipping to page three. She went over to stand near a bureau—just trying to get more reading light from the window above it, she could argue. Behind her, Adrian straightened her collar. His fingers made a whispery sound. "Why do you always wear a necklace?" he asked, very close to her ear.

"Hmm?" she said in a small voice. She turned another page, blindly.

"You always wear a string of pearls, or a cameo, or today this heart-shaped locket. Always something snug around your throat, and these little round innocent collars."

"It's only habit," she said, but her thoughts were racing. Did he mean that she looked silly, unsuited to her age?

He had never asked how old she was, and although she wouldn't have lied to him, she didn't feel any need to volunteer the truth. When he'd told her that he himself was thirty-two, she had said, "Thirty-two! Young enough to be my son!"—a deliberate exaggeration, calculated to make him laugh. She had not mentioned the ages of her children, even. Nor had he inquired, for like most childless people, he seemed ignorant of the enormous space that children occupy in a life.

Also, he had a slightly skewed image of her husband. She could tell from some of his remarks that he was picturing Sam as beefy and athletic (because he jogged) and perhaps possessed of a jealous disposition. And Delia had not set him straight.

All it would take was bringing the two men together once—inviting Adrian for supper, say, as a neighbor left wifeless and forced to cook for himself—and the situation would lose all its potential for drama. Sam would start referring to "your pal Bly-Brice," in that sardonic way of his; the children would roll their eyes if she talked to him too long on the phone. But Delia made no move to arrange such a meeting. She had not so much as spoken his name to anyone in her family. And when Adrian's hands left her collar to settle on both her shoulders and draw her closer, she didn't resist but tipped her head back to rest it against his chest. "You're such a little person," he said. She heard the rumble of his voice within his rib cage. "You're so little and dainty and delicate."

Compared with his wife, she supposed he meant; and the notion pulled her upright. She walked away from him, briskly realigning pages. She circled the bed (Rosemary's bed! covered with a rather seedy sateen quilt) and approached the closet. "What I want to know," she said over her shoulder, "is can you really make a living this way? Because a magazine like yours is kind of specialized, isn't it?"

"Oh, I'm not so much as breaking even," Adrian told her offhandedly. "Pretty soon I'll have to fold, I guess. Switch to something new. But I'm used to that. Before this, I published a bulletin for rotisserie-baseball owners."

The closet was filled with Rosemary's clothes—tops, then dresses, then pants, so there was an orderly progression from short to long; and they hung evenly spaced, not bunched together as in Delia's closet. According to Adrian, Rosemary had abandoned every single one of her possessions when she left. All she took was the black silk jumpsuit she was wearing and a slim black purse tucked under her arm. Why did Delia find that so alluring? This was not the first time she had stood mesmerized in front of Rosemary's closet.

"And before that," Adrian said, "I had a quarterly for *M*A*S*H* fans." He was behind her again. He reached out one finger to stroke the point of her bent elbow.

Delia said, "How've you been supporting yourself all this time?"

"Well, Rosemary had a bit of an inheritance."

She closed the closet door. She said, "Did you know that before you married her?"

"Why do you ask?"

"Lately I've been wondering if Sam married me for my father's practice," she said.

She shouldn't have told him. Adrian would look at her and think, *Yes, she is rather homely, and her elbows are chapped besides.*

But he smiled and said, "If it were me, I'd have married you for your freckles."

She went over to Rosemary's side of the bed. She knew it was Rosemary's because a blown-glass perfume bottle sat next to the lamp. First she laid Dr. Adwater's article on the nightstand, and then, as if it were the logical next step, she opened the little drawer underneath. She gazed into a clutter of manicure scissors, emery boards, and nail polish bottles.

How fitting, the name Rosemary! Rosemary was such a sophisticated herb, so sharp-tasting, almost chemical. Put too much in a recipe, and you'd swear you were eating a petroleum product. There was nothing plain about it, nothing mild or dull. Nothing freckled.

Adrian came up behind her. He turned her to face him and wrapped his arms around her, and this time she didn't move away but set her hands at his waist and strained upward to meet his kisses. He kissed her mouth, her eyelids, her mouth once more. He whispered, "Lie down with me, Delia."

Then the phone rang.

He didn't seem to hear it; he never heard it.

And he never answered it. He said it was his mother-in-law, who liked him better than she liked her own daughter and was always trying to get them back together. "How do you know it's not Rosemary?" Delia once asked, and Adrian, shrugging, said, "The telephone isn't Rosemary's instrument of choice." Now he didn't flinch, didn't even tense. Delia would have felt it if he had. He kissed the curve where her neck met her shoulder, and she began to notice the bed pressing the backs of her knees. But the phone continued to ring. Ten rings, eleven. Subconsciously, she must be counting. The realization enabled her, somehow, to pull away, although she felt that she was dragging her limbs through water. "Oh, my," she said, out of breath, and she made a great business of tucking her blouse more securely into her skirt. "I really should be . . . did I leave my purse downstairs?"

He was out of breath too. He didn't speak. She said, "Yes, I remember! On the chair. I have to hurry; Sam's mother is coming to dinner."

Meanwhile she was clattering down the stairs. The extension phone in the living room was on its fourteenth ring. Its fifteenth. She reached the front hall and seized her purse and turned at the door to say, "You know we're leaving tomorrow for—"

"You never stay," he said. "You're always rushing off as soon as you get here."

"Oh, well, I—"

"What are you afraid of?"

*I'm afraid of getting undressed in front of some-one thirty-two years old,* she did not say. She smiled up at him, falsely. She said, "I'll see you after the beach, I guess."

"Can't you ever manage a solid block of time? A whole night? Can't you tell them you're visiting one of your girlfriends?"

"I don't have a girlfriend," she said.

She really didn't, come to think of it. When she married Sam she had switched generations and left everyone behind, all her old high-school classmates. "Although it's true there's Bootsy Fisher," she said. (Whom Sam called Bootsy Officious: the thought rose out of nowhere.) "Her kids and mine used to carpool."

"Can't you say you're at Bootsy's?"

"Oh, no, I don't see how I—"

And then, because she guessed from the way his mouth seemed to soften that he was about to kiss her again, she gave him a fluttery wave and hurried out the door, nearly tripping over Butch on the mat.

Funny, she thought, as she settled herself in her car, how often lately her high-school days came to mind. It must be this dizzy, damp, rumpled feeling as she rushed home from secret meetings; her telltale flushed cheeks, the used and smushed look of her lips when she risked a glance in the rearview mirror. At a stop sign she made sure that all her buttons were buttoned, and she patted her locket into place between her collarbones. Once again she heard Adrian say, "Why do you always wear a necklace?" And then, "Lie down with me, Delia," and just as in her high-school days, she felt stirred even more by the memory than by the event itself. If she hadn't already been seated, her legs might have buckled.

Maybe she *could* say she was visiting Bootsy. Not for a whole night, of course, but for an evening. Certainly no one in her family would bother checking up on her.

She parked in the driveway, which was clear now of all cars except for Sam's. Smoke billowed from the yard on the other side of the house. He must be firing up the grill for dinner.

She followed the trail of smoke to the little flagstone rectangle beneath the office windows. Yes, there he was, peering at the grill's thermometer with his glasses raised. He still wore his shirt and tie and his suit trousers, minus his white coat. He looked so professional that Delia felt a flash of anxiety. Didn't he know everything? But when he straightened, lowering his glasses, all he said was, "Hi, Dee. Where've you been?"

"Oh, I was . . . running a few errands," she said.

She was amazed that he didn't ask why, then,

she had returned empty-handed. He just nodded and tapped the thermometer with his index finger.

Climbing the steps to the kitchen door, she felt like a woman emerging from a deep, thick daytime sleep. She walked past Eliza and drifted toward the hall. "Are you going to grill the vegetables too? Or put them in the oven?" Eliza called after her.

There wouldn't be space for them on the grill. They would have to go in the oven, and she meant to say as much to Eliza but forgot, lost the words, and merely floated into the study. It was unoccupied, thank heaven. She didn't believe she could have waited till she reached the phone upstairs. She lifted the receiver, dialed Adrian's number, let his phone ring twice, and then hung up—her way of letting him know that this was not his mother-in-law. She redialed, and he answered halfway through the first ring. "Is that you?" he asked. His voice sounded urgent, intense. She sank onto a footstool and gripped the receiver more tightly.

"Yes," she whispered.

"Come back here, Delia."

"I wish I could."

"Come back and stay with me."

"I want to. I do want to," she said.

Sam's mother said, "Delia?"

Delia slammed the phone down and jumped

to her feet. "Eleanor!" she cried. She thrust her hands in the folds of her skirt to hide their tremor. "I was just—I was just—"

"Sorry to barge in," Eleanor said, "but nobody answered the door." She advanced to kiss the air near Delia's ear. She smelled of soap; she was an unperfumed, unfrilled woman, sensibly clad in a drip-dry shirtdress and Nikes, with a handsome face and clipped white monkish hair. "Didn't mean to interrupt your conversation."

"No, I was just winding it up," Delia told her.

"It appears that someone has left some articles on your front porch."

"Articles?"

Delia had a fleeting vision of Dr. Adwater's article on charisma.

"Badminton sets and rafts and such, scattered all about where anyone might stumble on them."

Eleanor was the kind of guest who felt it her duty to point out alarming flaws in the household. How long had their toilet been making that noise? Did they know they had a tree limb about to come down? Delia always countered by pretending that she was a guest herself. "Imagine that!" she said. "Let me take you to Sam. He's out by the grill."

"Now, I thought you weren't going to any fuss," Eleanor told her, leading the way from the study. Instead of a purse, she had one of those belt packs, glow-in-the-dark chartreuse ny-

lon, riding in front of her stomach like some sort
of add-on pregnancy. It caused her to walk
slightly swaybacked, although ordinarily her posture was perfect.

"I'm only serving grilled chicken," Delia said
as they crossed the hall. "Nothing complicated."

"Tinned soup would have been plenty,"
Eleanor said. She eyed a browning apple core
centered on the newel post. "Particularly in view
of all you need to do for your beach trip."

Did she mean this as a reproach? Every
year, Sam suggested inviting his mother along
to the beach, and every year Delia talked him
out of it, which was why they always held this
placatory family dinner the night before they
left. It wasn't that Delia disliked his mother. She
knew that Eleanor was admirable. She knew
that she herself would never have coped so mag-
nificently in Eleanor's circumstances—widowed
early, forced to take a secretarial job to support herself and her young son. (And to hear
Sam tell it, his father had not been much use
anyhow—a weak and ineffectual, watery sort of
man.) The trouble was, in Eleanor's presence
Delia felt so inadequate. She felt so frivolous
and spendthrift and disorganized. Their vacation
was the one time she could hope to shake off
that feeling.

Besides, she couldn't imagine the Iron Mama
lolling on a beach towel.

"Did Linda get here?" Eleanor was asking as they entered the kitchen. "Are the twins just huge? Where are they all?"

It was Eliza, standing at the sink, who answered. "The twins are at the pool," she said. "Linda just left with Susie to fetch them home. How're you doing, Eleanor?"

"Oh, couldn't be better. Is that asparagus I see? Delia, my word, do you know what asparagus *costs*?"

"I found some on sale," Delia lied. "I'm going to roast it in the oven in this new way, really simple. No fuss," she added craftily.

"Well, if your idea of simple is asparagus and roast squab!"

"Chicken, actually."

"Just an old withered carrot would have been good enough for me," Eleanor said.

She headed for the back door, with Delia meekly shadowing her.

In the side yard, Sam was tinkering with the grill knobs. "Looks about the right temperature," he told Delia. "Hello, Mother. Good to see you."

"What's going on with the shrubbery, son?" Eleanor asked, looking past him.

"We're having it taken out," he said. "Putting in a whole new bunch of plantings."

"Why, that must cost a fortune! Couldn't you just work with what you had, for gracious sake?"

"We wanted totally new," Sam told her. (*We?* Delia thought.) "We're tired of working with what we had. Dee, believe I'm ready to start cooking."

As Delia walked toward the house, she heard Eleanor say, "Well, I don't know, son. This life of yours seems mighty rich for *my* blood, what with asparagus for dinner and grilled pheasant."

"Chicken!" Delia called back.

Eliza must have heard too, for she was grinning to herself when Delia opened the screen door. "You bring it to him," Delia told her. "I can't stand another minute."

"Oh, now, you take her too much to heart," Eliza said as she went over to the refrigerator. Eliza seemed to find Eleanor merely amusing. But then, Eliza wasn't Eleanor's daughter-in-law. She didn't have Eleanor held up before her daily as a paragon of thrift, with her professional-quality tool chest and her twelve-column budget book and her thrice-used, washed-and-dried sandwich bags.

Did it ever occur to Sam that Delia and his father might well have been kindred spirits?

She gathered up the silverware, ten of everything, and went into the dining room. Here the sounds from the yard were muted, and she could let her mind return to Adrian. She traveled around the table, doling out knives and forks and remembering the rustle of Adrian's fingers on her collar, his warm breath when he kissed her. But she could no longer truly feel the kiss, she discovered. Eleanor's interruption must have startled all feeling out of her, as in the old days when the telephone rang while she and Sam were making love and she had lost her place, so to speak, and not been able to fall back into it afterward.

She returned to the kitchen and found Eliza pondering in front of the glassware cupboard. "Which do we want?" Eliza asked her. "Iced tea or wine?"

"Wine," Delia answered promptly.

From the side yard, Eleanor's confident voice came sailing: "Have you checked the price of asparagus lately?"

"Pretty steep, is it," Sam said equably.

"Sky-high," Eleanor told him. "But that's what we're having for dinner tonight: asparagus and grilled peacock."

Eliza was the only one who laughed.

Supper was late, for one reason or another. First Linda and Susie took forever bringing the twins from the pool, and then Ramsay didn't appear till seven although he'd promised faithfully to be home by six, and when he did show up he had his girlfriend in tow and her wan and silent six-year-old daughter. This enthralled the twins, of course, but Delia was furious. It had been understood that tonight would be strictly family. However, she didn't have quite what it took to face Ramsay down in public. Seething inwardly, she scrunched two extra, mismatched place settings in among the others before she called everyone to the table.

Velma, the girlfriend, was a tiny, elfin woman with a cap of glassy hair and a pert little figure set off by trim white shorts. Delia could see what her appeal was, sort of. For one thing, when she entered the dining room she went straight to one of the orphan place settings, as if she were accustomed to existing on the edges of events. And for another, she was so inexhaustibly vivacious that even Carroll—surly Carroll—brightened in her presence, and Sam made a point of giving her the largest piece of chicken. ("Got to put some meat on your bones," he said—not his type of remark at all.) Then she endeared herself to Linda by marveling at the twins' names. "I'm crazy about things that sound French—I guess you can tell from me naming my daughter Rosalie," she said. "Shoot, I'd like to *go* to France. The furtherest I've been is Hagerstown a few times for hair shows."

Velma was a beautician. She worked in one of those unisex places, which was how she and Ramsay had met. He had come in for a haircut and invited her on the spot to a tea at the house of his freshman adviser. Now he sat proudly next to her, one arm resting on the back of her chair, and beamed around the table at his family. Short though he was (he took after Delia's father), he seemed manly and imposing alongside Velma.

"Although last fall I did attend a color conference in Pittsburgh," Velma was recalling. "I stayed overnight and left Rosalie with my mother."

Rosalie, perched behind the other odd plate, raised her enormous, liquid eyes and gave Velma a look that struck Delia as despairing.

"Everybody in our whole entire shop has been trained to do your colors," Velma went on. Was she speaking to Eleanor, of all people? Eleanor nodded encouragingly, wearing her most gracious expression.

"Some people ought to wear cool colors and some people ought to wear warm," Velma told her, "and they should never, ever cross over, though you'd be shocked at how many try."

"Would that be determined by temperament, dear?" Eleanor asked.

"Ma'am?"

But Eleanor was sidetracked just then by the plate that Sam was filling for her. "Oh, mercy, Sam," she said, "not such a great big helping!"

"I thought you asked for a breast."

"Well, I did, but just a little one. That one's way too big for me."

He forked another and held it up. "This okay?"

"Oh, that's huge!"

"Well, there's nothing smaller, Mother."

"Can't you just cut it in half? I could never manage to eat all that."

He put it back on the platter to cut it.

"This one lady," Velma told the others, "she was wearing pink when she came in and I'm like, 'Lady, you are so, so wrong. You should be all in cools,' I tell her, 'with the tone of skin you got.' She says, 'Oh, but that's why I head for warm.' Says, 'I go for what's my opposite.' I could not believe her. I really could not believe her."

"Sam, dear, that's about six times as much asparagus as I can possibly handle," Eleanor said.

"It's three spears, Mother. How can I give you a sixth of that?"

"I just want a half a spear, if it isn't too much trouble."

"You, now," Velma told Eliza, "you would look stunning in magenta. With your coal-black hair? That tan color doesn't do a thing for you."

"However, I'm partial to tan," Eliza said in her declarative way.

"And Susie, I bet you had your colors done already. Right? That aqua's real becoming."

"It was the only thing not in the laundry," Susie said. But she was fighting down a pleased expression around the mouth.

"I dress Rosalie in nothing *but* aqua, just

about. She turns washed out in any other color."

"Sam, I hate to be a nuisance," Eleanor said, "but I'm going to send my plate back to you so you can take a teensy little bit of that potato salad off and give it to someone else."

"Well, why not just keep it, Mother."

"But it's much too large a helping, dear."

"Then eat what you can and leave the rest, why don't you."

"Now, you know how I hate to waste food."

"Oh, just force yourself to choke the damn stuff down, then, Mother!"

"Goodness," Eleanor said.

The telephone rang.

Delia said, "Carroll, would you answer that? If it's a patient, tell them we're eating."

Not that she imagined a patient could be so easily dissuaded.

Carroll slouched off to the kitchen, muttering something about the grown-ups' phone, and Delia took a bite of her drumstick. It was dry and stringy as old bark from being kept warm in the oven too long.

"For you, Mom," Carroll said, poking his head through the door.

"Well, see who it is and ask if I can call back."

"He says it's about a time machine."

"Oh!"

Sam said, "Time machine?"

"I'll just be a minute," Delia said, setting aside her napkin.

"Someone wants to sell you a *time* machine?" Sam asked her.

"No! Not that I know of. Or, I don't know . . ." She sank back in her seat. "Tell him we don't need a thing," she told Carroll.

Carroll withdrew his head.

It seemed to Delia that her one bite of chicken was stuck halfway down her throat. She picked up the basket of rolls and said, "Thérèse? Marie-Claire? Take one and pass them on, please."

When Carroll returned to the table, she didn't so much as glance at him. She sent the butter plate after the rolls, and only then looked up to face Eliza's steady gaze.

It was Eliza she had to watch out for. Eliza was uncanny sometimes.

"This china belonged to your great-grand-mother," Linda was telling the twins. "Cynthia Ramsay, her name was. She was a famous Baltimore beauty, and the whole town wondered why she ever said yes to that short, stumpy no-body, Isaiah Felson. But he was a doctor, you see, and he promised that if she married him she would never get TB. See, just about her whole family had died of TB. So sure enough, she married him and moved out to Roland Park and stayed healthy as a horse all her days and bore two healthy children besides, one of them your grandpa. You remember your grandpa."

"He wouldn't let us roller-skate in the house."

"Right. Anyhow, your great-grandmother ordered her wedding china all the way from Europe, these very plates you are eating from tonight."

"Except for Rosalie," Marie-Claire said.

"What, sweet?"

"*Rosalie's* plate is not wedding china."

"No, Rosalie's comes from Kmart," Linda said, and she passed the butter to Eleanor, not noticing how Rosalie's eyes started growing even more liquid.

"Heavens, no butter for *me*, dear," Eleanor said.

Why had he phoned her? Delia wondered. How unlike him. He must have had something crucial to tell her. She should have taken the call.

She would go to the kitchen for water or something and call him back.

Grabbing the water pitcher, she stood up, and just then the doorbell rang. She froze. Her first, heart-pounding thought was that this was Adrian. He had come to take her away; he would no longer listen to reason. A whole scenario played itself out rapidly in her mind—her family's bewilderment as she allowed herself to be led from the house, her journey through the night with him (in a horse-drawn carriage, it seemed), and their blissful life together in a sunlit, whitewashed room on some Mediterranean

shore. Meanwhile Sam was saying, "I've told
them and told them . . . ," and he rose and strode
out to the hall, apparently assuming that this was
a patient. Well, maybe it was. Delia remained
on her feet, straining to hear. One of the twins
said, "*Rosalie's* napkin is plain old paper," and
Delia had an urge to bat her voice away phys-
ically.

It was a woman. An elderly, querulous
woman, saying something unintelligible. So. A
patient after all. Delia felt more relieved than
she would have expected. She said, "Well! Anybody want anything from the kitchen?" But before she could turn to go, Sam was ushering in
his visitor.

Easily past seventy, doughy and wrinkled beneath her heap of dyed black curls and her plastering of red rouge and dark-red lipstick, the
woman advanced on absurdly small, open-toed
shoes that barely poked forth from the hem of
her shapeless black dress. She was clutching a
drawstring purse in both fat, ringed hands, and
diamond teardrops swung from her long ear-
lobes. All of this Delia somehow took in while
at the same time registering Sam's astonished
face just beyond the woman's shoulder. "Dee?"
he said. "This person's saying—"

The woman asked, "Are you Mrs. Delia
Grinstead?"

"Well, yes."

"I want you to leave my daughter's husband alone."

Around the table there was a sort of snapping to attention. Delia sensed it, even though she forced her eyes to remain on the woman. She said, "I can't imagine what you're talking about."

"You know who I mean! My son-in-law, Adrian Bly-Brice. Or don't you even keep track? Have you collected so many paramours you can't tell one from another?"

Somebody snickered. Ramsay. Delia felt slightly affronted by this, but she made herself focus on the issue at hand. She said, "Mrs., um, really I . . ."

She hated how little-girlish her voice came out.

"That is a happy marriage you're destroying," the old woman told her. She was stationed now at the far end of the table, just behind Sam's empty chair. She glared at Delia from underneath lashes so thickly beaded with mascara that they shaded her face like awnings. "They may have their ups and downs, like any other young couple," she said, "but they're trying to work things out, I tell you! They're dating again, has he mentioned that? Twice they've gone to dinner at the restaurant where they got engaged. They're thinking it might help if they started a baby. But every time I look out of my house, what do I find? Your car, parked across the street. You at his front door kissing him, all over him, can't get enough of him, going up the stairs with him to paw him at his bedroom window for all the neighbors to gawk at."

Adrian's mother-in-law lived across the street from him?

Delia felt burning hot. She sensed the others' thunderstruck expressions.

Sam said, quietly, "Delia, do you know anything about this?"

"No! Nothing!" she cried. "She's making it up! She's confused me with somebody else!"

"Then what's this?" the old woman asked, and she started tweaking at her purse. The drawstring was held tight by some sort of sliding clasp, and it took her whole minutes, it seemed, to work it loose, while everybody watched in riveted silence. Delia realized she had not released a breath in some time. She was prepared for absolutely anything to emerge from that purse —something steamy and lurid and reeking of sex, although what would that be, precisely? But all the old woman brought forth in the end was a photograph. "See? See?" she demanded, and she held it up and swung slowly from left to right.

It was a Polaroid snapshot, so underexposed that it amounted to no more than a square of mangled darkness. But not till Ramsay snickered once again did Delia understand that she was safe.

"Now, there," Sam was saying, "don't you worry, I'm sure your daughter is *very* happily married. . . ." In the most chivalrous fashion, he was turning the old woman toward the door. "May I see you to your car?" he asked.

"Oh. Well . . . yes, maybe . . . yes, maybe so," she said. She was still fumbling with her purse, but she let him guide her out. She walked beneath the shelter of his arm in a dazed, uncertain manner that filled Delia with sudden pity.

"Who was *that*?" Marie-Claire asked distinctly.

Ramsay said, "Oh, just somebody for your aunt Delia; you know what a siren she is," and everybody stirred and chuckled.

It was perverse of her, she knew, but for one split second Delia actually considered confessing, just to show them. She didn't, of course. She smiled around the table and sat back down and placed the water pitcher on her left. "Who's for more chicken?" she asked, and she looked brazenly into Eliza's measuring eyes.

It was Susie's night to do the dishes, and Eleanor said she would help. She wouldn't think of letting Delia lift a finger, she said, after that extravagant meal. So Delia backed out of the kitchen, pretending reluctance, but instead of heading toward the porch with the others, she sped up the stairs and into her bedroom. She shut the door behind her, sat on the edge of the bed, and picked up the phone.

He answered almost instantly. She had braced herself to go through that whole two-ring rigmarole, but right away he said, "Hello?"

"Adrian?"

"Oh, God, Delia, did she come?"

"She came."

"I tried to warn you. I called your house, and even after your husband answered I went ahead and—"

"My husband answered? When?"

"Wasn't that your husband?"

"Oh, Carroll. My son. At suppertime, you mean."

"Yes, and I was hoping you would . . . That was your son?"

"Yes, my younger son. Carroll."

"But he was so old."

"Old? He's not old!"

"He sounded like a grown man."

"Well, he isn't," Delia said curtly. "Adrian, why did you stand there kissing me in doors and windows when you knew your mother-in-law lived across the street?"

"So she did what she said she would, did she?"

"She came and told my family I had a 'paramour,' if that's what you mean."

"Lord, Delia, what did they say?"

"I think they just thought she was crazy or

something, but . . . Adrian. She claimed you were happily married."

"Of course she did. You know she would want to believe that."

"She claimed you and Rosemary have started dating; you've gone out together twice to the restaurant where you got engaged."

"Well, that much is true."

"It is?"

"Just to talk things over; sure. We do have a lot in common, after all. A lot of shared history."

"I see."

"But it wasn't how you imagine. We met for dinner! Just to eat dinner!"

"And you're thinking of starting a baby."

"Is that what she told you?"

"Yes."

"Well, naturally it came up."

"Naturally?" Delia cried.

"I mean, Rosemary isn't getting any younger."

"No, that's right, she must be all of thirty," Delia said with some bitterness. She twined the telephone cord between her fingers. The connection was the kind with a rushing sound in the background, like long distance.

"Well, probably she's not the maternal type, though, anyhow," Adrian said cheerfully. "Weird, isn't it? The very thing that attracts you to someone can end up putting you off. When

Rosemary and I first met, she was so . . . cool, I guess you'd say, so cool-mannered I was bewitched, but now I see she might be too cool to be a good mother."

"How about me?" Delia asked him.

"You?"

"What is it about *me* that attracts you but puts you off?"

"Oh, why, nothing, Delia. Why do you ask?"

"Nothing attracts you?"

"Oh! Well, maybe . . . well, when we met, you acted so fresh and sweet and childish, I mean childlike, you know? But then when we reached the point where most people would, for example, um, get more involved, you were *still* so damn sweet and childlike. Turning all flustered, saying you should leave: you'd think we were teenagers or something."

"I see," Delia said.

Adrian said, "Delia. Just how old is your son, anyway?"

"Ancient," she told him. But it was herself she was referring to.

She hung up and walked out of the room.

Downstairs, she heard water running in the kitchen, and dishes clattering, and Eleanor saying, "Susie, dear, you're not planning to *discard* that, surely." Delia crossed the hall to stand at the screen door, gazing out toward the porch. She saw no sign of the boys, who had not stayed

to talk after dinner in years; no sign of Velma
or Rosalie. But Sam and Linda sat sniping at
each other in the swing. "Some of those azaleas
were planted by our grandfather," Linda said,
"not that that would be any concern of yours,"
and Sam said, "Or yours either, unless you plan
to start sharing a little of the burden here," and
Eliza, rocking in the cane rocker, said, "Oh, just
quit it, both of you." The twins were twirling on
the front walk beneath the pole lamp, with grass
blades stuck to their skin and white moths flick-
ering above them. They had reached that high-
pitched, overwrought state that seizes children
outdoors on summer evenings, and they were
chanting at breakneck speed:
  "*What's* life?"
  "Fifteen cents a copy."
  "But I only have a dime."
  "Well, that's life."
  "*What's* life?"
  "Fifteen cents a copy."
  "But I only have a dime."

# 5

It rained during their first evening at the beach, and their cottage roof turned out to have a leak. This was not a very fancy cottage, not an ocean-front, resort-style cottage, but a dumpy little house on the inland side of Highway 1. Delia could imagine an ordinary Delaware feed-store clerk living there until about a week ago. The kitchen sink was skirted in chintz, the living-room floor was blue linoleum squiggled to suggest a hooked rug, and all the beds sagged toward the middle and creaked at the slightest movement. Still, Sam said, they shouldn't have to endure a puddle in the upstairs hall. He phoned the rental agent at once, using the after-hours emergency number, and insisted that the problem be seen to the first thing the following morning.

"What," Linda asked him, "do you have to have your crew of workmen even on vacation?"

And Eliza said, "Let's just mop it up and forget it. It surely won't rain again while we're here, because if it does I'm going to sue God."

Delia herself said nothing. She really couldn't gather the strength.

In their own house back in Baltimore, work-men would be using the week to sand down the floors and refinish them. This meant that Delia had had to bring the cat along. (He wouldn't tolerate boarding—had nearly pined away the one time they had tried it.) Sam claimed they were sure to be evicted, since pets were expressly forbidden, but Delia told him that was impossible. How would anyone ever guess Vernon was there? For he'd been so incensed by the car trip that the instant he was set down in the cottage, he streaked to the back of a kitchen cabinet. Delia knew enough to leave him tactfully alone, but the twins wouldn't rest, and after supper they hovered at the cabinet door with a plate of left-overs, trying to coax him out. "Here, Vernon! *Nice* Vernon." His only response was that dis-heartening, numb silence cats seem to radiate when they're determined to keep to themselves. "Oh," Marie-Claire wailed, "what'll we do? He's going to starve to death!"

"Good riddance," Sam told her. "It's only live pets that we're not allowed."

Sam had been out of sorts all day, it seemed to Delia.

So that first evening, when they should have been taking a stroll on the beach or walking into town for ice cream, the grown-ups sat in the kerosene-smelling, poorly lighted living room, reading tattered magazines left behind by earlier tenants and listening to the pecking of the rain against the windows. The twins were still in the kitchen, badgering Vernon. Susie and the boys had borrowed the Plymouth and driven to Ocean City, which made Delia anxious because she always pictured Ocean City as a gigantic arena of bumper cars manned by drunken college students. But she tried to keep her mind on *American Deck and Patio*.

"If tomorrow isn't sunny," Linda said, "maybe we could take a little day trip out past Salisbury. I want the twins to get some sense of their heritage."

"Oh, Linda, not that damn cemetery again," Eliza said.

"Well, fine, then. Just lend me a car and I'll take them myself. That's what happened last year, as I recall."

"Yes, and last year both twins came back bored to tears and cranky. What do they care for a bunch of dead Carrolls and Webers?"

"They had a wonderful time! And I'd like to find Great-Uncle Roscoe's place too, if I can."

"Well, good hunting, is all I can say. I'm sure it's a parking lot by now, and anyhow, Mother never got along with Uncle Roscoe."

"Eliza, why do you have to run me down at every turn?" Linda demanded. "Why is it that every little thing I propose you have to mock and denigrate?"

"Now, ladies," Sam said absently, leafing through *Offshore Angler*.

Linda turned on him. She said, "Don't you 'Now, ladies' *me*, Sam Grinstead."

"Sorry," Sam murmured.

"Mr. Voice of Reason, here!"

"My mistake."

She rose in a huff and went off to check the twins. Eliza closed her *Yachting World* and stared bleakly at the cover.

Linda and Eliza were in their Day Two Mode, was how Delia always thought of it—that edgy, prickly stage after the first flush of Linda's arrival had faded. Once, Delia had asked Eliza why she and Linda weren't closer, and Eliza had said, "Oh, people who've shared an unhappy childhood rarely *are* close, I've found." Delia was surprised. Their childhood had been unhappy? Hers had been idyllic. But she refrained from saying so.

Linda returned with the twins, who were still fretting over Vernon, and Sam set aside his magazine and suggested a game of rummy. "Did you bring the cards?" he asked Delia.

She had not. She realized it the instant he asked, but made a show of rooting through the shopping bag on the coffee table. Jigsaw puzzles, Monopoly, and a Parcheesi board emerged, but no cards. "Um . . . ," she said.

"Oh, well," Sam said, "we'll play Parcheesi,

then." His tone was weightily patient, which seemed worse than shouting.

At the bottom of the bag, Delia came across her current library book. *Captive of Clarion Castle*, it was called. She had started it last week and found it slow, but anything was preferable to deck plans. When Sam asked, "Are you playing too, Delia?" she said, "I think I'll go read in bed."

"Now? It's not even nine o'clock."

"Well, I'm tired," she told him. She said good night to the others and walked out with the front of her book concealed, although no one made any attempt to see the title.

Upstairs, a new ribbon of water meandered from the sodden bath mat alongside the chimney. She ignored it and proceeded to the room she was sharing with Sam. It was small and musty-smelling, with one, uncurtained window. For privacy's sake she changed into her nightgown in the dark, and then she washed up in the bathroom across the hall. Back in the bedroom, she switched on the lamp and aimed its weak yellow beam in the direction of her pillow. Then she slid under the covers, wriggled her toes luxuriously, and opened her book.

The heroine of this book was a woman named Eleanora, which unfortunately brought Eleanor to Delia's mind. Eleanora's long raven tresses and "piquant" face kept giving way to Eleanor's no-nonsense haircut and Iron Mama jawline; and when Kendall, the hero, crushed her to him, Delia saw Eleanor's judging gaze directed past his broad shoulder. Kendall was Eleanora's future brother-in-law, the younger brother of her aristocratic, suave fiancé. Impetuously, Kendall kidnapped Eleanora the first time he laid eyes on her, which happened to be about fifteen minutes before her wedding. "I will never love you! Never!" Eleanora cried, pummeling his chest with her tiny fists, but Kendall seized her wrists and waited, masterful and confident, until she subsided.

Delia closed the book, leaving one finger inside as a marker. She stared down at the couple embracing on the cover.

Not once, from the moment they met, had Adrian truly pursued her. It had all been a matter of happenstance. Happenstance had led him to ask her to pose as his girlfriend (Who else was remotely eligible? The woman with the baby? The old lady at the checkout counter?), and happenstance had brought them together again a few nights later. In addition, his every act had betrayed that he was still in love with his wife. He loved her so much that he couldn't face her on his own in the supermarket; he couldn't sleep in their bedroom after she left. But Delia, like some self-deluded teenage ninny, had chosen not to see.

And she had overlooked other clues as well—clues that revealed the very nature of his character. For instance, his behavior at that first encounter: his rearrangement of her shopping plans, his condescending reference to Roland Park names, his trendy groceries. He was not a *bad* person, surely, but his mind was on his own concerns. And he was just the least bit shallow.

In romance novels, this realization would have made her turn thankfully to the man who had been waiting in the wings all along. But in real life, when she heard Sam's step on the stairs she closed her eyes and pretended to be asleep. She felt him standing over her, and then he slipped her book from her hands and switched off the lamp and left the room.

By morning the rain had stopped and the sun was out, shining all the brighter in the washed-clean air. The whole family set off for the ocean shortly before noon—the grown-ups in Sam's Buick, the younger ones in the Plymouth with Ramsay at the wheel. Scattered puddles hissed beneath their tires as they drove across Highway I and threaded past the higher-priced cottages, closer to the water. When the road dead-ended, they parked and fed two meters with quarters and unloaded the day's supplies—the thermos jugs and blankets, towels, Styrofoam coolers, rafts, and beach bags. Delia carried a stack of towels, along with her straw tote stuffed so full of emergency provisions that the handles dug a furrow in her bare shoulder. She was wearing her pink gingham swimsuit with the eyelet-edged skirt, and navy canvas espadrilles, but no robe or cover-up, because she didn't care *what* Sam said, she wanted to get at least a hint of a tan.

"Watch it, girls," Linda told the twins as they lugged a cooler between them up the wooden walkway. "You're letting the bottom drag."

"It's Thérèse's fault—she's making me do all the work!"

"Am not."

"Are so."

"Didn't I tell you to take something lighter?" Linda asked them. "Didn't I offer you the blankets, or the—"

But then they crested the low, sandy rise, and there was the ocean, reminding them what they had come all this way for. Oh, every year it seemed Delia forgot. That vast, slaty, limitless sweep, that fertile, rotting, dog's-breath smell, that continual to-and-fro shushing that had been going on forever while she'd been elsewhere, stewing over trivia! She paused, letting her eyes take rest in the dapples of yellow sunlight that skated the water, and then Carroll's armload of rafts crashed into her from behind, and he said, "Geez, Mom."

"Oh, excuse me," she said. She started down the wooden steps to the beach.

There were advantages to coming so early in

the season. True, the water had not had time to warm up yet, but also the beach was less crowded. Blankets were spread at civilized intervals, with space between. Only a few children splashed at the edge of the breakers, and Delia could easily count the heads that bobbed farther out.

She and Eliza unfolded a blanket and arranged themselves on it, while Sam worked an umbrella pole into the sand. Susie and the boys, however, walked a good twenty feet beyond before stopping to set up their own station. They had been keeping apart for several years now; it no longer hurt Delia's feelings. But she did always notice.

"Now, you two are not stirring from here," Linda told the twins, "until I get every inch of you covered with sunblock." She held them close, one after the other, and slathered lotion on their skinny arms and legs. As soon as she let go of them, off they raced to the young people's blanket.

Susie's radio was playing "Under the Boardwalk," which had always seemed to Delia a very lonesome song. In fact, "Under the Boardwalk" was rising from other radios as well, on other blankets, so that the Atlantic Ocean seemed to have acquired its own melancholy background music.

"Believe I'll go for a jog," Sam told Delia.

"Oh, Sam. You're on vacation!"

"So?"

He shucked off his beach robe and adjusted the leather band of his watch. (The watch was evidently part of his new exercise routine; in just what way, Delia wasn't sure.) Then he walked down to the surf, turned, and started loping northward, a lanky figure in beige trunks and gigantic white sneakers.

"At least here they have all these lifeguards who've been trained in CPR," Delia told her sisters. She folded Sam's robe and packed it away in her tote.

"Oh, he'll be fine," Eliza said. "The doctors told him to jog."

"Not to overdo, though!"

"To me he looks just the same as always," Linda said. "If you consider that a good thing." She was shading her forehead to gaze after him. "I never would have known he'd had a heart attack."

"It wasn't a heart attack! It was chest pains."

"Whatever," Linda said carelessly.

She was wearing a one-piece swimsuit held up by a center cord that encircled her neck. It made her breasts appear to droop at either side like a pair of weary eyes. Eliza, who scorned the notion of a whole separate outfit for one week of swimming per year, wore denim shorts and a black knit tank top rolled up beneath her bra.

Delia took off her shoes and dropped them

into her tote. Then she lay down flat on her back, with the sun's mild warmth soaking into her skin. Gradually sounds grew fainter, like remembered sounds—the voices of other sunbathers nearby, the high, sad cries of the seagulls, the music from the radios (Paul McCartney now, singing "Uncle Albert"), and under everything, so she almost stopped hearing it, the ocean's rush, as constant and unvaried as the ocean inside a seashell.

She and Sam had come to this beach on their honeymoon. They had stayed at an inn down-town that no longer existed, and every morning, lying out here side by side with their bare, fuzzed arms just touching, they had reached such a state that, eventually, they had to rise and rush back to their room. Once even that had seemed too far, and they'd plunged into the ocean instead, out past the breakers, and she could still remember the layers of contrast—his warm, bony legs brushing hers beneath the cool, silky water—and the fishy scent of his wet face when they kissed. But the summer after that they had the baby with them (little Susie, two months old and fussy, fussy, fussy) and in later years the boys, and they had seldom managed even to stretch out on their blanket together, let alone steal back to their cottage. Eliza started coming too, and Linda before she married, and their father because he never could have kept house on his own; and Delia spent her days ankle-deep in the surf tending children, making sure they didn't drown, admiring each new skill they mastered. "Watch this, Mom." "No, watch *this*!" They used to think she was so important in their lives.

Someone's feet passed in the sand with a sound like rubbing velvet, and she opened her eyes and sat up. For a moment she felt light-headed. "Your face is burning," Eliza told her. "Better put some lotion on." She herself was sitting sensibly in the shade of the umbrella. Linda was down in the surf, braced for an incoming wave with both plump arms outflung and her hands posed as liltingly as bird wings, and the twins had returned from the other blanket and were filling buckets near Delia. Damp sand caked Marie-Claire's knees and made two circles on the empty-looking seat of Thérèse's swimsuit.

"Did Sam get back from jogging?" Delia asked Eliza.

"Not yet. Want to go for a dip?"

Delia didn't dignify that with an answer. (As everyone in her family well knew, the temperature had to be blistering, the ocean flat as glass, and not a sea nettle sighted all day before she would venture in.) Instead, she reached for her tote bag. Delving past espadrilles, Sam's robe, and her billfold, she came up with *Captive of Clarion Castle*. Eliza humphed when she saw the cover. "Guess I'll leave you to your *literature*," she told Delia. She got to her feet and set off, dusting the back of her shorts in a businesslike manner.

"Aunt Eliza, can we come too?" Marie-Claire shrilled.

"Wait for us, Aunt Liza!"

When they ran after her, they looked as skittery and high-bottomed as two little hermit crabs.

Eleanora was beginning to notice that Kendall was not the monster she had imagined. He brought trays of food to her locked tower room and let it be known he had cooked all the dishes himself. Eleanora pretended to be unimpressed, but later, after he left, she reflected on the incongruity of someone so brawny and virile stirring pots at a stove.

"Whew!" Sam said. He was back. Sweat trickled down the ridged bones of his chest, and he had the drawn, strained, gasping look that always distressed Delia after his runs. "Sam," she said, setting aside her book, "you're going to kill yourself! Sit here and rest."

"No, I have to wind down gradually," he told her. He started walking in circles around the blanket, stopping every now and then to bend over and grip his kneecaps. Drops of sweat fell from his forehead to the sand. "What have we got to drink?" he asked her.

"Lemonade, Pepsi, iced tea—"

"Iced tea sounds good."

She stood to fill a paper cup and hand it to

him. He was no longer breathing so hard, at least. He drained the cup in a single draft and set it on the lid of the cooler. "Your nose is burning," he told her.

"I want to get a *little* tan."

"Melanoma is what you're going to get."

"Well, maybe after lunch I'll put on some—"

But he had already picked up Linda's bottle of sunblock. "Hold still," he said, unscrewing the cap. He started smoothing lotion across her face. It smelled like bruised peaches, an artificial, trashy smell that made her wrinkle her nose. "Turn around and I'll do your back," he told her.

Obediently, she turned. She faced inland now, where the roofs of cottages hulked beyond the sand fence. A flock of tiny dark birds crossed the blue sky in the distance, keeping a perfectly triangular formation so that they seemed connected by invisible wires. They swung around and caught the sun, and suddenly they were white, in fact almost silver, like a veil of sequins; and then they swung again, and once more they were plain black specks. Sam smoothed lotion over Delia's shoulders. It went on warm but cooled in the breeze, tingling slightly.

"Delia," he said.

"Hmm?"

"I was wondering about the old woman who came by the house Saturday night."

She grew still beneath his palm, but she felt

that every one of her nerves was thrumming like a twanged string.

"I know she was, maybe, peculiar," he said. "But she had an actual photograph, and she seemed to think it really did show you and that who's-it, that what's-his-name . . ."

She had already turned toward him to deny it when he said, "That Adrian Fried Rice."

"Bly-Brice," she said.

For he had twisted the name on purpose. He always did that. The maid of honor at their wedding, Missy Pringle, he had kept referring to as Prissy Mingle. It was just like him to be so belittling! So contemptuous of her friends, with that ironic glint to his voice! Her entire marriage unrolled itself before her: ancient hurts and humiliations and resentments, theoretically forgotten but just waiting to revive at moments such as this.

"His name is Adrian, Bly, Brice," she told him.

"I see," Sam said. His face had a sheeted look.

"But that woman got it all wrong. He's nothing but an acquaintance."

"I see."

In silence, he replaced the bottle of sunblock.

"You don't believe me."

"I never said that."

"No, but you implied it."

"I surely can't be blamed for what you imagine

I might have implied," Sam said. "Of course he's just an acquaintance. You're not exactly the type to have an affair. But I'm wondering how it seems to outsiders, Dee. You know?"

"No, I don't know," she said, between set teeth. "And my name is not *Dee*."

"All right," he said. "Delia. Now, why don't you just calm down."

And he leveled the air between them with both palms, in that patronizing gesture she always found so infuriating, and turned away from her and walked toward the water.

Every quarrel they had ever had, he had walked off before it was resolved. He would get her all riled up and then loftily remove himself, giving the impression that he, at least, could behave like an adult. Adult? Old man was more the case. Who else would wade into the surf in his sneakers? Who else would pat water so fastidiously on his chest and upper arms before ducking under? And check his watch, for Lord's sake, when he rose? To Delia it seemed he was timing the waves, engaging in some precise and picky ritual that filled her with irritation.

She snatched her tote bag from the blanket, spun on one bare heel, and stamped off down the beach.

More people had arrived without her noticing. Only a slender path wound among the umbrellas and canvas chairs and mesh playpens, and so after a few yards she changed course till she was marching alongside the ocean, on wet, packed sand that cooled the soles of her feet.

This part of the beach belonged to the walkers. They walked in twos, mostly: young couples, old couples, almost always holding hands or at least matching their strides. From time to time small children cut in front of them. Delia pictured a map of the entire East Coast from Nova Scotia to Florida—an irregular strip of beige sand dotted with tiny humans, a wash of blue Atlantic next to it even more sparsely dotted. She herself was a dot in motion, heading south. She would keep going till she fell off the bottom of the continent, she decided. By and by Sam would think to ask, "Have you seen Delia?" "Why, no, where could she have got to?" the others would say, but she would keep on the move, like someone running between raindrops, and they would never, ever find her.

Already, though, something was slowing her down. The first of the Sea Colony condominiums towered ahead—ugly Sea Colony with its impassive monochrome high-rises, like a settlement from an alien galaxy. She could have made her way past, but that mysterious, Star Wars hum that the buildings always emitted chilled her so that she stopped short. In her childhood, this had been grassy marshland, with a few plain-faced cottages scattered about. In her childhood, she was almost certain, she and her father had flown homemade kites right where that complex of orange plastic pyramids now shaded a modernistic sundeck. For an instant she could feel her father's blunt fingers closing over hers on the kite string. She brushed a hand across her eyes. Then she turned and started walking back.

A lifeguard slouched on his chair, surveying the bathers inscrutably from behind his dark glasses. A lardy young boy on a raft landed in the foam at Delia's feet. She stepped around him and, looking ahead, spotted her family's green-and-white umbrella and her children on their blanket just beyond. They were sitting up now, and Sam stood some distance away, still shiny after his swim. From here it didn't seem that anyone was speaking, for the children faced the horizon and Sam was studying his watch.

Just that abruptly, Delia veered inland. She left the ocean behind and picked her way around sand tunnels and forts and collections of toys. When she had traversed the wooden walkway to the road, she stopped to dust her feet off and dig her espadrilles from her tote. Sam's beach robe lay beneath them—a wad of navy broadcloth—and after a moment's consideration, she shook it out and put it on. Her shoulders were so burned by now that they seemed to give off heat.

If she had thought to get the car keys from

Ramsay, she could have driven. She wasn't looking forward to that trek to the cottage. In fact,
she could return for the keys right now. But then
some of the others might want to come with her,
and so she decided against it.

Already the ocean seemed far away and long
ago, a mere whisper on this sunny paved road
with its silent cottages and empty, baking
automobiles and motionless rows of swimsuits
on clotheslines. She cut through someone's
backyard—mostly sand—and circled an enclo-
sure of garbage cans that smelled of crab and
buzzed with glittery blue flies. Then she was facing Highway 1. Traffic whizzed by so fast that
she had to wait several minutes before she could
cross.

On the other side of the highway, her footsteps
were the loudest sound around—her stiff straw
soles clopping out a rhythm. Perhaps because
she'd been thinking of her father, the rhythm
seemed to keep time with the song he used to
sing when she was small. She stalked past
screened porches, with her shoes beating out
"Delia's Gone"—asking where she'd been so
long, saying her lover couldn't sleep, saying all
around his bed at night he kept hearing little
Delia's bare feet. She especially liked that last
line; she always had. Except, wasn't the other
Delia dead? Yes, obviously: there was mention
in the very first verse of little Delia dead and

gone. But she preferred to believe the woman had simply walked out. It was more satisfying that way.

Her face felt sticky, and her shoulder hurt where the handles of her tote bag chafed her sunburn. She switched the tote to her other side. She was almost there now, anyhow. She was planning on a tall iced tea as soon as she stepped through the door, and after that a cool bath and a little private visit with her cat. It was time to lure Vernon from under her bed, where he had taken up residence at some point during the night. In fact, maybe she ought to do that first.

She smiled at a woman carrying a suitcase out of the cottage next to theirs. "Lovely beach weather!" the woman called. "Hate to leave it!"

"It's perfect," Delia said, and she rounded a van parked in the driveway and climbed her own steps.

Inside, the dimness turned her momentarily blind. She peered up the stairwell and called, "Vernon?"

"What."

She gasped.

"Somebody page me?" a man's voice asked.

He lumbered down the stairs—a chubby young man with a clipboard, dressed in jeans and a red plaid shirt. His moon-shaped face, with its round pink cheeks and nubbin nose and buttonhole mouth, reassured her somewhat, but

even so she could barely draw breath to ask,
"Who . . . ?"

"I'm Vernon, didn't you holler my name? I'm
here about the roof."

"Oh," she said. She gave a shaky laugh and
clutched her tote bag to her chest. "I was just
calling my cat," she told him.

"Well, I haven't seen no cat about. Sorry if I
scared you."

"You didn't scare me!"

He squinted at her doubtfully. The satiny skin
beneath his eyes glistened with sweat, which
made him look earnest and boyish. "Anyhow,"
he said. "Seems I'll need to replace that flashing
up top round the chimney. I won't be doing it
today, though; I got to get on back. So if those
folks at the realtor's phone, tell them I'll be in
touch, okay?"

"Okay," Delia said.

He waved his clipboard amiably and headed
past her out the door. On the steps, he turned
and asked, "How you like my vehicle?"

"Vehicle?"

"Ain't it something?"

It was, in fact. She wondered how she could
have missed it. Big as a house trailer, painted a
metallic bronze with a desert landscape lighting
up one side, it occupied the whole driveway.
"Got a microwave," Vernon was saying, "got a
dinky little 'frigerator—"

"You mean it's for living in?"

"Sure, what else?"

"I thought vans would just have rows and rows of seats."

"Ain't you ever been inside a RV before? Shoot, come on and I'll show you."

"Oh, I don't know if I—"

"Come on! This'll knock your socks off."

"Well, maybe I *will* take a peek," Delia said, and she followed him, still hugging her tote bag. One section of the desert scene proved to be a sliding panel. Vernon slid it open and stood back to let her see inside. When she poked her head in she found gold shag carpeting halfway up the walls, and built-in cabinets, and a platform bed at the rear with storage drawers underneath. Two high-backed seats faced the windshield— the only sign that this was, after all, a means of transportation.

"Gosh," Delia said.

"Climb in. Get a load of my entertainment center."

"You have an entertainment center?"

"State of the art," he told her. He climbed in himself, causing the van to tilt beneath his weight, and then turned to offer a hand as big as a baseball glove. She accepted it and clambered inside. The oily, exciting smell of new carpet reminded her of airports and travel.

"Ta-daah!" Vernon said. He flung open a cabinet. "What it is," he said, "in the bottom of this here TV is a slot for a videotape, see? Integrated VCR. Evenings, I just swivel it out and watch the latest hit movies from the bed."

"You stay here all the time?"

"Just about," he said. "Well, more or less. Well, for now I do." Then he sent her a look, with his head ducked. "I'll tell you the honest truth," he said. "This van belongs to my brother."

He seemed to think the news would disappoint her deeply. He fixed her with a worried blue gaze and waited, scarcely breathing, until she said, "Oh, really?"

"I guess I kind of gave the impression it was mine," he said. "But see, my brother's off on this fishing trip, him and his wife. Left his van at our mom's house in Nanticoke Landing. Told her to watch over it and not let nobody drive it. Me is who he meant. But he's due back this afternoon and so yesterday I got to thinking. 'Well, durn,' I got to thinking. 'Here's this fully equipped RV, been setting in Mom's yard all week and I have not so much as tried that little microwave.' So last night I stayed in it, and this morning I took it out to make my estimates. Mom said she don't even want to know about it. Said not to drag her into it. But what can he do to me, right? What's he going to do to me—haul me off to jail?"

"Maybe he won't find out," Delia said.

"Oh, he'll find out, all right. Be just like him to have wrote down the mileage before he left," Vernon told her gloomily.

"You could always say you thought the battery needed charging."

"Battery. Sure."

"Does he live here? In the van, I mean?"

"Naw."

"Well, I would," Delia said. She bent to raise the seat of an upholstered bench. Just as she had expected, there was storage space underneath. She glimpsed woolens of some kind—blankets or jackets. "I would make it my year-round home," she said. "Really! Who needs a big old house and all those extra rooms?"

"Yeah, but my brother's got three kids," Vernon said.

"Have you ever seen those under-cabinet coffeemakers?" Delia asked him.

"Huh?"

She was inspecting the kitchen area now. It was a model of miniaturization, with a sink the size of a salad bowl and a two-burner stovetop. A dented metal percolator stood on one of the burners. "They have these coffeepots," she told Vernon, "that you permanently install beneath the overhang of a cabinet. So you don't waste any space."

"Is that a fact."

"Actually, there's a whole line of under-cabinet equipment. Toaster ovens, can openers . . . electric can opener you install beneath the—"

"I believe my brother just uses the hand-cranked kind," Vernon said.

"Well, if this were mine, I'd have everything under-cabinet."

"Hand-cranked don't take no space at all, to speak of."

"I'd have nothing rattling around," Delia said, "nothing interfering, so at a moment's notice I could hop behind the wheel and go. Travel with my house on my back, like a snail. Stop when I got tired. Park in whatever campground caught my fancy."

"Well, but campgrounds," Vernon said. "Mostly you'd need to reserve ahead, for a campground."

"And next morning I'd say, 'Okay! That's it for this place!' And move on."

"The rates are kind of steep too, if the camp-ground's halfway decent," Vernon said. "Durn. Is that the time?"

He was looking at the clock above the sink. Delia was glad to see that the clock, at least, was attached to the wall. In her opinion, there was far too much loose and adrift here—not just the percolator but sloppily refolded newspapers and videotapes out of their boxes and cast-off pieces of clothing. "What I can't fathom," she said, "is how you manage to drive with these things sliding all over. Wouldn't you have flying objects every time you hit a speed bump?"

"Not as I've noticed," Vernon said. "But remember this ain't my property. And speaking of which, my brother's due back in like a couple of hours so I reckon I better be going."

"I wish I could come too," Delia said.

"Yeah. Right. Well, look, it's been great talking with you—"

"Maybe I could just ride along for a little tiny part of the way," Delia said.

"When—now?"

"Just to see how it handles on the road."

"Well, it . . . handles fine on the road," Vernon said. "But I'm going inland, you know? I'm nowhere near any beaches. Going down Three eighty past Ashford, *way* past Ashford, over to—"

"I'll just ride to, um, Ashford," Delia said.

She knew she was making him nervous. He stood staring at her, his eyebrows crinkled and his mouth slightly open, his clipboard dangling forgotten from one hand. Never mind: any moment now she would let him off the hook. She would give a little coming-to-her-senses laugh and tell him that on second thought, she couldn't possibly ride to Ashford. She did have a family after all, and already they must be wondering where she was.

And yet here stood this van, this beautiful,

completely stocked, entirely self-sufficient van
that you could travel in forever, unentangled
with anyone else. Oh, couldn't she offer to buy
it? How much did such things cost? Or steal it,
even—shove Vernon out the door and zoom off,
careening west on little back roads where no one
could ever track her.

But: "Well," she said regretfully, "I do have
a family."

"Family in Ashford? Oh, in that case," Vernon said.

It took her a minute to understand. His eyebrows smoothed themselves out, and he leaned
past her to slide the door shut. Then he flung his
clipboard on the bench and said, "Long as you've
got transportation back, then . . ."

Speechless, Delia made her way to the front.
She sat in the passenger seat and perched her
tote bag on her knees. Next to her, Vernon was
settling behind the wheel. When he switched on
the ignition, the van roared to life so suddenly
that she fancied it had been jittering with impatience all this time.

"Hear that?" Vernon asked her.

She nodded. She supposed it must be the engine's vibration that caused her teeth to start
chattering.

Traveling down Highway 1 toward the Maryland
border, past giant beach-furniture stores and
brand-new "Victorian" developments and the

jumbled cafés and apartments of Fenwick Island, Delia kept telling herself that she could still get back on her own. It would mean a long walk, was all (which stretched longer moment by moment). And when they entered Ocean City, with its honky-tonk razzle-dazzle—well, Ocean City had buses, she happened to know. She could take a bus to its northernmost edge and *then* walk back. So she rode quietly, beginning to feel almost relaxed, while Vernon hunched over the wheel and steered with his forearms. He was one of those drivers who talked to traffic. "Not to pressure you or anything, fella," he said when a car ahead of him stalled, and he clucked at four teenage boys crossing the street with their surfboards. "Aren't *you*-all hotshots," he told them. Delia gazed after them. The tallest boy wore ticking-striped shorts exactly like a pair Carroll owned—that voluminous new fashion that billowed to mid-knee.

When her family discovered she was gone, they would be baffled. Flummoxed. If she stayed away long enough, they would wonder if she'd met with an accident. "Or could she have left on purpose?" Sam would at last ask the children. "Did one of you say something? Did *I* say something? Was I mistaken to believe she wasn't the type for an affair?"

An airy sense of exhilaration filled her chest. She felt so lightweight, all at once.

Then after they had had time to get really

concerned, she would phone. Find a booth before night fell and, "It's me," she would announce. "Just took a little jaunt to the country;
could one of you come pick me up?" No harm
done.

So when Vernon turned onto Highway 50 and
started inland (talking now about the "differ-
ential," whatever that was), she still said nothing
to stop him. The percolator clanked on the stovetop; they rattled across a bridge she'd never seen
before and entered a bleached, pale country entirely unfamiliar to her. She merely stared out
the window. They passed yellowing, papery
houses set in the middle of careful lawns that
appeared to have been hand clipped, blade by
blade. They flickered through leafy woodlands.
"One place he flubbed up is not opting for a
CB," Vernon said, referring evidently to his
brother, but Delia was just then picturing how
Sam's lips always formed a straight line when he
was angry. And it occurred to her that what he
might tell the children was, "Well, at least we
can get things done right, now she's gone."

"Besides which you will notice there's no
stereo," Vernon said. "That's my brother for
you: he don't care much for music. I say there's
something lacking in a man who don't like
music."

Maybe Eleanor would step in (speaking of
doing things right). Oh, Eleanor would take over

gladly—plan all the menus a year in advance and set up one of her Iron Mama budgets.

"I guess you think that's awful," Vernon said. "To pick fault with my own brother."

Delia said, "No, no . . ."

Here and there, now, gaunt old dignified farmhouses stood at the end of long driveways, with crops growing all around them and lightning rods bristling on their rooftops. Imagine living in such a place! It would be so wholesome. Delia saw herself feeding chickens, flinging corn or wheat or whatever from her capacious country apron. First she'd have to marry a farmer, though. You always had to begin by finding some man to set things in motion, it seemed.

"But I'll be honest," Vernon was saying. "Me and him never have been what you'd call close. He is three years older than me and never lets me forget it. Keeps yammering about head of the family, when fact is he hardly lays eyes on our family from one month to the next. *I'm* the one takes Mom grocery shopping. *I'm* the one runs her hither and yon for her bingo nights and her covered-dish suppers and what all."

Why did everyone maintain that men were uncommunicative? In Delia's experience, they talked a blue streak, especially repairmen. And Sam was no exception. Sam communicated all too well, if you asked Delia.

She let her eyes follow a trailer park as they

passed it. Each trailer was anchored by awnings and cinder-block steps and sometimes a screened extension. Whole menageries of plaster animals filled the little yards.

"Now, you take this fishing trip: know who's tending his kids? Me and Mom. Course mostly it's Mom, but time I come home from work nights, she is so wore out the rest is up to me. But don't expect Vincent to thank me. No, sir. And if he gets wind I drove his van, he'll have my head."

In her tote bag Delia had five hundred dollars of vacation money, split between her billfold and a deceptive little vinyl cosmetic kit. She could stay away overnight, if she really wanted to alarm them—take a room in some motel or even a picturesque inn. However, all she had on was her swimsuit. Oh, Lord. Her scrunchy-skirted swimsuit and her espadrilles and Sam's beach robe. But supposing she kept the robe tightly closed . . . Viewed in a certain way, it was not all that different from a dress. The sleeves were three-quarter length; the hem covered her knees. And hotels around here must be used to tourists, in their skimpy tourist outfits.

They were approaching the edge of a town now. Vernon slowed for a traffic light. He was talking about his brother's wife, Eunice. "I feel kind of sorry for her, if you really want to know," he said. "Picture being married to Vincent!"

"What town is this?" Delia asked him.

"This? Why, Salisbury."

The light changed, and he resumed driving. Delia was thinking that maybe she could just get out here. Maybe at the next red light. But the lights from then on were green, and also they had reached a residential section, very middle class and staid. And then beyond were unappealing malls, and messy commercial establishments, and somehow nothing struck her as very inviting.

"It's my belief he hits her," Vernon was saying. "Or at least, like, sort of pushes her. Anyways I know they fight a lot, because half the time when they come over she won't look him in the face."

They were riding through open country again, and Delia was beginning to fear she had missed her last chance. It was such *empty* country, so cardboard flat and desolate. She gripped her door handle and gazed at a naked dirt field in which violently uprooted trees lay every which way, their roots and branches clawing air. Unexpectedly Vernon braked, then took a sharp left onto a narrow paved road. "Three eighty," he informed her. He didn't seem to notice the clattering of the percolator behind them. "But this fishing trip they're on is supposed to be a second honeymoon."

"Honeymoon!" Delia said. She was looking

at a pasture filled with rusted-out cars. Around
the next curve lay a ramshackle barn halfway
returned to the earth—the ridgepole almost
U-shaped, the warped gray boards slumping into
waist-high weeds. Every minute, she saw, she
was traveling farther from civilization.

"Well, how Eunice put it to my mom," Vernon said, "she put it that her and Vincent were
going off on the boat by themselves, just the two
of them together."

Delia thought that a trip alone on a fishing
boat would strain the best of marriages, but all
she said was, "Well, I wish them luck."

"That's what I told Mom," Vernon said. He
swerved around an antique tractor, whose driver
was wearing what looked like a duster. "I told
Mom, I said, 'Lots of luck, when her husband is
Vincent the Dweeb.' "

"She should give up on him," Delia said, forgetting it was none of her business. "Especially
if he hits her."

"Oh, I'm pretty sure he hits her."

Was that a brick building in the distance? Yes,
and a grove of dark trees that cooled and relieved
Delia's eyes, and beyond them a sparkling white
steeple. She knew there must be guest accom-
modations here. She gathered up her tote bag
and smoothed her robe around her knees.

"One time Eunice dropped by the house with
a puffy place on her cheekbone," Vernon said.

"And when Mom asked where she got it she said, 'I walked into a wall,' which if it had been me I could have come up with a lot better story than that."

"She should leave him," Delia said, but her mind was on the town ahead. They were passing the outskirts now—small white houses, a diner, a collection of men talking in front of a service station. "There's no point trying to mend a marriage that's got to the point of violence," she told Vernon.

Now they had reached the brick building, which turned out to be a school. DOROTHY G. UNDERWOOD HIGH SCHOOL. A street leading off just past that ended, evidently, in a park, for Delia glimpsed distant greenery and a statue of some kind. And now they were nearing the church that the steeple belonged to. Vernon was saying, "Well, I don't know; maybe you're right. Like I was telling Mom the other day, I told her—"

"I believe I'll get out here," Delia said.

"What?" he said. He slowed.

"Here is where I think I'll get out."

He brought the van to a stop and looked at the church. Two ladies in straw hats were weeding a patch of geraniums at the foot of the announcement board. "But I thought you were going to Ashford," he said. "*This* is not Ashford."

"Well, still," she said, looping the handles of
her tote bag over her shoulder. She opened the
passenger door and said, "Thanks for the ride."

"I hope I didn't say nothing to upset you,"
Vernon told her.

"No! Honest! I just think I'll—"

"Was it Eunice?"

"Eunice?"

"Vincent hitting her and all? I won't talk about
it no more if it upsets you."

"No, really, I enjoyed our talk," she told him.
And she hopped to the ground and sent him a
brilliant smile as she closed the door. She started
walking briskly in the direction they had come
from, and when she reached the street where she
had seen the statue she turned down it, not even
slowing, as if she had some specific destination
in mind.

Behind her, she heard the van shift gears and
roar off again. Then a deep silence fell, like the
silence after some shocking remark. It seemed
this town felt as stunned as Delia by what she
had gone and done.

# 6

What kind of trees lined this street? Beeches, she believed, judging by the high, arched corridor they formed. But she had never been very good at identifying trees.

Identifying the town itself, though, was easy. First she passed an imposing old house with a sign in one ground-floor window: MIKE POTTS— "BAY BOROUGH'S FRIENDLIEST INSURANCE AGENT." Then the Bay Borough Federal Savings Bank. And she was traveling down Bay Street, as she discovered when she reached the first intersection. But would the bay in question be the Chesapeake? She was fairly sure she had not come so far west. Also, this didn't have the feel of a waterside town. It smelled only of asphalt.

She found her explanation in the square. There, where scanty blades of grass struggled with plantain beneath more trees, a plaque at the base of the single bronze statue proclaimed:

ON THIS SPOT, IN AUGUST 1863,
GEORGE PENDLE BAY,
A UNION SOLDIER ENCAMPED OVERNIGHT
WITH HIS COMPANY,

DREAMED THAT A MIGHTY ANGEL
APPEARED TO HIM AND SAID,
"YE ARE SITTING IN THE BARBER'S CHAIR
OF INFINITY,"
WHICH HE INTERPRETED AS INSTRUCTION
TO ABSENT HIMSELF
FROM THE REMAINDER OF THE WAR
AND STAY ON TO FOUND THIS TOWNSHIP.

Delia blinked and took a step backward. Mr. Bay, a round-faced man in a bulging suit, did happen to be sitting, but his chair was the ordinary, non-barber kind, as near as she could make out, with a skirt of twisted bronze fringe. He gripped the chair's arms in a manner that squashed his fingertips; evidently he had been a nail biter. This struck Delia as comical. She gave a snuffle of laughter and then glanced over her shoulder, fearing someone had heard. But the square was empty, its four green benches uninhabited. Around the perimeter, cars cruised past, one or two at a time, and people walked in and out of the low brick and clapboard buildings, but nobody seemed to notice her.

Still, she was conscious all at once of her outfit. It wasn't so much the beach robe as the swimsuit underneath, the *feeling* of it, crumpled and bunchy and saggy. She'd give anything for some underwear. So she crossed the little square and gazed toward the row of storefronts on the other side of the street.

Clearly, modern times had overtaken the town. Buildings that must have been standing for a century—the bricks worn down like old pencil erasers, the clapboards gently rubbed to gray wood—now held the Wild Applause Video Shop, Tricia's House of Hair, and a Potpourri Palace. One place that seemed unchanged, though, was the dime store on the corner, with its curlicued red-and-gilt sign and a window full of flags and bunting.

She had been taught to buy only top-quality underwear, however else she might economize, but this was an emergency. She crossed the street and entered the dime-store smells of caramel and cheap cosmetics and old wooden floors. Apparently the notion of consolidated checkout lanes had not caught on here. At each and every counter, a clerk stood by a cash register. A floss-haired girl rang up a coloring book for a child; an elderly woman bagged a younger woman's cookie sheets. The lingerie department was staffed by a man, oddly enough; so Delia made her selections in haste and handed them over without quite raising her eyes. A plain white nylon bra, white cotton underpants. The underpants came three to a pack. Other styles could be purchased singly, but it was the pack of three that her fingers alighted on. *Just in case I'm away*

*for more than one night,* she caught herself thinking. Then, as she counted out her money, she
thought, *But I can always use them at home, of
course, too. This doesn't mean a thing.*

Now she had her underclothes but no place to
get into them, for she didn't see a rest room in
the dime store. She went back outside, tucking
her parcel into her tote, and looked up the street.
Next door was Debbi's Dress Shoppe. Nineteen-
forties mannequins with painted-on hair sported
the latest fashions—broad-shouldered business
suits or linen sheaths shaped like upside-down
triangles. Not Delia's style at all, but at least she
would find a changing booth here. She breezed
in, trying to look purposeful, and snatched the
nearest dress off a rack and hurried toward a row
of compartments at the rear. "May I help you?"
a woman called after her, but Delia said, "Oh,
thanks, I'm only . . ." and disappeared behind
a curtain.

The underwear fit, thank heaven. (She did her
best to silence the rustling of the bag.) It was a
relief to feel *contained* again. She folded her
swimsuit into her tote. Then she reached for
Sam's robe, but the sight of it gave her pause.
It seemed so obviously a beach robe, all at once.
She looked toward the dress she'd snatched up
—a gray knit of some sort. Way too long, she
could tell at a glance, but still she slipped it off
its hanger and drew it over her head. The acrid

smell of new fabric engulfed her. She smoothed down the skirt, zipped the side zipper, and turned to confront her reflection.

She had assumed she would resemble a child playing dress-up, for the hem nearly brushed her ankles. What she found, though, was someone entirely unexpected: a somber, serious-minded woman in a slender column of pearl gray. She might be a librarian or a secretary, one of those managerial executive secretaries who actually run the whole office from behind the scenes. "You'll find it in the Jones file, Mr. Smith," she imagined herself saying curtly. "And don't forget you're lunching with the mayor today; you'll want to take along the materials on the—"

"How're we doing in there?" the saleswoman called.

"Oh, fine."

"Can I bring you anything else to try?"

"No," Delia said. "This is perfect."

She stuffed Sam's robe into her tote and emerged from the booth to ask, "Could you just take the tags off, please? I think I'll wear it home."

The saleswoman—an overtanned blond in a geometric black-and-white print—directed a dubious frown toward the hemline. "We do offer alterations," she said. "Would you like that shortened a bit?"

"No, thanks," Delia told her in a starchy, secretarial voice.

The saleswoman adjusted seamlessly. "Well, it certainly becomes you," she said.

Delia raised her left arm, and the woman reached for her scissors and snipped off the tags that dangled from the zipper pull.

Seventy-nine ninety-five, the dress cost, not including tax. But Delia paid without a moment's hesitation and strode out of the shop.

The momentum of her exit carried her some distance, past the dime store again and across an intersection to a row of smaller shops—a copy center, a travel agent, a florist. She noticed she walked differently now, not with her usual bouncy gait but more levelly, because of her slim skirt. *Here is the secretary, Miss X, speeding back to her office after lunch. Preparing to type up her notes for the board of directors.*

Just as a game, she started choosing her office, the same way she used to choose her house when riding through a posh neighborhood. NICHOLS & TRIMBLE FAMILY DENTISTS. But there she might have to clean teeth or something. VALUE VISION OPTICIANS. But did opticians use secretaries? EZEKIEL POMFRET, ATTORNEY. Possibly defunct, from the expressionless look of the lowered window shade. And none of these places bore a HELP WANTED sign. Not that that made any practical difference.

At the next intersection, she took a left. She passed a pet supply and an antique store, so called (its window full of Fiesta ware and aqua plastic ashtrays shaped like boomerangs). A pharmacy. Two frame houses. A mom-and-pop grocery. Then another frame house, set so close to the street that its porch floor seemed an extension of the sidewalk. Propped in the dusty front window stood a cardboard notice, ROOM FOR RENT, bracketed by limp gauze curtains.

Room for rent.

This would be, of course, a "boardinghouse." The word summoned a picture of the secretary tidying the covers on her spinsterly white bed; her fellow boarders shuffling down the hall in their carpet slippers; her ancient landlady, dressed in black, setting the dining-room table— the "board"—for tomorrow's breakfast. In the time it took Delia to cross the porch and ring the bell, she became so well entrenched that she hardly felt the need to introduce herself to the woman who appeared at the door. "Well, hi!" the woman said. "Can I help you?"

She didn't fit Delia's vision of a landlady. She was plump and fortyish, heavily rouged, wearing a towering dessert tray of lavish golden curls and a hot-pink pantsuit. Still, she seemed to be the one in charge, so Delia said, "I'm inquiring about the room."

"Room?"

"The room for rent," Delia reminded her.

"Oh, the room," the woman said. "Well. I was hoping to rent to a man."

Was that even legal, nowadays? Delia didn't know what to say next.

"Up to last April," the woman told her, opening the baggy screen door, "I just always had men. It just always seemed to work that way. I only rent out two rooms, you know, and so I had these two men, Mr. Lamb who travels weekdays and Larry Watts who was separated. But when Larry got back with his wife last April, why, I rented his room to a woman. And did I ever regret it!"

She turned, leaving the door to Delia, and started up a flight of stairs. Uncertainly, Delia followed. She had an impression of a house that had long ago been abandoned. Ovals of lighter wallpaper showed where pictures must once have hung, and the floorboards of the upstairs hall revealed the ghost of a rug.

"Katie O'Connell, her name was," the woman said. Even so short a climb had winded her. She patted her wide pink bosom with little spanking sounds. "A Delaware girl, I believe. She came to town to work for Zeke Pomfret—Zeke had just had his dear old Miss Percy *die* on him— and so Katie needed a place to stay and I said, 'Fine,' not having the slightest inkling: 'Fine,' I told her, thinking this would be no different from renting to a man. But, oh, it was, 'Where's this, where's that, where's my fresh towels daily, where's my little bar of soap . . . ?' I am not a bed-and-breakfast, mind you. I hope you don't think I'm a bed-and-breakfast.''

"Of course not," Delia said.

"I'm only renting out rooms, you know? I bought this place three years ago. Fixer-upper, they called it. I bought it after I passed my real estate exam, thought I'd fix it up and sell it, but the way the market's been doing I just never have found the money for that, and so I'm living here myself and renting out two of the rooms. But there's no meals involved; I hope you're not looking for meals. This Katie, she was, 'Oh, let me just keep this quart of milk in your fridge,' and not two shakes later she was cooking in my kitchen. Why, *I* don't even cook in my kitchen! This is a bare-bones operation."

Proving it, she opened the door to the right of the stairs. Delia followed her into a long, narrow room, its outside wall slanting inward under the eaves, a window at each end. A metal cot extended from beneath the front window, and a low, orange-brown bureau sat against the inside wall. There was a smell like a hornet's nest—a dry, sharp, moldering smell that came, perhaps, from the brittle-looking tan wallpaper traced with mottled roses.

"Now, Katie had drapes on these windows,"

the woman said, "but she took them when she left. Left last Thursday with Larry Watts; we think they went to Hawaii."

"The . . . Larry Watts who was separated?" Delia asked in confusion.

"Oh, I didn't realize you knew him. Yes, once I put it all together, I recalled he did come back for his raincoat—raincoat he'd left in the down-stairs closet. That must be how they met. Next thing anyone knows, he's flown the coop, leaving that little wife of his for the second time in two years. Not to mention Zeke Pomfret needing to hunt up a whole new girl now, so soon after losing poor Miss Percy."

She flung open a door at the rear, exposing a shallow closet. Three hangers tinkled faintly. "Bathroom's off the hall, full bath with tub and shower," she said, "and you wouldn't have to share it but on weekends, when Mr. Lamb gets back from his sales trips. I stay downstairs, my-self. Rent is forty-two dollars a week. You want it?"

Forty-two dollars was less than a single night in most hotels. And a hotel would not be any-thing like so satisfyingly Spartan. Delia said, "You mean it's all right I'm not a man?"

The woman shrugged. "No one *else* has come along," she said.

Delia walked over to the cot, which was made up with white sheets and a white woolen blanket washed bald. When she tested the mattress with one palm, it sounded the same tinny note as the hangers.

She said, "Definitely I want it."

"Well, great. I'm Belle Flint, by the way."

"I'm Delia Grinstead," Delia said, and then she wondered if she should have used an alias. But Belle seemed reassuringly uninterested. She was fluffing her curls now in the mirror over the bureau. "So," Delia said, "would I have to . . . sign a contract?"

"Contract?"

"I mean . . ."

It must be painfully apparent that she had never arranged for her own housing before. "I mean a . . . lease or something?" she asked.

"Lord, no, just pay in advance, every Saturday morning," Belle said, baring her front teeth to the mirror. "Let's see. Today's Monday. . . . Pay me thirty dollars; that'll cover this week. You plan on staying here long?"

"Oh, maybe," Delia said, deliberately vague, and she started making a to-do over digging through her tote. Belle was tilting her chin now to study the cushion of flesh beneath it. Her entire face was a cushion; she resembled one of those lush, soft flowers, a peony or a big floppy iris.

"Well, here," Delia told her, "ten, twenty . . . ," and only then did Belle turn away from the mirror. If she was surprised to receive cash, she didn't show it. She folded the bills and tucked them into her breast pocket.

"I guess you'll want to go fetch your belongings," she said, "and meantime I'll put your key on the bureau, just in case I'm out when you get back. I'm showing a house at four-thirty. You won't be bringing a lot of *stuff*, I hope."

"No, I—"

"Because this room doesn't have much storage space, and I hate for things to spill over. That's how all that happened with Larry Watts and Katie: his raincoat spilled into the downstairs closet, and so naturally he forgot it when he moved."

"I'm bringing very little," Delia said.

She would wait to come back till, say, five o'clock, when Belle was sure to be out. That way Belle wouldn't see she was really bringing nothing. It was now . . . Surreptitiously, she checked her watch. Three forty-five. Belle was clattering out of the room in her wedge-heeled sandals. "Rules are, the first floor is mine," she said, pausing in the hall, "and that includes the kitchen. Café across the street is pretty good: Rick-Rack's. There's a laundromat on East Street, and Mrs. Auburn comes Fridays to clean the rooms. We never lock the front door, but that key to your room does work, if you're the nervous type. You got all that?"

"Yes, thanks."

"And I don't suppose you'll have guests," Belle said. She gave Delia a sudden appraising look. "Men guests, that is."

"Oh! No, I won't."

"Your private life is your private life, but that forty-two dollars covers utilities for one. Sheets and towels for one, too."

"I don't even know anybody to invite," Delia assured her.

"You're not a local girl, huh?"

"Well, no."

"Me neither. Till I came here with a fella, I never heard of Bay Borough," Belle said cheerfully. "The fella didn't work out, but I stayed on anyhow."

Delia knew she should volunteer some information in exchange, but all she said was, "I guess I'll wash up before I go get my things."

"Help yourself," Belle said with a wave. And she went clomping down the stairs.

Delia waited a polite half second before stepping into the bathroom. She hadn't peed since ten o'clock that morning.

The bathroom wallpaper—seahorses breathing silver bubbles—curled at the seams, and the fixtures were old and rust-stained, but everything looked clean. First Delia used the toilet, and then she patted her face with cool water and let it air-dry. (The one towel belonged to the other boarder, she assumed.) She avoided her face in the mirror; she preferred to hang on to the image she'd seen in the changing booth. She did glance down at her dress, though, checking it for neatness, for secretarial properness. And just before walking out, she slipped her wedding ring off her finger and dropped it into her tote.

Then she made a brief return trip to her room. She didn't go inside but merely stood in the doorway, claiming it—reveling in its starkness, now that she had it completely to herself.

Clop-clop back up the street, eyes front, as if she knew where she was headed. Well, she did, more or less. Already the little town held pockets of familiar sights: the faded red soft-drink machine outside the Gobble-Up Grocery, the chipped Fiesta ware in Bob's Antiques, the stacked bags of kibble for overweight dogs in Pet Heaven. She took a right at the corner, and the green square in the distance seemed as comfortable, as well known and faintly boring, as if she had spent her childhood at the foot of Mr. Bay's fringed chair.

Ezekiel Pomfret still had his shade pulled down, but when Delia tried the door it yielded. A steep flight of stairs climbed straight ahead. A ground-floor door to the right bore, on its cloudy, pebbled glass, Ezekiel Pomfret's name once again and WILLS & ESTATES—DOMESTIC-CRIMINAL LAW. That door, too, opened when

Delia tried it. She stepped into a walnut-lined room with a reception desk in the center. No one sat at the desk, she was pleased to see. No one was visible anywhere, but behind another door, this one ornately paneled, she heard a man's voice. It stopped and started, interspersed by silence, so she knew he must be talking on the phone.

She crossed to the desk, which was bare except for a telephone and a typewriter. She lifted a corner of the typewriter's gray rubber hood. Manual; not even electric. (She had worried she would find a computer.) She gave a small, testing spin to the swivel chair behind it.

*Good afternoon,* she would say. *I'm here to ask if . . .*

No, not *ask. Ask* was too tentative.

She reached up to pat her hair, which felt as crumbly as dry sand on the beach. (The beach! No: shoo that thought away.) She smoothed her skirt around her hips and made sure that the trim on her tote—a flashy pink bow, ridiculous—was hidden beneath her arm.

*It just seemed so fateful, Mr. Pomfret, it seemed almost like a direct command, that I should learn about poor Miss Percy exactly at the moment when . . .*

The voice behind the door gathered energy and volume. Mr. Pomfret must be winding up his conversation.

*Like having something accidentally break my*

*fall, does that make any sense? Like I've been*
*falling, falling all day and then was snagged by*
*a random hook, or caught by an outjutting ledge,*
*and this is where I happened to land, so I was*
*wondering whether . . .*

Slam of receiver, squeak of caster wheels,
heavy tread on carpet. The paneled door swung
open, and a big-bellied middle-aged man in a
seersucker suit surveyed her over his half-
glasses. "I *thought* I heard someone," he said.

"Mr. Pomfret, I'm Delia Grinstead," she told
him. "I've come to be your secretary."

At four-fifteen she returned to the dime store
and bought one cotton nightgown, white, and
two pairs of nylon panty hose. At four twenty-
five she crossed the square to Bassett Bros. Shoe
Store and bought a large black leather handbag.
The bag cost fifty-seven dollars. When she first
saw the price she considered settling for vinyl,
but then she decided that only genuine leather
would pass muster with Miss Grinstead.

Miss Grinstead was Delia—the new Delia; for
after one grimacing, acidic "Ms.," that was how
Mr. Pomfret had addressed her throughout their
interview. It seemed apt that she should accept
this compromise—the unmarried title, the married surname. Certainly the aproned, complacent sound of "Mrs." no longer applied, and yet
she couldn't go back to being giggly young Miss

Felson. Besides, her Social Security card said Grinstead. She had drawn it from her wallet and read off the number to Mr. Pomfret (not having had enough use of it, all these years, to know it by heart). She had told him she was relocating after burying her mother. A whole unspoken history insinuated itself in the air between them: the puttery female household, the daughter's nunnish devotion. She said she had worked in a doctor's office her entire adult life. "Twenty-two years," she told Mr. Pomfret, "and I felt so sad to leave, but I simply couldn't stay on in Baltimore with all those memories." She seemed to have been infected with Miss Grinstead's manner of speaking. She would never herself have used "simply" in casual conversation, and the word "memories" in that context had a certain mealy-mouthed tone that was unlike her.

If references had been called for, she was prepared to say that her employer had recently died as well. (She was killing off people right and left today.) But Mr. Pomfret didn't mention references. His sole concern was the nature of her past duties. Had she typed, had she filed, taken shorthand? She answered truthfully, but it felt like lies. "I typed all the bills and correspondence and the doctor's charts," she said. Sam's worn face rose up before her, along with his mended white coat and the paisley tie that he called his "paramecium tie." She sat straighter in her chair. "I filed and manned the phone and kept the appointment book, but unfortunately I do not take shorthand."

"Well, no matter," Mr. Pomfret said. "Neither did Miss Percy or Miss What's-her-name. I've always dreamed of having a secretary with shorthand, but I guess it's not meant to be."

There was an uncomfortable moment when he asked for her address, since she had no idea what it was. But when she mentioned Belle Flint he said, "Oh, yes, on George Street." He added, as he made a notation, "Belle's a real fun gal." That was the advantage to a small town, Delia supposed. Or the disadvantage, depending on how you looked at it.

He said she should start tomorrow; her hours were nine to five. Sorry the pay was just minimum wage, he said (sliding his eyes over subtly to gauge her reaction). Also, she was expected to brew the coffee; he hoped that wasn't a problem.

Of course it wasn't, Delia said brusquely, and she rose and terminated the interview. Her impression of Mr. Pomfret was that he was a man without any grain to him, someone benign but not especially interesting, and that was fine with her. In fact, she didn't much like him, and that was fine too. For the impersonal new life she seemed to be manufacturing for herself, Mr. Pomfret was ideal.

Her watch said twenty minutes till five, and

she hadn't eaten since breakfast. Before heading back to her room, therefore, she walked to the café that Belle had recommended. It turned out to be not directly across from Belle's but a few doors farther west, next to a hardware. Still, she could see the boardinghouse from the window; so she sat in the booth that offered the best view and kept watch against Belle's return. Maybe she should have purchased a suitcase, just so she could move in openly. But it was foolish to spend money on appearances. Already her five hundred dollars had dwindled to . . . what? Mentally she tallied it up and then winced. When the waitress arrived, she confined her order to a bowl of vegetable soup and a glass of milk.

Rick-Rack's was the kind of place where she might have eaten in high school—a diner, basically, linoleum floored and tile walled, with six or eight booths and a row of stools along a Formica counter. One little redhead served the whole room, and a blue-black young man, gigantically muscled and shaven skulled, did the cooking. He was grilling a cheese sandwich for the only other customer, a boy about Ramsay's age. The smell of fried food gave Delia hunger pangs even as she was spooning her soup, but she reminded herself that soup provided more vitamins for the money, and she declined the homemade pie for dessert. She paid at the register. The cook, after wiping his hands on his apron, rang up her total without comment. Next time she'd bring something to read, she decided. She had felt awkward, munching her saltines and staring fixedly out the window.

No sign of Belle back at the house. Delia unlatched the front door and felt a thin, bare silence all around her. She climbed the stairs, thinking, *Here comes the executive secretary, returning from her lone meal to the solitude of her room.* It wasn't a complaint, though. It was a boast. An exultation.

When she opened her own door the hornet's-nest smell seemed stronger, perhaps because of the afternoon heat that had penetrated the eaves. She set her belongings on the bureau and went to raise both windows. The rear window offered a view of the tiny backyard and an alley. The front window showed the porch overhang and the buildings across the street. Delia leaned her forehead against the screen and picked out the café (B. J. "RICK" RACKLEY, PROP.) and the hardware store and a brown shingled house with the bars of a crib or a playpen visible in one upstairs window. The only sounds were soothing sounds—occasional cars swishing past and footsteps on the sidewalk.

Belle had left an old-fashioned, spindly key on the bureau, and Delia fitted it into the door and turned the lock. Then she took the tags off her new handbag, dropped her wallet inside, and hung the bag from a hook in the closet. She stowed her other purchases in the bureau. (The drawers stuck and slid out crookedly; they were cheaply made, like the house itself.) She hung Sam's beach robe on a hanger. She placed her cosmetic kit in a drawer. Her tote, with its remaining litter of sun lotions and swimsuit and rubber bands and such, she boosted onto the closet shelf. Then she closed the closet door and went over to the cot and sat down.

So.

She was settled.

She could look around the room and detect not the slightest hint that anybody lived here.

It was twilight before Belle returned. Delia heard the clunk of a car door out front, then loud heels on the porch. But neither woman called out a greeting. In fact, Delia, who had been staring into space for who knows how long, rose from the cot as soundlessly as possible, and tiptoed when she went over to collect some things from the bureau, and took care not to creak any floorboards when she crossed the hall to the bathroom.

While she waited for the shower to run warm, she brushed her teeth and undressed, putting her underwear to soak in the sink. A second towel and washcloth now hung on the other towel bar, she saw. She took the washcloth with her and stepped behind the shower curtain, which was crackly with age and slightly mildewed.

Grime and sweat and sunblock streamed off

her, uncovering a whole new layer of skin. The soles of her feet, which felt ironed flat from all that walking, seemed to be drinking up water. She lifted her face to the spray and let her hair get wet. Finally, regretfully, she shut off the faucets and stepped out to towel herself dry. The new nightgown drifted airily over her scorched shoulders.

She chose not to leave her toothbrush in the holder above the sink. Instead, she returned it to her cosmetic kit and carried everything back to her room. Her wrung-out underclothes she draped on one of the hangers in the closet. This meant she would have to keep the closet door open during the night—a blot on the room's sterility. Better that, though, than letting her laundry clutter the bathroom. She approved of Belle's house rules; she did not intend to "spill over."

She turned the bedcovers back and lay down, drawing up just the top sheet. The breeze from the window chilled her damp head, but not so much that she needed a blanket.

Outside, children were playing. It wasn't even completely dark yet. She lay on her back with her eyes open, keeping her mind as blank as the ceiling above her. Once, though, perhaps hours later, a single thought did present itself. *Oh, God,* she thought, *how am I going to get out of this?* But immediately afterward she closed her eyes, and that was how she fell asleep.

# 7

*Baltimore Woman Disappears,* Delia read, and she felt a sudden thud in her stomach, as if she'd been punched. *Baltimore Woman Disappears During Family Vacation.*

She had been checking the Baltimore news-papers daily, morning and evening. There was nothing in either paper Tuesday, nothing Wednesday, nothing Thursday morning. But the Thursday evening edition, which arrived in the vending box near the square in time for Delia's lunch hour, carried a notice in the Metro section. *Delaware State Police announced early today . . .*

She folded the paper open to the article, glanc-ing around as she did so. On the park bench opposite hers, a young woman was handing her toddler bits of something to feed the pigeons, piece by piece. On the bench to her right, a very old man was leafing through a magazine. No one seemed aware of Delia's presence.

*Mrs. Grinstead was last seen around noon this past Monday, walking south along the stretch of sand between . . .*

Probably the police had some rule that people were not considered missing till a certain amount of time had passed. That must be why there'd been no announcement earlier. (Searching each paper before this, Delia had felt relieved and wounded, both. Did no one realize she was gone? Or maybe she *wasn't* gone; this whole experience had been so dreamlike. Maybe she was still moving through her previous life the same as always, and the Delia here in Bay Borough had somehow just split off from the original.)

It hurt to read her physical description: *fair or light-brown hair . . . eyes are blue or gray or perhaps green . . .* For heaven's sake, hadn't anyone in her family ever looked at her? And how could Sam have made her clothing sound so silly? *Kind of baby-doll,* indeed! She refolded the paper with a snap and then darted another glance around her. The toddler was throwing a tantrum now, a silent little stomping dance, because he'd run out of pigeon food. The old man was licking a finger to turn a page. Delia hated when he did that. Every lunch hour he came here with a magazine and licked his way clear through it, and Delia could only hope that no one else was planning to read it after him.

Like a commuter who always chooses the same seat on the train, like a guest who always settles in the same chair in the living room, Delia had managed in just three days to establish a routine for herself. Breakfast at Rick-Rack's, over the morning paper. Lunch in the square—yogurt and fresh fruit purchased earlier from the Gobble-Up Grocery. Always on the southeast park bench, always with the evening paper. Then some kind of shopping task to fill the hour: Tuesday, a pair of low-heeled black shoes because her espadrilles were blistering her heels. Wednesday, a goosenecked reading lamp. Today she had planned to look for one of those immersion coils so she could brew herself a cup of tea first thing every morning. But now, with this newspaper item, she didn't know. She felt so exposed, all at once. She just wanted to scuttle back to the office.

She dropped her lunch leavings into a wire trash basket and buried the newspaper underneath them. As a rule she left the paper on the bench for others, but not today.

The mother was trying to stuff the toddler into his stroller. The toddler was resisting, refusing to bend in the middle. The old man had finished his magazine and was fussily fitting his glasses into their case. None of the three looked at Delia when she walked past them. Or maybe they were pretending, even the toddler; maybe they'd been instructed not to alarm her. No. She gave her shoulders a shake. *Get ahold of yourself.* It wasn't as if she'd committed any crime. She decided to go on with her routine—drop by the dime store as she'd planned.

Funny how life contrived to build up layers of *things* around a person. Already she had that goosenecked lamp, because the overhead bulb had proved inadequate for reading in bed; and she kept a stack of paper cups and a box of tea bags on her closet shelf, making do till now with hot water from the bathroom faucet; and it was becoming clear she needed a second dress. Last night, the first really warm night of summer, she had thought, *I should buy a fan.* Then she had told herself, *Stop. Stop while you're ahead.*

She walked into the dime store and paused. Housewares, maybe? The old woman presiding over the cookie sheets and saucepans stood idle, twiddling her beads; so Delia approached her. "Would you have one of those immersion coils?" she asked. "Those things you put in a cup to heat up water?"

"Well, I know what you mean," the old woman said. "I can see it just as plain as the nose on your face. Electric, right?"

"Right," Delia said.

"My grandson took one to college with him, but would you believe it? He didn't read the directions. Tried to heat a bowl of soup when the directions said only water. Stink? He said you couldn't imagine the stink! But I don't have any here. Maybe try the hardware department."

"Thanks," Delia said crisply, and she moved away.

Sure enough, she found it in Hardware, hanging on a rack among the extension cords and three-prong adapters. She paid in exact change. The clerk—a gray-haired man in a bow tie—winked when he handed her the bag. "Have a nice day, young lady," he said. He probably thought he was flattering her. Delia didn't bother smiling.

She had noticed that Miss Grinstead was not a very friendly person. The people involved in her daily routine remained two-dimensional to her, like the drawings in those children's books about the different occupations. She hadn't developed the easy, bantering relationships Delia was accustomed to.

Leaving the dime store, she crossed Bay Street and passed the row of little shops. The clock in the optician's window said 1:45. She always tried her best to fill her whole lunch hour, one o'clock to two o'clock, but so far had not succeeded.

And what would she do in wintertime, when it grew too cold to eat in the square? For she was looking that far ahead now, it seemed—this Miss Grinstead with her endless, unmarked, unchanging string of days.

But in Bay Borough it was always summer. That was the only season she could picture here.

She opened Mr. Pomfret's outside door, then the pebble-paned inner door. He was already back from his own lunch, talking on his office phone as usual. *Wurlitzer, wurlitzer,* it sounded like from here. Delia shut her handbag in the bottom desk drawer, smoothed her skirt beneath her, and seated herself in the swivel chair. She had left a letter half finished, and now she resumed typing, keeping her back very straight and her hands almost level as she had been taught in high school.

*Authorities do not suspect drowning,* the paper had said. It hadn't occurred to her they might. *Since Mrs. Grinstead professed a—*how had they put it?—*professed an aversion to water.* Or something of the sort. Made her sound like a woman who never bathed. She slammed the carriage return more violently than was necessary. And that business about Eliza saying she'd been a cat! People must think the both of them were lunatics.

This typewriter had a stiffer action than the one in Sam's office. Her first day at work, she'd broken two fingernails. After that she had filed all her nails down blunt, which was more appropriate anyhow to Miss Grinstead's general style. Besides, it had used up twenty minutes of an evening. She was devoting a lot of thought these days to how to use up her evenings.

"Well, let's do that! We'll have to get together and do that!" Mr. Pomfret was saying, suddenly louder and heartier. Delia typed the closing ("Esquire," he called himself) and rolled the letter out of the carriage. Mr. Pomfret burst through the door. "Miss Grinstead, when Mr. Miller shows up I'll need you in here taking notes," he said. "We're going to send a . . . What's that you've got?"

"Letter to Gerald Elliott?" Delia reminded him.

"Elliott! I met with Elliott back in . . ."

She checked the date at the top of the page. "May," she said. "May fourteenth."

"Damn."

It had come to light that Delia's immediate predecessor had stowed her more irksome chores in the filing cabinet under *Ongoing*. Anything red-inked by Mr. Pomfret had conveniently vanished. (And a great deal had been red-inked, since Katie O'Connell couldn't spell and apparently did not believe in paragraphs.) Mr. Pomfret had turned purple when Delia brought him the evidence, but Delia was secretly pleased. This way she looked so capable herself—so efficient, so take-charge. (She felt a bit like a grade-school tattletale.) Also, the retyping job amounted to a low-key training course. She would be sorry when she finished.

"Mr. Miller is due at two-thirty," Mr. Pomfret told her. He was leaning over her desk to sign the letter. "I want you to write down word for word everything he specifies."

"Yes, Mr. Pomfret."

He straightened, capping his pen, and gave her a sudden sharp look over his lizardy lower lids. Sometimes Delia carried her secretary act a bit too far, she suspected. She flashed him an insincere smile and gathered up the letter. His signature was large and sweeping, smeared on the curves. He used one of those expensive German fountain pens that leaked.

"And we'll want coffee, so you might as well fix it ahead," he told her.

"Yes, Mr.—. Certainly," she said.

She went into his office for the carafe, then took it to the sink in the powder room. When she came back he was seated at the credenza, short thighs twisted sideways, tapping once again at his computer. For he did have a computer. He had bought it sometime just recently and fallen under its spell, which might explain his failure to notice Katie O'Connell's filing methods. Theoretically, he was going to learn the machine's mysterious ways and then teach Delia, but after her first morning Delia knew she had nothing to fear. The computer would sit forever in its temporary position while Mr. Pomfret wrestled happily with questions of "backups" and "macros." Right now he was recording every dinner party he and his wife had ever hosted—guest list, menu, wines, and even seating arrangements—so their variables could be rotated into infinity. Delia gave the screen a scornful glance and circled it widely, heading for the cof-feemaker at the other end of the credenza.

Water, filter, French roast. This coffeemaker was top-of-the-line: it ground its own beans. She supposed it came from one of those catalogs that weighed down the office mail. Whenever Mr. Pomfret spotted an item he liked, he had Delia place an order. ("Yes, Mr. Pomfret . . .") She called 1-800 numbers clear across the country, requesting a bedside clock that talked, a pocket-sized electronic dictionary, a black leather map case for the glove compartment. Her employer's greed, like his huge belly, made Delia feel trim and virtuous. She didn't at all mind placing the orders. She enjoyed everything about this job, especially its dryness. No one received word of inoperable cancer in a lawyer's office. No one told Delia how it felt to be going blind. No one claimed to remember Delia's babyhood.

She pressed a button on the coffeemaker, and it started grinding. "Help!" Mr. Pomfret shouted over the din. He was goggling at his computer screen, where the lines of text shivered and shim-mied. For some reason, it never occurred to him that this always happened when the grinder was running. Delia left the office, closing the door discreetly behind her.

She typed another letter, this one enumerating the corporate bylaws of an accounting firm. ("Buy-laws," Katie O'Connell had spelled it.)

*Pursuant to our discussion,* she typed, and *fiscal liability,* and *consent of those not in attendance.* She sacrificed speed for accuracy, as befitted Miss Grinstead, and corrected her rare mistakes with Wite-Out fluid on original and carbon both.

Mr. Miller arrived—a big, handsome, olive-skinned man with a narrow band of black hair. Delia followed him into Mr. Pomfret's office to serve their coffee and then perched on a chair, pen and pad ready. She had worried she couldn't write fast enough, but there wasn't much to write. The question was how often Mr. Miller's ex-wife could see their son, and the answer, according to Mr. Miller, was "Never," which Mr. Pomfret amended to once a week and alternate holidays, hours to be arranged at client's convenience. Then the conversation drifted to computers, and when it didn't drift back again, Delia cleared her throat and asked, "Will that be all?"

Mr. Pomfret said, "Hmm? Oh. Yes, thank you, Miss Grinstead." As she left, she heard him tell Mr. Miller, "We'll see to that right away. I'll have my girl mail it out this afternoon."

Delia settled in her swivel chair, rolled paper into the carriage, and started typing. You could have balanced a glass of water on the back of each of her hands.

The only other appointment was at four—a woman with some stock certificates belonging to her late mother—but Delia's services were not required for that. She addressed a number of envelopes and folded and inserted the letters Mr. Pomfret had signed. She sealed the flaps, licked stamps. She answered a call from a Mrs. Darnell, who made an appointment for Monday. Mr. Pomfret walked past her, cramming his arms into his suit coat. "Good night, Miss Grinstead," he said.

"Good night, Mr. Pomfret."

She sorted her carbons and filed them. She returned what was left of the Ongoing file to its drawer. She answered a call from a man who was disappointed to find Mr. Pomfret gone but would try him at home. She cleaned the coffee-maker. At five o'clock exactly she lowered all the shades, gathered the letters and her handbag, and left the office.

Mr. Pomfret had given her her own key, and she already knew the crotchets of the pebble-paned door—the way you had to push it inward a bit before it would lock.

Outside, the sun was still shining and the air felt warm and heavy after the air-conditioning. Delia walked at a leisurely pace, letting others pass her—men in business suits hurrying home from work, women rushing by with plastic bags from the Food King. She dropped her letters into the mailbox on the corner, but instead of turning left there, she continued north to the library—the next stop in her routine.

By now she had a sense of the town's layout.
It was a perfect grid, with the square mathe-
matically centered between three streets north
and south of it, two streets east and west. Look
west as you crossed an intersection, and you'd
see pasture, sometimes even a cow. (In the
mornings, when Delia woke, she heard distant
roosters crowing.) The sidewalks were crumpled
and given over in spots to grass, breaking off
entirely when a tree stood in the way. The streets
farther from the square had a tendency to slant
into scabby asphalt mixed with weeds at the
edges, like country highways.

On Border Street, the town's northern bound-
ary, the Bay Borough Public Library crouched
between a church and an Exxon station. It was
hardly more than a cottage, but the instant Delia
stepped inside she always felt its seriousness, its
officialness. A smell of aged paper and glue hung
above the four tables with their wooden chairs,
the librarian's high varnished counter, the book-
cases chockablock with elderly books. No CDs
or videotapes here, no spin racks of paperback
novels; just plain, sturdy volumes in buckram
bindings with their Dewey decimal numbers
handwritten on the spines in white ink. It was a
matter of finances, Delia supposed. Nothing
seemed to have been added in the last decade.
Best-sellers were nowhere to be seen, but there
was plenty of Jane Austen, and Edith Wharton,

and various solemn works of history and biography. The children's corner gave off a glassy shine from all the layers of Scotch tape holding the tattered picture books together.

Closing time was five-thirty, which meant that the librarian was busy with her last-minute shelving. Delia could place yesterday's book on the counter without any chitchat; she could hunt down a book for today unobserved, since at this hour all the tables were empty. But what to choose? She wished this place carried romances. Dickens or Dostoyevsky she would never finish in one evening (she had an arrangement with herself where she read a book an evening). George Eliot, Faulkner, Fitzgerald . . .

She settled on *The Great Gatsby*, which she dimly remembered from sophomore English. She took it to the counter, and the librarian (a cocoa-colored woman in her fifties) stopped her shelving to come wait on her. "Oh, *Gatsby!*" she said. Delia merely said, "Mmhmm," and handed over her card.

The card had her new address on it: 14 George Street. A dash in the space for her telephone number. She had never been unreachable by phone before.

Tucking the book in her handbag, she left the library and headed south. The Pinchpenny Thrift Shop had changed its window display, she noticed. Now a navy knit dress hung alongside a shell-pink tuxedo. Would it be tacky to buy her second dress from a thrift shop? In a town this size, no doubt everyone could name the previous owner.

But after all, what did she care? She made a mental note to come try on the dress tomorrow during lunch hour.

Taking a right onto George Street, she met up with the mother and toddler who fed the pigeons in the square. The mother smiled at her, and before Delia thought, she smiled back. Immediately afterward, though, she averted her eyes.

Next stop was Rick-Rack's Café. She glanced over at the boardinghouse as she passed. No cars were parked in front, she was glad to see. With luck, Belle would be out all evening. She seemed to lead a very busy life.

Rick-Rack's smelled of crab cakes, but whoever had ordered them had already eaten and gone. The little redheaded waitress was filling salt shakers. The cook was scraping down his griddle. "Well, hey!" he said, turning as Delia walked in.

"Hello," she said, smiling. (She had nothing against simple courtesy, as long as it went no further.) She settled in her usual booth. By the time the waitress came over, she was already deep in her library book, and all she said was, "Milk and the chicken pot pie, please." Then she went on reading.

Last night she'd had soup and whole-wheat toast; the night before that, tuna salad. Her plan was to alternate soup nights with protein nights. Just inexpensive proteins, though. She couldn't afford the crab cakes, at least not till she got her first salary check.

Paying for her new shoes on Tuesday, she had wished she could use the credit card she was carrying in her wallet. If only a credit-card trail were not so easily traced! And then a peculiar thought had struck her. *Most untraceable of all,* she had thought, *would be dying.*

But of course she hadn't meant that the way it sounded.

The print in her library book was so large, she worried she had chosen something that wouldn't last the evening. She forced her eyes to travel more slowly, and when her meal arrived she stopped reading altogether. She kept the book open, though, next to her plate, in case somebody approached.

The waitress set out scalloped paper place mats for the supper crowd. The cook stirred something on the burner. Two creases traversed the base of his skull; his smooth black scalp seemed overlaid with a pattern of embroidery knots. He had made the pot pie from scratch, Delia suspected. The crust shattered beneath her fork. And the potatoes accompanying it seemed hand mashed, not all gluey and machine mashed.

She wondered whether her family had thought to thaw the casseroles she'd packed.

"If he do come," the cook was telling the waitress, "you got to keep him occupied. Because *I* ain't going to."

"You have to be around some, though," the waitress said.

"I ain't saying I won't be around. I say I won't keep him occupied."

The waitress looked toward Delia before Delia could look away. She had those bachelor's-button eyes you often see in redheads, and a round-chinned, innocent face. "My dad is planning a visit," she told Delia.

"Ah," Delia said, reaching for her book.

"He wasn't all that thrilled when me and Rick here got married."

The waitress and the cook were married? Delia was afraid that if she started reading now, they would think she disapproved too; so she marked her place on the page with one finger and said, "I'm sure he'll accept it eventually."

"Oh, he's accepted it, all right! Or says he has. But now whenever Rick sees him, he always gets to remembering how ugly Daddy acted at the start."

"I can't stand to be around the man," Rick said sadly.

"Daddy walks into a room and Rick is like, *whap!* and his mouth slams shut."

"Then Teensy here feels the pressure and goes to talking a mile a minute, nothing but pure silliness."

Delia knew what that was like. When her sister Linda was married to the Frenchman, whom their father had detested . . .

But she couldn't tell them that. She was sitting in this booth alone, utterly alone, without the conversational padding of father, sisters, husband, children. She was a person without a past. She took a breath to speak and then had nothing to say. It was Teensy who finally broke the silence. "Well," Teensy said, "at least we've got ourselves a few days to prepare for this." And she went off to wait on a couple who had just entered.

When Delia walked out of the café, she felt she was surrounded by a lighter kind of air than usual—thinner, more transparent—and she crossed the street with a floating gait. Just inside Belle's front door she found an array of letters scattered beneath the mail slot, but she didn't pick them up, didn't even check the names on the envelopes, because she knew for a fact that none of them was hers.

Upstairs, she went about her coming-home routine: putting away her things, showering, doing her laundry. Meanwhile she kept an ear out for Belle's return, because she would have moved more quietly with someone else in the

house. But she could tell she had the place to
herself.

When every last task was completed, she
climbed into bed with her library book. If there
had been a chair she would have sat up to read,
but this was her only choice. She wondered
whether Mr. Lamb's room was any better
equipped. She supposed she could request a
chair from Belle. That would mean a conversation, though, and Delia was avoiding conversation as much as possible. Heaven forbid they
should get to be two cozy, chatty lady friends,
exchanging news of their workdays every evening.

She propped her pillow against the metal rail
at the head of the cot and leaned back. For this
first little bit, the light from outdoors was enough
to read by—a slant of warm gold that made her
feel pleasantly lazy. She could hear a baby crying
in the house across the street. A woman far away
called, "Robbie! Kenny!" in that bell-like, two-
note tune that mothers everywhere fetch their
children home with. Delia read on, turning pages
with a restful sound. She was interested in Gatsby's story but not what you would call carried
away. It would serve to pass the evening, was
all.

The light grew dimmer, and she switched on
the goosenecked lamp that craned over her
shoulder from the windowsill. Now the children

across the street, released from the supper table, were playing something argumentative outdoors. Delia heard them for a while but gradually forgot to listen, and when she thought of them again she realized they must have gone in to bed. Night had fallen, and moths were thumping against the screen. Down in the street, a car door closed; heels clopped across the porch; Belle entered the house and went directly to the front room, where she started talking on the phone. "You know it's got great resale value," Delia heard, before forgetting to listen to that as well. Later she stopped reading for a moment and heard only silence, inside and out, except for the distant traffic on 380. It was cooler now, and she felt grateful for the lamp's small circle of warmth.

She came to the end of her book, but she kept rereading the final sentence till her eyes blurred over with tears. Then she placed the book on the floor and reached up to switch the lamp off so she could sit weeping in the dark—the very last step in her daily routine.

She wept without a thought in her head, heaving silent sobs that racked her chest and contorted her mouth. Every few minutes she blew her nose on the strip of toilet paper she kept under her pillow. When she felt completely drained, she gave a deep, shuddering sigh and said aloud, "Ah, well." Then she blew her nose one last time and lay down to sleep.

It amazed her that she always slept so soundly.

The toddler wanted the pigeons to eat from his fingers. He squatted in their midst, his bulky corduroy bottom just inches from the ground, and held a crouton toward them. But the pigeons strutted around him with shrewd, evasive glances, and when it dawned on him that they would never come closer he suddenly toppled backward, not giving the slightest warning, and pedaled the air in a fury. Delia smiled, but only behind the shield of her newspaper.

Today there was no further mention of her disappearance. She wondered if the authorities had forgotten her that quickly.

She folded the Metro section and laid it on the bench beside her. She reached for the cup of yogurt at her left and then noticed, out of the corner of her eye, the woman who stood watching her from several yards away.

Her heart gave a lurch. She said, "Eliza?"

Eliza moved forward abruptly, as if she had just this second determined something.

There was no one beside her. No one behind her.

No one.

She was wearing a dress—a tailored tan shirt-waist that dated from the time when they still had a Stewart's department store. Eliza almost never wore dresses. This must be a special occasion, Delia thought, and then she thought, *Why, I am the occasion.* She rose, fumbling with her yogurt cup. "Hello, Eliza," she said.

"Hello, Delia."

They stood awkwardly facing each other, Eliza gripping a boxy leather purse in both hands, until Delia recollected the old man on the east bench. He appeared to be intent on his magazine, but that didn't fool her in the least. "Would you like to take a walk?" she asked Eliza.

"We could," Eliza said stiffly.

She was probably angry. Well, of course she was angry. Bundling her lunch things into the trash basket, Delia felt like a little girl hiding some mischief. She sensed she was blushing, too. Hateful thin-skinned complexion, always giving her away. She slung the strap of her handbag over her shoulder and set off across the square, with Eliza lagging a step behind as if to accentuate Delia's willfulness, her lack of consideration. When they reached the street, Delia stopped and turned to face her. "I guess you think I shouldn't have done this," she said.

"I didn't say that. I'm waiting to hear your reasons."

Delia started walking again. If she had known Eliza would pop up this way, she would have invented some reasons ahead of time. It was ridiculous not to have any.

"Mr. Sudler thought you were a battered wife," Eliza said.

"Who?"

"The roofer. Vernon Sudler."

"Oh, Vernon," Delia said. Yes, of course: he would have seen the newspaper.

They crossed the street and headed north. Delia had planned to visit the thrift shop, but now she didn't know where she was going.

"He phoned us in Baltimore," Eliza said. "He asked for—"

"Baltimore! What were you doing in Baltimore?"

"Why, we packed up and drove there after you left. Surely you didn't think we'd stay at the beach."

Actually, Delia *had* thought that. But she could see now it would have looked strange: everybody slathering on the suntan lotion as usual, industriously blowing air into their rafts while the policemen gave their bloodhounds a sniff of Delia's slippers.

"We thought at first you'd gone to Baltimore yourself," Eliza was saying. "You can imagine the fuss with the floor refinishers when all of us walked in. And when we didn't find you there . . . Well, thank goodness Mr. Sudler called. He called the house last night, inquiring how to get in touch with me personally, and as luck would have it I was the one who answered. So he said he could swear you hadn't been kidnapped, but he hesitated to tell the police because he believed you'd had good cause to run away. He said you got out of his van at a church that counsels battered women.''

"I did?''

Delia stopped in front of the florist's shop.

"You saw their signboard and asked him to let you out, he said.''

"Signboard?''

"And also there'd been some discussion, he said, something you two were discussing that made him wonder later if . . . But he wouldn't tell me your whereabouts, in case your husband was dangerous. 'Dangerous!' I said. 'Why, Sam Grinstead is the kindest man alive!' I said. But Mr. Sudler was very fixed in his mind. He said, 'I only called to tell you she's all right, and I want to say too I didn't know at the time that she was running away. She just begged me for a ride to this certain town,' he said, 'and claimed that she had family there, so I didn't see the harm.' Then he said not to tell Sam, but of course I did tell Sam; I could hardly keep it a secret. I told Sam I would come talk to you first and find out how things stood.''

She waited. She was going to make Delia ask.

All right. "And what did Sam say back?" Delia
asked.

"He said well *naturally* I should come. He
agreed completely."

"Oh."

Another wait.

"And he quite understood that I couldn't di-
vulge which town it was till we'd talked."

"I see," Delia said.

Then she said, "But how did *you* know the
town?"

"Why, because you told Mr. Sudler you had
family there."

"Family. Um . . ."

"Our mother's family! In Bay Borough."

"Mother's family lives in Bay Borough?"

"Well, they used to. Maybe some still do, but
nobody I would have heard of. You knew that.
Bay Borough? Where Aunt Henny lived? And
Great-Uncle Roscoe had his chicken farm just
west of?"

"That was in Bay Borough?"

"Where else!"

"I never realized," Delia said.

"I can't imagine why not. Shoot, there's even
a Weber Street—Grandmother Carroll's maiden
name. I crossed it coming in from Three eighty.
And a Carroll Street just south of here, if I remember correctly. Isn't there a Carroll Street?"

"Well, yes," Delia said, "but I thought that

was the other Carrolls. The Declaration of Independence Carrolls.''

''No, dear heart, it's our Carrolls,'' Eliza said comfortably. Proving her point had evidently put her in a better mood.

They started walking again, passing the dentists' office and the optician's. ''In fact, I believe we're related to the man who started this town,'' Eliza said. ''But only by marriage.''

''The man . . . You mean George Bay?''

''Right.''

''George Bay the deserter?''

''Well, you're a fine one to talk, might I mention.''

Delia flinched.

''So I drove on over this morning,'' Eliza said, ''and inquired anywhere I thought you might be staying. Turns out there's only one inn, not counting that sleazy little motel on Union Street. And when I didn't find you there I figured I'd keep an eye on the square, because it looked to be the kind of square that everybody in town passes through at one time of day or another.''

They were abreast of Mr. Pomfret's office now. If he had returned from lunch he could glance out the front window and see her walking by. Miss Grinstead with a companion! Acting sociable! She hoped he was still in the Bay Arms Restaurant with his cronies. At George Street she steered Eliza left. They passed Pet Heaven, where a boy was arranging chew toys next to the sacks of kibble.

"Delia," Eliza said, "Mr. Sudler had it wrong, didn't he? I mean, is there some . . . problem you want to tell me about?"

"Oh, no," Delia said.

"Ah." Eliza suddenly looked almost pretty. "See there? I told him so!" she cried. "I told him I was positive you just needed a little breather. You know what the police said? When we called them, this one policeman said, 'Folks,' he said, 'I'll wager any amount she is perfectly safe and healthy.' Said, 'The most surprising number of women seem to take it into their heads to walk out during family vacations.' Did you know that? Isn't that odd?"

"Hmm," Delia said. Her feet felt very burdensome. She could just barely drag them along.

"I guess he'd had lots of experience, working in Bethany Beach and all."

"Yes, I guess he had," Delia said.

"So should we collect your things, Dee?"

"My things," Delia said. She stopped short.

"I'm parked down next to the square. Do you have any luggage?"

Something hard rose up in Delia's throat—a kind of stubbornness, only fiercer. She was taken aback by the force of it. "No!" she said. She swallowed. "I mean, no, I'm not going with you."

"Pardon?"

"I want . . . I need . . . I have a place now, I mean a job, a position, and a place to stay. See? There's where I live," Delia said, gesturing toward Belle's. The gauze curtains in the downstairs windows looked like bandages, she noticed.

"You have a house?" Eliza asked incredulously.

"Well, a room. Come see! Come inside!"

She took Eliza's elbow and drew her toward the porch. Eliza hung back, her arm as rigid as a chicken wing. "A real estate agent owns it," Delia told her as she opened the door. "A *woman* real estate agent, very nice. The rent is extremely reasonable."

"I should think so," Eliza said, gazing about.

"I work for a lawyer just around the corner. He's the only lawyer in town and he handles everything, wills, estates . . . and I have total charge of his office. I bet you didn't think I could do that, did you? You probably thought it was just because I was Daddy's daughter that I worked in the office at home, but now I'm finding . . ."

They were climbing the stairs, Delia in front. She wished Belle would hang some pictures. Either that or put up new wallpaper. "Basically this whole floor is mine," she said, "because the other boarder travels during the week. So I have a private bathroom, see?" She waved toward it. She unlocked the door to her room and walked in. "All mine," she said, setting her handbag on the bureau.

Eliza advanced slowly.

"Isn't it perfect?" Delia asked. "I know it might seem a bit bare, but—"

"Delia, are you telling me you plan to live here?"

"I do live here!"

"But . . . forever?"

"Yes, why not?" Delia said.

She kept feeling the urge to swallow again, but she didn't give in to it. "Sit down," she told Eliza. "Could I offer you some tea?"

"Oh, I . . . no, thanks." Eliza took a tighter grip on her purse. She seemed out of place in these surroundings—somebody from home, with that humble, faded look that home people always have. "Let me make sure I'm understanding this," she said.

"I could heat up the water in no time. Just have a seat on the bed."

"You are telling me you're leaving us forever," Eliza said, not moving. "You plan to stay on permanently in Bay Borough. You're leaving your husband, and you're leaving all three of your children, one of whom is still in high school."

"In high school, yes, and fifteen years old, and

able to manage without me fine and dandy," Delia said. To her horror, she felt tears beginning to warm her eyelids. "Better than with me, in fact," she continued firmly. "How are the kids, by the way?"

"They're bewildered; what would you expect?" Eliza said.

"But are they doing all right otherwise?"

"Do you care?" Eliza asked her.

"Of course I care!"

Eliza moved away. Delia thought she planned to relent and take a seat, but no, she went to gaze out the front window. "Sam, as you might imagine, is just dumbfounded," she announced, with her back to Delia.

"Yes, he must wish now he'd chosen Daughter One or Two instead," Delia said.

Eliza wheeled around. She said, "Delia, what is the *matter* with you? Have you totally lost your senses? Here's this wonderful, model husband roaming the house like a zombie, and your children not knowing *what* to think, and the neighbors all atwitter, and the TV people and newspapers spreading our names across the state of Maryland—"

"It's been on TV?"

"Every station in Baltimore! Big color photograph flashing on the screen: 'Have you seen this woman?' "

"What photo did they use?" Delia asked.

"The one from Linda's wedding."

"That was years ago!"

"Well, most other times you were the one snapping the picture. We didn't have much to choose from."

"But that awful bridesmaid gown! With the shoulders that looked like the hanger was still inside!"

"Delia," Eliza said, "ever since Mr. Sudler phoned, I've been trying to figure out what could have made you walk away from us like that. Till now I'd thought you'd had it so easy. Baby of the family. Cute as a button. Miss Popularity in high school. Daddy's pet. It's true you lacked a mother, but you never seemed to notice. Well, you were only four years old when she died, and anyhow she was bedridden all your life. But now I think four years old was plenty old! Of course you noticed! You'd spent those afternoons playing in her room, for God's sake!"

"I don't remember," Delia said.

"Oh, you must. You and she had those paper dolls. You kept them in a shoe box on the floor of her closet, and every afternoon—"

"I don't remember anything about it!" Delia said. "Why do you keep insisting? I have no memory of her at all!"

"And then being Daddy's pet was kind of a mixed blessing, I guess. When he discouraged you from applying to college, took it for granted you'd come to work in the office . . . well, I wouldn't blame you for resenting that."

"I didn't resent it!"

"And then his dying: of course his dying would hit you harder than—"

"I don't see why in the world you're bringing all this up!" Delia said.

"Just hear me out, please. Dee, you know I believe that human beings live many lives."

Ordinarily, Delia would have groaned. Now, though, she was glad to see the talk veering in a new direction.

"Each life is a kind of assignment, I believe," Eliza told her. "You're given this one assigned slot each time you come to earth, this little square of experience to work through. So even if your life has been troubled, I believe it's what you're meant to deal with on this particular go-round."

"How do you know my assignment doesn't include Bay Borough?" Delia asked her.

A ripple of uncertainty crossed Eliza's forehead.

Delia said, "Eliza, um, I was wondering . . ."

"Yes?" Eliza said eagerly.

"Can you tell me if they brought the cat home from the beach?"

A mistake. Something closed over behind Eliza's eyes. "The cat!" she said. "Is that all you care about?"

"Of course it's not all I care about, but he *was* kind of skulking under furniture when I left, and I didn't know if they'd remember to—"

"They remembered," Eliza said shortly. "What for, I can't imagine. Durn creature is getting so old he snores even when he's awake."

"Old?" Delia said.

"They packed all your clothes and your casseroles too," Eliza said. "Poor Susie had to pack your— Delia? Are you crying?"

"No," Delia said in a muffled voice.

"Are you crying about the *cat*?"

"No, I said!"

Well, she knew he wasn't a kitten anymore. (Such a *merry* kitten he'd been—a kitten with a sense of humor, slinking theatrically around the forbidden houseplants and then giving her a smirk.) But she had thought of him as still in his prime, and only now did she recall how he had started pausing lately as if to assemble himself before attempting the smallest leap. How she had swatted him off the counter once this spring and he had fallen clumsily, scrabbling with his claws, landing in an embarrassed heap and then hastily licking one haunch as if he had intended to take that pose all along.

She widened her eyes to keep the tears from spilling over.

"Delia," Eliza said, "is there something you're

not telling me? Does this have something to do with that . . . man back home?''

Delia didn't bother acting puzzled. She said, ''No, it's not about him.'' Then she went to the head of the bed, causing Eliza to take a step back. She reached under her pillow for the toilet paper and blew her nose. ''I must be going crazy,'' she said.

''No, no! You're not crazy! Just a little, oh, tired, maybe. Just a little run-down. You know what I think?'' Eliza asked. ''I think it took more out of you than any of us realized, tending Daddy's last illness. You're probably anemic too! What you need is plain old physical rest. A vacation on your own. Yes, this wasn't such a bad idea, coming to Bay Borough! Few more days, couple of weeks, and you'll be home again, a new woman.''

''Maybe so,'' Delia said unsteadily.

''And that's what I'm going to tell the police. 'She just went back to our people's place for some R and R,' I'll say. Because I do have to inform them, you know.''

''I know.''

''And I'll have to tell Sam.''

''Yes.''

''And then I expect he'll want to come talk things over.''

Delia pressed the toilet paper to each eye.

''I'm not very good in these situations,'' Eliza

said. She lifted one hand from her purse and placed it on Delia's shoulder.

"You're fine," Delia told her. "It's not your fault."

She felt saddened, all at once, by the fact that Eliza was wearing lipstick. (A sugary pink, lurid against her murky skin.) Eliza never bothered with makeup, as a rule. She must have felt the need to armor herself for this visit.

"I'll have Sam bring some of your clothes with him, shall I?" she was asking.

"No, thanks."

"A dress or two?"

"Nothing."

Eliza dropped her hand.

They left the room, Eliza walking ahead, and started down the stairs. Delia said, "So how's your *gardening*?" in a forced and sprightly tone.

"Oh . . . ," Eliza said. She arrived in the downstairs hall. "You'll need money," she told Delia.

"No, I won't."

"If I'd realized you weren't coming back with me . . . I don't have very much on me, but you're welcome to what there is."

"Honest, I don't want it," Delia said. "I'm making this huge, enormous salary at the lawyer's; I couldn't believe how much when he told me." She ushered Eliza out the door. "And you know I took the vacation cash. Five hundred dollars. I feel bad enough about that."

"Oh, we managed all right," Eliza said, eyeing a fibrous area in one porch floorboard.

Delia could have walked her to her car, or at least as far as the office, but that would have meant prolonging their parting. She had left her handbag upstairs, therefore, and she stood on the porch with her arms folded, in the attitude of someone about to go back indoors. "I'm sure you *managed*," she told Eliza. "It's not that. It's just that I feel bad I didn't start out with nothing. Start out . . . I don't know. Even."

"Even?"

"Even with the homeless or something. I don't know," Delia said. "I don't know what I mean!"

Eliza leaned forward and set her cheek against Delia's. "You're going to be fine," she told her. "This little rest is going to work wonders, take my word. And meanwhile, Dee—" She was about to turn away, but one last thought must have struck her. "Meanwhile, remember Great-Uncle Roscoe's favorite motto."

"What was that?"

" 'Never do anything you can't undo.' "

"I'll bear it in mind," Delia told her.

"Uncle Roscoe may have been a grump," Eliza said, "but he did show common sense now and then."

Delia said, "Drive safely."

She stood watching after Eliza—that short, economical, energetic figure—until she disappeared down the sidewalk. Then she went back in the house for her bag.

Climbing the stairs, she thought, *But if you never did anything you couldn't undo*—she set a hand on the splintery railing—*you'd end up doing nothing at all,* she thought. She was tempted to turn around and run after Eliza to tell her that, but then she couldn't have borne saying goodbye all over again.

# 8

Her book that night was *The Sun Also Rises*, but she didn't manage to finish it because she kept getting distracted. It was Friday, the start of the weekend. The traffic beneath her window had a livelier, more festive sound, and the voices of passersby were louder. "Hoo-*ee*! Here we come!" a teenage boy cried out. Momentarily, Delia lost track of the sentence she was reading. Around eight o'clock someone crossed the porch—not Belle but someone in flat-soled shoes walking slowly, as if weary or sad—and she lowered her book and listened. The front door opened, he entered the house, the stairs creaked upward one step at a time. Then the doorknob across the hall gave a rattle, and she thought, *Oh. The other boarder.*

She returned to her book, but every now and then a sound would break through her concentration—a hollow cough, the sliding of metal hangers along a closet rod. When she heard the shower running, she rose and tiptoed over to her door to make sure it was locked. Then she climbed back into bed and reread the paragraph she had just finished.

An hour or so later, Belle arrived. She had a
man with her. Delia heard his hearty, booming
laugh—not a laugh belonging to anyone she
knew. "Now, be serious!" Belle said once. The
TV came on downstairs, and the refrigerator
door slammed shut with a dull clunk.

Mr. Lamb turned out to be an emaciated man
in his forties, with straight brown hair and
sunken eyes. Delia met him in the upstairs hall
as she was setting out on some errands the following morning. "Hello," she said, and passed
on, having resolved in advance to keep their exchange to a minimum. But she needn't have worried. Mr. Lamb flattened his back against the
wall and smiled miserably at his shoes, mumbling
something unintelligible. He was probably no
happier than she about having to share the
bathroom.

She was looking for a bank that kept Saturday
hours. She wanted to cash Friday's paycheck.
The check was drawn on First Farmers', just
north of the square, but she found First Farmers'
closed, and so she walked on to Bay Borough
Federal. It was a cool, breezy day, with dark
clouds overhead that turned the air almost lilac;
and this part of town, which she had not seen
since the afternoon she arrived, now looked
completely different to her. It looked out of date,
somehow. The buildings were so faded they

seemed not colored but hand tinted, like an antique photograph.

"Would you be able to cash this for me?" she asked the teller at Bay Borough Federal.

The teller—a woman in squinty rhinestoned glasses—barely glanced at the signature before nodding. "Zeke Pomfret? No problem," she said.

So Delia signed over the first real paycheck of her life and received a few crisp bills in return. She was surprised at how much the taxes and whatnot could eat away from a salary.

Weber Street, East Street. Diagonally across the square. She carried her head high and set her feet down with precision. She might have been the heroine in some play or movie. And her intended audience, of course, was Sam.

It wasn't that she looked forward to his visit, certainly. She dreaded having to explain herself; she knew how lame and contradictory all her reasons would sound to him. And yet as early as yesterday afternoon, some part of her mind had been making its devious calculations. *Let's say it's two hours to Baltimore. Eliza could get home around, oh, say, four-thirty, so Sam could be here by six-thirty. Maybe seven. Or supposing he decided to finish up at the office first, supposing he had to buy gas . . .* And then later that night: *He must be waiting for the weekend. That would be much more sensible.*

Imagine if he came upon her this minute,

heading toward the library for Saturday's book. Or pausing on the way home to rummage through a table of mugs in front of Katy's Kitchenware. Or stepping out of the Pinchpenny with the navy knit dress in a bag. Imagine if he were watching from the boardinghouse porch as she rounded the corner of George Street. He would see her skimming along, wearing professional gray, entirely at ease in this town he had never laid eyes on before. He would think, *Could that really be Delia?*

Or imagine if she climbed the stairs and found him waiting at the door of her room. "Why, Sam," she would say serenely, and she would draw her keys from her handbag—so official-looking, room key and office key on Mr. Pomfret's chrome ring—and open the door and tilt her head, inviting him inside. Or he would be inside already, having persuaded Belle to admit him. He would be standing at one of the windows. He would turn and see her entering with her burdens—her library book and her tea mug and new dress—and, "Here, let me help you with those," he would say, and she would say, "Thanks. I can manage."

But he wasn't there after all, and she set her things on the bed in total silence.

She went downstairs to pay her rent. Belle was home, she could tell. She heard sounds from behind the celery-colored door leading off the hall. She knocked and Belle called, "Come in!" meanwhile squeaking something, whirring something. It was a stationary bicycle, Delia discovered when she stepped inside. Belle was pedaling madly, flushed and overheated in a pink sweat suit strewn with tiny satin bows. "Whew!" she said when she saw Delia. Her living room, like the rest of the house, seemed furnished with pieces earlier tenants had discarded. A dingy plush sofa faced the TV; the coffee table bore a loopy design of ring-shaped water stains.

"I just wanted to pay my rent," Delia told her.

"Oh, thanks," Belle said, and without slowing her pedaling she stuffed the folded bills up one sleeve. "Everything all right?"

"Yes, fine."

"Great," Belle said, and she leaned diligently over the handlebars as Delia closed the door again.

Delia planned to go next to the Gobble-Up for some lunch things, but just as she was leaving the house a young man in uniform arrived on the porch. She thought at first he was some kind of soldier; the uniform was a khaki color, and his hair was prickly short. "Miz Grinstead?" he said.

"Yes."

"I'm Chuck Akers, from the Polies."

It took her a moment to translate that.

"Think I could have a word with you?" he asked.

"Certainly," she said. She turned to lead him inside and then realized she had nowhere to take him. Her bedroom was out of the question, and she couldn't very well use Belle's living room. So she turned back and asked, "What can I do for you?" and they ended up conducting their business right there on the porch.

"You *are* Miz Cordelia F. Grinstead," he said.

"Yes."

"I understand you came here of your own free will."

"Yes, I did."

"Nobody kidnapped you, coerced you . . ."

"Nobody else had anything to do with it."

"Well, I surely wish you had thought to make that clear before you left."

"I'm sorry," she said. "Next time I will."

Next time!

She wondered when on earth she supposed that would be.


Saturday, Sunday. The elaborate filling of empty white hours, the glad pounce upon the most inconsequential task. Saturday evening she ate at home, little cartons of Chinese takeout, and she read *Daisy Miller* late into the night. Sunday breakfast was tea and a grocery-store muffin in bed, but she made an event of lunch. She ate at the Bay Arms Restaurant, a stodgy, heavily draped and carpeted establishment, where all the other tables were occupied by families in church clothes. Her inclination was to get the meal over with as fast as possible, but she forced herself to order a soup course, a main course, and a dessert, and she worked her way through all this in a measured and leisurely fashion, fixing her gaze upon a point in the middle distance.

Once Susie had announced, during a particularly feminist stage in her life, that every woman ought to learn how to dine alone in a formal restaurant without a book. Delia wished Susie could see her now.

In fact, maybe Sam would bring the children with him when he came. Maybe they would walk right into the Bay Arms; it was not impossible that they would track her down. She was wearing her new navy dress from the Pinchpenny. It looked very becoming, she thought. She requested a second cup of coffee and sat on awhile.

Out of nowhere, she longed for a cigarette, although she had not smoked since tenth grade.

When she left the restaurant she headed north to the library, planning to choose that night's reading. But the library door was locked tight and the venetian blinds were slanted shut. She should have realized the place would be closed on Sundays. Now she would have to *buy* a book—invest actual money.

In the pharmacy on George Street, she found one rack of paperbacks—mostly mysteries, a few romances. She chose a romance called *Moon Above Wyndham Moor*. A woman in a long cloak was swooning on the cover, precariously supported by a bearded man who encircled her waist with his left arm while he brandished a sword with his right. Delia hid the book in her purse after she had paid for it. Then she continued toward Belle's, taking quick, firm steps so that anybody watching would think, *That woman looks completely self-reliant.*

But there was no one watching.

She remembered how, as a child, she used to arrange herself in the front yard whenever visitors were due. She remembered one time when her great-uncle Roscoe was expected, and she had placed her doll cradle on the grass and assumed a pretty pose next to it till Uncle Roscoe stepped out of his car. "Why, looky there!" he cried. "It's little Lady Delia." He smelled of cough drops, the bitter kind. She had thought she retained no mental picture of Uncle Roscoe, and she was startled to find him bobbing up like this, shifting his veiny leather gladstone bag to his other hand so he could clamp her shoulder as they proceeded toward the house. But what had the occasion been? Why had he come to visit, wearing his rusty black suit? She suspected she would rather not know the answer.

"I was singing my doll a lullaby," she had told him in a confiding tone.

She had always been such a *false* child, so eager to conform to the grown-ups' views of her.

*Moon Above Wyndham Moor* was a disappointment. It just didn't seem very believable, somehow. Delia kept lowering it to stare blankly at the dim, far corners of the room. She checked to see how many pages remained. She cocked her head toward the sound of Mr. Lamb's radio. He had been playing it all weekend, though never so loudly that she could decipher the announcer's words. On the porch overhang outside, raindrops were falling one by one. She missed the noises of the family across the street. They must have closed their windows against the weather.

*Is he not going to come at all, then?*

On Monday morning Mr. Pomfret let her know, in a roundabout way, that he had learned the truth. "I see you have a new dress, *Mrs*. Grinstead," he said, eyeing her significantly. But she pretended not to understand, and by noon he had drifted back to "Miss." Not that she much cared. She felt oddly lackluster today. The rain didn't help. She had been forced to buy an umbrella at the pharmacy, and during lunch hour she went to the dime store and purchased an inexpensive gray cardigan made of something synthetic. Miss Grinstead's standards were slipping, it appeared. She poked her hands dispiritedly through the clingy, tubelike sleeves.

Because of the rain, she couldn't picnic on her usual park bench, and she wasn't up to the social demands of Rick-Rack's or the Bay Arms; so she took her cup of yogurt back to her room. She opened the front door, stepping over the mail, and started up the stairs. Then she halted and turned to look back at one of the envelopes on the floor.

A cream-colored envelope—or more like custard-colored, really. She knew that shade well. And she knew the name embossed in brown on the upper-left-hand corner: SAMUEL A. GRINSTEAD, M.D.

He would settle for just writing her a letter?

She stooped to pick it up. *Mrs. Delia Grinstead*, the address read (Miss Manners would be appalled). *George Street, house w/ low front porch next door to Gobble-Up Grocery. Bay Borough, Maryland.*

She took it to her room before she opened it. *Delia*, he wrote. No *Dear. Delia, it is my understanding from Eliza that . . .*

He had used the office typewriter, the one with the tipsy *e*, and he hadn't bothered to change the margins from when she'd done the bills. The body of the letter was scarcely four inches wide.

*Delia, it is my understanding from Eliza that you have requested some time on your own due to various stresses including your father's recent death, etc.*

*Naturally, I would much rather you had fore-warned us. You cannot have been unaware of the anxiety you would cause, simply strolling off down the beach like that and disappearing.* ~~*Do you have any idea how it feels to*~~

*Nor am I entirely clear on what "stresses" you are referring to. Of course I realize you and your father were close. But his death after all occurred four and a half months ago.*~~*and frankly I feel*~~ *Perhaps you view me as one of the stresses. If so this is regrettable but I* ~~*have always tried to be a satisfactory husb*~~ *vowed while I was growing up that I would be a rock for my wife and children and to the best of my belief I have fulfilled that vow* ~~*and I don't understand what*~~ *but if you have any complaints against me I am certainly willing to hear what they are.*

*In the meantime you may rest assured that I will not invade your privacy.* ~~xxxxxxxxxxxxx xxxxxxxxxxxxxxxxxxxxxxxxxxxxxxxxxxxxxxxxx xxxxxxxxxxxxxxxxxxxxxxxxxxxxxxxxxxxxxxxx~~

*Sam*

He had made his first four corrections with the hyphen key—easy for Delia to read through—

but the fifth was so thoroughly x-ed over that she couldn't figure it out even when she held the letter up to the light. Well, no doubt that was for the best. It was probably something even more obtuse than his other remarks, and Lord knows those were obtuse enough.

Not invade her privacy! Just sit back and give up on her, as if she were a missing pet or mitten or dropped penny!

She might have known, she reflected. All this proved was how right she had been to leave.

Her teeth were chattering, and her new sweater was no help. Instead of eating her lunch, she slipped off her shoes and climbed into bed. She lay shivering beneath the one blanket, with her jaw set against the cold and her arms wrapped around her ribs, hugging her own self tightly.

# 9

No wonder she'd been unable to picture winter in Bay Borough! Underneath, she realized now, she had expected Sam to come fetch her long before then. She resembled those runaway children who never, no matter how far they travel, truly mean to leave home.

So anyhow. Here she was. And the entire rest of her life was stretching out empty before her.

She took to sitting on her bed in the evenings and staring into space. It was too much to say that she was thinking. She certainly had no conscious thoughts, or at any rate, none that mattered. Most often she was, oh, just watching the air, as she used to do when she was small. She used to gaze for hours at those multicolored specks that swarm in a room's atmosphere. Then Linda had informed her they were dust motes. That took the pleasure out of it, somehow. Who cares about mere dust? But now she thought Linda was wrong. It was air she watched, an infinity of air endlessly rearranging itself, and the longer she watched the more soothed she felt, the more mesmerized, the more peaceful.

She was learning the value of boredom. She was clearing out her mind. She had always known that her body was just a shell she lived in, but it occurred to her now that her mind was yet another shell—in which case, who was "she"? She was clearing out her mind to see what was left. Maybe there would be nothing.

Often she didn't begin the night's reading till nine or nine-thirty, which meant she could no longer finish a novel in one sitting; so she switched to short stories instead. She would read a story, watch the air awhile, and read another. She would mark her page with a library slip and listen to the sounds from outdoors—the swish of cars, the chirring of insects, the voices of the children in the house across the street. On hot nights the older children slept on a second-floor porch, and they always talked among themselves until their parents intervened. "Am I going to have to *come upstairs?*" was their father's direst threat. That would quiet them, but only for a minute.

Delia wondered if Sam knew that Carroll was scheduled for tennis lessons the middle two weeks in July. You couldn't depend on Carroll to remember on his own. And did anyone recall that this was dentist month? Well, probably Eliza did. Without Eliza, Delia could never have left her family so easily.

She wasn't sure if that was something to be thankful for.

The fact was, Delia was expendable. She was an extra. She had lived out her married life like a little girl playing house, and always there'd been a grown-up standing ready to take over— her sister or her husband or her father.

Logically, she should have found that a comfort. (She used to be so afraid of dying while her children were small.) But instead, she had suffered pangs of jealousy. Why was it Sam, for instance, that everybody turned to in times of crisis? He always got to be the reasonable one, the steady and reliable one; she was purely decorative. But how had that come about? Where had she been looking while that state of affairs developed?

She read another story, which contained several lengthy nature descriptions. She enjoyed nature as much as the next person, but you could carry it too far, she felt.

And was anybody keeping an eye on Sam's health? He had that tendency, lately, to overdo the exercise. But, *It's none of my concern,* Delia reminded herself. His letter had freed her. No more need to count cholesterol grams; pointless to note that the Gobble-Up carried fat-free mayonnaise.

She called back some of the letter's phrases: *You cannot have been unaware* and *Nor am I entirely clear.* Bloodless phrases, emotionless phrases. She supposed the whole neighborhood knew he hadn't married her for love.

Again she saw the three daughters arrayed on the couch—Sam's memory, originally, but she seemed to have adopted it. She saw her father in his armchair and Sam in the Boston rocker. The two of them discussed a new arthritis drug while Delia sipped her sherry and slid glances toward Sam's hands, reflecting on how skilled they looked, how doctorly and knowing. It might have been the unaccustomed sherry that made her feel so giddy.

Just a few scattered moments, she thought, have a way of summing up a person's life. Just five or six tableaux that flip past again and again, like tarot cards constantly reshuffled and redealt. A patch of sunlight on a window seat where someone big was scrubbing Delia's hands with a washcloth. A grade-school spelling bee where Eliza showed up unannounced and Delia saw her for an instant as a stranger. The gleam of Sam's fair head against the molasses-dark wood of the rocker. Her father propped on two pillows, struggling to speak. And Delia walking south alongside the Atlantic Ocean.

In this last picture, she wore her gray secretary dress. (Not all such memories are absolutely accurate.) She wore the black leather shoes she had bought at Bassett Bros. The clothes were wrong, but the look was right—the firmness, the decisiveness. That was the image that bolstered her.

"Whenever I hear the word 'summer,' " one of the three marriageable maidens announced (Eliza, of course), "I smell this sort of melting smell, this yellow, heated, melting smell." And Linda chimed in, "Yes, that's the way she is! Eliza can smell nutmeg day at the spice plant clear downtown! Also anger." And Delia smiled at her sherry. "Ah," Sam murmured thoughtfully. Did he guess their ulterior motives? That Eliza was trying to sound interesting, that Linda was pointing out Eliza's queerness, that Delia was hoping to demonstrate the dimple in her right cheek?

The washcloth scrubbing her hands was as rough and warm as a mother cat's tongue. The squat, unhappy-looking young woman approaching Miss Sutherland's desk changed into Delia's sister. "I wish . . . ," her father whispered, and his cracked lips seemed to tear apart rather than separate, and he turned his face away from her. The evening after he died, she went to bed with a sleeping pill. She was so susceptible to drugs that she seldom took even an aspirin, but she gratefully swallowed the pill Sam gave her and slept through the night. Only it was more like *burrowing* through the night, tunneling through with some blunt, inadequate instrument like a soup spoon, and she woke in the morning muddled and tired and convinced that she had missed something. Now she thought what she had missed was her own grief. Why that rush toward forgetfulness? she asked herself. Why the hurry to leap past grief to the next stage?

She wondered what her father had been wishing for. She hadn't been able to figure it out at the time, and maybe he had assumed she just didn't care. Tears filled her eyes and rolled down her cheeks. She made no effort to stop them.

Didn't it often happen, she thought, that aged parents die exactly at the moment when other people (your husband, your adolescent children) have stopped being thrilled to see you coming? But a parent is always thrilled, always dwells so lovingly on your face as you are speaking. One of life's many ironies.

She reached for her store of toilet paper and blew her nose. She felt that something was loosening inside her, and she hoped she would go on crying all night.

In the house across the street, a child called, "Ma, Jerry's kicking me." But the voice was distant and dreamy, and the response was mild. "Now, Jerry . . ." Gradually, it seemed, the children were dropping off. Those who remained awake allowed longer pauses to stretch between their words, and spoke more and more languidly, until finally the house was silent and no one said anything more.

———

Independence Day had passed nearly unobserved in Bay Borough—no parades, no fireworks, nothing but a few red-white-and-blue store windows. Bay Day, however, was another matter. Bay Day marked the anniversary of George Pendle Bay's famous dream. It was celebrated on the first Saturday in August, with a baseball game and a picnic in the town square. Delia knew all about it because Mr. Pomfret was chairman of the Recreation Committee. He had had her type a letter proposing they replace the baseball game with a sport that demanded less space—for instance, horseshoes. The square, he argued, was so small and so thickly treed. But Mayor Frick, who was the son and grandson of earlier mayors and evidently reigned supreme, wrote back to say that the baseball game was a "time-honored tradition" and should continue.

"Tradition!" Mr. Pomfret fumed. "Bill Frick wouldn't know a tradition if it bit him in the rear end. Why, at the start it was *always* horseshoes. Then Ab Bennett came back from the minors with his tail between his legs, and Bill Frick Senior got up a baseball game to make him look good. But Ab doesn't even play anymore! He's too old. He runs the lemonade stand."

Delia had no interest in Bay Day. She planned to spend the morning on errands and give the square a wide berth. But first she found everything closed, and then the peculiar weather (a

fog as dense as oatmeal and almost palpably soft)
lured her to keep walking, and by the time she
reached the crowd she felt so safe in her cloak
of mist that she joined in.

The four streets surrounding the square were
blocked off and spread with picnic blankets.
Food booths lined the sidewalks, and strolling
vendors hawked pennants and balloons. Even
this much, though, Delia had trouble making
out, because of the fog. People approaching
seemed to be materializing, their features assembling themselves at the very last instant. The
effect was especially unsettling in the case of
young boys on skateboards. Elated by the closed
streets, they careened through the crowd recklessly, looming up entire and then dissolving. All
sounds were muffled, cotton-padded, and yet
eerily distinct. Even smells were more distinct:
the scent of bergamot hung tentlike over two old
ladies pouring tea from a thermos.

"Delia!" someone said.

Delia turned to see Belle Flint unfolding a
striped canvas sand chair. She was wearing a
vivid pink romper and an armload of bangle
bracelets that jingled when she sat down. Delia
hadn't been sure till now that Belle remembered
her name; so she reacted out of surprise. "Why,
hello, Belle," she said, and Belle said, "Do you
know Vanessa?"

The woman she waved a hand toward was the

young mother from the square. She was seated just beyond Belle on a bedspread the same color as the fog, with her toddler between her knees. "Have some of my spread," she told Delia.

"Oh, thanks, but—" Delia said. And then she said, "Yes, maybe I will," and she went over to sit next to her.

"Get a load of the picnic lunches," Belle told Delia. "It's some kind of contest; they ought to give prizes. What did you bring?"

"Well, nothing," Delia said.

"A woman after my own heart," Belle said, and then she leaned closer to whisper, "Selma Frick's brought assorted hors d'oeuvres in stacked bamboo baskets. Polly Pomfret's brought whole fresh artichokes on a bed of curried crayfish."

"Me, I'm with the teenagers," Vanessa said, handing her son an animal cracker. "I grab something from a booth whenever I get hungry."

She reminded Delia of those girl-next-door movie stars from the 1940s, slim and dark and pretty in a white blouse and flared red shorts, with shoulder-length black hair and bright-red lipstick. Her son was overdressed, Delia thought—typical for a first child. In his corduroys and long-sleeved shirt, he looked cross and squirmy, and for good reason; Delia could feel the heat of the pavement rising through the bedspread.

"How old is your little boy?" she asked Vanessa.

"Eighteen months last Wednesday."

Eighteen months! Delia could have said. Why, she remembered that age. When Ramsay was eighteen months, he used to . . . and Susie, that was when Susie learned to . . .

Such a temptation, it was, to prove her claims to membership—the labor pains, the teething, the time when she too could have told her baby's age to the day. But she resisted. She merely smiled at the child's shimmer of blond hair and said, "I suppose he gets his coloring from his father."

"Most likely," Vanessa said carelessly.

"Vanessa's a single parent," Belle told Delia.

"Oh!"

"I have no idea who Greggie's father might be," Vanessa said, wiping her son's mouth with a tissue. "Or rather, I have a few ideas, but I could never narrow it down to just one."

"Oh, I see," Delia said, and she turned quickly toward the ball game.

Not that there was much to look at, in the fog. Apparently home plate lay in the southeast corner. It was from there she heard the *plock!* of a hit. But all she could discern was second base, which was marked by a park bench. While she watched, a runner loped up to settle on the bench, and the player already seated there rose and caught a ball out of nowhere and threw it back into the mist. Then he sat down again. The runner leaned forward with his elbows on his knees and stared intently toward home plate, although how he hoped to see that far Delia couldn't imagine.

"Derek Ames," Belle informed her. "One of our best hitters."

Delia said, "I would think the statue would get in the way."

"Oh, George plays shortstop," Belle said, giggling. "No, seriously: there's a rule. Bean the statue and you walk to first. It used to count as an automatic run till Rick Rackley moved here. But you know professional athletes: they excel at *any* sport. It got so every time Rick came to bat, he laid old Georgie low."

"Rick Rackley's a professional athlete?"

"Or was, till his knee went. Where've you been living—Mars? Of course, his game was football, but believe me, the Blues are lucky to have him on their side. That's who we're watching, in case you didn't know: the Blues versus the Grays. Blues are the new folks in town; Grays have been here all along. Whoops! That sounds to me like a homer."

Another *plock!* had broken through from the southeast corner. Delia gazed upward but saw only opaque white flannel. In the outfield, such as it was (a triangle of grass behind second base), one player called to another, "Where's it headed?"

"Damned if I know," the second player said. Then, with a startled grunt, he caught the ball as it arrived in front of him. "Got it," he called to the first man.

"You see it?"

"I caught it."

"It came down already?"

"Right."

"Bobby caught that!" the first man shouted toward home plate.

"What say?"

"He caught it," someone relayed. "Batter's out."

"He's what?"

"He's out!"

"Where is the batter?"

"*Who* is the batter?"

Vanessa fed her son another animal cracker. "Fog on Bay Day is kind of a rule here," she told Delia. "I don't believe anyone's ever once got a good look at that game. So! Delia. How do you like working for Zeke Pomfret?"

"Well . . . he's okay," Delia said. She supposed she should have expected that her job would be common knowledge.

"He's a real fine lawyer, you know. If you decide to go ahead with your divorce, you could do worse than hire Zeke."

Delia blinked.

"Yes, he did just great with my ex-boy-friend's," Belle told her. "And he got Vanessa here's brother Jip out of jail, when Jip hit a spell of bad luck once."

"I haven't given much thought to, um, divorce," Delia said.

"Well, sure! No hurry! And anyhow, my ex-boyfriend's case was totally different from yours."

What did they imagine Delia's case was? She decided not to ask.

Belle was rummaging through her big purse. She pulled forth a pale-green bottle and a stack of paper cups. "Wine?" she asked the others. "It's a screw top. Don't tell Polly Pomfret. Yes, Norton's case was so straightforward, for one thing. He'd only been married a year. In fact, we met on his first anniversary. Met at a Gamblers' Weekend Special in Atlantic City, where he'd brought his wife to celebrate. He and I just sort of . . . gravitated, you know?" She passed Delia a cup of white wine. "It helped that his wife was one of those people who end up soldered to their slot machines. So one-two-three I move to Bay Borough, and we rent a little apartment together, and Zeke Pomfret goes to work on Norton's divorce."

The wine had a metallic aftertaste, like tinned grapefruit juice. Delia cradled the cup in both

hands. She said, "I'm not really planning anything that definite just yet."

"Well, of course you're not."

"I'm really feeling sort of . . . blank right now.
You know?"

"Of course you are!" both women said si-
multaneously.

In the square, the inning must have ended.
The players they had been watching vanished
and new players took shape, a new second base-
man floating up by degrees and solidifying on
the bench.

She dreamed Sam was driving a truck across the
front lawn in Baltimore and the children were
playing hide-and-seek directly in his path. They
were little, though; not their present-day selves.
She tried to call out and warn them, but her voice
didn't work, and they were all run over. Then
Ramsay stood up again, holding his wrist, and
Sam climbed out of the truck and he fell down
and tried to get up again, fell down and tried to
get up, and the sight made Delia feel as if a huge,
ragged wound had ripped open in her chest.

When she woke, her cheeks were wet. She had
thought she was starting to lose her habit of
crying at night, but now tears flooded her eyes
and she gave in to wrenching sobs. She was
haunted by the picture of Ramsay in those little brown sandals she'd forgotten he'd ever

owned. She saw her children lined up on the lawn, still in their younger versions before they'd turned hard-shelled and spiky, before the boys had grown whiskers and Susie bought a diary with an unpickable brass lock. Those were the children she longed for.

One evening in September, she returned from work to find several envelopes bearing her name scattered across the hall floor. She knew they must be birthday cards—she was turning forty-one tomorrow—and she could tell they were from her family because of the wordy address. *(House w/ low front porch . . .)* The first card showed a wheelbarrow full of daisies. *A BIRTHDAY WISH,* it said, and inside, *Friendship and health / Laughter and cheer / Now and through / The coming year.* The signature was just *Ramsay*, with the tail of the *y* wandering off across the page in a halfhearted manner.

She carried the rest of her mail upstairs. No sense facing this in public.

*Susie,* the next card was signed. *(Heartiest Congratulations and Many Happy Returns.)* And nothing at all from Carroll, though she riffled through the envelopes twice. Well, it was easy to see what had happened. These cards were Eliza's idea. She had coaxed and cajoled the whole family into sending them. "All I'm asking," was a phrase she would have used. Or,

"No one should have to pass a birthday without . . ." But Carroll, the stubborn one, had flatly refused. And Sam? Delia opened his envelope next. A color photo of roses in a blue-and-white porcelain vase. *Barrels of joy / Bushels of glee* . . . Signed, *Sam*.

Then a letter from Linda, in Michigan. *I want you to know that I sincerely wish you a happy birthday*, she wrote. *I don't hold it against you that you absconded like that even though it did mean we had to cut short our vacation which is the twins' only chance each year to get some sense of their heritage but anyhow, have a good day.* Below her signature were Marie-Claire's and Thérèse's—a prim strand of copperplate and a left-hander's gnarly crumple.

*Dear Delia,* Eliza wrote, on yet another rhymed card.

> *We are all fine but we hope you'll soon be home. I am taking care of the office paperwork for now, and all three kids have started back to school.*
>
> *Bootsy Fisher has phoned several times and also some of the neighbors but I tell everyone you're visiting relatives at the moment.*
>
> *I hope you have a good birthday. I remember the night you were born as if it were just last week. Daddy let Linda and me wait in the waiting room with the fathers, and when the nurse came out she told us, "Congratulations, kids,*

*you can form a singing trio now and go on
Arthur Godfrey,*" *and that's how we knew you
were a girl. I do miss you.*

*Love, Eliza*

Delia kept that one. The others she discarded.
Then she decided she might as well discard Eliza's too. Afterward she sat on her bed a long
while, pressing her fingertips to her lips.

On her actual birthday, a package arrived from
Sam's mother. It was roughly the size of a book,
too thick to fit through the mail slot, so it stood
inside the screen door, where Delia found it
when she came home. She groaned when she recognized the writing. Eleanor was known for her
extremely practical gifts—a metric-conversion
tape measure, say, or a battery recharger, always
wrapped in wrinkled paper saved from Christmas. This time, as Delia discovered when she
took the package upstairs, it was a miniature
reading light on a neck cord. Well, in fact . . . ,
she reflected. It would probably work much better than her lamp. She tucked it under her pillow,
next to her stash of toilet paper.

There was a letter too, on Eleanor's plain buff
stationery:

*Dear Delia,*
    *This is just a little something I thought you
might find helpful. On the few occasions when*

*I've traveled myself, the reading light has gen-
erally been miserable. Perhaps you're having
the same experience. If not, just pass this along
to your favorite charity. (Lately I've been most
dissatisfied with Goodwill but continue to feel
that Retarded Citizens is a worthwhile organi-
zation.)*

*My best wishes for your birthday.*

*Love, Eleanor*

Delia flipped it over, but all she found on the
back was RECYCLED PAPER RECYCLED PAPER
RECYCLED PAPER running across the bottom. She
had expected indignation, or at least a few
reproaches.

She remembered how, when she and Sam
were first engaged, she had entertained such
high hopes for Eleanor. She had thought she
was finally getting a mother of her own. But
that was before they met. Eleanor came to supper at the Felsons', arriving directly from the
Home for Wayward Girls, where she volunteered as a typing teacher twice a week. Once
the introductions were over, she hardly gave
Delia a glance. All she talked about was the terrible, terrible poverty endured by the wayward
girls and the staggering contrast of this meal—
which, by the way, was merely pot roast sprin-
kled with onion-soup mix and an iceberg lettuce
salad. "I asked this one poor child," Eleanor

said, "I asked, 'Dear, could your people buy you a typewriter so you could work from your house after the baby arrives?' And she said, 'Miss, my family's so poor they can't even afford shampoo.' " A basket of rolls appeared before her. Eleanor gazed into it, looking puzzled, and passed it on. "I don't know what made her choose that example, of all things," she said. "Shampoo."

(Why was it that so many voices came wafting back to Delia these days? Sometimes as she fell asleep she heard them nattering on without her, as if everybody she'd ever known sat around her, conversing. Like people in a sickroom, she thought. Like people at a deathbed.)

Another present Eleanor had once given her was a tiny electric steamer gadget to freshen clothes during trips. This was some years back; Delia couldn't remember what she'd done with it. But the thing was, here in Bay Borough she could have put it to use. She could have touched up her office dresses, both of which had grown somewhat puckery at the seams after repeated hand laundering. It would certainly have been preferable to buying an iron and ironing board. Oh, why hadn't she kept the steamer? Why hadn't she brought it with her? How could she have been so shortsighted, and so ungrateful?

———

She didn't answer any of the birthday cards, but etiquette demanded a thank-you note to Eleanor. *The little light is very convenient,* she wrote. *Much better than the goosenecked lamp I've been reading by up till now. So I've moved the lamp to the bureau which means I don't have to use the ceiling bulb and therefore the room looks much softer.* In this manner she contrived to cover the entire writing area of a U.S. postcard without really saying anything at all.

The next morning, while she was dropping the card in the mailbox near the office, she was suddenly struck by the fact that Eleanor had once worked in an office. She had put her son through college on a high-school secretary's salary—no small feat, as Delia could now appreciate. She wished she had thought to mention her job in her thank-you note. But maybe Eliza had said something. "Delia's employed by a lawyer," Eliza might have said. "She handles every detail for him. You should see her all dressed up for work; if you met her on the street, you wouldn't know her."

"Is that so?" Sam would ask. (Somehow, the listener had changed from Eleanor to Sam.) "Handles everything, you say. Not mislaying important files? Not lounging around the waiting room, reading trashy novels?"

Well, she'd spent more than half her life trying to win Sam's approval. She supposed she

couldn't expect to break a habit like that overnight.

October came, and the weather grew cooler. The
square filled up with yellow leaves. Some nights,
Delia had to shut her windows. She bought a
flannel nightgown and two long-sleeved dresses
—one gray pinstripe, one forest green—and she
started keeping an eye out for a good second-
hand coat. It was not yet cold enough for a coat,
but she wanted to be prepared.

On rainy days, now, she ate lunch at the Cue
Stick 'n' Cola on Bay Street. She ordered coffee
and a sandwich and watched the action at the
one pool table. Vanessa often wheeled her
stroller in to join her. While Greggie lurched
among the chair legs like a brightly colored top,
Vanessa would offer Delia thumbnail sketches
of the players. "See the guy breaking? Buck Baxter. Moved here eight or ten years ago. Baxter
as in Baxter Janitorial Supplies, but they say his
father's disowned him. No, Greggie, the man
doesn't want your cookie. Now, her I don't
know," she said. She meant the diminutive,
dark-haired young woman who was leaning
across the pool table to shoot on tiptoe, her purple canvas pocketbook still slung over her shoulder. "Must be from outside. Leave him *alone*,
Greggie. And the fellow in the cowboy boots,
that's Belle's ex-boyfriend, Norton Grove. Belle

was out of her mind to fall for him. Fickle? That man put fickle in the dictionary."

Delia was gathering an impression of Bay Borough as a town of misfits. Almost everybody here had run away from someplace else, or been run away *from*. And no longer did it seem so idyllic. Rick and Teensy Rackley were treated very coolly by some of the older citizens; the only two gay men she knew of seemed to walk about with no one but each other; there was talk of serious drug use in the consolidated high school; and Mr. Pomfret's appointment book was crammed with people feuding over property lines and challenging drunk-driving arrests.

Still, she felt contented here. She had her comfortable routine, her niche in the general scheme of things. Making her way from office to library, from library to café, she thought that her exterior self was instructing her interior self, much like someone closing his eyes and mimicking sleep in order to persuade sleep to come. It was not that her sadness had left her, but she seemed to operate on a smooth surface several inches above the sadness. She deposited her check each Saturday; she dined each Sunday at the Bay Arms Restaurant. People nodded now when they saw her, which she took not just for greeting but for confirmation: *Ah, yes, there's Miss Grinstead, exactly where she belongs.*

Although every so often something would stab

her. A song from Ramsay's Deadhead period about knock-knock-knocking on heaven's door, for instance. Or a mother and a little girl hugging each other in front of the house across the street. "She's leaving me!" the mother called mock-plaintively to Delia. "Going off to her very first slumber party!"

Maybe Delia could pretend to herself that she was back in the days before her marriage. That she didn't miss her children at all because they hadn't been born yet.

But in retrospect it seemed she had missed them even then. Was it possible there had been a time when she hadn't known her children?

*Dear Delia,* Eleanor wrote. (She addressed her letter to 14 George Street this time.)

> *I was so pleased to get your postcard. It's good to know that my little gift came in handy, and I'm glad you're doing some reading.*
>
> *I myself find it impossible to sleep if I don't read at least a few pages first, preferably from something instructive like biography or current events. For a while after Sam's father died I used to read the dictionary. It was the only thing with small enough divisions to fit my attention span. Also the information was so definite.*
>
> *Probably Sam has been marked by losing his father at such an early age. I meant to say that*

*in my last note but I don't believe I did. And
his father never had a strong personality. He
was the kind of man who let all the bathwater
drain away before he got out of the tub. Maybe
it would worry a boy to think he might grow
up to do the same.*

  *I hope I haven't overstepped.*

                              *Love, Eleanor*


Delia didn't know what to make of that. She
understood it better when the next note came,
some two weeks later. *Please forgive me if you
felt I sounded "mother-in-lawish" and that's why
you didn't answer my letter. I had no intention
of offering excuses for my son. I've always said
he was forty years old when he was born, and I
realize that's not easy to live with.*

  Delia bought another postcard—this one the
kind with a picture on it, a rectangle of unblem-
ished white captioned *Bay Day in Bay Borough,*
so there was even less space to write on. *Dear
Eleanor,* she wrote. *I'm not here because of Sam,
so much. I'm here because*

  Then she sat back, not knowing how to end
the sentence. She considered starting over, but
these postcards cost money, and so she settled,
finally, for *I'm here because I just like the thought
of beginning again from scratch.* She signed it,
*Love, Delia,* and mailed it the following morning
on her way to work.

And after all, wasn't that the true reason? Truer than she had realized when she wrote it, in fact. Her leaving had very little to do with any specific person.

Unlocking the office door, she noticed the pleasure she took in the emptiness of the room. She raised the white window shades; she turned the calendar to a fresh page; she sat down and rolled a clean sheet of paper into the typewriter. It was possible to review her entire morning thus far and find not a single misstep.

Mr. Pomfret sometimes employed a detective named Pete Murphy. This was not the swaggery character Delia would have envisioned, but a baby-faced fat boy from Easton. It seemed he was hired less often to locate people than to *fail* to locate them. Whenever a will or a title search required his services, Pete would plod in, whistling tunelessly, and trill his pudgy fingers at Delia and proceed to the inner office. He never spoke to her, and he probably didn't know her name.

One rainy afternoon, though, he arrived with something bulging and struggling inside the front of his windbreaker. "Got a present for you," he told Delia.

"For me?"

"Found it out in the street."

He lowered his zipper, and a small, damp gray-

and-black cat bounded to the floor and made a dash for the radiator. "Oh!" Delia said.

Pete said, "Shoot. Come out of there, you little dickens."

Beneath the radiator, silence.

"It'll never come if you order it to," Delia said. "You have to back away a bit. Turn your face away. Pretend you're not looking."

"Well, I'll let you see to that," Pete decided. He brushed cat hairs off his sleeves and started for the office.

"Me! But . . . wait! I can't do this!" Delia said. She was speaking now to Mr. Pomfret; he had come to his door to see what all the fuss was about. "He's brought a stray cat! I can't take care of a cat!"

"Now, now, I'm sure you'll think of something," Mr. Pomfret said genially. "Miss Grinstead was a cat in her last incarnation, you know," he told Pete.

"Is that a fact," Pete said. They walked into the office, and Mr. Pomfret closed the door.

For the next half hour, Delia worked with one eye on the radiator. She watched a gray-and-black tiger tail unfurl from behind a pipe, gradually fluffing as it dried. She had a sense of being under surveillance.

When Pete reemerged, she said, "Maybe the cat belongs to someone. Have you thought of that?"

"I doubt it," he told her. "I didn't see no collar." He trilled his fingers and left. When the door slammed behind him, the tail gave a twitch.

Delia rose and went to the office. "Excuse me," she said.

Mr. Pomfret said, "Hmm?" He was back at his computer already. This morning he had discovered something called Search-and-Replace that was apparently very exciting. *Tap-tap,* his fingers went, while he craned his sloping neck earnestly toward the screen.

"Mr. Pomfret, that cat is still under the radiator and *I* can't take it anywhere! I don't even have a car!"

"Maybe get a box from the supply closet," he said. "Damn!" He hit several keys in succession. "Just see to it, will you, Miss Grinstead? There's a good girl."

"I live in a boardinghouse!" Delia said.

Mr. Pomfret reached for his computer manual and started thumbing through it. "Who wrote this damn thing, anyhow?" he asked. "No human being, that's for sure. Look, Miss Grinstead, why don't you leave early and take the kitty wherever you think best. I'll lock up for you, how's that?"

Delia sighed and headed for the supply closet.

Pet Heaven: they might help. She emptied a carton of manila envelopes and carried it to the other room. Kneeling in front of the radiator, she placed a palm on the floor. "Tsk-tsk!" she said. She waited. After a minute, she felt a tiny wince of cold on the back of her middle finger. "Tsk-tsk-tsk!" The cat peered out at her, only its whiskers and heart-shaped nose visible. Gently, Delia curved her hand around the frail body and drew it forward.

This was hardly more than a kitten, she saw —a scrawny male with large feet and spindly legs. His fur was almost startlingly soft. It reminded her of milkweed. When she stroked him, he shrank beneath her hand, but he seemed to realize he had nowhere to run. She gathered him up and set him in the carton and folded the flaps shut. He gave a single woebegone mew before falling silent.

It was still raining, and she didn't have a free hand to open her umbrella, so she hurried along the sidewalk unprotected. The carton rocked in her arms as if it contained a bowling ball. For such a little thing, he certainly was heavy.

She rounded the corner and burst through the door of Pet Heaven. A gray-haired woman stood behind the counter, checking off a list. "You wouldn't happen to know if Bay Borough has an S.P.C.A.," Delia said.

The woman looked at her a moment, slowly refocusing vague blue eyes. Then she said, "No; the nearest one's in Ashford."

"Or any other place that takes homeless animals?"

"Sorry."

"Maybe *you'd* like a cat."

"Gracious! If I brought home another stray my husband would kill me."

So Delia gave up, for now, and bought a box of kibble and a sack of litter-box filler, the smallest size of each just to get her through one night. Then she lugged the cat home.

Belle was there ahead of her, talking on the phone in the kitchen. Delia heard her laugh. She tiptoed up the stairs, unlocked the door of her room, set the carton on the floor, and shut the door behind her. In the mirror she looked like a crazy woman. Tendrils of wet hair were plastered to her forehead. The shoulders of her sweater were dark with rain, and her handbag was spotted and streaked.

She bent over the carton and raised the flaps. Inside, the cat sat hunched in a snail shape, glaring up at her. Delia retreated, settled on the edge of her bed, looked pointedly in another direction. Eventually, the cat sprang out of the carton. He started sniffing around the baseboards. Delia stayed where she was. He ducked beneath the bureau and returned with linty whiskers. He approached the bed obliquely, gazing elsewhere. Delia turned her head away. A moment later she felt the delicate denting of the mattress as he landed on it. He passed behind her, lightly brushing the length of his body against her back as if by chance. Delia didn't move a muscle. She felt

they were performing a dance together, something courtly and elaborate and dignified.

But she couldn't possibly keep him.

Then Belle's clacky shoes started climbing the
stairs. Belle almost never came upstairs. But she
did today. Delia threw a glance at the cat, willing
him to hide. All he did was freeze and direct a
wide-eyed stare toward the door. *Knock-knock.*
He was smack in the center of the pillow, with
his bottle-brush tail standing vertical. You
couldn't overlook him if you tried.

Delia scooped him up beneath his hot little
downy armpits. She could feel the rapid patter
of his heart. "Just a minute," she called. She
reached for the carton.

But Belle must have misheard, for she breezed
on in, caroling, "Delia, here's a—" Then she
said, "Why!"

Delia straightened. "I'm just trying to find a
home for him," she said.

"Aww. What a honey!"

"Don't worry, I'm not keeping him."

"Oh, why not? Er, that is . . . he is housebroken, isn't he?"

"All cats are housebroken," Delia said. "For
goodness' sake!"

"Well, then! Not keep this little socky-paws?
This dinky little pookums?" Belle was bending
over the cat now and offering him her polished
fingernails to sniff. "Is it a prinky-nose," she

crooned. "Is it a frowzy-head. Is it a fluffer-bunch."

"Mr. Pomfret's detective found him out in the rain," Delia said. "He just dumped him on me; nothing I could do. I mean, I knew I couldn't keep him myself. Where would I put a litter box, for one thing?"

"In the bathroom?" Belle asked. She started scratching behind the cat's ears.

"But how would he get out to use it?"

"You could leave your door cracked open, let him go in and out as he likes," Belle said. "Ooh, feel how soft! I don't know why you ever lock it, anyhow. Little town like this, who do you think's going to rob you? Who's going to creep in and ravish you?"

"Well . . ."

"Believe me, Mr. Lamb couldn't gather up the enthusiasm."

Belle stroked beneath the cat's chin, and the cat tipped his head back blissfully. He had one of those putt-putt purrs, like a Model T Ford.

"I don't know if I want my life to get that complicated," Delia said.

"Is he a complication. Is he a bundle of trouble."

Belle was holding an envelope in her free hand, Delia saw. That must be what had brought her upstairs. Eleanor's stalky print marched

across the front. Delia felt suddenly overbur-
dened. Things were crowding in on her so!

But when Belle said, "Are you going to keep
this itty-bitty, or am I?" Delia said, "I am, I
guess."

"Well, good. Let's call him Puffball, what do
you say?"

"Hmm," Delia said, pretending to consider it.

But she had never approved of cutesy names
for cats. And besides, it seemed that at some
point she had already started thinking of him as
George.

She was in bed that night before she got around
to reading Eleanor's letter. It was more of the
same: a thank you for Delia's last postcard, news
of her Meals on Wheels work. *I can certainly
empathize with your desire to start over!* she
wrote. (That careful word, *empathize*, revealing
her effort to say just the right thing.)

> *And I'm relieved it's the reason you left. I had
> assumed it was Sam. I've wondered if maybe
> he expressly* wanted *a flighty wife, in which case
> you could hardly be held to blame.*
>
> *But when you've finished starting over, do
> you picture working up to the present again and
> coming home? Just asking.*
>
> > *All my love, dear,*
> > *Eleanor*

A furry paw reached out to bat the page, and Delia laid the letter aside. The cat had found a resting place next to her on the blankets. He had eaten an enormous meal and paid two visits to the makeshift litter box in the bathroom. She could tell he was beginning to feel at home.

She reached for her book—Carson McCullers—and turned to where she had stopped reading last night. She read two stories and started a third. Then she found she was growing sleepy; so she set the book on the windowsill and clicked off her little reader's light and placed it on top of the book. Light continued to shine through the partly open door, sending a rod of yellow across the floorboards. She slid downward in bed very cautiously so as not to disturb the cat. He was giving himself a bath now. He pressed against her ribs with each movement in a way that seemed accidental, but she could tell he meant to do it.

How strange it was, when you thought about it, that animals would share quarters with humans! If Delia had been out in the wilderness, if this were some woodland creature nestling so close, she would have been astounded.

She yawned and shut her eyes and pulled the blanket up around her shoulders.

One of the stories she had read tonight was called "A Tree, a Rock, a Cloud." A man in this story said people should begin by loving eas-

ier things before they worked up to another person. Begin with something less complex, he
proposed. Like a tree. Or a rock. Or a cloud.
The rhythm of these words kept tapping across
Delia's mind: tree, rock, cloud.

First a time alone, then a casual acquaintance
or two, then a small, undemanding animal. Delia
wondered what came after that, and where it
would end up.

# 10

The Sunday before Thanksgiving, Belle waylaid Delia at the bottom of the stairs. "Say, Dee," she said. "What're you doing for the holiday?"

"Oh, um . . ."

"Want to have dinner at my place?"

"Well, I'd love to," Delia said.

"I'm serving this real hokey meal: turkey and dressing, cranberry relish . . ."

"I didn't know you cooked!"

"I don't," Belle said grimly. "It's a plot. I'm trying to look domestic for this fella I've been seeing."

At the moment, she looked anything but domestic. Sunday was always a busy day at the real estate office, and she was dressed to go out in her huge purple coat, the one with the shoulders not just padded but flaring to sharp points like an alien's space suit. Lilac trousers swam beneath it, and the smell of her fruity, overripe perfume freighted the air all around her.

"Vanessa is coming with Greggie," she said. "Nice touch to invite a child, don't you think? And these out-of-towners I just sold a house to, married couple; that's always good. . . ."

"And I would help in the food department," Delia guessed.

"Oh, I'm bringing in the food from outside, just between you and me. But I was thinking you could add a little, call it, class. I need for this guy to see me as all proper and respectable. And also you could advise me on the wifely touches: the centerpiece and et cetera. You must've used to do that stuff back home, didn't you? Do you have one of those baskety things that look like a cornucopia?"

"Well, not right handy," Delia said. "But I'll be glad to do what I can."

"Great," Belle said. She toed the cat aside— he had followed Delia downstairs—and opened the front door. They stepped out into a chilly, tin-colored day. "This fella's name is Henry McIlwain, did I mention that?" she asked. "We've been dating several weeks now and I'd like to start getting more purposeful. I don't want him thinking I'm just a good-time gal! Maybe you could drop a few remarks in front of him. Something like, 'Gosh, Belle, I hope you made your famous brussels-sprout dish.' "

"You're serving him brussels sprouts?"

"I don't have any choice. It's the only green vegetable Copp Catering offers that will fit in my toaster oven."

Delia said, "How did you manage the meals when you were living with Norton?"

"We ate out. But this time I want to do things

differently. Maybe while Henry's listening you could ask me for one of my recipes."

"I can hardly wait to hear how you'll answer," Delia said.

"Dinner's at one, but could you come down a bit early to help set up? And wear your gray pinstripe. Your gray pinstripe is so . . . gray; know what I mean?"

On Thanksgiving Day Delia slept late, and she idled the morning away drinking tea and reading in bed, with the cat curled up beside her. Across the hall, in Mr. Lamb's room, an announcer's voice droned steadily. This was a TV announcer, Delia had figured out; not radio. Now that she kept her door cracked open, she could hear how the music swelled and diminished without apparent reason, responding to some visual cue; and today she caught distinct phrases each time she emerged for more tea water. "The mother bear leads her cubs . . . ," she heard, and, "The female spider injects her victims . . ." Evidently Mr. Lamb was watching nature shows.

Shortly after noon, she rose and started dressing. It was a pity she didn't have a string of pearls to add a festive note, she thought. Or at least a scarf. Didn't she own a paisley scarf with gray commas around the edges? Yes, she did—back in Baltimore. She could see it lying folded in her grandmother's lacquer glove box.

She applied an extra-bright coat of lipstick,

and then she leaned toward the mirror to smooth her hair. It was longer now, which made her curls look flatter and somehow calmer—very suitable for Miss Grinstead. Although when she stepped back to gauge the total effect, the person who came to mind was not Miss Grinstead at all. It was Rosemary Bly-Brice.

She turned sharply from the mirror and picked up the vase of autumn flowers she had bought the day before.

The cat came along when she left. He scampered after her down the stairs, and he tumbled around her ankles while she knocked at the living-room door. When nobody answered she tried the other door, the one to the right, and finally she turned the knob and poked her head into the dining room. "Anybody home?" she asked.

Goodness, Belle did need her services. The table—one of those long, narrow, wood-grain affairs you see at PTA bazaars—was not even spread with a cloth yet. Delia put her flowers down and walked on into the kitchen. "Belle?" she said.

Belle was leaning against the sink. Her arms were clamped across the bosom of a violently frilled white apron, and tears were streaming down her face.

"Belle? What's happened?" Delia asked.

"He's not coming," Belle said thickly.

"Your date?"

"He's back with his wife."

"I didn't know he *had* a wife."

"Well, he does."

"Oh, I'm sorry."

In fact, she was shocked, but she tried not to show it. No wonder Belle had been so eager to look respectable! Delia gave her a tentative pat, just in case she wanted consoling. She did, it turned out. She fell into Delia's arms, sobbing hotly against her neck.

"He was perfect for me!" she wailed. "He was exactly what I wanted! And then this morning he calls up and—oh, I should have known from how low he was speaking, mumbly low secretive voice like he was scared somebody might hear him—"

She drew back from Delia's embrace to snap a paper towel off the roll above the sink. Blotting first one eye and then the other, she said, " 'Belle,' he tells me, 'about today. Something's come up,' he tells me. 'Oh?' I ask. 'What's that?' Thinking maybe he couldn't start the car, or wanted to bring a friend. 'Well, it's like this,' he tells me. 'Seems like Pansy and I have gotten back together.' "

"Pansy would be his wife," Delia guessed.

"Yes, and the baby's name is Daffodil, can you believe it?"

"There's a baby?"

"And it wasn't even a springtime baby! It was born in October!"

"You're talking about . . . this *past* October?"

Belle nodded, loudly blowing her nose.

"So the baby is, what, a month old?"

"Six weeks."

"Ah."

Belle's apron was so new that the pinholes still showed from the packaging. Her hairdo was even larger than usual, and she wore the first actual dress Delia had ever seen her in—or presumably it was a dress, for her legs were visible beneath the apron, encased in nylon stockings with a frosty white sheen like the bloom on plums. But her face was a disaster—blurred lipstick and blackened eyes and gray dribbles of tears. "You'll have to get in touch with the others," she was saying as she dabbed the tears. "I can't possibly go through with dinner."

"But everything's all ready," Delia said. She was taking stock of the foil-wrapped, disposable pans covering one counter, and the plates and silver heaped on the kitchen table, and the empty serving dishes waiting to be filled. Through the oven's lighted window she could make out a brown turkey, although she wasn't able to smell it, for some reason. "That turkey looks about done," she told Belle.

"It arrived done. I'm just reheating it. I had to keep it in the fridge overnight."

"So, why not go ahead with your party? Maybe it'll cheer you up."

"Nothing could cheer me up," Belle said.

"Oh, now, you sit here and I'll see to things."

"I wish I was dead and buried," Belle said, pulling out one of the kitchen chairs. She sank into it and picked up the cat. "I'm getting too old to be jilted! I'm thirty-eight years old. It's *tiring* to keep going on first dates."

Delia didn't answer, because she was hunting a tablecloth. No telling where Belle kept her linens. This was one of those fifties kitchens with shiny bare walls and enormous white appliances and rust-specked white metal cabinets and drawers. She slid open every drawer with a clanking sound. Most were empty. Eventually she located a jumble of fabrics in the space below the sink. "Aha!" she said, shaking out a wrinkled damask cloth. She carried it into the dining room and spread it over the table, resettling her flowers in the center. "I know you must have candlesticks," she called.

"We met last spring," Belle said. "I was the one who sold off their house. They were moving to a bigger place on account of the baby coming. And wouldn't you know it took me six months, with the market the way it's been."

Delia opened all the drawers of the apple-green bureau that served as a dining room buffet. She found two brass candlesticks lying in a nest of extension cords, and she placed them on either side of the flowers. Meanwhile, in the kitchen, Belle had sold the house just as Daffodil arrived.

"Settlement date was two days before due date,"
she said. "Kid was born three days later. So
naturally I stopped by the hospital with a giftie;
these things are tax-deductible. And there was
Henry all proud and fatherly, took me down the
hall to that baby window they have and showed
me how smart and cute and blah-blah-blah.
Well, he just got to me, you know? I stood there
not hearing a word he said, watching how his
mouth moved, and all at once I thought, *Suppose
I was to step forward and kiss him, what do you
guess he'd do?*"

"Candles?" Delia asked.

"Try the broom cupboard." Belle blew her
nose with a honking sound that caused the cat
to spring off her lap. "And this was not even my
usual style of man," she said. "He was skinny!
And pale! And computerish! But there I stood,
thinking, *Suppose I unbuttoned my blouse right
here in front of the baby window, staring at his
mouth the whole time and running the tip of my
tongue across my lower lip.*"

The candles were not in the broom cupboard
but on top of the refrigerator, in a yellowing
white box. Even the candles were yellowed, and
also a bit warped, but Delia fitted them into the
holders anyway. Then she collected the dishes
and silver from the kitchen table and dealt them
out. Belle proceeded through the baby's colic,
the new parents' cranky quarrels, her own warm-
eyed, cooing sympathy. "I schemed and plotted,

I lay in wait," she said. "I told him my door was always open. Two, three, four o'clock in the morning he would leave that spit-up milk and dirty-diaper smell and find me here in my spaghetti-strap nightie from Victoria's Secret."

And to think all this had been going on while Delia was sound asleep! She checked the turkey. It appeared to have caved in around the breast-bone. She found the brussels sprouts in their foil pan and set them in the toaster oven at 350 degrees. There were biscuits too, but she would wait to warm those till the very last minute.

"Two weeks ago, Pansy goes back to her mom's," Belle said. "Takes Daffodil and leaves. I was in heaven. Didn't you notice I've had this radiant glow about me lately? Oh, Delia, how can you stand it, going without a love life?"

Holding a pack of paper napkins printed all over with pilgrims, Delia paused to reflect upon the question. "Well," she said, "I do miss *hugs*, I guess. But nowadays when I think about, um, the rest of it, I just feel sort of perplexed. I think, *Why did that seem like such a big deal, once upon a time?* But I suppose it's only—"

The doorbell rang.

"Oh, Lord, we didn't call off dinner," Belle said, as if she had not been sitting in the midst of Delia's preparations. "Shoot! I can't cope with this! See who's there, will you, while I try to fix my face."

As Delia walked through the dining room to

the hall, she felt drab and thin and virginal, like somebody's spinster aunt fulfilling her duties.

It was Vanessa at the door. She wore a leather blazer and blue jeans, and she toted Greggie on one hip. Behind her, just stepping out of their car, were a man and a woman who must have been Belle's married couple. Delia barely had time to whisper the news to Vanessa—"Henry McIlwain's gone back to his wife"—before the couple arrived on the porch. "Why! What have we here!" the husband told Greggie. He was young, no more than thirty, but as staid as a middle-aged man, Delia thought, with his receding tuft of black hair and his long black formal overcoat. His wife was a trim, attractive brunette in a tidy red woolen suit that reminded Delia of a Barbie-doll outfit. "I'm Delia Grinstead," Delia told her. "This is Vanessa Linley—do you know each other?—and Greggie."

"We're the Hawsers," the husband said for both of them. "Donald and Melinda."

"Won't you come in?"

She planned to lead them into the living room, but when she turned she found Belle at the door of the dining room. She was showing all her teeth and adjusting the plunging neckline of a flowered, button-front dress. "Happy Thanksgiving!" she sang out. Whatever repairs she had made to her face had not done much good. Gray tracks still ran down her cheeks, and her eyes were pink and puffy. But she caroled, "So glad you could come! Step in and have a seat!"

There was nowhere to sit but around the table. "Donald, you're on my right," Belle said, "and Vanessa's on my left. I've put Greggie next to you, Vanessa. Get some phone books from the kitchen if he needs a booster. And Melinda's on the other side of Greggie."

Well, maybe this was the local custom: proceeding directly to the food. But even Vanessa seemed taken aback. And the husband (still wearing his overcoat) stood frozen in place for a moment before approaching his chair. "Are we . . . late?" he asked Belle.

"Late! Not at all!" she said, and she let out a cascade of musical laughter. "Delia, you'll sit next to—"

She broke off. "Oh!" she cried. "Delia! Honestly!"

"What's the matter?" Delia asked.

"You've gone and laid too many places!"

It was true. Delia had doled out all she'd found on the kitchen table, and that must have included a setting for Henry McIlwain. Belle gazed toward the chair at the far end, her eyes brimming over with fresh tears.

"I'm sorry," Delia told her. "We could just—"

"Run fetch Mr. Lamb," Belle ordered.

"Mr. Lamb? From upstairs?"

"Hurry, though. We're all waiting. Tell him

we'll eat without him if he doesn't get down here pronto."

What they would have eaten Delia couldn't imagine, since there wasn't a morsel of food anywhere in sight. But Vanessa, returning from the kitchen with several phone books, told Delia, "Go ahead. I'll get the meal on."

Delia went out to the hall, which seemed very quiet after the bustle in the dining room. With the cat twining underfoot, she climbed the stairs and knocked on Mr. Lamb's door. "Desperately, the salmon fling themselves against the current," a stern voice announced. The door opened on a sliver of Mr. Lamb's rag-and-bone face. "Yes?" he said, and then, "Oh!" for George had somehow managed to wriggle through the crack.

Delia said, "Belle sent me up to invite you for Thanksgiving dinner."

"But it seems your animal's got into my room!"

"Sorry," Delia said. "Here, George."

She reached in for the cat, and Mr. Lamb grudgingly opened the door another few inches. Delia caught the hazelnut smell of clothes worn once and then stuffed into drawers unwashed. The television's icy light flickered in the dimness. She scooped George up and backed away.

"I've been meaning to mention the toilet arrangements under the bathroom sink," Mr. Lamb told her.

"The . . . ?"

"Couldn't your animal use the outdoors?"

"Not in the middle of the night," Delia said. She clutched George more tightly and asked, "Are you coming to dinner, or aren't you?"

"What time?"

"Um . . . now?"

"Well, I suppose I could make it," Mr. Lamb said.

He looked down at what he was wearing—a limp T-shirt, baggy dark pants—and then sadly closed the door in her face.

Delia wondered how a man so fond of nature programs could object to a harmless cat.

Downstairs, Vanessa had finished setting everything on the table—turkey, brussels sprouts, cranberry relish, mashed sweet potatoes dotted with marshmallows, all in their original pans. Still wearing her leather blazer, she was spooning the stuffing out of the turkey. Greggie lolled on the stack of phone books, sucking his thumb and watching his mother with heavy-lidded eyes. It must be naptime.

Belle was discussing Henry with the Hawsers. "What I can't figure," she was saying, "is when all this came about. Last night as of ten o'clock, everything was jim-dandy. Henry and I had a real nice dinner over in Ocean City. Then this noon on the phone—poof! He's a totally changed man."

"So his wife showed up in the morning," Donald Hawser said sagely. He had draped his coat over the back of his chair, and he was lighting the warped candles with a silver lighter. "She got out of bed this morning and, 'Here I am,' she must have said, 'away from home on Thanksgiving. A family holiday,' she said."

Delia placed the cat on the floor and sat down next to Donald. *A family holiday,* she thought, *and I'm eating a store-cooked turkey with strangers.* She felt madcap and adventurous.

" 'Here I am with my mom when I ought to be with my husband,' she said, and she packed her suitcase then and there and went back to him, but he couldn't let you know till noon because what was he going to do—excuse himself and run phone you the minute she walked in?"

"Donald has an expert opinion to offer on every subject," his wife announced with a brittle laugh.

She was sitting very tensely, her spine not touching the chair. Her hair was scrolled upward at the ends like the sound holes in a violin.

"Yes; you might call it a gift," Donald agreed, unruffled. "I'm able to envision. See, first there's the business of settling her into the house. Don't forget she has that baby with her, and a diaper bag no doubt and one of those infant car seats—"

"But he could have just turned her away!"

Belle exploded. "He doesn't even love her! He told me he didn't!"

"Well, of course that's what he would claim," Donald said, leaning back expansively.

By now Vanessa was carving the turkey. Delia began passing around the other foods. The brussels sprouts were barely warm, she discovered. The sweet potatoes were refrigerator cold, but everybody took some anyhow.

"You're right," Belle said. "Oh, when will I learn? Seems this happens to me about every other week. Norton Grove was the only one who actually divorced his wife for me, and look how that ended up!"

"How *did* it end up?" Delia asked.

"He fell in love with a lady plumber who came to unstop our sink."

Donald nodded, implying he could have predicted as much.

"It's just the way Ann Landers keeps saying in her column," Belle told them. "She says a man who would leave his wife will most likely leave you, too, by and by."

"Maybe you ought to look for someone who doesn't *have* a wife," Vanessa suggested, handing her son a turkey wing.

"Yes, but it's kind of like I lack imagination. I mean, I can't seem to picture marrying a man till I see him married to someone else. Then I say, 'Why! He'd make a good husband for *me*!' "

The hallway door opened and Mr. Lamb stood on the threshold, wearing a shiny black suit that turned his skin to ashes. "Oh, God, you have guests," he said.

"Yes, Mr. Lamb, and you're one of them," Belle said. "Donald Hawser, Melinda Hawser . . . Vanessa and Greggie you've seen around, I bet. This is Horace Lamb," she told the others. She waved carelessly toward the one empty chair. "Have a seat."

"Well, I can't stay long."

"Have a *seat*, Mr. Lamb."

He entered the room with a skimming sound that made Delia glance downward. On his feet he wore the kind of backless paper slippers given out free in hospitals. "This afternoon will be sports, sports, sports," he said as he fell into his chair. "All regular programs are preempted. I'm reduced to the educational channels."

"Say!" Donald cried. "Who you going to root for?"

"Pardon? Weekday afternoons, I like to watch the soaps. Oh, I confess. I admit it. I make a point of stopping for *All My Children* every blessed day I'm on the road."

"What's your line of business, Horace? Okay if I call you Horace?"

"I sell storm windows," Mr. Lamb told him. He accepted the container of sweet potatoes and peered down into it. "This looks exceedingly rich," he said. His long front teeth were so prominent that his lips had to labor to stretch across them. His whole face seemed stretched, and too intricately hinged at the jawbone. He raised his deep-set eyes to Belle and said, "Regrettably, I'm afflicted with a touchy stomach."

"Oh, eat up, it'll do you good," Belle snapped. "We were discussing married men."

"Pardon?"

"Another problem I have is, I look at a married man and I can't believe he won't find me irresistible."

"Irresistible?"

"I'm speaking to the table at large, Mr. Lamb. Eat your dinner. I see a man with his wife, mousy boring wife who isn't even attempting to keep herself up, and I think, *Why wouldn't he prefer me instead? I'm a hell of a lot more fun, and better-looking to boot.* But it's like there's some—I don't know—some hold wives have, and I can't seem to break it. Is it a secret? Is it some secret you-all pass around among yourselves?"

She was asking Melinda Hawser, but Melinda just gave another shattered laugh and started crumbling bits of biscuit onto her plate. "Is it?" Belle asked Delia.

"Oh, no," Delia told her. "It's more like just . . . what's the word? The word from science class. Momentum?"

"Inertia," Mr. Lamb supplied.

"Right." She glanced over at him. "It's just a matter of people staying where they are."

"Well, if that's all it is," Belle said, "how come Katie O'Connell got to waltz off to Hawaii with Larry Watts? *She* must have found out the secret. Why, when Larry Watts was boarding here, he never even gave me a look! He almost seemed to be avoiding me. He acted like I was some floozy the one time I asked him downstairs for a friendly little drink!"

Her mouth collapsed, and she covered her eyes with one hand. Donald said, "Oh, now! Hey!" and Vanessa said, "Aw, Belle, don't cry," while Mr. Lamb started tugging ferociously at his nose.

"To be honest," Melinda said in a crystal voice, "I can't think what you want with a husband anyhow."

There was a pause, a kind of reconsidering among the other diners.

"Who first thought marriage up, do you suppose?" Melinda asked Greggie. He goggled at her from behind a greasy fistful of turkey wing. "Everyone pushes it so, especially the women. Your mother and your aunts and your girlfriends. Then after you're married you see how he's always so full of himself and always going on about something, always got these theories and pronouncements, always crowing over these triumphs at his business. 'I told them this,' and 'I told them that,' and you ask, 'What did they say back?' and he says, 'Oh, *you* know, but then I told them such and such, and I let them have it outright, I put it to them straight, I said . . .' And if you mention this to your mother and your aunts and so forth, 'Oh,' they say, 'marriage is a pain, all right.' 'Well, if that's the way you feel,' you want to ask them, 'why didn't you speak up before? Where were you when I was announcing my engagement?' "

"Ha. Yes," her husband said. He glanced around the table. "They're going to think you mean *our* marriage. Dear."

Everybody waited, but Melinda just speared a brussels sprout.

"Oh," Belle assured him, "we would never think that." She was sitting erect now, her tears already drying on her cheeks. "A gorgeous man like you? Of course we wouldn't." She told the others, "Donald and Melinda are customers of mine. They bought the old Meers place—lovely place. Donald's an important executive at the furniture plant."

Melinda was chewing her brussels sprout very noisily, or maybe it only seemed that way because the room was so quiet.

"*Mrs.* Meers had gone into the nursing home," Belle said, "but Mr. Meers was still living there. Took us through the house himself;

taught us how to work the trash compactor. Told us, 'Here in the freezer are one hundred forty-four egg whites, no charge.' "

"Folks who made their own mayonnaise," Mr. Lamb surmised.

Belle was about to go on speaking, but she stopped and looked at him.

"I don't guess you'd be in the market for storm windows," Mr. Lamb told Donald.

"Not really," Donald said, with his eyes on his wife.

"Ah, well, I didn't think so."

"That house needs absolutely nothing," Belle said. "The Meerses kept after it every minute. And Donald here, Don . . ." She smiled at him. "Don spotted that the first time he walked through."

"Melinda and I have a *fine* marriage. Married seven years," Donald said, still watching his wife. "We were one of those recognized campus couples at our college. Went steady, got pinned: the works."

"I know the type you mean," Belle said.

"Why, Melinda's known me so long she still calls me Hawk! Hawk Hawser," he added, turning at last to meet Belle's gaze. "I was on the basketball team. Kind of a star, some people might say, though I never had the height to go professional."

"Is that right!" Belle exclaimed.

"Hawk Hawser," he repeated lingeringly.

"I believe I might've heard of you."

"Well, maybe so if you were ever in Illinois. Jerry Bingle College?"

"Jerry Bingle. Hmm."

"I played center."

"Really!"

"And midway through my senior year—"

"Marshmallow," Greggie demanded.

He didn't have the usual small child's trouble pronouncing *l*'s. He spoke very precisely and daintily. "Mama? Marshmallow!"

It was Delia, finally, who plucked a marshmallow from the sweet potatoes and reached across the table to set it on his plate. Everyone else was watching Belle. Open-mouthed and breathless, miraculously recovered, Belle stroked her topmost button with a hypnotic, circular motion and kept her damp-lashed eyes focused raptly on Donald's lips.

# ||

Sometimes Mr. Pomfret ordered Delia to go out and feed the parking meter for a client. Sometimes he snapped his fingers when he needed her. Once, he tossed her his raincoat and told her to take it down the block to the one-hour cleaner's. "Yes, Mr. Pomfret," she murmured. When she returned, she placed the receipt on his palm as smartly as a surgical nurse dealing out a scalpel.

But now she began to feel a little itch of rebellion.

"Miss Grinstead, can't you see I'm *merging*?" he demanded when she brought in some letters to sign, and she said, "Sorry, Mr. Pomfret," but neutrally, too evenly, with her expression set in granite. And back at her desk, she seethed with imaginary retorts. *You and your crummy computer! You and your "merging" and your Search-and-Destroy or whatever!*

One Friday in early December, a stooped, gray-haired man in a baseball jacket arrived without an appointment. "I'm Mr. Leon Wesley," he told Delia. "This is about my son Juval. Do you think Mr. Pomfret might have a minute for me?"

Mr. Pomfret's office door was closed—it was early morning, his time to peruse new catalogs —but when Delia inquired, he said, "Leon? Why, Leon resurfaced my driveway for me. Send him in. And make us a pot of coffee while you're at it."

It was impossible to avoid overhearing Mr. Wesley's reason for coming. He poured it out even before he was seated, speaking through the grinding of the coffee beans so Mr. Pomfret had to ask him to repeat himself. Juval, Mr. Wesley said, was scheduled to join the navy first thing after Christmas. He had a highly promising future; special interest had been taken on account of his qualifications, which seemed to involve some technical know-how that Delia couldn't quite follow. And last night, clear out of the blue, he had been arrested for breaking and entering. Caught climbing through the Hanffs' dining-room window at ten o'clock in the evening.

"The Hanffs!" Mr. Pomfret said. The Hanffs owned the furniture factory, as even Delia knew—the town's one industry. "Well, of all the doggone folks to up and burglarize," he said.

Delia went to the supply closet for more sugar, and when she came back Mr. Pomfret was still marveling at Juval's choice of victims. "I mean, here you've got Reba Hanff, who disapproves of jewelry and doesn't own a piece of silver," he said, "gives every cent of their profits to some

religious honcho in India . . . What did the boy
hope to steal, for God's sake?"

"And why, is what I'd like to know," Mr.
Wesley said. "That's the part I can't figure. Was
he in need of money? For what? He doesn't even
drink, let alone take drugs. Doesn't even have
a girlfriend."

"Not to mention the Hanffs own the only
house alarm in all of Bay Borough," Mr. Pomfret
mused.

"And with such a hotshot career ahead!" Mr.
Wesley said. "You can bet that's all down the
drain now. How come he went and ruined things,
so close to time he was leaving?"

"Maybe *that's* how come," Delia spoke up,
setting two mugs on a tray.

"Ma'am?"

"Maybe he ruined things so he wouldn't have
to leave after all."

Mr. Wesley gaped at her.

Mr. Pomfret said, "You may go now, Miss
Grinstead."

"Yes, Mr. Pomfret."

"Shut the door behind you, please."

She shut the door with such conspicuous care
that every part of the latch declared itself.

*In regard to the establishment of a designated
fund,* she typed, and then Mr. Pomfret emerged
from his office, stuffing his arms into his overcoat
as he walked, forging a trail for Mr. Wesley.
"Cancel my ten o'clock," he told Delia.

"Yes, Mr. Pomfret."

He opened the outer door, ushered Mr. Wesley through it, and then closed it and came back to stand at Delia's desk. "Miss Grinstead," he said, "from now on, please do not volunteer comments during my consultations."

She stared at him stubbornly, keeping her eyes wide and innocent.

"You're paid for your secretarial skills, not for your opinions," he said.

"Yes, Mr. Pomfret."

He left.

She knew she had deserved that, but still she felt a flare of righteous anger once he was gone. She typed rapidly and badly, flinging the carriage so hard that the typewriter kept skidding across the desk. When she called to cancel the ten o'clock appointment, her voice shook. And when she left the office at lunchtime, she picked up a Bay Borough *Bugle* so she could look for another job.

Well, not that she would actually go through with it, of course. It was just that she needed to fantasize awhile.

The weather was raw and dismal, and she hadn't brought any food with her, but she walked to the square even so because she couldn't deal with the Cue Stick 'n' Cola today. She found the park benches deserted. The statue looked huddled and dense, like a bird with all its feathers reared against the cold. She wrapped her coat around her and sat down on the very edge of one damp, chilly slat.

How satisfying it would be to announce her resignation! "I regret to inform you, Mr. Pompous . . . ," she would say. He would be helpless. He didn't even know where she kept the carbon paper.

She opened the *Bugle* and searched for the classified section. As a rule she didn't read the *Bugle*, which was little more than an advertising handout—several pages of half-price specials and extremely local news, stacked weekly in various storefronts. She flipped past a choral call for the Christmas Eve Sing on the square, a two-for-one day at the shoe store, and a progress report on the Mitten Drive. On the next-to-last page she discovered four Help Wanted ads: baby-sitter, baby-sitter, lathe operator, and "live-in woman." This town must have unemployment problems. After that came the For Sale ads. A person named Dwayne wished to sell two wedding rings, cheap. Her eyes slid back to *Live-in Woman*.

> Single father desires help w/ lively, bright, engaging, 12-yr-old son. Must be willing to wake boy in a.m., serve breakfast, see off to school, do light cleaning / errands / shopping, assist w/ homework, provide transportation to dentist / doctor /grandfather /

playmates, attend athletic meets & cheer appropriate team, host groups of 11–13 yr olds,
cook supper, show enthusiasm for TV sports
programs / computer games / paperback war
novels, be available nights for bad dreams /
illness. Driver's license a must. Non-smokers
only. Room, board, generous salary. Weekends & most daytimes free except school holidays / sick days / snow days. Call Mr. Miller
at Underwood High 8–5 Mon–Fri.

Delia clucked. The nerve of the man! Some
people wanted the moon. She rattled the paper
impatiently and refolded it. You can't expect a
mere hireling to serve as a genuine mother,
which was really what he was asking.

She rose and placed the *Bugle* in the trash
basket. So much for that.

Crossing West Street, she glanced toward the
shops—Debbi's and the dime store and the florist. How about a job in sales? No, she was too
quiet-natured. As for waitressing, she used to
forget her own family's dessert orders in the time
it took to walk to the kitchen. And she knew
from her talks with Mrs. Lincoln at the library
that the town was having to struggle to support
even one librarian.

Actually, she reflected, passing the sterile
white blinds of the Fingernail Clinic, a hireling
would in some ways be *better* than a mother—
less emotionally ensnarled, less likely to cause

damage. Certainly less likely to suffer damage herself. When the employer's child was unhappy, it would never occur to the live-in woman to feel personally responsible.

She turned into Value Vision and took another *Bugle* from the stack just inside the door.

"I wouldn't like for my son to think people are checking him over," Mr. Miller said. "Filing through to see if he's up to standard. That's why I asked you to come while he was out. Then if you find you're interested, you could stay on and meet him. He's eating supper at a friend's, but he'll be home in half an hour or so."

He sat across from her in a chintz armchair that he seemed to dwarf, as he dwarfed the whole overstuffed, overdecorated living room of this little ranch house on the edge of town. To Delia's surprise, he'd turned out to be someone she recognized. Joel Miller: he had consulted Mr. Pomfret several months ago on a visitation matter. She remembered admiring his undisguised baldness. Men who scorned the subterfuge of artfully draped strands of hair, she felt, conveyed an attractive air of masculine assurance; and Mr. Miller, with his large, regular features and his olive skin and loose gray suit, seemed positively serene. Underneath, though, she detected some tension. He had told her three times—contradicting the entire gist of his ad—that his son would be at school for the vast majority of every day, in essence *all* day, and that even when he was home he required not much more than a token adult in the wings. Delia had the feeling that no one else had applied for this position.

"He eats at friends' houses often, in fact," Mr. Miller was saying. "And in summer—I don't think I mentioned this—he spends two weeks at sleep-away camp. Besides which there's computer day camp, soccer clinic—"

"Summer!" Delia said. She rocked back in her chintz-padded rocking chair. Summer, with its soft, lazy afternoons, tinkling glasses of lemonade, children's peach-colored bodies in swimsuits! "Oh, Mr. Miller," she said. "The truth is, I seem to be in a changeable stage of life right now. I'm not sure I could get that . . . invested."

"And in summer I'm around more myself," Mr. Miller went on, as if she hadn't spoken. "Not the whole day, exactly—a principal doesn't have quite the same leeway his teachers do—but quite a lot."

"I probably shouldn't have come," Delia said. "A child your son's age needs continuity."

*Then why* did *you come?* he might reasonably have asked, but instead, poor man, he seized on her last sentence. "You sound experienced," he said. "Do you have children of your own, Miss Grinstead? Oh." The corners of his mouth jerked briefly downward. "I'm sorry. Of course not."

"Yes, I do," she told him.

"So it's *Mrs.* Grinstead?"

"I prefer 'Miss.' "

"I see."

He thought this over.

"But, so, you *are* experienced," he said finally. "That's excellent! And do you come from this area?"

Evidently he didn't keep up with Bay Borough gossip. "No, I don't," she told him.

"You don't."

She could see him reconsidering. Desperate he might be, but not foolhardy. He wouldn't want to hire an ax murderer.

"I'm from Baltimore," she volunteered at last. "I'm perfectly respectable, I promise, but I've put that part of my life behind me."

"Ah."

Oh, Lord, now he was envisioning some drama. He surveyed her with interest, his head slightly tilted.

"But!" she exclaimed. "As far as the job goes—"

"I know: you don't want it," he said sadly.

"It's nothing to do with the job itself. I'm sure your son is a very nice boy."

"Oh, he's more than nice," Mr. Miller said. "He's really, he's such a good kid, Miss Grinstead. He's wonderful! But I guess I overestimated how well we could do on our own. I thought as long as we knew how to work the washing machine . . . But things have gotten away from me."

He waved a hand toward the room in general, which puzzled Delia, because it seemed painfully neat. Fat little cushions with buttons in their middles filled the skirted couch, each one propped at a careful angle. Glossy fashion magazines lapped at mathematical intervals across the coffee table. But Mr. Miller, following her glance, said, "Oh, the *surface* I can handle. I've posted a chart in the kitchen. Each day has its special job. This afternoon we vacuumed, yesterday we dusted. But it seems there are other issues. Last weekend, for example, he asked if we could have penny soup. 'Penny soup!' I said. Sounded kind of weird to me. He said his mother used to serve it for lunch when he was little. I asked him what was in it, and it turns out he meant plain old vegetable soup. I guess they call it penny soup because it's cheap. So I said, 'Well, I can make *that*.' I heat up a tin of Campbell's, he takes one look, and what does he do? Starts crying. Twelve years old and he falls apart, kid who didn't so much as whimper the time he broke his arm. I said, 'Well, what? What did I do wrong?' He said it had to be homemade. I said, 'God Almighty, Noah.' Still, I'm not stupid. I knew this soup had some meaning for him. So I haul out a cookbook and set to work making homemade. But when he saw what I was doing, he told me

to forget it. 'Just forget the whole thing,' he told
me. 'I'm not hungry anyhow.' And off he went
to his room, leaving me with a pile of diced
carrots."

"Sliced," Delia told him.

He raised his straight black eyebrows.

"You should have *sliced* the carrots," she told
him, "and also zucchini, yellow squash, new
potatoes—everything coin-shaped. That's why
they call it penny soup. It's nothing to do with
the cost. I doubt you'd find it in cookbooks,
because it's more a . . . mother's recipe, you
know?"

"Miss Grinstead," Mr. Miller said, "let me
show you where you'd stay if you took the job."

"No, really, I—"

"Just to look at! It's the guest room. Has its
own private bath."

She rose when he did, but only because she
wanted to make her escape. What had she been
thinking of, coming here? It seemed she could
feel within the curl of her fingers the urge to slice
those vegetables as they ought to be sliced, to
set the soup in front of the boy and turn away
briskly (twelve was too old to cuddle) and pretend she hadn't noticed his tears. "I'm sure it's
a lovely room," she said. "Somebody's going to
love it! Somebody young, maybe, who still has
enough . . ."

She was trailing Mr. Miller down a short, carpeted hall lined with open doors. At the last door, Mr. Miller stood back to let her see in. It was the sort of room where people were expected to spend no more than a night or two. The high double bed allowed barely a yard of space on either side. The nightstand bore a thoughtful supply of guest-type reading (more magazines, two books that looked like anthologies). The framed sampler on the wall read WELCOME in six languages.

"Large walk-in closet," Mr. Miller said. "Private bath, as I believe I've mentioned."

In another part of the house, a door slammed and a child called, "Dad?"

"Ah," Mr. Miller said. "Coming!" he called. "Now you get to meet Noah," he told Delia.

She took a step backward.

"Just to say hello," he assured her. "What harm could that do?"

She had no choice but to follow him down the hall again.

In the kitchen (cabinets the color of toffees, wallpaper printed with butter churns), a wiry little boy stood tugging off a red jacket. He had a tumble of rough brown hair and a thin, freckled face and his father's long dark eyes. As soon as they entered the room, he started talking. "Hey, Dad, guess what Jack's mother gave us for dinner! This, like, cubes of meat that you dunk into this . . ." He registered Delia's presence, flicked a look at her, and went on. ". . . dunk into this pot and then—"

"Noah, I'd like you to meet Miss Grinstead," his father said. "Should we call you Delia?" he asked her. She nodded; it hardly mattered. "I'm Joel," he said, "and this is Noah. My son."

Noah said, "Oh. Hi." He wore the guarded, deadpan expression that children assume for introductions. "So the pot is full of hot oil, I guess it is, and each of us got—"

"Fondue," his father said. "You're talking about fondue."

"Right, and each of us got our own fork to cook our meat on, with different, like, animals on the handles so we could keep straight whose was whose. Like mine was a giraffe, and guess what Jack's little sister's was?"

"I can't imagine," his father said. "Son, Delia is here to—"

"A pig!" Noah squawked. "His little sister got the pig!"

"Is that right."

"And she cried about it too, but Carrie cries about everything. Then for dessert we each had a bag of chocolate marbles, but I turned mine down. I was polite about it, though. I go to his mom, I go—"

"Said."

"Huh?"

"You *said* to his mom."

"Right, I'm all, 'Thanks a lot, Mrs. Newell, but I'm so full I guess I better pass.' "

"I thought you liked chocolate marbles," his father said.

"Are you kidding? Not after what I know now." Noah turned to Delia. "Chocolate marbles are coated with ground-up beetle shells," he told her.

"No!" she said.

"No," Mr. Miller agreed. "Where'd you get *that* information?" he asked his son.

"Kenny Moss told me."

"Well, then! If Kenny Moss said it, how can we doubt it?"

"I'm serious! He heard it from his uncle who's in the business."

"What business—tabloid newspapers?"

"Huh?"

"There are no beetle shells in chocolate marbles. Take my word for it. The FDA would never allow it."

"And guess what's in corn chips," Noah told Delia. "Those yellow corn chips? Seagull do."

"I never knew that!"

"That's what makes them so crackly."

"Noah—" his father said.

"Honest, Dad! Kenny Moss swears it!"

"Noah, Delia came to talk about keeping house for us."

Delia shot Mr. Miller a frown. He wore an

oblivious, bland expression, as if he had no idea what he'd done. "Actually," she said, turning to Noah, "I was only . . . inquiring."

"She's going to think about it," Mr. Miller amended.

Noah said, "That'd be great! I've been having to fix my own school lunches."

"Horrors," his father said. "Don't let on to the child-labor authorities."

"Well, how would *you* feel? You open your lunch box: 'Gee, I wonder what I surprised myself with today.' "

Delia laughed. She said, "I should be going. It was nice to meet you, Noah."

"Goodbye," Noah said. Unexpectedly, he held out his hand. "I hope you decide to come."

His hand was small but callused. When he looked up at her, his eyes showed an underlay of gold, like sunshine filtered through brown water.

Outside the front door, Delia told his father, "I thought you didn't want him to feel people were checking him over."

"Ah," Mr. Miller said. "Yes. Well."

"I thought you were trying to spare him! Then you went and told him what I was here for."

"I realize I shouldn't have done that," Mr. Miller said. He spread one hand distractedly across his scalp, like a cap. "It's just that I wanted so badly for you to say you'd come."

"And you haven't seen my references, even! You don't know the first thing about me!"

"No, but I approve of your English."

"English?"

"It kills me to hear him speak so sloppily. 'Like' this and 'like' that, and 'I go' instead of 'I said.' It drives me bats."

"Well, of all things," Delia said. She turned to leave.

"Miss Grinstead? Delia?"

"What."

"Will you at least think it over?"

"Of course," she said.

But she knew she wouldn't.


Vanessa said Joel Miller was the most pitiful man she knew of. "Ever since his wife left, the guy has been barely coping," she told Delia.

"Isn't anyone in Bay Borough happily married?" Delia wondered.

"Yes, lots of folks," Vanessa said. "Just not who you choose to hang out with."

They were sitting in Vanessa's kitchen the following morning, a cold, sunny Saturday. Really it was her grandmother's kitchen; Vanessa and all three of her brothers lived with their father's mother. Vanessa was filling out labels with an old-fashioned steel-nibbed pen. *Highly Effective Insect Repellent,* she wrote, in hair-thin brown script on ivory paper ovals. Highly Effective was

an ancient family recipe. When Vanessa had finished her daily allotment of labels, her youngest
brother would glue them onto the slender glass
phials in which various dried sprigs and berries
bobbed mysteriously underwater. Delia found it
hard to believe that people could make a living
this way, but evidently the Linleys did all right.
The house was large and comfortable, and the
grandmother could afford to travel once a year
to Disney World. Vanessa said the trick was pennyroyal. "Don't let this get around," she'd told
Delia, "but insects *despise* pennyroyal. The
other herbs are mostly for show."

On the floor, Greggie was building a tower
with stacks of corks. After Vanessa finished her
labels, she and Delia were going to take him to
visit Santa. Then Delia might do a little Christmas shopping. Or maybe not; she couldn't decide. She had always disliked Christmas, with its
possibilities for disappointing her family's secret
hopes, and this year would be worse than ever.
Should she just, maybe, skip the whole business?
Oh, why wasn't there an etiquette book for runaway wives?

Which brought her back to Mr. Miller. "How
come his wife left him, does anyone know?" she
asked Vanessa.

"Oh, sure; everyone knows. Here they were,
together for years, sweet little boy, nice house,
and one day last spring Ellie, that's his wife,

found a lump in her breast. Went to the doctor and he said, yup, looked like cancer. So she came home and told her husband, 'In the time that I have left to me, I want to make the very best of my life. I want to do exactly what I've dreamed of.' And by nightfall she had packed up and gone. That was her deepest, dearest wish—did you ever hear such a thing?"

"So where is she now?"

"Oh, she's a TV weather lady over in Kellerton," Vanessa said. "The lump was nothing at all; they removed it under local anesthetic. Now Mr. Miller and Noah can turn on their TV and watch her every evening. Or you might have seen her in *Boardwalk Bulletin*. They ran a profile of her last August. Real pretty blond? Hair like that shredded straw we pack our bottles in. Course, no one here was impressed in the slightest—person who'd leave her own child."

Delia looked down at her lap.

"All the women in town have been trying to help Mr. Miller out," Vanessa said. "Bringing pans of lasagna, taking his kid for the afternoon. But I guess by summer he realized it wasn't enough, because that's when he put the ad in the *Bugle*."

"The ad's been in since summer?"

"Right, but his neighbor tells me the onliest answers were teenaged girls from the high school. Every girl at Dorothy Underwood's got

a crush on Mr. Miller. I did too; it's part of being
a student there. I was a senior the first year he
was principal, and I thought he was the sexiest
man I'd ever laid eyes on. But of course he can't
hire some airhead, so he's just kept running the
ad. It never crossed my mind you'd want the job
yourself."

"Well, I don't, really," Delia said. She
watched Greggie start a cork train across the
linoleum. His little hands reminded her of biscuits, that kind with a row of fork holes pricked
on top. She had forgotten what a joy it was to
rest your eyes on young children. "It's just that
I'm so fed up with Mr. Pomfret," she said. "Do
you suppose they have any openings at the furniture factory?"

"Oh, the furniture factory," Vanessa said,
dipping her pen. "All's they ever need there is
oilers. Stand all day rubbing oil into chair legs
with these big mittens on your hands."

"But they must have office positions. Typist,
filing clerk . . ."

"How come you're not taking the job at Mr.
Miller's?"

"I don't want to just . . . step into a little boy's
life like that, in case I decide to leave," Delia
told her.

"Do you always up and leave a place?"

Delia wasn't sure how that question was intended. She looked at Vanessa suspiciously.
"No, not always," she said.

"I mean I never heard you speak a word against Zeke Pomfret. Now you want to quit."

"He's so bossy, though. So condescending. Also, the pay is ridiculous," Delia said. "I didn't realize how ridiculous when I took the job. And he doesn't even provide health insurance! What if I got sick?"

Vanessa sat back to watch her.

"Well," Delia told her, "yes, I *do* seem to up and leave a lot."

As she spoke, she saw a lone, straight figure marching down the coastline. It was strange, the feeling of affection the image summoned up in her.

For her family's Christmas, she decided to buy nothing at all. Maybe Greggie's trip to Santa had depressed her. He had appeared to grasp the concept before they went, but once they got there he started screaming and had to be carried out. Vanessa was crushed; even the Santa looked crushed. And their shopping expedition afterward was spiritless, with Greggie hiccuping tearfully and slouching in his stroller in a brooding, insulted manner. Delia told Vanessa she thought she would call it a day. "I need to go to the laundromat anyhow," she said—a flimsy excuse.

When she got home, Belle hailed her from the living-room doorway. "You had a phone call," she said.

"I did?"

Her knees seemed to melt. She thought first of the children, then of Sam's heart.

But Belle said, "Mr. Miller from the high school. He wants you to call him back."

"Oh."

"*I* didn't know you knew Joel Miller."

Delia hadn't mentioned him to Belle because working for him would mean moving out of this house, and how could she ever do that? This house was perfect. Even Mr. Pomfret had his good points. Somehow the visit to Santa had shown her that. So she nonchalantly accepted the number Belle had scrawled on the corner of a takeout menu. Might as well get this over with. She perched on one arm of the couch and reached for the phone and dialed. Meanwhile Belle hovered in the background, supposedly absorbed with the cat. "Is you a nice little kitty. Is you a sweet little kitty," she crooned. Delia listened to the ringing at the other end of the line, letting her eyes travel gratefully over the blank white walls and bare floorboards.

"Hello?" Noah said.

She said, "This is Delia Grinstead."

"Oh, hi! I'm supposed to tell you I'm sorry."

"Sorry? For what?"

"Dad says a guy shouldn't talk about seagull do in front of ladies."

"Oh. Well—"

A man said something in the background.

"Women," Noah said.

"Excuse me?"

" 'Women,' I meant to say, not 'ladies.' "

All pretext, of course. Mr. Miller surely didn't think she would be offended by seagull do. *Or* the word "ladies." This was mere strategy. But Noah himself probably had no inkling of that, and so Delia told him, "It's quite all right."

"Kenny Moss's uncle drives a snack truck; that's how Kenny knows about the you-know-what. But Dad claims his uncle was teasing him. Dad goes, 'Right, the corn-chip factory really does take the time to send their workers out to the beach with shovels.' "

Another mutter in the background.

"Okay, 'said.' He *said*," Noah told Delia. "And on top of that he *said*"—heavy stress, meaningful pause—"he said how come it's not in the list of ingredients, if they use seagull do? Oops."

"Oh, you know those lists," Delia told him. "All those scientific terms. They can cover up just about anything with some chemical-sounding name."

"They can?"

"Why, sure! They probably call it 'dihydroxyexymexylene' or some such."

Noah giggled. "Hey, Dad," he said, his voice retreating slightly. "Delia says it probably *is* on the list; it's probably dihydroxy . . ."

Belle had carried the cat over to the window now. She was holding him up to the glass, which was nearly opaque with dust. And cobwebs clouded the tops of the curtains, and the philodendron plant on the sill was leggy and bedraggled. The whole room seemed drained of color, as if, already, it had slipped into the dimmest reaches of Delia's memory.

# 12

Mr. Pomfret said, "Moving on, eh," without so much as a change of expression. (You would think she was a piece of office equipment.) All he asked, he said, was that she finish out the week—tie up any dangling odds and ends. Which of course she agreed to do, even though there were no odds and ends; just the usual busywork of rat-a-tat letters and robot phone calls and Mr. Pomfret's daily sheaf of marked catalogs.

It seemed he urgently required a pair of perforated leather driving gloves. A radio antenna the size and shape of a breakfast plate. A solid-walnut display rack for souvenir golf balls.

When she turned in her office key on Friday afternoon, he told her he might wait till after New Year's to replace her. "This time," he said, "I believe I'll hire a word processor, assuming I can find one."

Delia was confused, for an instant. She pictured hiring a machine. Just try asking a machine to debate his glove size with an 800 operator! she thought. Then she realized her mistake. But still, somehow, she felt hurt, and she shouldered

her bag abruptly and left without saying goodbye.

All she owned fit easily in a cardboard carton
begged from Rick-Rack's. The goosenecked
lamp poked its head out, though. She could have
left it that way (Belle was giving her a ride), but
she liked the notion of a life no larger than a
single, compact box; and so she shifted things
until the flaps closed securely. Then she took her
coat and handbag from the bed, and she picked
the carton up and walked out.

No point sending one last look backward. She
knew every detail of that room by heart—every
nail hole, every seam in the wallpaper, and the
way the paw-footed radiator, in the furry half-
light of this overcast Saturday morning, resembled some skeletal animal sitting on its haunches.

At the bottom of the stairs, she set down her
load and put her coat on. She could hear Belle
talking to George in the kitchen. He was staying
here another week or two, just till Delia was
settled. It was Delia's belief that she had to let
her own smell permeate the new place first; otherwise he'd keep running back to the old place.

Mr. Miller had told her George was more than
welcome. He'd been meaning to buy a cat anyhow, he said. (But notice how he'd used the word
"buy," apparently unaware that true animal lovers would not be caught dead in a pet shop.)

Still buttoning her coat, she walked through the dining room to knock on the kitchen door. "Coming," Belle called. Delia returned to the hall. Upstairs, Mr. Lamb was creaking the floorboards, and his TV had started its level, fluent murmur. She wondered when he would get around to noticing she was gone. Maybe never, she thought.

It was still not too late to change her mind.

"I gave George a can of tuna," Belle said when she emerged. "That ought to keep him occupied."

"Oh, Belle, you'll spoil him."

"Nothing's too good for my whiskums! I'm hoping he'll refuse to leave me when it's time. 'No, no, Mommy!' " she squeaked. " 'I want to stay here with Aunt Belle!' "

Meanwhile she was flouncing into her winged coat, fluffing her curls, jingling her car keys. "All set?" she asked.

"All set."

They walked out to her enormous old Ford. Delia fitted her carton among a tangle of real estate signs in the trunk, and then the two of them got in the car and Belle started the engine. With the seat-belt alarm insistently dinging, they pulled away from the curb.

It was months since Delia had ridden in a car. The scenery glided past so quickly, and so smoothly! She gripped her door handle as they

swung around the corner, and then *zip! zip! zip!*
went the dentist, the dime store, the Potpourri
Palace. In no time, they were turning onto Pendle Street and parking in the Millers' gravel
driveway—a trip that had taken her at least ten
minutes, walking.

"My parents live in a house like this," Belle
said. She was peering through the windshield at
the cut-out designs of covered wagons on the
shutters. "In a suburb of York, P.A. Dee, are
you sure you want to do this?"

"Oh, yes," Delia said weakly.

"You'll be nothing but a servant!"

"It's better than being a typewriter," Delia
told her.

"Well, if you're going to put it *that* way."

Delia climbed out of the car, and Belle came
around to help her maneuver her box from the
trunk. "Thanks," Delia said. "You have my
phone number."

"I have it."

"I'll let you know when's a good time to bring
the cat."

"Or before then," Belle said. "Or supposing
you want to move back! I'll wait a few days before I try renting your room."

They might have gone on this way forever, but
at that moment Noah burst out the front door.
"Delia! Hi!" he called.

"Ms. Grinstead to *you*," Belle muttered under

her breath. She told Delia, "Don't you let them treat you like a peon."

Delia just hugged her and turned toward the house. How the Millers treated her was the least of her concerns, she thought. The question was how to treat *them*—what distance to maintain from this mop-headed, blue-jeaned boy. It was so easy to fall back into being someone's mother! She smiled at him as he lifted the carton from her arms. "I can manage that," she said.

"I'm *supposed* to carry your luggage. Dad told me. Don't you have anything more?" he asked. Belle was already backing the car out of the driveway.

"This is it," Delia said.

"Dad's over at the school, so I'm supposed to show you where everything is. We've got your room all made up for you. We changed the bed-sheets even though they were clean."

"Oh, then why did you change them?"

"Dad said if they didn't still have their laundry smell you might think someone else had slept in them."

"I wouldn't think that," she assured him.

They walked through the living room, where the cushions lined the couch in last week's exact formation and the magazines had not varied their positions by an inch. The carpet in the hall was freshly vacuumed, though. She could see the roller marks in the nap. And when they entered the guest room, Noah placed her box on a folding luggage stand that had definitely not been there earlier. "It's new," he said, noticing her glance. "We bought it at Home 'n' Hearth."

"It's very nice."

"And lookit here," he said. On the bureau sat a tiny television set. "Color TV! From Lawson Appliance. Dad says a live-in woman always has her own TV."

"Oh, I don't need a—"

"Clock radio," Noah said, "decorator box of Kleenex . . ."

What touched her most, though, was how they'd turned the bedcovers down—that effortful white triangle. She said, "You shouldn't have." And she meant it, for the sight made her feel indebted, somehow.

She followed Noah to the closet, where he was displaying the hangers. "Three dozen matching hangers, solid plastic, pink. Not a wire one in the bunch. We had our choice between pink or white or brown."

"Pink is perfect," she told him.

Three dozen! It would disappoint them to find out how few clothes she owned.

"Now I'm supposed to leave you in private," Noah said. "But I'll be in my room if there's anything you need."

"Thank you, Noah."

"You know where my room is?"

"I can find it."

"And you're supposed to unpack and put your stuff in drawers and all."

"I'll do that," she promised.

As he left he glanced back at her doubtfully, as if he worried she wouldn't follow instructions.

Her carton looked so shabby, resting on the needlepoint webbing of the luggage stand. She walked over to it and lifted the flaps, and out floated the lonesome, stale, hornet's-nest smell of the room on George Street. Well. She took off her coat, hung it on one of the hangers. Draped her purse strap over a hook. Drew the goosenecked lamp from the box but then had nowhere to put it, for the room already contained two lamps, shaded in rigid white satin. Still holding the goosenecked lamp (with its helmet of army-green metal and the dent at its base from when the cat had knocked it over one night), she sat down limply on the edge of the bed. She had to brace her feet so as not to slide off the slick coverlet. It was one of those hotel-type beds that seem at once too springy and too hard, and she couldn't imagine getting used to it.

Elsewhere in the house she heard a door open, a set of heavy footsteps, a man's voice calling and Noah answering. She would have to rearrange her face and go join them. Any minute

now, she would. But for a while she went on
sitting there, clutching her homely little lamp and
gathering courage.

At the rear of the house, divided from the
kitchen by only a counter, lay what the Millers
called the family room. Here the stuffy decorat-
ing style relaxed into something more casual. A
long, low couch faced a TV, an office desk stood
against one wall, and three armchairs were
grouped in a corner. It was this room that became, within the next few days, Delia's territory.
(She had always wanted a more modern house,
without cubbies or nooks or crannies.) In the
mornings, when she was through cleaning, she
sat at the desk to write her grocery list. She went
out for several hours then—usually on foot, even
though she had a car at her disposal—but afternoons would find her puttering between family
room and kitchen while Noah did his homework
on the couch. Evenings, she read in one of the
armchairs while Noah watched TV. Sometimes
Mr. Miller watched too—or Joel, as she had to
remind herself to call him—in which case she
retired early with her book. She was a little shy
with Mr. Miller: Joel. This was such an awkward
situation, businesslike and yet at the same time
necessarily intimate. But usually he had meetings
to go to, or he spent the evening at his workbench in the garage. She suspected he felt the

awkwardness too. He couldn't possibly have stayed away so much before she came here.

They liked plain food, plainly prepared—roast beef and broiled chicken and burgers. Noah hated vegetables but was required to eat one spoonful each night. Mr. Miller was probably no fonder of them, but he worked his way conscientiously through everything, and he always told her, "Dinner is delicious, Delia." She suspected he would have said that no matter what she served. He asked her several courteous questions at every meal (had her day gone well? was she finding what she needed?), but she sensed he didn't listen to her answers. This was a sad, sad man underneath, and sometimes even when his own son spoke there was a moment of silence before he pulled himself together to reply.

"Guess what!" Noah might say. "Kenny Moss just got a humongous golden retriever. Dad, can we get a golden retriever?"

Long pause. Clinking of china. Then finally: "There is no such word as 'humongous.' "

"Sure there is, or how come I just used it?"

And the two of them would be off on one of their arguments. Delia had never known anyone as particular about words as Joel Miller. He despised all terms that were trendy (including "trendy" itself). He refused to agree that something was "neat" unless it was, literally, tidy. He interrupted one of Noah's most animated stories with the observation that no one could be "into" mountain climbing. But he always spoke with good humor, which probably explained why Noah still ventured to open his mouth.

Fastened to Delia's bathroom door was a full-length mirror, the first she had faced in six months, outside of a changing booth; and she was startled to see how thin she had grown. Her hipbones were sharp little chips, and the tops of her dresses looked hollow. So she served herself large helpings at these suppers, and she break-fasted with Noah every morning, and she walked to Rick-Rack's each noon to dine on something hefty—even crab cakes, for she was making good money now and had nothing else to spend it on.

Rick also served pork barbecue, the vinegary kind she was partial to, as it turned out. "You know," she told him, "I never had much of a chance to try a real meal here. I knew you were a good cook, but I didn't know *how* good."

"And here you been taking your Sunday dinners at that la-di-da Bay Arms!" he said.

Was there anything about her this whole town didn't know?

After lunch, she crossed the street to pay a visit to George. He was in a snit with her for leaving. He showed up as soon as she let herself in but then turned his back pointedly and stalked off. "George?" she wheedled. No response. He marched into Belle's living room and vanished.

Delia waited in the hall, and a moment later a telltale sprig of whiskers poked around the edge of the door. A nose, an ear, an accusing green eye. "Georgie-boy!" she said. He sidled out, dusting the door with his fur and seeming to hang back even as he drew close enough to let her pat him.

Why couldn't Delia's children miss her this much?

All around town the streets were festooned with bristly silver ropes and honeycombed red tissue bells. There was a wreath above Mrs. Lincoln's desk in the library. Vanessa had tied a red bow to Greggie's stroller.

The thought of spending Christmas with the Millers—poor Noah bearing the full weight of it—filled Delia with dread. But maybe they didn't celebrate Christmas. Maybe they were Jewish, or some kind of fundamentalists who frowned on pagan ritual. It was true that so far, with just a week remaining, they hadn't given a sign they knew what season this was.

Delia went out to the garage to talk to Mr. Miller. "Um, Joel?" she said.

He was measuring a board at his workbench, wearing a raveled black sweater and frayed corduroys. Delia waited for him to look up—it took a minute—and then she said, "I wanted to ask about Christmas."

"Christmas," he said. He reeled in his measuring tape.

"Do you observe it?"

"Well, yes. Normally," he said.

By "normally," he must mean when he still had his wife. This would be their first Christmas without her, after all. Delia watched the thought travel across his face, deepening the lines at either side of his mouth. But he said, "Let's see. Ah, you would get the day off, of course. Noah will be at his mother's, and some friends in Wilmington have been asking me to visit. School is closed through New Year's, so if you need more time in Baltimore—"

"I won't be going to Baltimore."

He stopped speaking.

"I just wondered how you celebrate," she told him. "Do you put up a tree? Should I take Noah shopping for gifts?"

"Gifts."

"Something for his mother, maybe?"

"Oh, God," he said, and he sank onto the high stool behind him. He clamped the top of his head with one large hand—his usual sign of distress. "Yes, certainly for his mother, and also for Nat, Ellie's father. He and Noah are pretty close. And for me, I guess; aren't we supposed to encourage that? And I should get something for him. Oh, God Almighty."

"I'll take him tomorrow," she said. She hadn't intended to plunge the man into despair.

"That's a Saturday. Your weekend."

"I don't mind."

Seated on the stool, Mr. Miller was closer to Delia's eye level. He looked across at her for a moment. He said, "Don't you have any family around? For weekend visits and such?"

"No."

It was a mark of his isolation, she thought, that he had apparently not heard so much as a whisper about her past. For all he knew, Delia had dropped from the sky. Clearly he would have liked to ask more, but in the end he just said, "Well, thanks, Delia. As far as a tree goes, I figure since Noah won't be here for the day itself, we don't need to bother."

Delia would have bothered anyhow, if it had been up to her. But she didn't argue. When she left, Mr. Miller was still slumped on his stool, staring down at the measuring tape in his hands.

She and Noah did all his Christmas shopping at the hardware store—dark, old-fashioned, wooden-floored Brent Hardware, across the street from Belle's. Noah had very definite ideas, Delia discovered. For his mother he chose a screwdriver with interchangeable shafts, because she lived alone now and would need to make her own repairs. For his grandfather, who had trouble bending, a tonglike instrument called a "grabber" that would help him retrieve dropped objects. And for his father, a device to hold a

nail in position while he was hammering it in.
"Dad is all the time banging his thumb," Noah
told Delia. "He's not a real great carpenter."

"What is it that he builds, exactly?" Delia
asked.

"Shadow boxes."

"Shadow boxes?"

For an instant she pictured Charlie Chaplin
shadowboxing in baggy trunks.

"Those, like, partitioned-up wooden shelves.
You know? To hang on a wall?"

"Oh, yes."

"Because my mom collects miniatures. Teeny
little kitchen utensils and furniture and like that,
and he used to make these shadow boxes for her
to keep them in."

And now? Delia wanted to ask.

As if he had read her mind, Noah said, "Now
he just piles them behind the tires in the garage."

"I see."

She couldn't tell from Noah's tone how he felt
about his parents' separation. He had mentioned
his mother only in passing, and this coming visit
would be his first since Delia's arrival.

"I want to pick out one more thing," he told
her. "You go wait outside a minute."

So he was buying her a present too. She wished
he wouldn't. She would have to act appreciative;
she would have to make a big show of putting
whatever it was to use, not to mention the ne-
cessity of buying something for *him* that was nei-

ther more nor less serious than what he'd bought
her. Oh, how had she worked her way back to
this? She should have stayed at Belle's; she'd
known it all along.

But Noah was so gleeful as he hustled her out
the door, she couldn't help smiling.

"Will you need money?" she asked him.

"I've been saving up my allowance."

He closed the door after her and made a comic
shooing motion through the glass.

She waited on the sidewalk, watching the passersby. It was hard to resist getting caught up in
the spirit of things. Everyone carried shopping
bags and brightly wrapped parcels. From Rick-
Rack's Café, next door, the cheering smells of
bacon and hot pancakes drifted into the frosty
air. When Noah rejoined her, hugging his own
bag, she said, "How about I buy you a soda at
Rick-Rack's?"

He hesitated. "You going to put it in the
book?" he asked.

He meant the little notebook Mr. Miller had
given her. She was supposed to keep a record of
reimbursable expenses, and Noah always worried she might shortchange herself. (He viewed
her as someone *less fortunate*, which she found
both amusing and slightly humiliating.) "Today
it's my treat," she told him firmly, and even as
he opened his mouth to protest, she was nudging
him toward the café.

Rick waved a spatula in their direction; he was

busy at the grill. Teensy, though, made a big fuss. "It's Delia! And Mr. Miller's boy. Look, Pop!" she chirped, turning to an old man seated at the counter. "This is Delia Grinstead! She used to live across the street! My father, Mr. Bragg," she told Delia. "He's come to stay with us awhile."

Teensy's father, Delia seemed to recall, was a snarky man who had not behaved very graciously toward his son-in-law; so she was unprepared for his timid, meek expression and wilted posture. He sat up close to his breakfast like a child. When she said, "Hello," he had to work his mouth a minute before the words formed.

"I'm having cocoa," was what he finally said.

"How nice!"

Her voice came out sounding as false as Teensy's had.

"That your boy?" he asked.

"This is . . . Noah," she told him, not bothering with a full explanation.

"Come sit here, boy."

"Oh, we'd better take a booth, with all we're carrying." Delia gestured toward Noah's shopping bag. The handles of his grandfather's grabber extended from it a good two feet.

In the rear corner booth, Mr. Lamb sat hanging his head over a bowl of cereal. Two teenage girls had a window table—Underwood students, Delia assumed, judging by how they perked up at the sight of Noah. (Already she had turned several away from the house, briskly thanking them for their plates of homemade fudge and pretending not to notice how they gazed beyond her for Joel.) One of them sang out, "Hey there, Noah!" Noah rolled his eyes at Delia.

"What can I get you?" Teensy asked, standing over their table.

"Coffee, please," Noah said.

"Coffee!"

"Can't I?" He was addressing Delia. "Dad lets me have it, sometimes on special occasions."

"Well, all right. Make that two," Delia told Teensy.

"Sure thing," Teensy said. Then she bent so close that Delia could smell her starched-fabric scent, and she whispered, "When you leave here, could you say goodbye real loud to Rick, so Pop can hear you?"

"Of course," Delia said.

"Pop can act so hurtful to him sometimes."

"I'd have said goodbye anyhow, you know that."

"I know, but . . ." Teensy flapped a hand toward her father. He still appeared harmless, the X of his suspenders curving with the hunch of his back.

Noah was one of those people who like gloating over their purchases even before they get them home. He was rustling through his bag, first pulling out the screwdriver, then burrowing to the bottom for a furtive look at something there and shooting a tucked, sly glance at Delia. When she craned across the table, pretending to be angling for a peek, he laughed delightedly and crumpled the bag shut again. His two front teeth were still new enough to seem too big for his mouth.

And see how his hair fell over his eyes—the bouncy thickness of it, the soft sheen that made her want to press it with her palm. And the tilt at the tip of his nose, the knobby cluster of little-boy warts that showed on the bend of his index finger when he gripped the mug Teensy brought him. One point of his jacket collar stuck up crookedly. The knit shirt beneath it bore scratches of ballpoint-pen ink. His jeans, she knew, were ripped at the knees, and his sneakers were those elaborate, puffy high-tops that could have been designed for walking on the moon.

He was telling her a dream he'd had—something boring and impossible to follow. His teacher changed into a dog, the dog came to visit at Noah's house, which was somehow the school auditorium too, if Delia knew what he meant . . .

Delia nodded, smiling, smiling, and folded her hands tightly so as not to reach across to him. When they left, she told Rick goodbye with such feeling that her voice broke.

———

Belle claimed the cat had developed an eating disorder. She brought him over in a Grape-Nuts carton late Monday morning, so he could adjust to the house while Delia was the only one home. Still in the carton, he was borne directly to Delia's room and set on the floor. "It's like he's bulimic," Belle was saying. She sank onto the edge of the bed to watch him nose his way out of the carton. "The minute his bowl is half empty he starts nagging me for more; I swear I never knew a cat could plan ahead that way. And if, God forbid, he should finish every bit of it, we have this heartrending melodrama the second I walk in from work. Great yowling and wringing of paws, and as soon as I fill the bowl he staggers over all weak-kneed to eat and makes these disgusting gobbling sounds and then darned if he doesn't throw up in a corner not ten minutes after he's done."

"Oh, George, did I do this to you?" Delia asked him. He was investigating the room now, sniffing daintily at the luggage stand.

"About six times a day he goes to the cupboard and looks up at his sack of kibble, checking to make sure I'm keeping enough in stock."

"All my life," Delia said, "I've been the ideal cat-owner. I lived in one place; I had a routine. I was motionless, in fact. Now I'm flitting about like a . . . He must feel so insecure!"

She bent to stroke the black M on his fore-

head, while Belle gazed around her. "This room
is awfully small, isn't it?" she asked. "Your old
one was a whole lot bigger."

"It's okay." Delia was trying to lure George
into the bathroom now. "See? Your litter box,"
she told him. "Store-bought; not just cardboard."

"What're you doing for Christmas, Dee?"
Belle called after her.

"Oh, staying here."

"Christmas with strangers?"

"They'll be gone, at least for the day."

"That's even worse," Belle told her.

"I'm sort of looking forward to it."

George stepped into the litter box and then
out again, as if demonstrating that he knew what
it was.

"Come along with me to my folks'," Belle told
her. "They'd be thrilled to have you."

"No, really, thanks."

"Or get Vanessa to invite you to her
grandma's."

"She already did, but I said no."

"Well, granted it's kind of hectic there," Belle
said. "I'm a little peeved at Vanessa these days."

"Oh? How come?"

"You know what she had the nerve to ask
me?" Belle stood up to follow Delia into the
hall; they were heading for the bowl of cat food
in the kitchen. George wafted after them in a

shadowy, indecisive way. "I was complaining about my love life," Belle said. "Can't find a man to save my soul, I told her, and she asked why I'd never thought of Mr. Lamb."

"Mr. Lamb!"

"Can you imagine? That dreary, gloomy man, that . . . Eeyore! I said, 'Vanessa, just what sort of idea do you have of me? Do you honestly believe I would date a man who's spent his entire adulthood in rented bedrooms?' I mean, think about it: no one even calls him by his first name, have you noticed? Quick: what's Mr. Lamb's first name?"

"Um . . ."

"Horace," Belle said grimly. She plunked herself at the kitchen table. "I may be single, but I'm not suicidal. What's that I see on the fridge?"

She meant Mr. Miller's map of the household. "It's to keep things in the living room the way Mrs. Miller left them," Delia said. "He's charted all the doodads, exactly where she used to set them out."

Belle leaned forward for a closer look. On the rectangle representing the mantel, tiny block letters spelled *blue vase, pine-cone candle, sandbox photo, clock.*

"Well, that's just pathetic," Belle said. "And why would he need it? What makes him think these things would go and lose themselves, for Lord's sake?"

"You wouldn't ask if you could see him around the house," Delia said. "For someone so set on order, he's awfully . . . discombobulated. He's just plain incompetent! Oh, everything's fine on the surface, but when you look in the back of a cupboard you find pans with scorched bottoms that will never come clean, dish towels with big charred holes in them . . ."

Belle was peering at the diagram of the coffee table. "*Large paperweight, small paperweight, magazines*," she read.

"He keeps these magazines that still come to the house in her name, all about clothing styles and cellulite and such."

"Ellie Miller never had a speck of cellulite in her life," Belle said.

"A new magazine comes, he fits it in the spot where the old one was and throws the old one away."

"That's what you get for worshiping a person," Belle said. "Poor man, he thought she walked on water! In fact, she was kind of silly, but you know how the smartest men will sometimes go so gaga over silly women. I asked him to a picnic after she left, and he said, 'Oh, I'm afraid I wouldn't know anyone; thank you just the same.' This is a high-school principal we're talking about! He ought to know the whole town! But he always depended on Ellie for that. Ellie was real outgoing and social, threw these parties with themes to them like Hawaiian Luau, Wild West Barbecue . . . and a Grade Mothers' Tea in the fall, but Joel hasn't kept that up. He just let the grade mothers flounder this year, when needless to say, every gal in town was dying to help him."

"I wish . . . ," Delia began.

She wished Sam Grinstead had felt like that about her, she'd been going to say. But she stopped herself.

"Oh, I'm sure he'll let *you* help," Belle said, misunderstanding. "You just have to do it inch by inch, you know? Pretty soon, you'll be indispensable."

"Well, yes, of course," Delia agreed.

That much she simply assumed. Already, only ten days into her stay, Mr. Miller had requested another of "her" meat loaves; he had wordlessly laid out a shirt in need of a button; he no longer left his compulsive lists of instructions on the breakfast table.

But wasn't it odd that she had assumed it? She seemed to have changed into someone else—a woman people looked to automatically for sustenance.

The cat wove around her ankles, purring. "See?" Delia told Belle. "He doesn't have an eating disorder. All he ate was a couple of kibbles, just to be polite."

"You're amazing, Dee," Belle said.

Belle had also brought Delia's mail—a package
from Eleanor and a letter from Eliza. Eleanor's
package contained a knitted jacket for reading
in bed. Eliza's letter said she'd invited the Allinghams for Christmas dinner. *I won't press you
but you know you're welcome too,* she wrote,
and then she hurried on to news of Linda. *She
says the twins are getting to the age where they
want to spend the holidays at home, so I guess it
will be just the Allinghams and us and then
Eleanor too of course.* . . . The stationery gave
off that faint scent of cloves (for positive
thoughts) that always hung in the air of Eliza's
bedroom.

Noah was very excited about the cat. He came
straight home from school that day, and he flung
his books any old where and raced through the
house, calling, "George? George?" George, of
course, hid. Delia had to explain to Noah how
cats operated—that you shouldn't pursue them,
shouldn't face them head-on; should do everything at a diagonal, so to speak, with a cat. "Sit
at his level," she said when George finally
showed himself. "Look a little sideways to him.
Talk in a crooning tone of voice."

"Talk? What should I say?"

"Tell him he's beautiful. Cats love the word
'beautiful.' I guess it must be something in your
tone, because they're not the least bit good at

language, but if you draw out that *u* sound long and thin and twangy . . .''

"Bee-yoo-tee-ful," Noah said, and sure enough, George slitted his eyes in a sleek, self-satisfied smile.

On Christmas Eve, Delia picked Noah up at school and drove him to his mother's. The Millers' car was a Volkswagen Beetle. She didn't yet feel completely at home with the stick shift, so it was a rocky ride. Noah was nice enough not to comment. He sat forward and watched for the turnoff to Kellerton. "Most times Mom comes to get me," he said, "but her car's in the shop right now. She's had five wrecks in the last nine months."

"Five!" Delia said.

"None of them were her fault, though."

"I see."

"She's just, like, unlucky. This last time, a guy backed into her while she was looking for a parking spot. Here's where you turn."

Delia signaled and took a right onto a patchy highway that ran between fields of frozen stubble. This countryside was so flat, at least she didn't need to shift gears all that often. They were heading east, in the direction of the beaches. Mr. Miller had told her it was a half-hour drive.

"Tonight at six you want to watch WKMD,"

Noah said. "It's not like I'll be on it or anything, but at least you'll know I'm sitting there in the station."

It must feel eerie to see your absent mother deliver the weather report every night. Although Noah never did, to the best of Delia's knowledge. Six o'clock was *The MacNeil / Lehrer NewsHour*, which Mr. Miller watched instead.

The fields gave way to hamburger joints and used-car lots and liquor stores, implying the approach of a town, but soon Delia realized this *was* the town—this scattering of buildings flung across the farmland. Noah pointed out the television station beneath its Erector-set tower. He showed her where his mother did her grocery shopping and where she got her hair done, and then he directed her two blocks south to a low, beige-brick apartment building. "Should I come in with you?" Delia asked, parking at the curb.

"Naw. I've got a key if she's not there."

Delia was disappointed, but she didn't argue.

"When you wake up tomorrow," Noah told her as she unlocked the trunk, "look on my closet shelf and you'll find your present."

"And when *you* wake up, look in the inside end pocket of your duffel bag."

He grinned and took the bag from her. "So, okay," he said. "See you, I guess."

"Have a good Christmas."

Instead of hugging him, she tousled his hair. She'd been longing to do that anyhow.

By the time she got back to the house, Mr. Miller was waiting at the front window. They barely crossed paths in the doorway—Mr. Miller holding out a palm for the car keys, wishing her a Merry Christmas, saying he'd be back with Noah tomorrow evening—and then he was gone. The cat mewed anxiously and trailed Delia to her room.

On her bureau, she found a Christmas card with a check for a hundred dollars. *Season's Greetings,* the card read, followed by Mr. Miller's block print: *Just a token thank you for setting our lives back in order. Gratefully, Joel and Noah.*

That was nice of him, she thought. Also, he had shown tact in clearing out of the house when he did. It would have been a strain without Noah to serve as buffer.

She spent the afternoon on the couch, reading an extra-thick library book: *Doctor Zhivago.* The wind dashed bits of leaves against the picture windows. George slept curled at her feet. Twilight fell, and her lamp formed a nest of honey-colored light.

A few minutes before six, she took the remote control from the end table and clicked the TV on. WKMD had a one-eyed pirate advertising choice waterfront lots. Then a housewife spraying a room with aerosol. Then a deskful of newscasters—a bearded black man, a pink-faced white man, and a glamorous blonde in a business suit. Delia thought at first the blonde was Ellie Miller, till the black man called her Doris. Doris told about a bank heist in Ocean City. The robber had been dressed as Santa Claus, she said. She spoke in such a way that her lipstick never came in contact with her teeth.

Delia was disconcerted by the speed at which everything moved. She had lost the knack of watching television, it seemed. She felt her eyes had experienced an overload, and during the next round of commercials she looked away for awhile.

"Now here's Ellie with the weather," the bearded man said. "So tell us, Ellie, any chance of a white Christmas?"

"Not a prayer, Dave," Ellie told him in that sporty, bosom-buddy tone that TV people affect. Her face, though, didn't match her voice. It was too soft, too open—a pretty face with a large red mouth, surprised blue eyes, and circlets of pink rouge. Her hair was silvery fluff. Her white sweater, a scoop-necked angora, seemed uncertain around the edges.

Delia rose and went to stand in front of the TV. Ellie slid weather maps along an aluminum groove. Somewhere behind that painted backdrop of marsh and improbable cattails, Noah would be sitting, but at the moment Delia wasn't thinking of Noah. She was memorizing Ellie, trying to see what lay beneath her sky-blue, doll-like stare.

"Continued cold . . . gale-force winds . . ." Delia listened with her head cocked, her fingertips supporting her cheek.

The weather was followed by sports, and Delia turned and wandered out of the family room and through the kitchen, down the hall to the master bedroom. She opened the closet door and studied the clothes hanging inside. Mr. Miller's suits straggled across the rod toward the empty space at the right. The shelf above was empty on the right as well. It appeared that Ellie, unlike Rosemary Bly-Brice, had taken everything with her when she went. Even so, Delia next pulled out each drawer in Ellie's bureau. All she found was a button, trailing a wisp of blue thread.

Back in the family room, the TV was showing the national news. It was months since she had watched the news, but she could see she hadn't missed anything: the planet was still hurtling toward disaster. She switched the TV off in midsentence and went to make her supper.

When she woke the next morning, the sun was out. Something about the hard, bright light told her it was very cold. Also, George lay nestled close under her arm, which he wouldn't do in warmer weather.

Not until she was drinking her tea did she consider the fact that it was Christmas. Christmas, all by herself! She supposed that would strike most people as tragic, but to her the prospect was enjoyable. She liked carrying her cup through the silent house, still wearing her night-gown and beach robe, humming a snatch of "We Three Kings" with no one to hear her. In Noah's room she rooted through the top drawer for a pair of woolen socks to wear as slippers. Then she remembered he'd left her a gift, and she pulled it down from his closet shelf—a squarish shape wrapped in red foil. The tag read, *Because you don't have house-type clothes,* which puzzled her till she tore off the foil and saw a canvas carpenter's apron with pockets across the front. She smiled and slipped the neck strap over her head. Till now she'd been using the cocktail apron she'd found among the dish towels, which protected no more than the laps of her dresses.

Her gift to Noah had been a survival kit from Kemp's Kamping Store. Boys seemed to go for such things. And this kit was so ingenious— hardly bigger than a credit card, with streamlined foldout gadgets, including a magnifying lens for starting fires.

She fed George, and then she dressed and settled on the couch again with *Doctor Zhivago.* Periodically, she looked up from the book and let her eyes travel around the room. Wintry sun-light, almost white, fell across the carpet. The cat was giving himself a bath in a square of sun-light on the blue armchair. Everything had a pleasantly shallow look, like a painting.

At home they must be opening their presents now. It was nothing like the old days, when they used to rise before dawn. Now they ambled downstairs in midmorning, and they passed out presents decorously, one person at a time. Then for dinner they always had goose, a contribution from one of Sam's patients who hunted. For dessert, plum pudding with hard sauce, and they would complain it was too heavy but eat it anyhow and spend the rest of the afternoon moaning and clutching their stomachs.

Every so often it took her breath away to realize how easily her family had accepted her leaving.

Although it *did* seem acceptable, come to think of it. It seemed almost inevitable. Almost . . . foreordained. In retrospect she saw all the events of the past year—her father's death, Sam's illness, Adrian's arrival—as waves that had rolled her forward, one wave after another, closer and closer together. Not sideways, after all, but forward, for now she thought that her move to the Millers' must surely represent some kind of progress.

She had imagined that her holiday would not last nearly long enough, but when Joel and Noah turned into the driveway at dusk, she was already watching at the window. She dropped the curtain as soon as she saw the headlights, and she rushed to open the door and welcome them home.

# 13

Once a week, generally on Wednesday afternoons, Delia drove Noah a few miles west on
Highway 50 to visit his grandfather. The old man
lived in a place called Senior City—four stories
of new red brick on the edge of a marshy golf
course. Delia would pull up in the U-shaped
drive, let Noah out, and leave, maneuvering past
a fleet of gigantic Buicks and Cadillacs. She came
back to collect him at the front door an hour
later. It was an inconvenient length of time, just
slightly too short to make returning to Bay Borough worth her while, and so she formed the
habit of heading for a nearby shopping center.
There she browsed in a bookstore, or picked up
some treat for supper at the gourmet food store.

She was dropping Noah off one Wednesday in
mid-January, when he announced that she
should come in with him. "Me? What for?" she
asked.

"Grandpa wants to see you."

"Well, but . . ."

She glanced down. Beneath her coat she was
wearing a housedress, a dark cotton print she
had bought at an after-Christmas sale. "How
about next week?" she suggested.

"He asked me to bring you today. I forgot."

She pulled into one of the visitors' parking slots. "If you'd warned me, I would have dressed up," she said.

"It's only Grandpa."

"I look a mess! What's his name?"

"Nat."

"I meant his last name," she said, getting out of the car. Years of experience had taught her not to rely on children's formal introductions. "I have to call him Mister *something*."

"Everybody just says Nat."

She gave up and followed Noah past a row of Handicapped license plates. "Does he want to see me for any particular reason?" she asked.

"He says he doesn't know who to picture when I talk about you."

They approached the double doors, which slid open to admit them. The lobby was carpeted with some nubby, hard substance, probably to accommodate wheelchairs. It made a winching sound beneath their feet. On their right was a glassed-in gift shop, and through an entrance at their left Delia glimpsed a cafeteria, deserted at this hour but still giving off that unmistakable steamed-vegetable smell. Several old women waited in front of the elevators. One sat in a motorized cart, and two leaned on walkers. This was like visiting a war zone, Delia thought. But the women were elegantly coiffed and dressed, and at the sight of Noah their faces lit up in smiles. *Valiant* smiles, they seemed to Delia. She was familiar with old people's tribulations, having observed Sam's patients for so long.

The elevator opened to expose a slim, blue-haired old woman in a designer dress. "Sorry!" she caroled. "I'm going down."

"You *are* down, Pooky," the woman on the cart said. "This is the bottom floor."

"Well, you're welcome to come along for the ride, but I've pressed One, I regret to say."

"This *is* One, Pooky."

The others didn't bother to argue. They entered laboriously, most of them clinging to various surfaces for support. Noah and Delia came last. The door closed behind them, and they began rising. Meanwhile everyone beamed at Noah—even Pooky, who seemed unfazed that they were not, in fact, going down. At the second floor, a woman with a shopping bag got off. At the third floor, Noah said, "This is us," and he and Delia stepped into a long corridor. Several women followed, with metallic clanking sounds and a whirring of wheels. Pooky, however, remained on board, gazing contentedly straight ahead as the elevator door slid shut.

"She rides up and down all day sometimes," Noah told Delia.

Nothing here seemed any different from a standard apartment building, except for the handrails that ran along both walls. Blond flush

doors appeared at intervals, each with a peep-
hole at eye level. Noah stopped at the fourth
door on the right. *Nathaniel A. Moffat, Photographer*, a business card read, with a Cambridge,
Maryland, street address crossed out. When
Noah pressed the doorbell, a single golden note
sounded from within.

"Is that my favorite grandson?" a man
shouted.

"Yes, it is," Noah called back.

"It's his *only* grandson," he told Delia with a
giggle.

The door opened, but instead of the old man
Delia had expected, a short, chunky woman
stood smiling at them. She could not have been
out of her thirties. She had a round apricot of a
face and pink-tinted curls, and she wore an orange sweater-dress with a keyhole neckline. Her
shoes were orange too—tiny, open-toed pumps,
as Delia found when she checked, reflexively,
for nurse shoes to explain the woman's presence.
"Hi! I'm Binky," she told Delia. "Hey there,
Noah. Come on in."

The living room they entered must have been
as modern as the rest of the building, but Delia
couldn't see beyond the furniture, which was
dark and tangled, ornate, ponderously antique.
Also, there was far too much of it, set far too
close together, as if it had once filled several
larger rooms. For a moment Delia had trouble

locating Noah's grandfather. He was rising from
the depths of a maroon velvet chair with viny
arms. A four-pronged metal cane stood next to
him, but he moved forward on his own to shake
her hand. "You're Delia," he said. "I'm Nat."

He was one of those men who look better old,
probably, than they ever did young—clipped
white beard, ruddy face, and a lean, energetic
body. He wore a tweed sports coat and gray
trousers. His handshake was muscular and
brisk.

"Thank you for coming," he told her. "I
wanted to get a look at this person my grandson's
so taken with."

"Well, thank you for inviting me."

"Won't you give Binky your coat?"

Delia was about to tell him she would keep
her coat, she could only stay a second; but then
she saw that the table in front of the couch was
laid for tea. There were plates of cakes, four
china cups and saucers, and a teapot already
steeping in a swaddling of ivory linen. Thank
goodness Noah had remembered she was invited.

She handed her coat to Binky and then sat
where Nat indicated, at one end of the couch.
Nat reclaimed his chair, and Noah took a seat
in the little rocker next to him. Binky, when she
returned from the coat closet, settled on the
other end of the couch and bent forward to un-
wrap the teapot.

"Noah always likes mint instead of plain," she told Delia. "I hope you don't mind."

"Not at all."

Noah had this tea party every time he came here, then? Delia had imagined he was, oh, playing checkers or something. She looked over at his grandfather, who nodded gravely.

"Noah's been taking tea with me since the days when he drank from a training mug," he told her. "He's the only boy in the family! We men have to stick together."

Binky handed Delia her cup and said, "So how do you like keeping house for Noah's father, Delia?"

"Oh, very much," Delia said.

"Joel's a good man," Nat said placidly. "I make it a point not to choose sides in my daughters' domestic disputes," he told Delia. "Back when they were wee little girls, I swore an oath to myself I would approve of whoever they married."

Enough of a pause hung after his words so that Delia felt pushed to ask, "And do you?"

"Oh, absolutely," he said. His chuckle, filtered through his beard, had a wheezy sound. "I love my sons-in-law to death! And they think I'm just wonderful."

"Well, you *are* wonderful," Binky told him staunchly.

He bowed from the waist. "Thank you, madam."

"Maybe not quite as wonderful as they imagine, mind you . . ."

He grimaced at her, and she gave Delia a mischievous wink.

Was this Binky a paid companion? Was she one of the daughters? But her merry face bore no resemblance to Nat's. And she didn't seem all that connected to his grandson. "Have some butter," she was telling Noah, not noticing he had nothing to put it on.

"Have some low-cholesterol vegetable-oil spread," Nat corrected her. "First I wolf down my I Can't Believe It's Not Butter," he told Delia, "and then I go wash my hair in Gee, Your Hair Smells Terrific."

Delia found this remark mystifying, but Noah tittered. His grandfather glanced over at him; his lips twitched as if he were trying not to smile. Then he turned back to Delia. "You're from Baltimore, I hear."

"Yes," she said.

"Got family there?"

"Some."

He raised his eyebrows, but she offered nothing further.

"Ninety percent of the people in this building come from Baltimore," he said finally.

"They do?"

"Rich folks, retiring to the Eastern Shore. Roland Park and Guilford folks."

Delia kept her face blank, giving no sign she had ever heard of Roland Park or Guilford.

"You surely don't suppose all those chichi ladies are locals," he said. "Lord, no. I wouldn't be here myself if I hadn't married a Murray. That's Murray as in Murray Crab Spice. You think a two-bit, hole-in-the-wall photographer could afford these exorbitant prices?"

"They're going to raise the rates again in July, I hear," Binky told him.

Delia was looking around the room. The mention of photography had alerted her to the pictures hanging everywhere—large black-and-white photos, professionally framed. "Are these your work?" she asked him.

"These? If only."

He stood, this time reaching for his cane. "These were taken by the masters," he said, stumping over to a study of a voluptuous green pepper. "Edward Weston, Margaret Bourke-White . . ." He pivoted to inspect the picture at his left—factory chimneys, lined up like notes of music. "Me, I photographed brides," he said. "Forty-two years of brides. Few golden-anniversary couples thrown in from time to time. Then I started getting my, what I call, flashbacks." He gave a downward jab with his beard. Delia thought at first he was indicating the rug. "Old boyhood polio came bouncing back on me," he said. "Thelma—that was my wife—

she'd passed on by then, but she had put our names on the waiting list when they first drew up the plans for Senior City. Just why, I couldn't tell you, since she refused to budge from our big old house long after the girls were grown and gone. She always said, what if they wanted to come back for any reason? And come back they did, you know they did: all four of them rushing home at every minor crisis, just because of the very fact they had a home to rush to, if you want my honest opinion. 'Lord God, Thel,' I told her, 'we can't be rearing those girls for all time! Look at how cats do,' I told her. 'Raise up their kittens, wean them, don't know who the hell they are when they meet them in the alley a few months later. You think humans should be any different?' "

"Well, of course they should!" Binky protested, and she and Delia exchanged a smile.

But Nat hissed derisively behind his beard. "Hogwash," he told Noah. Noah merely licked a dab of frosting from his thumb. "In any event," Nat said, "I started getting these flashbacks. Times the one leg would clean give out on me, along about the end of day. Reached the point where I barely made it up the stairs some nights; I knew I couldn't go on living where I was. So I phoned the people here and said, 'Listen,' I said, 'didn't my wife put our names on your waiting list once upon a time?' And that's how I happened to end up in Senior City. Senior City: God. Abominable name."

"It seems very . . . well-organized, though," Delia said.

"Precisely. Organized. That's the word!" He spun around (there was something explosive, barely contained, about even his most painful movements) and returned to his chair. "Like files in a filing cabinet," he said, reseating himself by degrees. "We're organized on the vertical. Feebler we get, higher up we live. Floor below this one is the hale-and-hearty. Some people there go to work still, or clip their coupons or whatever it is they do; use the golf course and the Ping-Pong tables, travel south for Christmas. This floor here is for the moderately, er, challenged. Those of us who need wheelchair-height counters or perhaps a little help coping. Fourth floor is total care. Nurses, beds with railings . . . Everybody hopes to die before they're sent to Four."

"Oh, they do not!" Binky said indignantly. "It's lovely up on Four! Have a cupcake, Noah."

" 'Lovely' isn't the word that first comes to *my* mind," Nat told Delia. "Not that I don't applaud Senior City in theory, understand. It's certainly preferable to burdening your children. But something about the whole setup strikes me as uncomfortably, shall we say, symbolic. See, I've always pictured life as one of those ladders you find on playground sliding boards—a sort of ladder of years where you climb higher and higher, and then, *oops!,* you fall over the edge and others move up behind you. I keep asking myself: couldn't Thelma have found us a place with a few more levels to it?"

Delia laughed, and Nat sat back in his chair and grinned at her. "Well," he said, "don't let me ramble on. I'm glad we finally got to meet you, Delia. Noah's told me how much you've done for the two of them."

She recognized her cue. "It was good to meet you too," she said, rising.

"From now on, stop in and have tea whenever you come for Noah, why don't you?"

"I'll do that," she promised.

She slid her arms into the coat Binky held for her, and Noah wrangled his jacket on. "Drive carefully, now," Binky said as she opened the door. Her keyhole neckline showed a teardrop of plump, powdered pink, bisected by the tight crevice between her breasts. Was it that, or was it the memory of Nat's roguish grin, that made Delia wonder suddenly whether Binky might in fact be his girlfriend?

Joel told her he had no idea who Binky was. He hadn't realized she existed, even. "Binky? Binky who?" he asked. "What kind of a name is Binky?"

They were eating supper in the kitchen, just the two of them. Noah had accepted a last-minute invitation to the Mosses'. At first Delia had contrived to be on her feet most of the time, but finally Joel said, "Sit down, Delia," in a kindly tone that made her feel he'd seen straight through her. "Tell me how you think Noah's doing," he said.

That took about three seconds. (Noah was doing fine.) Then they had to find a new topic, and so Delia thought to mention Binky.

"How old is she, would you guess?" Joel asked.

"Oh, thirty-five, thirty-six . . ."

"So: too young to be a fellow resident. And I doubt Nat needs a nurse. What did Noah say about her?"

"He said she's just 'around.' I asked who she was, and he said, 'I don't know; someone who's just around a lot.' "

"Hmm."

"Well, anyhow," Delia said. "It's really none of my business. I can't think why I brought it up."

But then she remembered why, because they were back to an uneasy silence.

"His wife was a paragon of virtue," Joel said

while he was helping himself to another roll. "Noah's grandma, that is."

"Oh, really?"

"To hear *her* tell it."

"Oh."

"I never could abide that woman. Always interfering. Nudging into our lives. Inquiring after the welfare of her gifts. 'Do you ever use the such and such?' 'How come I never see you in the so-and-so?' "

Delia laughed.

"So if this Binky is his mistress," Joel said—the bald, bold word giving Delia a slight shock—"I say more power to him. He deserves a little happiness."

"Well, I didn't mean—"

"Why not? He's only sixty-seven. If it weren't for those damn flashbacks, he'd be out sailing his boat still."

Delia hadn't known that Nat sailed, but she could easily picture it: his spiky figure all over the deck, everywhere at once.

"She liked to say she was 'there' for people," Joel was reminiscing. He must be on the subject of Noah's grandma again. "First person I ever heard say that, though Lord knows it's grown common enough since. 'I'm always *there* for my daughters,' " he mocked. "You want to ask, 'Where's that, exactly?' It's one of my least favorite terms."

Delia hoped she hadn't used it herself. She was fairly sure she had not.

"That and 'survivor,' " Joel said. "Well, unless it's meant in the literal sense."

"Survivor?"

"Nowadays you're a survivor if all you did was make it through childhood."

"Ah."

"And another word I hate is . . ."

It was lucky he held so many strong opinions. Delia wouldn't need to make conversation after all. Instead, she sat watching his mouth, that long, firm, fine-edged mouth with the distinctive notch at the center of the upper lip, and she reflected that for someone so absorbed in questions of language, he certainly didn't reveal very much.

Now when she went to the gourmet food store after dropping Noah off on Wednesday afternoons, she chose some additional item—sour French cornichons, hot-pepper jelly—and paid for it with her own money and brought it to tea at Nat's. "How did you guess I like such things?" Nat would ask. "Most people come with chocolates. Fruit preserves. Sweet stuff."

She didn't tell him it was because her father, too, had been fond of pickly foods, for something gallant and slightly flirtatious in Nat's manner suggested he didn't view himself as all that old.

Often he poked fun at Senior City, as if to prove
he didn't really belong there. "House of the Living Dead," he called it. He claimed to believe
that the seagulls drifting above the building were
vultures, and he spoke jocularly of the "poor
dears" on floor Four. And then there was his
romance with Binky.

For Binky *was* his girlfriend; Delia couldn't
doubt that. Three times Delia arrived for tea and
found her perched on his couch, playing hostess.
And the fourth time, when she was missing, Nat
found it necessary to explain that she'd been
called away at the last minute. Her son had
chipped a tooth, he said.

"Binky has a son?" Delia asked.

"Two sons, in fact."

"I didn't know that."

"So Noah has been doing the honors today."

Delia settled on the couch, laying her coat over
the arm. She watched Noah pour an unsteady
stream of tea.

"I didn't even know she was married," she
said.

She chose her words carefully; she didn't say
*had been* married, because it could be that Binky
was married still. And Nat's response left her
none the wiser. "Oh, yes," was all he said. "To
a dentist."

Inspired, she said, "Well, then, the chipped
tooth should be no problem."

"Correct," Nat said. He sent her a glint of a look from under his tufted gray eyebrows. Then he relented. "Assuming she doesn't mind flying her son to an office in Wyoming."

"Oh."

"They're divorced."

"Oh, I see."

"*Bitterly* divorced," Nat said with some relish. "Months in court, lawyers and replacement lawyers, forty thousand dollars spent to win five thousand . . . you get the picture."

"I'm sorry to hear that."

"She ended up almost penniless, had to take a job in the Senior City gift shop."

"She works in the gift shop?"

"Well, for now."

He glanced over at Noah, who was passing around a plate of brownies at a perilous tilt. "Fact is," Nat said, "Binky and I are getting married."

Noah let the plate tilt more sharply. Delia said, "Oh! Congratulations," and bent to pick a brownie off the rug.

"Honest?" Noah asked his grandfather.

"Honest. But don't mention it to the girls yet, will you? I should have told your mom and your aunts before anyone."

"So then will you move out of here?" Noah asked.

"Afraid not, son." Nat turned to Delia. "Noah liked my old place better," he said.

"The old place had this real cool tree house out back," Noah told her.

"However, it did not have an elevator. Or a handgrip above the bathtub. Or a physical-therapy room for ancient codgers."

"You're not an ancient codger!" Noah said.

"Plus there's the little detail of my contract with Senior City," Nat told Delia. "Bit of a problem with the board of directors, as you might imagine. All my life savings are sunk in this apartment, but the minimum age of entrance is sixty-five. Binky's thirty-eight."

"And how about her sons?" Delia asked.

"Yes, that *would* have been a poser! Rock music in the cafeteria, skateboards down the halls . . . However, her sons will stay on with her parents. One is already in college, and the other's about to go. But even so, the board is having hissy fits, and then a few neighbors are mad at me too, because men are mighty scarce in these parts. Plan was, I would marry one of the residents, not some luscious babe in the gift shop."

"Well, I think you've made the perfect choice," Delia said.

She meant it, too. She had developed a liking for Binky, who edged all their conversations with a ruffle of admiring murmurs and encouraging remarks.

So when Delia stopped by the following week,

she made a point of telling Binky that Nat was a lucky man.

"Well, thank you," Binky said, beaming.

"Have you set a date yet?"

"We've talked about maybe June."

"Or March," Nat amended.

Binky rounded her eyes comically at Delia. March was right around the corner; they were halfway through February. "He has no idea what goes into these things," she said.

"Oh, are you planning a big wedding?"

"Well, not *that* big, but . . . My first wedding, I eloped. I was a freshman at Washington College and wore what I'd worn to class that day. So this time I'd like all the trimmings."

"I'm going to be best man," Noah told Delia.

"You are!"

"I get to hold the ring."

"You'll come too, won't you, Delia?" Nat asked.

"If I'm invited, of course I will."

"Oh, you'll be invited, all right," Binky said, and she patted Delia's hand and gave her a dimpled smile.

But later, riding home, Noah told Delia that Binky had been crying when he got there.

"Crying! What about?"

"I don't know, but her eyes were all red. She pretended she was fine, but I could tell. And then when she was in the kitchen the phone rang and Grandpa shouted out, 'Don't answer that!' and she didn't. And he didn't either, just let it ring and ring. So finally I said, 'Want me to get it?' but he said, 'Nah, never mind.' Said, 'It's probably just Dudi.' "

"Who's Dudi?"

"One of my aunts."

"Oh." Delia thought that over. "But why wouldn't he talk to her?"

He shrugged. "Beats me," he said. "You want to watch your speedometer, Delia."

"Thanks," Delia said.

She'd been issued two tickets in the last three weeks. It was something to do with this open country, she believed. The speed just seemed to inch up on her, and before she knew it she was flying.

Back in Bay Borough, Joel was already home and waiting to hear the latest. He took a rather gleeful interest in Nat's wedding plans. "Noah's going to be best man," Delia told him as she hung up her coat.

"No kidding!" He turned to Noah. "Where are you throwing the stag party?"

"Stag party?"

"Have you thought out your toasts yet?"

"Toasts!"

"Don't you pay any attention," Delia told Noah. He was looking worried.

It occurred to her that she was bound to run

into Ellie at the wedding. Scandalous that they hadn't met before; Delia was in charge of Ellie's son. What kind of mother entrusted her son to a stranger?

A couple of weeks before, passing through Nat's bedroom to use his bathroom, Delia had noticed a color photo of his daughters on the highboy. At least she assumed they were all his daughters—Ellie and three other blondes, linking arms and laughing. Ellie was the most vivid, the one you looked at first. She wore a cream dress splashed with strawberries that matched her strawberry mouth. Her shoes, though, were not very flattering. They were ballerina flats, *black* ballerina flats, papery and klutzy. They showed the bulges of her toes. They made her ankles look thick.

Why did Delia find this so gratifying? She had nothing against Ellie; she didn't even know her. But she bent closer to the photo and spent several moments hunting other flaws. Not that she found them. And not that she would have occasion, anyhow, to point them out to Joel.

# 14

On a Friday morning at the tail end of February—a day so mild and sunny that she would have supposed spring was here, if she hadn't known the tricky ways of winter—Delia walked to the Young Mister Shop to exchange some pajamas for Noah. (She had bought him a pair like an Orioles uniform, not realizing that for some strange reason, Noah preferred the Phillies.) And then, because it felt so pleasant to be out in nothing heavier than a sweater, she decided to walk to the library and visit with Mrs. Lincoln awhile. So she cut across the square and started up West Street. At the florist's window she slowed to admire a pot of paper-whites, and at Mr. Pomfret's window she slid her eyes sideways to check out his new secretary. Rumor had it he was limping along with a niece of his wife's who couldn't even type, let alone run a computer. But the way the light hit the glass, Delia would have had to step closer to see inside. All she could make out was her own silhouette and another just behind, both ivy-patterned from the sprawling new plant the niece must have set on the sill. Delia increased her speed and crossed George Street.

The window display in the Pinchpenny was little girls' dresses this week; so now the two silhouettes were made up of rosebud prints and plaids. She noticed that the second silhouette was storky and gangling, mostly joints, like an adolescent boy. Like Carroll.

She turned, and there he was. He looked even more startled than she felt, if that was possible. His expression froze and he drew back sharply, hands thrust into his windbreaker pockets, elbows jutting.

She said, "Carroll?"

"What."

"Oh, *Carroll*!" she cried, and the feeling that swept through her was so wrenching, like the grip of some deep, internal fist, that she understood for the first time how terribly much she had missed him. His face might have been her own face, not because it resembled hers (although it did), but because she had absorbed its every detail over the past fifteen years—the sprinkle of starry freckles across his delicate nose, the way the shadows beneath his eyes would darken at fraught moments. (Right now they were almost purple.) He raised his chin defiantly, and so at the very last second she merely reached out to lay a hand on his arm instead of kissing him. She said, "I'm so happy to see you! How'd you get here?"

"I had a ride."

She had forgotten that his voice had changed.

She had to adjust all over again. "And what are you doing on West Street?" she asked.

"I tried your boardinghouse first, but no one answered, and then I happened to see you crossing the square."

He must not have told the family he was coming, therefore. (She had sent Eliza her new address weeks ago.) She said, "Is something wrong at home? Are you all right? It's a school day!"

"Everything's fine," he said.

He was trying, unobtrusively, to step out from under her hand. He was darting embarrassed glances at passersby. Much as she hated to, she let go of him. She said, "Well, let's . . . would you like some lunch?"

"Lunch? I just had breakfast."

Yes, it was morning still, wasn't it. She felt dizzy and disoriented, almost drunk. "A Coke or something, then," she said.

"Okay."

Turning him in the direction of Rick-Rack's gave her an excuse to touch him again. She loved that hard tendon at the inside crook of his arm. Oh, she might have known it would be Carroll who finally came for her! (Her most attached child, when all was said and done—her most loving, her closest. Although she would probably have thought the same if it had been either of the other two.)

"There's so much you have to bring me up-to-date on," she told him. "How's tenth grade?"

He shrugged.

"Has your father had any more chest pains?"

"Not that I know of."

"Ramsay and Susie all right?"

"Sure."

*Then what is it?* she wanted to ask, but she didn't. Already she was falling back into the veiled, duplicitous manner required for teenage offspring. She led him west on George Street, very nearly holding her breath. "Is Ramsay still seeing that divorcée person? That Velma?" she said.

Another shrug. Obviously, he was.

"And how about Susie?"

"How about her."

"Has she figured out yet what she'll do after graduation?"

"Huh?" he said, looking toward a Bon Jovi poster in the record store.

He was as frustrating as ever, and he hadn't lost that habit of ostentatiously holding back a yawn each time he spoke. She forced herself to be patient. She steered him past Shearson Liquors, past Brent Hardware, and through the door of Rick-Rack's.

"Dee-babe!" Rick hailed her, lowering his copy of *Sports Illustrated*. She would have known from his greeting alone that his father-in-law was sitting at the counter. (Rick always put on a display for Mr. Bragg.) "Who's that you got with you?" he asked.

"This is my son Carroll." She told Carroll, "This is Rick Rackley."

"Hey, your son!" Rick said. "How about that!"

Carroll looked dazed. Delia felt a prickle of annoyance. Couldn't he at least act civil? "Let's sit in a booth," she said brusquely.

Teensy was nowhere in sight, so Delia took it upon herself to grab two menus from the pile on a stool. As soon as they were seated, she passed one to Carroll. "I know it's early," she said, "but you might want to try the pork barbecue sandwich. It's the North Carolina kind, not a bit sweet or—"

"Mom," Carroll whispered.

"What."

"Mom. Is that *Rick*-Rack?"

"What?"

"Rick Rackley, the football player?"

"Well, yes, I think so."

Carroll gaped at Rick, who was topping off his father-in-law's mug of coffee. He turned back to Delia and whispered, "You know Rick-Rack in person? Rick-Rack knows you?"

This was working out better than she could have hoped. She said, "Yes, certainly," in an airy tone, and then, showing off, she called, "Where's Teensy got to, Rick?"

"She's over at House of Hair," he said, setting the coffeepot back on the burner. "You-all going to have to shout your order direct to me."

"Well, is it too early to ask for pork barbecue?"

"Naw, we can do that," Rick said.

Carroll said, "I just had breakfast, Mom. I told you."

"Yes, but this is something you wouldn't want to miss," she said. "Not a drop of tomato sauce! And it comes with really good french fries and homemade coleslaw!"

She didn't know why she was making such a fuss about it. Carroll was clearly not hungry; he was still staring at Rick. But she called, "Two platters, please, Rick, and two large Cokes."

"You got it."

Mr. Bragg spun his stool around so he could study them. His thin white crew cut stood erect, giving him the look of someone flabbergasted. "Why!" he cried. "What's happened with this *boy*?"

Delia glanced toward Carroll in alarm.

"How'd he shoot up so fast?" Mr. Bragg asked. "How'd he get so big all at once?"

She wondered if the old man had somehow read her mind, but then he said, "Last Christmas he was only yea tall," and he set a palm down around the level of his shins.

"Oh," Delia said. "No, that's Noah you're thinking of."

It was common knowledge by now that Mr. Bragg was failing, which was why poor Rick and Teensy couldn't send him back wherever he came from.

"Who's Noah?" was his next question.

"Who's Noah?" Carroll echoed.

"Just the boy who . . ." She felt rattled, as if she had been caught in some disloyalty. "Just the son of my employer," she said. "So! Carroll. Tell me all that's been going on at home. Has the Casserole Harem descended? Lots of apple pies streaming in?"

"You haven't asked about Aunt Liza," Carroll told her.

"Eliza? Is she all right?"

"Well. All *right*, I guess," he said.

"What is that supposed to mean? Is she sick?"

"No, she's not sick."

"Last Christmas you were just a shrimp," Mr. Bragg called. "You and her were drinking coffee together, tee-heeing over the presents you'd bought."

"Eliza *is* still taking care of the house, isn't she?" Delia persevered.

But Carroll seemed distracted by Mr. Bragg. He said, "Who's he talking about?"

"I told you: my employer's son."

"Is that why you've got that bag with you? 'Tasteful Clothing for the Discerning Young

Man'? You buy this kid clothes? You tee-hee together? And what's that you're wearing, for God's sake?"

Delia looked down. She wasn't wearing anything odd—just her Miss Grinstead cardigan and the navy print housedress. "Wearing?" she said.

"You're so, like, *ensconced*."

Two plates appeared before them, clattering against the Formica. "Ketchup, anyone?" Rick asked.

"No, thanks." She told Carroll, "Honey, I—"

"*I* would like ketchup," Carroll announced belligerently.

"Oh. Sorry. Yes, please, Rick."

Carroll said, "Have you forgotten you have a son who puts ketchup on his french fries?"

"Honey, believe me," she said, "I would never forget. Well, maybe about the ketchup, but never about—"

A plastic squirt bottle arrived, along with their Cokes in tall paper cups. "Thank you, Rick," she said.

She waited till he had left again, and then she reached across the table and touched Carroll's hand. His knuckles were grained like leather. His lips were chapped. There was something too concrete about him; she was accustomed to the misty, soft-edged Carroll of her daydreams.

"I would never forget I have children," she told him.

"Right. That's why you sashayed off down the beach and didn't once look back at them."

Someone said, "Delia?"

She started. Two teenage girls stood over their table—Kim Brewster and Marietta something. Schwartz? Schmidt? (She brought Joel home-made fudge so sweet it zinged through your temples.) "Well! Hello there!" Delia said.

"You won't tell Mr. Miller you saw us here, will you?" Kim asked. Kim was one of Delia's remedial pupils; lately, Delia had been volunteering as a math tutor over at the school. "He would kill us if he found out!"

"We're cutting class," Marietta put in. "We saw you in here and we figured we'd ask: you know how Mr. Miller's birthday is coming up."

Delia hadn't known, but she nodded. Anything to get rid of them.

"So a bunch of us are chipping in on a present, and we thought you might could tell us what to buy him."

"Oh! Well . . ."

"I mean, you know him better than anyone. He doesn't smoke, does he? Seems like a lot of gifts for guys are smokers' stuff."

"He doesn't smoke, no," Delia said.

"Not even a pipe?"

"Not even a pipe."

"He's always so, you know, distinguished and all, we think he'd look great with a pipe. Maybe we should just get him one anyways."

"No, I really think he would hate that," Delia said firmly. "Well! It was good seeing you girls."

But Kim was studying Carroll now from beneath her long silky lashes. "*You* don't go to Old Underwear," she informed him.

Carroll flushed and said, "Underwear?"

"Our high school: Dorothy Underwood," she said, snapping her gum. "You must be from out of town."

"Yeah."

"I knew we hadn't seen you around."

Delia started eating her coleslaw; she felt it would be a kindness not to look at Carroll's face. But Carroll just picked up the ketchup and squirted it thoroughly and methodically over every single one of his french fries. "Well . . . ," Kim said at last, and the two of them moved on toward an empty booth, trailing crumbs of remarks behind them. "Thanks anyhow, Dee . . . ," they said, and, "If you think of something . . ."

Delia took a sip of Coke.

"So who's the guy?" Carroll asked, setting down the ketchup with a thump.

Confused, she glanced around the café.

"The guy with the pipe, Mom. The oh-so-distinguished guy that you know so extremely-emely well."

"Oh," she said. She laughed, not quite naturally. "It's nothing like that! He's my boss."

"Right."

He pushed his plate away. "It all fits together now," he said. "No wonder you weren't home for Labor Day."

"Labor Day?"

"Dad said you'd be back by then, but I guess it's pretty clear now why you weren't."

She stared at him. "Dad said I'd be back by Labor Day?"

"He said you just needed some time to yourself and you'd come home at the end of the summer. We were counting on it. He promised. Susie thought we should go get you, but he said, 'No,' he said, 'leave her be. I guarantee she'll be here for our Labor Day picnic,' he said. And look what happened: you went back on your word."

"*My* word!" Delia cried. "That was *his* word! I didn't have a thing to do with it! And what right was it of his, I'd like to know? Who is he to guarantee when I'll be home?"

"Now, Mom," Carroll said in an undertone. He glanced furtively toward Rick. "Let's not make a big thing of this, okay? Try and calm down."

"Don't you tell me to calm down!" she cried, and at the same time she caught herself wondering exactly how often she had uttered that sentence before. *Don't you tell me to calm down!* And, *I am completely cool and collected.* But to Sam; not to Carroll. Oh, it all came back to her now: that sense of being the wrong one, the flighty, unstable, excitable one. (And the more she protested, of course, the more excitable she appeared.) She gripped the edge of the table with both hands and said, "I am completely cool and collected."

"Well, fine," Carroll told her. "I'm glad to hear it." And he picked up a red-soaked french fry and threaded it into his mouth with elaborate indifference.

*I'm glad to hear it* was one of Sam's favorite responses. Along with *If you say so, Dee,* and *Have it your way.* After which he might serenely turn a page, or he would start talking with the boys about some unrelated subject. Always so sure he was right; and the fact was, he *was* right, generally. When he criticized people she liked, she would suddenly notice their faults; and when he criticized Delia, she saw herself all at once as the foolish little whiffet he believed her to be. Like now, for instance: he had promised she would slink home by summer's end, and the picture of that humbled return was so convincing that she almost felt it had happened. She couldn't even *desert* properly! Had only been off in a pout, anyhow. Just needed to get it out of her system.

Although, in fact, she had not slunk home. Not by summer's end and not afterward. Not to this day. She had actually made a life for herself in a town Sam had nothing to do with.

So when Belle sailed in, calling, "Hey, Dee,

I *thought* that was you I saw," Delia made a point of rising to give her a flamboyant hug.

"Belle!" she cried, and Belle (her purple-clad figure a luxurious, pillowy armful) had the grace to hug her back.

"Who's your new fella?" she asked.

"This is my son Carroll. This is Belle Flint," she told Carroll. She kept an arm around Belle's waist. "How're you *doing*, Belle?"

"Well, you're never going to guess what, not in a million years."

"What?" Delia asked, a little too enthusiastically.

"Swear you won't tell Vanessa, now. This is just between the two of us."

But the whole demonstration went for nothing, because just then Carroll stood up and pushed his way out of the booth. "So long," he mumbled, head down.

"Carroll?"

She dropped her arm from Belle's waist.

"Tomorrow night," Belle was saying, "I've asked Horace Lamb to the movies."

Horace Lamb? Delia felt an inner hitch of surprise even as she went hurrying after Carroll. He lunged out the café door. "Carroll, honey!" she called.

On the sidewalk, Teensy was mincing toward them beneath a gigantic new busby of exploding red ringlets. Carroll almost ran her down.

Teensy said, "Oh!" and took a step back, reaching up to feel for her hairdo as if she feared it might have toppled off. "Delia, tell me the truth," she said. "Do you honestly think I look silly?"

"Not a bit," Delia told her. "Carroll, wait!"

Carroll wheeled, his eyebrows beetling. "Never mind me, just tend to your pals!" he said. "Orphan Annie here and Mr. Distinguished and little Tee-hee Boy and Veranda or whoever . . ."

*Vanessa*, Delia almost corrected him, while behind her, Teensy asked, "Delia? Is everything all right?" and Belle, in the doorway, said, "Kids. But that's just how they are, I guess."

"I *was* going to do you a favor," Carroll said.

"What, honey?"

"I *was* going to tip you off to what's going on at home, but never mind. Just never mind now," he said.

Still, he didn't turn and leave. He seemed to be suspended, teetering on the squeaky rubber soles of his gym shoes. Cannily, Delia came no closer. She stayed six or eight feet away from him, her face a mask of smoothness. "What's going on at home?" she asked him.

"Oh, nothing. Not a thing! Except that your own blood sister is making a play for your husband," he said.

"Eliza?"

"And Dad's so out of it, he just laughs it off

when we tell him. But *we've* all noticed, me and
Susie and Ramsay notice plain as day, and we
can guess how it's going to end up, we bet, too.''

"Eliza would never do that," Delia said, but
she was trying out the notion even as she spoke.
She cast her mind back to the living-room couch,
the row of marriageable maidens. *Whenever I
hear the word "summer," I smell this sort of melting smell.* And now it seemed that Sam sent Eliza
a quick, alert, appreciative glance, as he had not
done in real life. It wasn't impossible, Delia saw.

But she told Carroll, "You must be imagining
things."

"Oh, what do *you* care?" Carroll burst out,
and he spun around again and started running
toward West Street.

"Carroll, don't go!"

She followed at a fast walk. (How far could
he get, after all?) He crossed George Street,
halting briefly for a mail truck, and disappeared
around the corner. Delia picked up her pace. On
West Street she saw him loping south, passing
Mr. Pomfret, who stood in front of his office
speaking with a UPS man. She raced by Mr.
Pomfret herself, with her face averted; the last
thing she needed just now was another acquaintance calling out her name. She lost sight of Carroll for an instant and then spotted him near the
florist's. He was jogging up and down on the
curb as he waited for a break in the traffic. Ev-

idently he was headed for the square. Good: they could sit on a bench together. Catch their breath. Talk this over.

But once he'd crossed the street, he stopped at one of the cars parked along the perimeter. A gray car, a Plymouth. *Her* Plymouth. With Ramsay at the wheel. She recognized his dear, blocky profile. Carroll opened the passenger door and got in. The engine ground to life, and the car swung out into traffic.

Even then she might have run after them. They were forced to drive very slowly at first. But she stayed where she was, brought up short on the sidewalk with one hand pressed to her throat.

Ramsay had been right here in town. He had driven all these miles and then not bothered to visit her. Susie too, perhaps, although Delia had glimpsed only two heads in the Plymouth.

She deserved this, of course. There was no denying that.

She turned and retraced her steps to Rick-Rack's, all but feeling her way.

An enormous amount had happened to her, but when she reached the café Belle and Teensy were still talking out front, Kim and Marietta were blowing sultry ribbons of cigarette smoke inside, and Rick was tucking her lunch bill under the ketchup container. She counted out her money in slow motion and paid, not forgetting to leave a tip on the table. She gathered her purse and her Young Mister bag and walked out the door, through the scorched, chemical smell of Teensy's hairdo, through the clack and tumble of Belle's chatter. "Have you ever noticed," Belle was saying, "that Horace Lamb looks the eentsiest little bit like Abraham Lincoln?"

At the corner, Delia turned south. The clock in the optician's window read eleven-fifteen—nowhere near time for lunch, and yet she regretted leaving that barbecue sandwich. And the coleslaw had been superb. It was the creamy kind, with lots of celery seeds. A seed or two still lodged in her mouth, woodsy and fragrant when she bit down. She savored the taste on her tongue. She felt the most amazing hunger, all at once. She felt absolutely hollow. You would think she hadn't eaten in months.

# 15

For a short while after Carroll's visit, half a dozen spots around town seemed haunted by his presence. Here was the ivy-filled window where he had first appeared, here the booth at Rick-Rack's where he'd sat, here Belle's front porch where he must have spent several minutes waiting for someone to answer the door. (Had he noticed the scaly paint? The hammocking of the floorboards under his tread?) In Delia's memory he seemed not surly now but sad, his porcupine behavior merely a sign of hurt feelings. She should have taken him with her when she left, she thought. Except that then she would have had to take Susie and Ramsay too. Otherwise it would have looked like favoritism. She saw herself striding down the coastline with her retinue—the two boys' ropy wrists in her grasp, Susie scurrying to keep up. *Where we going, Mom? Hush, don't ask; we're running away from home.*

Although her children had been partly what she was running from, as it happened.

Then she reflected that after all, Carroll had not appeared ruined by her leaving. He had survived just fine, and so had his brother and sister. And she remembered Nat's philosophy: we ought to forget our grown offspring as easily as cats forget theirs. She smiled to herself. Well, maybe not *quite* as easily.

Still, wasn't it true that over the past several years, her children had turned into semistrangers—at last even her youngest? That not only had she lost her central importance to them but they, in fact, had become just a bit less overwhelmingly all-important to her?

She sat stone still, staring into space, wondering how long ago she had first begun to know that.

Then, having watched her children slip free, she turned to what remained: her husband.

If he really did remain.

In her mind's eye he sat at the breakfast table while Eliza poured his coffee. Eliza wore her tan safari dress and even a bit of rouge. She was not unattractive, from certain angles. She had that smooth, yellowish skin that didn't go all fragile with age, and the rouge turned her dark eyes bright and snappy. She would insinuate herself into Sam's routine, take over his charts and bills, provide him with hot meals and a seamlessly organized household. "Why, thanks, Eliza," Sam would say feelingly. Men were so gullible sometimes! And he had more in common with Eliza than you might suspect. Granted, Eliza claimed she was living life over and over again until she got it right, while Sam said that for his part, he meant to get it right the first time. But both of them did assume that "getting it right" was possible. Delia herself had more or less given up trying.

Besides which, there was the fact that Eliza was Delia's sister. She had Delia's small, neat bone structure and her phenomenally sound teeth, her tendency to get out of hand after eating any sugar, her habit of letting her sentences trail away unfinished. Loving Eliza would come as naturally to Sam as appreciating a song he had already heard once before.

Delia felt an impulse to jump in the car and tear off to Baltimore, but she knew how trite that was—to want a man back the instant she learned he was wanted by someone else. She made herself sit still. *This is what you asked for,* she told herself.

This other woman's maimed husband and child, this too new ranch house with its walls that thunked like cardboard when you rapped them, this thin town propped on a countryside as flat and pale as paper.

Before dawn one morning, she came sharply awake, perhaps disturbed by a dream, although no fragments of it lingered. She lay in bed recalling, for some reason, the first dinner party

she'd given after she and Sam were married. He
had wanted to invite two of his old classmates,
along with their wives. For days she had pored
over possible menus. She had refused her sisters'
offers of help; she had extracted her family's
promise not to show their faces during the evening. It was essential that she prove she was a
grown-up. And yet from the moment the first
couple arrived, she had felt herself sinking back
into childhood. "Hey, Grin," the husband had
said to Sam. Grin! Would she ever feel so com-
radely as to call Sam that herself? she had wondered, twisting her skirt. "Hi, Joe," Sam had
said. "Delia, I'd like you to meet Joe and Amy
Guggles." Delia had not been informed of their
last name ahead of time, and in fact had never
heard the name Guggles in all her life. It had
struck her as funny, and she'd started laughing.
She slid into helpless cascades of laughter, her
breath dissolving in squeaks, her eyes streaming
tears, her cheeks beginning to ache. It was like
being in sixth grade again. She laughed herself
boneless, while the couple watched her with
kindly concern and Sam kept saying, "Delia?
Honey?"

"I'm sorry," she had told them, when finally
sheer embarrassment had sobered her. "I'm so
sorry, really I can't think what—"

At which point, the second couple arrived.
"Why, here you are!" Sam had cried in relief.

"Hon, these are my oldest friends, Frank and Mia Mewmew."

Oh, Lord.

But Sam had been very understanding. After the party, he had drawn her into his arms and told her, speaking warmly into the curls on top of her head, that these things could happen to anyone.

How young he'd been, back then! But Delia hadn't realized. To her he had seemed fully formed, immune to doubt, this unassailably self-possessed man who had all but arrived on a white horse to save her from eternal daughterhood. Around his eyes faint puckers were already evident, and she had found them both appealing and alarming. *If he dies first I don't want to go on living,* she had thought. *I'll find something in Daddy's office cabinet that's deadly poison.* In those days, she could say such things, not having had the children yet. She used to picture all sorts of catastrophes, in those days. Well, later too, to be honest. Oh, she'd always been a fearful kind of person, full of hunches and forebodings. But look what happened: the night of his chest pains, she hadn't felt the slightest premonition. She had sat there reading *Lucinda's Lover,* dumb as a post. Then the phone rang.

Although the news had not come as a shock, certainly. Listening to the nurse's diplomatic wording, she had thought, *Ah, yes, of course,* while a dank, heavy sense of confirmation had solidified inside her. *First Daddy, and now Sam.* He would die and they would bury him in Cow Hill Cemetery and he would lie there alone till Delia crept up to join him, as on those nights when she stayed awake watching some silly movie and then climbed the stairs afterward and slipped between the covers and laid one arm lightly across his chest while he went on sleeping.

She sat against her headboard, jostling the cat, and switched on the clock radio. They were playing jazz, at this hour. Lots of lonesome clarinets and plinkety-plonk pianos, and after every piece the announcer stated the place it was recorded and the date. A New York bar on an August night in 1955. A hotel in Chicago, New Year's Eve, 1949. Delia wondered how humans could bear to live in a world where the passage of time held so much power.

Nat and Binky were not going to have a June wedding after all. They moved the date up to a Saturday in March. Nat said he had exercised his seniority. "I used your basic how-much-longer-have-I-got approach," he confided to Noah and Delia. "Your take-pity-on-an-old-geezer approach."

Binky adapted cheerfully to the change in plans. "This way," she told Delia, "I'm Mrs. Nathaniel Moffat three months sooner, that's all.

So what if we skimp some on the frills? They're not such a very big deal." The two of them were alone in Nat's kitchen when she said this, leafing through cookbooks. (The wedding cake was one of the frills she was skimping on.) "And I do mean to be Mrs. Moffat," she said. "None of this 'Ms.' business for me! He's the first man I've ever known who's just totally, totally loved me." Then the skin around her eyes grew pink, as if she might start crying, and she turned quickly back to her cookbook.

"In that case, you ought to marry him this instant," Delia said.

"Well, I wish his daughters agreed," Binky said. "You heard Dudi cut all her hair off."

"Cut her hair off?"

"Threw a tantrum when Nat announced our engagement; ran into his bathroom, grabbed up these little scissors he trims his beard with and cut every bit of her hair off."

"Goodness," Delia said.

"And Pat and Donna refuse to come to the wedding, and when I asked Ellie to be an attendant—purely out of niceness; I've already got my sister and my nieces—she said maybe she wasn't coming either, she couldn't be sure, she might or might not, so she'd better say no. Then she went and told Nat he ought to have his lawyer draw up a prenuptial agreement. I guess they all think I'm some kind of . . . gold digger. It doesn't

occur to them what an insult that is to their father, not to believe a woman might love him for
his own self."

"They're just a little surprised," Delia said.
"They'll get over it."

Binky shook her head, smoothing a cookbook
page with her palm. "They phone him and the
very first thing, 'Is *she* around?' they ask. 'She,'
they call me; they never use my name if they can
help it. They hardly ever come to visit. Donna
says it's because I'm always here. She says I don't
allow them any time alone with him, but I try
to; it's just that—"

She broke off, blushing, and Delia wondered
why until Binky mumbled the end of her sentence. "I do sort of, kind of like, live here now,"
she said.

"Well, of course," Delia hastened to say.
"What do they expect?"

"Oh, well, I didn't start out to bore you with
all my troubles," Binky said. "You know why I
like to talk to you, Delia? You never interrupt
with *your* experiences. No wonder you're so
popular!"

"I'm so popular?"

"Don't be modest. Noah's told us how you're
friends with half of Bay Borough."

"Good grief! I hardly know anyone," Delia
said.

Although she was startled to see how her

friends did add up, now that she stopped to count.

"You're not just marking time while I'm speaking," Binky said. "Not jiggling your foot till you get a chance to jump in with your life history."

"Well, it isn't as if there's a whole lot I could jump in with," Delia told her.

Last week at supper, Joel had asked what part of Baltimore Delia hailed from. "Oh," she had said, "here and there," and he had dropped the subject—or so she'd thought. But a minute later he had said, "Strange, isn't it? A person who doesn't discuss her past is automatically assumed to *have* a past, I mean more of a past than usual, something rich and exotic."

"Is that right," she had said neutrally. It had struck her as an interesting theory; she had considered it until, noticing the silence, she looked up and found his eyes on her. "What?" she had asked.

"Oh, nothing."

Then Noah had reached between them for the salt—a disruptive swoop, a lunge forward on two legs of his chair—and the moment had passed.

Driving to the wedding, Delia kept glancing in the rearview mirror. She was afraid she might have put on too much makeup. "What do you think of my lipstick?" she asked Noah.

"It's okay," he said without looking.

He had worries of his own. Periodically he wriggled his fingers between the buttons of his winter jacket, checking for the ring in his shirt pocket.

"Are you sure it's not too heavy?" she asked him.

"Hmm?"

"My lipstick, Noah."

"Nah, it's okay."

"*You* look nice," she said.

"Well, I don't know why I had to get so dressed up."

"Dressed up! You call a shirt and no tie dressed up!"

"I look like one of those yo-yos who sing in the school chorus."

"You should just be thankful Nat didn't make you buy a suit," she told him.

"And what if I drop the ring? You know my hand will shake. I'll drop the ring and it will clink real loud and roll across the floor and fall into one of those grate things, *clang-ang-ang!* and we'll never get it back again."

"I wish I had a fancier outfit," Delia said. "I look like an old-maid aunt or something." Under her coat she was wearing her gray pinstripe. "Or at least a necklace or a locket or a string of beads."

"You're okay."

In her jewelry box back in Baltimore was a four-strand pearl choker. Fake, of course, but it would have been perfect with the pinstripe.

How long before she could say that her Baltimore things would have gone out of fashion anyway, or fallen apart or been used up even if she'd stayed? When would the things she had here become her *real* things?

She flicked her turn signal and swerved onto Highway 50. "U-u-urch!" Noah squealed, grabbing his door handle.

"Sorry." She slowed. "So," she said. "I guess I get to meet your mother, finally."

"Yup."

"She did decide to come, didn't she?"

"Last I heard she did."

Recently, Delia had found the *Boardwalk Bulletin* profile buried in the back of Noah's closet. (*Who's the gorgeous new weather wench on WKMD?* the article began.) But to look at Noah now, you wouldn't guess he spared his mother a thought. He was yawning and gazing out his window at the remains of last week's freak snowstorm. The woods were a scrawl of black against white, like an arty photograph.

*A snow warning or a hurricane watch can be a matter of life and death,* Ellie had told her interviewer. *It gives me a lot of warm fuzzies to know I'm making a contribution to my community.*

Delia wondered what Joel would have said about "warm fuzzies."

The red-brick cube of Senior City rose before them. Delia signaled and turned into the parking lot. "What if they want me to make a speech?" Noah was asking.

"You won't have to make a speech."

"Or what if somebody faints or something? I'm supposed to assist."

"Believe me," Delia said, "this will be a breeze."

They got out of the car and crossed the lot, which was not as well plowed as it might have been. Delia, who didn't own boots, had to hang on to Noah's arm as they picked their way around icy spots. "See?" she told him. "Already you're assisting!"

His arm was thin but fiercely strong, like a band of steel.

In the lobby, they asked an old man the way to the chapel. "Straight ahead, then left at the end of the hall," he said. "You must be going to the wedding."

They nodded.

"Well, I'll be along directly; wouldn't miss it. Everyone in the building's been invited, you know."

Delia thanked him, and they proceeded down the hall. Passing the elevators, with their gleaming metal doors, she checked her reflection. It seemed to her she looked pale and draggled, her coat a dreary, wilted shape clinging too low on her shins.

*Clothes are my biggest weakness,* Ellie had told *Boardwalk Bulletin. But luckily my figure's the kind that everything hangs really well on, so I don't have to spend a fortune to look good.*

At the end of the hall they turned left and entered the side door of a small chapel, carpeted wall to wall in beige and lined with sleek beige pews. Already the pews were nearly filled with elderly women and three or four widely spaced men. Most of the women wore stylish dresses; a few wore bathrobes. Several people in wheel-chairs formed an extra row at the rear. Delia and Noah stood gazing about until a dark young boy in a suit approached and offered Delia his arm. "We're seating everyone helter-skelter," he told her. "Wherever we can find room."

"Well, Noah here won't need a seat. He's the best man."

"Hey there, Noah. I'm Peter. Son of the bride," the boy said. He had not inherited Binky's small, pursed features or her rosy col-oring; just her easy manner of talking to people. He told Noah, "You're supposed to go through that door up front. Your grandpa's already waiting."

Noah sent Delia one last imploring glance, and she grinned at him and brushed his hair off his forehead. "Good luck," she said.

Then she let Peter escort her to one of the few

remaining seats, between a woman in a brown-
and-white dress and an old man fiddling with his
hearing aid. The old man had the aisle seat and
merely moved his bony knees to one side so she
could get past. It was the woman who helped
her out of her coat. "Isn't this exciting?" she
asked Delia. She had a freckled, finely wrinkled
face lit with a gracious expression, and a crimp
of orange-sherbet hair that must once have been
red. "It's our very first Senior City wedding! We
don't count Paul and Ginny Mellors; they
eloped. Are you a relation?"

"Just a friend."

"The board is in a tizzy, I can tell you. They
want to charge Binky higher rates because she's
underage. Otherwise the young folks will be
*flooding* in, they claim, on account of our security and our managed health care. My name's
Aileen, by the way."

"I'm Delia."

"It's nice to meet you, Delia. What I say is,
hell's bells, Binky's such a lambie-pie I think we
ought to pay *her*! She'll be a huge addition to
our Sunday Socials."

Just then, Ellie appeared at the side entrance.

Delia knew her immediately—the tinsel hair,
the pulpy red mouth. She wore a long, cream-
colored coat just one shade off from her skin,
and she stood poised, looking somehow stiller
than ordinary women, until an usher ap-

proached. This was not Peter but his brother, evidently—someone equally dark but more stockily built. Ellie took his arm and walked toward the front, the hem of her coat swaying classily. Where would she find a seat, though? All the pews were jam-packed. The usher seemed to be informing her of this; she listened, pooching her lips and frowning. They were crossing in front of the pulpit now. On the other side, several people—mostly kitchen staff, in aprons—lined the wall, and Ellie was deposited in their midst. What a pity, Delia thought, that the one daughter who'd shown up should have to stand!

But no, another daughter was here as well—a wan, wraithlike woman who rose from her seat and edged past a row of knees to join Ellie. The second woman had fair hair too, but it was cut so brutally short that in places it seemed scraped off her skull. Behind cupped fingers, she whispered something to Ellie. Then they both turned and looked straight at Delia.

Guiltily, Delia lowered her eyes. She should have smiled at the two of them, but instead she pretended to be absorbed in conversation with Aileen. "That's Mary Lou Simms playing the organ," Aileen was saying. Delia hadn't noticed there *was* an organ, but now she heard a wispy rendition of "Blessed Assurance." From the old man on her right came a piercing whistle, something to do with his hearing aid. "Oh, and there's Reverend Merrill," Aileen said. "Isn't he striking?"

Reverend Merrill was not all that striking in Delia's opinion, but he wore his black robe with a certain flair. He strode toward the pulpit, swinging a Bible in one hand. Behind him came Nat and Noah. Nat held himself rigidly erect; he was doing without his cane today. Noah was getting so tall, Delia realized. Now that he took his position next to Nat, she could see how he had shot up, just in the few months she'd known him.

The organ slithered into the "Wedding March." Everyone looked toward the rear.

First came a stouter, plainer version of Binky—the matron of honor, in a wide blue gown, with square-cut gray hair and a broad, pleasant face. Then Binky herself, in white. She looked lovely. She was carrying pink roses and beaming joyously as she floated down the aisle. Her two nieces, as bulky as their mother, plodded behind with fistfuls of her train.

"Oh, what a vision!" Aileen said. "Did you ever see anything sweeter?" Delia's other seatmate was gnawing open a blister pack of batteries. Over by the wall, Ellie's white face blazed fixedly, but it didn't seem to be Binky she was watching.

The bridal procession reached the front, and Nat, proudly stern, gave Binky his arm and turned toward the minister.

It was a very brief ceremony—just the vows and the exchange of rings. Noah did fine. He produced the ring on cue, and he didn't drop it. But all of this Delia observed with only part of her attention, while with another part—her tensed, wary, innermost part—she was conscious every moment of Ellie Miller's unwavering stare in her direction.

All the guests were invited to Nat's apartment afterward—anybody who wanted to come. There was a great press of frail bodies milling out of the chapel. Delia offered support to arms as withered and soft as day-old balloons. She packed mothball-smelling woolens into elevators, and then, upstairs, she settled more women than she would have thought possible onto the swampy cushions of Nat's couch. They were all looking forward to Binky's cake. It seemed they *preferred* homemade, and were glad she hadn't had time to order the towering pagoda she had dreamed of. "We get store-bought in the cafeteria all the time," one woman told Delia. "Sent over from Brinhart's Bakery. Tastes like Band-Aids."

Delia looked for Ellie but didn't see her, or Dudi either. Although in this crush, people were easily missed.

She threaded her way toward Binky, who was cutting squares of sheet cake, with her train looped over her arm. "Do you think it went all right?" Binky asked. Her headpiece of pink roses slanted toward one ear like a rakish halo.

"It went perfectly," Delia said. She started distributing the cake. Nat, meanwhile, was pouring champagne, which he sent around with Binky's two sons and her nieces. They ran out of stemware and had to open a pack of disposable tumblers.

When everyone was served, Nat proposed a toast. "To my beautiful, beautiful bride," he said, and he made a little speech about how life was not a straight line—either downward or upward, either one—but something more irregular, a zigzag or a corkscrew or sometimes a scribble. "And sometimes," he said, "you get to what you thought was the end and you find it's a whole new beginning." He raised his glass toward Binky, and his eyes were suspiciously shiny.

One of the women on the couch said Binky must have grated her own lemon zest. "I can always tell fresh-grated zest," she said. "It's no use trying to substitute that brown dust that comes in bottles." She licked crumbs off her fork in a contemplative way. Her face had gone past merely old to that stage where it seemed formed of disintegrating particles, without a single clear demarcation. Did there come a point, Delia wondered, after you'd outlived every one of your friends, when you began to believe you might be the first to escape death altogether?

She relieved Binky of her cake knife and cut more slices, which she carried around on a platter in case people wanted seconds. In the bedroom, a young woman in a nurse's white pantsuit was holding forth on various hospitals, referring familiarly to "Saint Joe" and "Holy Trin" while a circle of residents listened spellbound. Two men were playing chess in a corner; one of them asked Delia if he could take an extra piece of cake for his wife on Floor Four. Aileen, Delia's former seatmate, was nodding and smiling as a fur-stoled woman described other weddings she'd been to. "And then Lois: *she* was a lucky one! Married a man with all his major appliances, including convection oven."

Noah walked in with a glass of champagne, which he tried to hide when he saw Delia. "Give me that," she ordered.

"Aw, Delia."

She took it from him and set it on a passing tray. "By the way," she said, "where's your mother?"

"I don't know."

"She didn't come upstairs?"

He shrugged. "I guess she must have had other stuff to do," he said. Then he turned on his heel and left the room before she could comment— not that she would have been so tactless.

Binky's sister, the bearer of the tray, tut-tutted. "I saw her walk out directly after the vows," she said. "Her and her sister both. Doo-doo, is that what they call her?"

"Dudi."

"All this brouhaha about *his* family's reaction! How about ours? We could have said plenty, trust me: marrying a man old enough to be her father."

"Well," Delia said, "I'm just glad she and Nat found each other."

"Yes, I suppose," the sister said, sighing.

Then Nat popped up at Delia's elbow. "Have you met my sister-in-law?" he asked her. "Bernice, my new sister-in-law. Can you imagine someone my age getting a brand-new sister-in-law?" He was exultant, his voice unsteady, his face so firm-skinned and glowing that he looked like a *pretend* old man made up for a high-school play. If he'd noticed his daughters' disappearance, it hadn't dampened his happiness.

During the drive home, Delia told Noah she thought his mother was very pretty. In fact, this was not strictly true. She had decided Ellie had a garish quality; the high contrast of her coloring went over better on TV than in person. But she wanted an excuse to mention her. All Noah said in response was, "Yeah," and he drummed his fingers and looked out the side window.

"And you looked mighty handsome up there, too," she said.

"Oh, sure."

"You don't believe me? Just watch," she teased him. "The next wedding you're in might very well be your own."

But he didn't so much as smile. "Fat chance," he said.

"What—you're not getting married?"

"Me and Dad have blown it with women," he said glumly. "There must be something about them we don't understand."

In other circumstances, she might have been amused, but now she felt touched. She glanced at him. He went on staring out the window. Finally she reached over and gave him a pat on the knee, and they rode the rest of the way without speaking.

# 16

"If $x$ is the age Jenny is now, and $y$ is the age she was when she went to California . . . ," Delia said.

T. J. Renfro put his head on the kitchen table.

"Now, T.J., this is not so hard! See, we know that she was three years older than the girlfriend she was visiting in California, and we know that when her girlfriend was—"

"This is not going to do me one bit of good in real life," T.J. informed her in a smothered voice.

He had the kind of haircut that seemed half finished—medium length on top but trailing long black oily strands in back. Both of his upper arms were braceleted with barbed-wire tattoos, and his black leather vest bore more zippers than you'd find in most people's entire wardrobes. Unlike Delia's other pupils, who met with her in the counseling room over at the high school, T.J. came to the house. He had been suspended till May 1 and was not allowed to set foot on school property; showed up instead at the Millers' back door every Thursday afternoon at three o'clock. Delia didn't want to know what he'd been suspended for.

She told him, "Real life is full of problems like this! Finding the unknown quantity: there's lots of times you'll need to do that."

"Like I'm really going to walk up to some chick and ask how old she is," T.J. said, raising his head, "and she's going to say, 'Well, ten years ago I was twice the age my third cousin was when . . .' "

"Oh, now, you're missing the point," Delia said.

"And how come this Jenny would visit someone three years younger anyway? That don't make sense."

The phone rang, and Delia rose to answer it.

"She probably just *claimed* she was visiting, and then hid out in some motel with her boyfriend," T.J. said.

Delia lifted the receiver. "Hello?"

Silence.

"Hello!"

Whoever it was hung up. "That's happened a lot lately," Delia said, hanging up herself. She returned to her chair.

"It's electrical backwash," T.J. told her.

"Backwash?"

"If you don't use your line awhile, it, like, develops all this pent-up power that spills out in this kind of like overflow and sets your phone to ringing."

Delia cocked her head.

"Happens at my mom's house once or twice a week," T.J. told her.

"Well, here it's been happening more on the order of once or twice a day," Delia said.

The phone rang again. She said, "See?"

"Just don't answer."

"It *kills* me not to answer."

He tipped back in his chair and studied her. The phone gave a third ring, a fourth. Then the outside door burst open and Noah tumbled in, bringing along a gust of fresh air. "Hey, T.J.," he said. He shed his school knapsack and picked up the receiver. "Hello?"

In the pause that followed, T.J. and Delia watched him closely.

"Naw, I don't guess I can," Noah said. He turned away from them. "I just can't, that's all." Another pause. "It's nothing like that, honest! Just I got all this homework and stuff. Well, I better go now. Bye." He hung up.

"Who was that?" Delia asked.

"Nobody."

He slung his knapsack over one shoulder and walked off toward his room.

T.J. and Delia looked at each other.

The next afternoon, a cool, sunny Friday, Delia went with Vanessa to a knitwear sale at Young

Mister. Spring would be arriving any minute now, and Noah had outgrown all last spring's clothes. It was an excruciatingly slow trip, because Greggie was in the midst of his terrible twos and refused to ride in his stroller. He had to walk every inch of the way. Delia felt she had never seen Bay Borough in such detail—every plastic cup lid wheeling along the sidewalk, every sparrow pecking tinfoil in the gutter. They didn't start heading back until nearly three o'clock. "Oh-oh," Delia said, "look at the time. Noah will be home before I am."

"Isn't he going to his mother's?" Vanessa asked.

"Not this week."

"I thought he went every Friday."

"Well, I guess something must have come up."

They had reached the corner where they separated, and Delia said, "Bye, Greggie. Bye, Vanessa."

"So long, Dee," Vanessa said. "Let's ask Belle if she wants to get together over the weekend."

"Fine with me."

Belle was saving all her weekends for Mr. Lamb these days, but Delia had been ordered to keep that a secret.

At the grade school, children were already pouring onto the playground. Delia didn't try to find Noah, though. She knew he'd want to walk home with his friends. She sidestepped a runaway skateboard, smiled at a little girl collecting scattered papers, and politely ignored a mother and son quarreling next to their car.

But wait. The son was Noah. The mother was Ellie.

Wearing her cream-colored coat from the wedding but looking frazzled and disordered, Ellie was trying to wrestle Noah into the passenger seat. And Noah was pulling away from her, his jacket wrenched halfway off his arms. "Mom," he kept saying. "Mom. Stop."

Delia said, "Noah?"

They threw her an identical distracted stare and went on with their tussle. Ellie started mashing Noah's head down the way policemen did on TV, guiding their handcuffed suspects into squad cars.

"What's happening here?" Delia asked. She made a grab for Ellie's wrist. "Let go of him!"

Ellie flung her off so violently that she knocked Delia in the face; her sharp-stoned ring grazed Delia's forehead. Noah, meanwhile, managed to yank himself free. He stumbled several steps backward and adjusted his jacket. His knapsack was gaping open and spilling papers. (*Those* were the papers the little girl was collecting!) He wiped his fist across his nose and said, "Gee, Mom."

Ellie stood straighter, breathing harshly, glaring at him.

Reverently, the little girl presented Noah with his papers. He took them without looking at them. Now Delia saw that two of his friends were loitering nearby—Kenny Moss and a second boy, whose name she couldn't remember. They were watching but pretending not to, kicking the sidewalk. The other children, passing in groups, seemed unaware that anything was wrong.

"I just wanted you to come visit! Like always! Just a normal Friday visit!" Ellie cried. "Is that too much to ask?" She turned to Delia. "Is that so—?"

Something stopped her. Her mouth fell open.

Noah said, "Gosh!" He was staring at Delia's forehead. "Delia! Golly! You're all bloody!"

Delia raised her fingers to her forehead. They came away bright red. But she didn't feel much pain—only the least little sting at that spot in her temple where the pulse beat. She said, "Oh, it's nothing. I'll just go home and—"

But Noah's eyes were huge, and Kenny Moss said, "Holy moley!" and gripped the other boy's sleeve, and the little girl said, in an informative tone, "I pass out if I see blood."

She did seem about to pass out—her lips had an ashy pallor—and so Delia, attending to first things first, said crisply, "Don't look, then." She herself wasn't dizzy in the slightest. This was plainly one of those wounds that appear much worse than they are. However, she was concerned about her clothes. "Somewhere here . . . ," she said, hunting through her purse for a tissue. Her Young Mister bag hindered her, and she passed it to Noah, leaving sticky red fingerprints across the scrunched top. "I know I must have a—"

Soft, blossomy mounds of tissue were thrust under her chin—an offering from Ellie. "I am so, so sorry," she was saying. "It was an accident! Believe me, Delia, I never meant to harm you."

"Well, I know that," Delia said, accepting the tissues. She found it oddly flattering that Ellie called her by name. She pressed the tissues to her temple, and her pulse began to throb.

"Oh, God, we have to get you to a doctor," Ellie said.

"I don't need a doctor; goodness."

"You're no judge of that! You're not in your right mind," Ellie said. Although it was Ellie who seemed unhinged, thrusting more handfuls of tissues at her (did she carry them loose in her pockets, or what?) and shrilly ordering the others about. "Move! Give us room. Noah, you ride in back; we'll put Delia up in front."

"Isn't there a school nurse or something? Why don't we look for the nurse?" Delia asked.

But Ellie said, "You don't want to end up with a scar, do you? An ugly, disfiguring scar?"

Which was something to consider; so Delia allowed herself to be shepherded toward the front seat. Noah, who had folded the seat forward so he could climb into the rear, straightened it for Delia. When she was settled, he leaned over her shoulder to offer her a gray sweatshirt from his knapsack. "Here," he said. "You're going through those hankies like a spigot."

She would have argued (blood was so hard to launder), but it was true she had used up the tissues. She pressed the sweatshirt to her forehead and breathed in its smell of clean sweat and gym shoes. Meanwhile Ellie slid behind the wheel and started the engine. "You'll probably need stitches," she said, pulling into traffic. "Oh, lately it seems everything I touch goes galloping off in every direction! Leaves me staring after it amazed!"

"I know exactly what you mean," Delia told her. She took a peek from under the sweatshirt. Up close, Ellie seemed more likable. Her lipstick was worn to a tired outline, and her eyes sagged slightly at the outer corners.

"I'm not myself these days," Ellie said. "You hear people say that all the time, but up till now I'd assumed it was a figure of speech. Now I stand off to one side looking at myself like a whole other person, and I ask, 'What could she be *thinking* of?' "

They turned left, onto Weber Street. Delia folded the sweatshirt to a new section. She was beginning to understand why you often saw red roses planted near gray stone walls. The blood-stains looked so vivid against the sweatshirt fabric, she would have liked to show the others. But Ellie was still talking away. "I admit it was me who walked out on the marriage," she said. (Delia replayed the last few sentences, wondering if she had missed some key transition.) "You don't have to remind me! I started picturing how I'd get to heaven and God would say, 'Such a waste; I sent you into the world and you didn't even make use of it, just sat there in one spot complaining you were bored.' So I walked out. But when I saw you at the wedding, when I saw how—well, I guess I thought you'd be older and fatter and wearing a zip-front dress or something. I know I made a scene, phoning Joel like I did. . . ."

Ellie had phoned Joel?

"In fact I watched myself dialing, and I said, 'What a dumb thing to do!' But I went right on doing it. And I'd planned to be Madam Iceberg. 'I've been thinking, Joel,' I'd say. 'Perhaps you should grant me custody, now you've got a female companion.' But I guess he told you how it came out. I hear his voice, I'm like a woman possessed. 'How dare you do this to Noah! Exposing an innocent child to that tawdry little love nest you've set up!' "

Love nest! Delia was thrilled.

"And if that wasn't bad enough, then I go and drag Noah in too. I'm sorry, honey!" Ellie said, addressing the rearview mirror. But she didn't wait for Noah's reaction. "And you know how heartless kids can be. The minute you show you're upset, they pretend you don't exist. They stare right through you. They make up all these excuses why they can't come and visit you."

"Mom," Noah said.

Delia was curious to hear how he would handle this, but all he said was, "Mom, you just passed Dr. Norman's."

"Yes, I know," Ellie said. They were on Border Street now, heading toward Highway 380. "Every morning I'd wake up saying, 'Today I'll get ahold of myself. I'll just put it out of my mind,' I'd say, but there you were, regardless: this mystery woman no one knew a thing about, the very type Joel would fall for. I bet you speak perfect English too, don't you?"

"You have it all wrong," Delia said, much as she hated to. "It's not the way you—"

But Ellie was turning north on 380, and Noah broke in to ask, "Mom? Where you going?"

"There are scads of doctors in Easton," Ellie said.

"Easton!" Noah and Delia said together.

"Well, you surely don't think we could use Dr. Norman. He's right there in town! Anybody in town will believe I did this on purpose."

"Can't we just tell him you didn't?" Delia asked.

"Ha! You don't know Bay Borough like I do. People there make a scandal out of the simplest little trifle."

"Maybe a drugstore, then," Delia said. She was beginning to feel uneasy. "All I need is a bandage."

"Oh, Delia, Delia, Delia," Ellie said. "You are so naive. Sure as you live, the pharmacist would be some Underwood graduate who couldn't wait to get on the phone and start blabbing. 'Guess what!' " she mimicked. " 'Mr. Miller's demented wife tried to murder his girlfriend.' "

"I'm not his—"

"I bet *you* never say 'share,' do you?"

"Share?"

"As in communicate. As in, 'So-and-so shared his feelings with me.' Joel used to gnash his teeth when I said that. And he had this thing about putting in the objects of my verbs. 'Enjoy *what*?' he'd ask me. Or, 'Take care of *whom*? Where's the end of your sentence, Ellie?' "

Delia watched a field of dead autos slide past. In back, Noah was silent.

"Funny how men always worry ahead of time that marriage might confine them," Ellie said. "Women don't give it a thought. It's afterwards it hits them. Stuck for life! Imprisoned! Trapped forever with a man who won't let you say 'parenting.' "

She braked; they had reached the stoplight at Highway 50. While they waited for it to turn green, she started digging through her purse. "Do you have any cash?" she asked Delia. "I don't want to pay with a check. Even over in Easton, my name might ring a bell."

She was crazy, Delia decided. So far she had been able to see Ellie's side of things—had sympathized, even. But now she had a sense of panic. And besides that, her cut was starting to hurt. She imagined she could actually feel its widening mouth, the edges hardening into a permanent scar.

They would have to make a run for it, as soon as she could safely snatch Noah out of the back. Maybe when they got to the doctor's. *If* they got to the doctor's; for here they sat, on and on, at this eternal red light. "Green light, green light," she urged. She leaned forward, as if that would hurry things.

Ellie, misunderstanding, said, "Oh, sorry," and took her foot off the brake. They zoomed onto Highway 50, and an oil truck, horn blaring wildly, swerved around them and careened down the wrong side of the road. Ellie screamed. Delia was too terrified to scream. They veered onto the shoulder and bounced over a stretch of dry grass before coming to a stop.

"I thought you said the light was green!" Ellie shrieked.

"I only meant—oh, Lord," Delia said. She turned to check on Noah. "Are you all right?" she asked him.

He swallowed and then nodded.

Surreptitiously, in a movement that might have been oiled, Delia felt for her door handle. She gave it a smooth nudge downward and let the door inch open. Then she shouted, "Out, Noah! Quick!" and sprang from the car, at the same time slamming her seat forward so Noah could follow. He did, luckily. He had good reflexes. He landed almost on top of her, because she happened to step directly into some kind of hole or ditch concealed by the flattened grass. Her right ankle twisted beneath her and Noah came bruising into her shoulder, and of course she still had the sweatshirt pressed to the wound on her head, but at least they were safe.

Ellie, meanwhile, had opened her own door, causing yet another truck to honk as it passed. The bleat of the horn traveled straight through Delia's chest. All at once her heart caved in, as if only now receiving word of the danger. Why, they had run a red light! Whizzed into high-speed traffic without a glance in either direction! Her skin began to tingle with the memory of it. She imagined that her outermost surface had actually been brushed by their near miss.

"We could have been killed!" she cried, and Ellie, rushing toward her, called, "I know! I can't believe we're still alive!" She flung her arms around Delia and Noah. Noah said, "Mom," and struggled free, but Delia hugged her back. Both women were slightly teary. Ellie kept saying, "Oh, God, oh, God," and laughing and dabbing her eyes.

"Mom," Noah said again, from the sidelines. "Can we just go to Dr. Norman, please?"

"We'll tell him I bumped my head," Delia said. "He won't think a thing about it."

"Well, you're right," Ellie said. "We'll do that. Come on, if I can get up the nerve to drive again."

So they all climbed back in the car, which turned out to be a Plymouth, just a year or two newer than Delia's Plymouth; and Ellie waited till there wasn't another vehicle in sight before inching out onto the highway and executing a U-turn. Not until they were traveling back down 380 did she venture to speak, even; she was so intent on her driving. Then she asked Noah what he planned to tell his father.

Noah let a long pause develop, but finally he said, "Same thing we tell Dr. Norman, I guess. You gave us a ride home from school? Delia banged her head some way?"

"I knocked against the car door as I got in," Delia suggested.

"Oh, good," Ellie said, and her hands relaxed on the wheel.

Most likely it was Delia she had been worrying about. She must have known that Noah wouldn't tattle; he had that disconcertingly cold, stoic secretiveness you often see in children of troubled marriages.

"And in fact that's almost what happened," Ellie said. "We just got caught up in one of those, what you might call flurries of events, right? Am I right?"

"Well, of course," Delia told her.

Ellie slowed for the turn onto Border Street. "You may not believe this," she said, "but I'm a very stable person as a rule. It's just that lately, I've been under a lot of stress. Oh, working in front of the camera is way more pressure than I thought it would be! I have to watch my weight every instant, make sure I get my full eight hours' sleep, take care of my complexion. See this?" She was in the midst of parallel parking, but she paused to grab a strand of her hair. "Bleached, stripped, body-waved, color-treated . . ." She pulled the strand taut and released it. "See how it stretches out so long and thin and then just snaps, *boing?* That's not hair anymore; it's, I don't know, Silly Putty. And if only they'd give me a leave of absence till my eyebrows can grow back in!"

One tire scraped the curb. "Besides which there's my nutso sister losing her marbles over

Dad's marriage," she said, "and this leak in my apartment ceiling nobody knows where from, and not to mention Dad himself. What business does he have, starting all over at his age? He's sixty-seven years old and in constant pain to boot, were you aware of that? Why do you suppose he keeps Noah's visits so short? His favorite grandchild, but any more than an hour and Dad's exhausted!"

"Oh, the poor man," Delia said. She opened the door and got out, still holding the sweatshirt to her head. Somehow the urgency of their errand had receded, she noticed. She flipped the seat forward for Noah, and he piled out after her.

"When I think how hard I worked moving him into that place!" Ellie told her, slamming her own door. "All those boxes I packed! I felt like I was sending him off to camp or something. 'Do you have the right kind of clothes for this? What will the other kids be wearing?' And now they're threatening to evict him."

"Evict him!" Delia said.

They were climbing the steps of a large frame house with a wraparound porch. Noah led the way. Delia trailed behind because her ankle was slowing her down. She called, "I thought they said he could stay on after he married."

"That was before they found out his wife was expecting," Ellie said.

Delia halted on the top porch step and stared

at her. Even Noah stared. "Expecting what?"
Delia asked foolishly.

"Use your head, Delia! Why do you suppose
they moved the wedding up to March?"

"Well, because . . . did they tell you this? Or
are you just surmising?"

"Darn right they told me," Ellie said. "Made
a big announcement of it, just last week. Dad
asks Binky, 'Angel? Are you going to break the
news, or am I?' and Binky says, 'Oh, you do it,
honeybunch.' Don't you want to just gag? That
kind of talk seems so, I don't know, fake, when
it's a second marriage. So Dad clears his throat
and says, 'Ellie,' he says; says, 'you're going to
have a sister.' Well, I was kind of slow on the
uptake. I said, 'I *already* have a sister. Several.'
He said, 'I mean another sister. We're pregnant.'
That's an exact quote. 'We,' he said. You can
bet he didn't word it that way the first four times
around."

"But . . . when is this going to happen?" Delia
asked.

"September."

"September!"

Majestically, Ellie sailed through the front
door. Delia stood on the porch with her mouth
open. Binky had always been a rotund little person, rotund in the stomach as well, but . . . She
looked over at Noah. "Did *you* know about
this?" she asked.

He shook his head.

"Well," she said. "So you'll have a . . . baby aunt! Imagine!"

As she limped through the door, she heard Ellie's humorless snicker.

This was the first time Delia had been to Dr. Norman's office, although his telephone number was posted next to the Millers' kitchen phone. The instant she smelled that mixture of floor wax and isopropyl alcohol, she was overcome by a settling-in sensation—a feeling that she had returned to her rightful place; that all other places were counterfeit, temporary, foreign to her true nature. She stopped short in the foyer (stringy Oriental rug, ginger-jar lamp on a table), until Ellie took her arm and steered her toward the waiting room. "Is he in?" she asked the woman at the desk. The woman was much older than Delia and fifty pounds heavier, but still somebody Delia could identify with, seeing her fingers poised on the chrome-rimmed keys of an ancient typewriter. "We've got an emergency here!" Ellie told her.

Oh, yes, the emergency. Delia had almost forgotten. While Ellie explained the circumstances ("sharp metal corner on the . . . nothing *I* could do . . . tried to warn her but . . ."), Delia unstuck the sweatshirt from her forehead and discovered she was no longer bleeding. The bloodstains on the shirt had dried to a dull, blackish color. She glanced toward the other patients. Two women and a small girl sat watching her with interest, and she hastily clapped the sweatshirt back on her temple.

Dr. Norman was just hanging up the phone when the secretary led them in. He was a dumpy man with a flounce of white curls above his ears. "What have we here?" he asked, and he rose and came around the desk to peel away the sweatshirt with practiced fingers. His breath smelled of pipe tobacco. Delia would have liked to take hold of his hand and cradle it against her cheek. "Hmm," he said, peering. "Well, nothing you'll die of."

"Will it leave a scar?" Delia asked him.

"It shouldn't. Hard to tell for sure till I get it cleaned up."

"Of course I did everything humanly possible," Ellie said. "Warned her over and over again. 'Watch yourself getting in, Dee,' I told her; if I told her once, I told her half a dozen times—"

Dr. Norman said, with a touch of impatience, "Yes, fine, Ellie, I understand," and Ellie shut up. "Come next door," he told Delia. He ushered her into an adjoining room. Ellie and Noah followed, which may not have been what he had intended.

This second room held an examining table upholstered in cracked black leather. Delia boosted herself nimbly onto the end of it and settled her handbag in her lap. While Dr. Norman rummaged in a metal drawer the color of condensed milk, he asked Ellie about the weather; he asked Noah about his softball team; he told Delia he had heard she was a ba-a-ad tutor.

"Bad!" Delia said.

"Good, that means." He looked up from the rubber gloves he was slipping on. "In T. J. Renfro's language, 'bad' is good, and so is 'wicked.' You teach a wicked equation, he says."

"Oh," Delia said, relieved.

Ellie, who had been studying a poster on the Heimlich maneuver, looked over at her. "You tutor at Underwood?" she asked.

"Yes."

She sniffed. "Joel must be in heaven," she said. "He was always after me to volunteer."

Dr. Norman sent Ellie a quick glance that she probably didn't notice. Then he told Noah, "Excuse me, son," and stepped around him to peer again at Delia's forehead. She stilled her swinging feet as he came close. "This'll smart some," he said, tearing open an antiseptic wipe. The keen, authoritative smell filled her with longing. *I'm really not just a mere patient,* she could have told him. *I know this office top to bottom! I know you'll sit down to supper tonight and tell your family that that Ellie Miller sure acts mighty possessive of Joel, considering they're separated. I know you'll say you finally got to meet that live-in woman of his, and depending on how discreet you are, you might even voice some suspicion as to exactly how I was injured. Don't think I'm one of those outsiders who can't see beyond the white coat!*

But of course she said nothing, and Dr. Norman swabbed her wound and then laid dots of rubbery warmth on either side of it as he tested it with his fingertips. "What you've got," he said, "is a superficial scratch across the forehead, but a fairly deep gash at the temple. No need for stitches, though, and I doubt there'll be a scar if we keep the edges together while it heals." He turned back to the cabinet. "We'll just apply a butterfly closure. This nifty type of bandage that . . ."

Yes, Delia knew what a butterfly was—had plastered more than a few onto her own children's injuries. She shut her eyes as he set it in place. Next to her she heard Noah breathing; he was leaning in close to watch. "Cool!" he said.

"Now, if you want I could prescribe a pain medication," Dr. Norman said, "but I don't believe—"

"It hardly hurts at all," Delia told him, opening her eyes. "I won't need anything."

He scrawled a note for his secretary before he showed her out, and clapped Noah on the shoulder, and said, "Ellie, always good to see your clothes hanging so well on you."

"Oh, stop," Ellie said. She told Delia, "Everybody pokes fun at this remark I made in *Boardwalk Bulletin.*"

Delia's only response was, "Oh?" because she didn't want to let on she'd read it.

"But I was misquoted!" Ellie said. "Or at least, I didn't mean it that way. What I meant was, I dress economically."

She was still going on about that—telling Noah that this skirt, for instance, had cost thirteen ninety-five at Teenage World—when they reached the reception desk, which left Delia to pay the bill. She did think Ellie might have offered. But she had planned to decline anyhow, and so she held her tongue.

Out on the porch, she folded the sweatshirt and stuffed it in her bag. Then she followed Ellie and Noah down the steps. Ellie was discussing the clothing budget of someone named Doris. Doris? Oh, yes, the anchorwoman at WKMD. "What she spends on headbands alone," Ellie said, "to say nothing of those scarves she wears to hide her scraggy neck . . ."

Delia was reflecting that she should have accepted that prescription after all, not for her forehead but for her ankle. She had completely neglected to mention twisting her ankle. She limped painfully to the car and fell with a thud into the passenger seat.

"So I guess you want to go home now," Ellie said.

"Yes, please," Delia told her.

But Ellie had been speaking to Noah. "Honey?" she said, watching his face in the rear-view mirror.

"I guess," he said.

"Don't want to change your mind and visit *me*?"

"I've got this history test to study for."

Ellie's shoulders slumped. She didn't point out that he could do that anytime over the weekend.

They cruised down Weber Street, passing Copp Catering where Belle had bought Thanksgiving dinner, and the Sub Tub, where all the Underwood students headed for snacks after school. In Ellie's company, Delia felt that Bay Borough took on a different shading. It didn't look as happy as it usually did. The women walking home with their grocery bags seemed unknowingly ironic, like those plastic-faced, smiling housewives in kitchen-appliance ads from the fifties. Delia shook off the thought and turned to Ellie. "Well!" she said. "Maybe I'll run into you at your father's sometime."

"If I ever go back there," Ellie said gloomily.

"Oh, you have to go back! Why wouldn't you? He's such a pleasure to talk to."

"That's easy for you to say," Ellie said. "You're not his daughter."

She turned onto Pendle Street, braked for a jaywalking collie, and pulled into the Millers' driveway. (The glance she shot toward the front windows could have meant nothing at all.) "Bye, No-No," she said, blowing her son a kiss. "Delia, sorry again about the whatever."

"That's all right," Delia said.

Limping after Noah up the sidewalk, she remembered where she'd heard that phrase of Ellie's before. "Easy for *you*," Delia's sisters used to tell her. They said, "Naturally *you* get along with Dad. You arrived so late, is why. You don't have so much to hold against him."

But they never specified just what they held against him themselves. They hadn't been able to name it even when she asked, and she would be willing to bet that Ellie couldn't either.

When Delia changed into the shoes she wore around the house, she found that the strap of her pump had left a groove across her right instep. Her foot was so swollen, in fact, that she seemed to be wearing a *ghost* pump, pressing into her flesh. And her anklebone had become a mere dent. She doubted anything was broken, though. She could still wriggle her toes.

She drew a dishpan of cold water, added a few ice cubes, and sat down on a kitchen chair to let the ankle soak. And what else should she do for it? All those times she'd heard Sam advising his patients; you'd think she would remember. There was a mnemonic: R.I.C.E., he always told them. She tried it aloud. "Rest, ice . . ." But what was the *C* for? Caution? Coddling? She tried again. "Rest, ice . . ."

"Rest, ice, compression, elevation," Joel told her, setting his briefcase on the counter. "What happened to *you*? You look like a war orphan."

"Oh," Delia said, "you know that sharp corner they have on car doors . . ." Then she realized that this in no way explained her ankle. "It's just been one of those days," she finished vaguely.

He didn't pursue it. He opened an overhead cabinet and felt for something on the top shelf. "I know we have a first-aid kit," he said. "I had to take a course in— Here we go." He pulled out a gray metal tackle box. "When you're through soaking, I'll tape it."

"Oh, I'm through," Delia said. She should probably allow more time, but the ice was making her shiver. She lifted her foot and patted it dry with a dish towel. Joel bent over it. He whistled.

"Maybe you ought to get that x-rayed," he said. "Are you sure it's not broken?"

"Pretty sure. Everything works," Delia told him.

Moving aside the dishpan, he knelt and started unrolling a strip of flesh-colored elastic. Delia felt self-conscious about the puffiness of her ankle and the dead blue of her skin, but he showed no reaction. He began wrapping her foot, criss-crossing her instep, working his way upward in a series of perfectly symmetrical V's. "Oh, how neat! Tidy, I mean," Delia said. "You're very good at this."

"Part of a principal's education," Joel said. He wound the last of the bandage around her shin. Then he secured it with two metal clips the same shape as the butterfly closure on her temple. "How's that?" he asked. He took hold of her foot, as if weighing it. "Tight enough?"

"Oh, yes, it feels . . ."

It felt wonderful. Not just the bandage—although the support was a great relief—but the hand clasping her foot, the large palm warming her arch through the elastic. She wished she could push even harder against his grip. She was thirsty, it seemed, for that firmness. Till now she had never realized that the instep could be an erogenous zone.

As if he guessed, he went on kneeling there, looking into her face.

"Delia?" Noah said. "Can I invite—?"

Both of them jumped. Joel dropped her foot and stood up. He said, "Noah! I thought you were off at your mother's."

Noah stood in the doorway, frowning.

"We were just, ah, taping Delia's ankle," Joel told him. "It seems she must have sprained it."

Delia said, "Rest, ice, compression, elevation!

That's the menon . . . menonom . . ." She
laughed, short of breath. "Oh, Lord, I never can
pronounce it."

Noah just watched her. Finally he said, "Can
I invite Jack for supper?"

"Oh, of course!" she said. "Yes! Good idea!"

He looked at her a moment longer, looked at
his father, then turned and walked out.

Joel wouldn't let her cook that night. He settled
her on the family-room couch with her feet up
and the cat in her lap, and he went off to order
a pizza. Meanwhile Noah and Jack sprawled on
the floor in front of the TV. Some kind of thriller
was playing. During the more suspenseful scenes
a piano tinkled hypnotically. Delia loosened her
hold on George and leaned her head back and
closed her eyes.

Behind her lids, she saw the gritty surface of
Highway 50 rushing toward her. She saw the
Plymouth darting across a stream of traffic, miraculously avoiding collision like a blip in a video
game. She jerked awake, eyes wide and staring,
shaken all over again by the narrowness of her
escape.

# 17

The cut on Delia's forehead healed quickly, leaving just the faintest white fishhook of a scar. The sprain, though, took longer. She favored her right ankle for weeks. "This is not my actual walk," she wanted to tell passersby, for she felt, somehow, at a disadvantage—second rate, inferior. She wondered how people endured it when they knew they'd be disabled forever, like some of the residents in Senior City.

Senior City was the one place where her limp attracted no attention. She could proceed unhurriedly toward a waiting elevator, trusting the other passengers to hold it for her. When she finally stepped inside, she would find them conversing among themselves without a sign of impatience, one of them leaning absently on the Open button till Delia reminded her to release it. No longer did their own infirmities seem so apparent, either, or their wrinkles or white hair. Delia had adjusted her slant of vision over the past months.

And what a contrast Binky made! For anyone could see now that she was pregnant. By May she was in maternity clothes. By early June she was cupping her belly like an apronful of fruit as she rose from a chair. "Seems like things are *more so,* with this one," she told Delia. "When I had the boys I hardly showed till the end. I used to wear unzipped jeans and one of my husband's long-tailed shirts. But now I have to squeeze through car doors sideways and I've still got three months to go."

There was no question that this baby was unplanned. Binky said she'd been twelve weeks along before she suspected a thing—had continued proclaiming her June wedding date to all and sundry. "Then I said, 'What *is* this?' and I went to see my doctor. When he told me I was pregnant I just looked at him. He said, 'But nowadays, thirty-eight is nothing. Lots of women give birth at thirty-eight.' I said, 'How about sixty-seven?' He said, 'Sixty-seven?' I said, 'That's the age of the father.' He said, 'Oh.' Said, 'I see.' Said, 'Hmm.' "

"I view it this way," Nat told Delia. "What better place for childbirth than a retirement community? Here we have all these doctors and nurses, just standing by twiddling their thumbs on Floor Four."

Delia was horrified. She said, "You would go to Floor Four for this?"

"He's teasing," Binky told her.

"We'll turn the cardiac unit into a labor room," Nat went on impishly. "Use one of those railed hospital beds for a crib. And Lord knows these folks have got enough diapers around. Right, Noah?"

Noah grinned, but only at his teacup. He had reached that age where any talk of bodily functions was a monumental embarrassment.

"The best part is," Nat said, "whoever drew up the bylaws for Senior City never dreamed of this eventuality. All our contract says is, 'Applicants must be sixty-five before entering,' but this baby isn't an applicant. However, we did lose the Floor Two dispute. You heard we asked permission to move down to Floor Two? Now that I have Binky to look after me, I said . . . but the board said no. Said it wasn't the way the place worked. Progression was supposed to be up, they said; not down."

"Well, perhaps it's for the best," Binky told him. "Our neighbors on Three would be heartbroken to lose us, now the baby's coming."

"Yes, she certainly won't lack for sitters," Nat said dryly.

He kept insisting that the baby was a girl, even though they had chosen not to learn the sex. Girls were the only babies he'd had experience of, he said. He tried to convince Noah that *all* babies were girls but metamorphosed, some of them, into boys at about the same time their eyes darkened.

"You wouldn't believe how many old ladies

are working on booties right now," he told Delia. "Little knitted slippers, socks, embroidered Mary Janes . . . Kid is going to be the Imelda Marcos of the nursery set."

Still, both Nat and Binky must have misgivings, Delia thought. How could they not? She was awed by their determined good cheer—by Binky's habit of telling people, "We couldn't be more pleased," as if prompting them; and by Nat's solicitude, even as he hobbled around as fragile and easily overturned as something constructed of Tinkertoys.

"When my first wife was dying," he told Delia one afternoon, "I used to sit by her bed and I thought, *This is her true face.* It was all hollowed and sharpened. In her youth she'd been very pretty, but now I saw that her younger face had been just a kind of rough draft. Old age was the completed form, the final, finished version she'd been aiming at from the start. *The real thing at last!* I thought, and I can't tell you how that notion colored things for me from then on. Attractive young people I saw on the street looked so . . . temporary. I asked myself why they bothered dolling up. Didn't they understand where they were headed? But nobody ever does, it seems. All those years when I was a child, longing for it to be 'my turn,' it hadn't ever occurred to me that my turn would be over, by and by. Then Binky came along. Is it any wonder I feel I've been born again?"

Binky was present when he said this, and she leaned forward and kissed his cheek. "Me too, sweetheart," she told him.

Delia grew suddenly conscious of her own separateness—of her upright posture, her elbows pressed primly against her sides in an armchair all to herself.

Then it was summer, warm and green and buzzing with cicadas after a long, cool spring. School came to an end, and Noah started sleeping late and hanging around the house with his friends and complaining of boredom. Joel switched to vacation hours and was home by midafternoon. In the maple tree out back, a woodpecker couple built themselves a nest. Delia could hear their cries from time to time—high-pitched, excited squawks that reminded her of girls'-school girls attending their first mixed party. And on Highway 50, more and more cars sped toward the beach, their rooftops spinning with bicycle wheels, their back seats stuffed with children, their rear window ledges a coagulation of sand shovels, rubber flippers, and Utz potato chip cartons.

Would Delia's family be going to the beach themselves? she wondered. It was June, after all. It was a year since she had left them, although it seemed much longer. She had, by now, done everything at least once—observed a birthday alone as well as Thanksgiving, Christmas, and

New Year's. Paid her income taxes (married filing separately). Registered to vote. Taken the cat to the vet. She was a bona fide citizen of Bay Borough.

Then a letter arrived from Susie.

The envelope bore the correct address, which meant that Susie must have consulted Eliza or Eleanor. The handwriting was so rounded that *Borough* resembled a row of balloons anchored by a single string. Delia lifted the flap almost stealthily, unsealing it rather than tearing it, as if this would soften the impact of whatever waited inside.

*Hi Mom!*

*Just a quick note to fill you in! How you doing? Thanx for the graduation card! Commencement was kind of a drag but Tucky Pearson gave the most awesome party afterwards at her family's horse farm!*

*Nothing special to report except Dad is being so-o-o-o difficult right now! I know you'll see my side of things so could you maybe phone him and have a talk? Don't tell him I asked you to call—just say you got a letter from me and thought you should discuss my plans. You wouldn't believe how mean he's being! Or maybe you would! Honestly Mom sometimes I don't even blame you for going! See ya!*

*Luv, Susie*

Delia had a sudden sense of exhaustion. She refolded the letter and put it back in the envelope.

Well.

She couldn't phone from the house. She didn't want the call appearing on Joel's bill. Nor did she want to reverse the charges, which would give an impression of needfulness. So first she had to scrounge through her handbag and various pockets for change, and then she had to walk to the pay phone at Bay and Weber Streets, a block and a half away. She walked as fast as her ankle allowed, because if she made her call between eleven-thirty and twelve, she had a better chance of reaching Sam directly. He always broke for lunch then. Unless, in her absence, things had altered more than she had predicted.

Inside the booth—just one of those above-the-waist, partially enclosed affairs that let in every traffic sound—she lined up her coins on the shelf and then dialed the grown-ups' number. She had never called long distance from a pay phone before, and she was distressed to find that she had to wait to deposit the coins till her party answered. First the phone at the other end rang twice, then Sam said, "Dr. Grinstead," and then a recording issued instructions and Delia dropped her quarters in. *Whang! Whang!* It was humiliating—very nearly as bad as calling collect, and made worse by the fact that Sam didn't grasp what was going on. "Hello?" he kept saying. "Is anyone there?"

His deep, level voice, his habit of slanting downward even on questions.

Delia said, "Sam?"

"Where are you?" he asked immediately.

He assumed this was a plea for help, she realized. He thought she was admitting defeat—calling to say, "Come get me." He must have been expecting it for months. She stood straighter. "I'm calling about Susie," she told him.

A dead silence. Then: "Oh. Susie."

"I wonder if you know what's troubling her."

"I believe my feeble brain can encompass *that* much," he said icily. "But I suppose you're going to tell me anyhow, aren't you."

"What?" Delia pressed her fingers to her forehead. "No, wait—I mean I'm honestly asking! She wrote me there was some problem, but she didn't say what it was."

"Oh," Sam said again. Another silence. "Well," he said, "this would have to do with her wedding, I suspect."

"Susie's getting married?"

"She wants to. I'm opposed."

"But—" Delia said. *But she didn't talk to* me *about this!* she wanted to protest. *Didn't even consult me!* Unreasonable, she knew; so she changed it to, "But Driscoll's a very nice boy. It is Driscoll, isn't it?"

"Who else," Sam said. "However, that's not the issue. She can marry whoever she chooses, of course, but I told her she'll have to live on her own for one calendar year beforehand."

"A year! Why?"

"I hate to see her jumping straight from school to marriage. From her father's house to her husband's house."

Her *father's* house? *He* hated to see? How about her mother? Oh, all right . . . but her *husband's* house?

And the biggest offense of all: what he meant was, he didn't want Susie turning out like Delia. Who had never spent so much as a night on her own before *she* married; and just look at the results.

He'd been mulling that over all year, she supposed. Arriving at his own private theory.

"But if she lives alone," Delia said, "she'll be so . . . unprotected. And also she and Driscoll might . . . I mean, what if they end up, um, sleeping together or something like that?"

"Don't you suppose they already sleep together, Delia?"

Her mouth dropped open.

A taped voice said metallically, "To continue your call, please deposit another—"

"Hold on, I'm going to try to get these charges reversed," Sam told Delia.

She didn't argue. She was trying to reassemble her thoughts. Well, no doubt they *did* sleep together. On some level, she'd probably known that. Still, she felt bereft. She pictured herself waving goodbye while Susie and Driscoll dwindled into the distance, never once looking back.

"You know she doesn't have a job yet," Sam said when he'd dealt with the operator.

"I wondered about that."

Amazing, how easy it was to fall back into this matter-of-fact, almost chatty exchange of information. The *ordinariness* of it struck her as surreal.

"She sleeps till all hours," he was saying, "and then heads off to the swimming pool. No interviews set up, no mention of careers . . ."

*But if she's getting married,* Delia thought. That too, though, she censored. She asked, "How about Driscoll? Does he have a job?"

"Yes, he's hired on with his father."

Delia tried to think what Driscoll's father did, but she couldn't remember. Something businessy. She said, "Well, have you and Susie talked about this? Discussed what kind of work might interest her?"

"No," Sam said.

"And where could she afford to live? I mean, if she isn't earning money yet."

"We haven't gone into that," Sam said.

"Well, golly, Sam, what *have* you gone into?"

"Nothing," Sam said. He gave a slight cough. "It appears that we're not speaking."

Delia sighed. She said, "How about Eliza? I know Susie must talk to *her*."

"Not necessarily," Sam said.

"What do you mean?"

"I don't think they do talk, to tell the truth."

"They had a fight?"

"I'm not sure. Well, they did, I guess, but I'm not sure if it's still on or not. Actually, Eliza is out of town right now."

"Out of town!"

"She's visiting Linda awhile."

Delia digested this. She said, "Aren't you all taking your beach trip this year?"

"No, Delia," Sam told her, and the iciness was back in his voice. Delia understood his point as clearly as if he'd stated it: *Do you really imagine we'd go back to the beach, now that you've ruined it for all of us forever?*

Hastily she said, "So no one's sat Susie down and discussed her options with her."

"I fail to see how I can hold a discussion with someone who walks out of a room the instant I walk in," Sam said.

*You follow her, is how,* Delia wanted to tell him. *You walk out after her. What's so hard about that?* But for Sam it would be unthinkable, she knew. He wasn't a man who laid himself open to rebuff. He didn't like to plead, or bargain, or reverse himself; he had never made a mistake in all his life. (And was that why the people around him seemed to make so many?)

A delivery truck wheezed past, and she covered her free ear. "All right," she said, "here's what I propose. I'm going to write and tell her that if she wants you to pay for her wedding, she'll have to accept your conditions. And if she doesn't like those conditions, then she can pay for her own wedding. Either way, you will go along with it."

"I will?"

"You will."

"But then she might decide to marry him tomorrow."

"If she does, she does," Delia said. "That's up to her."

Sam was quiet. Delia's ankle had started to pound, but she didn't push him. Finally he said, "How about the not-speaking part?"

"How about it?"

"Could you tell her to talk all this over with me?"

"I could suggest it," she said.

"Thank you."

She felt uncomfortable in this new role. She said, "So! Everything else all right?"

"Oh, yes."

"Boys okay?"

"They're fine."

"Who's taking care of the office while Eliza's gone?"

"I am."

"Maybe *that's* a job for Susie."

"Never," he said flatly.

Another stab to the heart. *Never,* he meant, *would I let my daughter follow her mother's wretched example.* And she couldn't even argue with that. She said, "I guess I'll be going, then."

"Oh. Well. Goodbye," he said.

After she hung up, it occurred to her that on the other hand, maybe he was just saying Susie would be a disaster in the office. It was true that she was hopeless when it came to organizational matters. Unlike Delia, who had a gift for them.

Could that have been what he'd meant?

In her letter to Susie she included one request that she hadn't mentioned to Sam beforehand. *When you do get married,* she wrote, *whatever kind of wedding it may be, will you let me come? I couldn't blame you if you didn't, but . . .*

She wrote that afternoon, using the desk in the family room, choosing a time when she had the house to herself. Before she was finished, though, Joel came home. He said, "Oh, here you are." Then he stood about for a while, jingling coins deep in his pocket. At last she stopped writing and looked up at him.

"Was there something you wanted?" she asked.

"No, no," he said, and he moved away, went off to another part of the house. But as soon as she had finished the letter, he was back again. He must have heard her starting supper preparations. He stood in the kitchen doorway, once again jingling his coins. "Saw you on Weber Street today," he said.

"Weber Street?"

"Making a phone call."

"Ah."

"You know you're welcome to use the phone here," he said.

Delia had one of those flashes where she saw herself through someone else's eyes: huddling over the receiver and shielding her ear with one hand. She almost laughed. The Mystery Woman Strikes Again. She said, "Oh, well, it's just that I . . . had to call on the spur of the moment, that was all."

He waited, as if hoping for more, but she said nothing else.

Sometimes Delia noticed some detail in Joel —the play of muscles under the skin of his forearms, or the casual drape of his suit coat across his back—and she felt a pull so deep that she had to remind herself she hardly knew this man. In fact, they barely talked to each other. Ever since he'd bandaged her ankle they seemed to have grown tongue-tied and shy. And anyhow, they had Noah to think of.

Watchful, mistrustful Noah! Always lurking about, lately, scanning their faces for signs of guilt. One night when Joel and Delia came home from a Volunteer Tutors' Supper (potluck, each woman meditatively eating just her own dish, for the most part), they found him waiting at the front door with his arms clamped across his chest. "What took you so long?" he demanded. "That supper was supposed to get over at nine. It's nine forty-three, for gosh sake, and the Brookses' house is not but five minutes away!"

Well, think about it: in October he would turn thirteen. Not an easy age, as Delia knew far too well. Already there were signs. For instance, he had spurned those clothes she'd bought him this spring. And he wanted her to leave his laundry in the hall outside his room from now on, not bring it in. And one morning after his friends had slept over, he asked her, "Do you have to wear that beachy-looking cover-up at breakfast? Don't you own a bathrobe like normal people?"

Yes, it was clear where he was headed.

"He's getting so tall all at once; I went to kiss him the other day and his face was just about even with mine," Ellie said. (Often, now, the two of them talked on the phone awhile before Delia summoned Noah.) "Every time I see him, he's changed some way! He's started listening to this horrible music in the car, these singers who might as well be gossiping amongst themselves except every now and then you manage to over-hear a stray word or two."

"And he says he's going to start a rock band," Delia told her. "He and Kenny Moss."

"But he doesn't play an instrument!"

"Well, *I* don't know. They've already got a name picked out: Does Your Mother Have Any Children?"

"That's a band name?"

"So he tells me."

"I don't get it," Ellie said.

"You're not supposed to, I guess. And you heard he doesn't want to go to camp this sum-mer."

"But he loves camp!"

"He says it's babyish."

"What will he do instead, then?"

"Oh, he's going, willy-nilly," Delia told her. "Joel says he has to." She felt odd, mentioning Joel so familiarly to Ellie. She hurried on. "He's already paid the deposit, he says, and anyhow, I won't be here to tend him. I'll be on vacation."

"You will? Where?"

"Ocean City, the middle two weeks in July.

Belle Flint set it up with this friend of hers who runs a motel."

"You and I should get together while you're there," Ellie told her. "Have dinner one night in my favorite restaurant. I hang out in Ocean City all the time!"

Evidently she no longer thought Delia was Joel's girlfriend. Delia wondered why. Was it seeing Delia up close that had changed her mind?

Delia felt a little bit disappointed, to be honest.

She dreamed she ran into Sam in front of Senior City. He was standing outside the double doors in his starched white coat, with his hands in his pockets, and she walked directly up to him and said, in her most positive tone, "At the Millers' I have a full-sized bike I built all by myself out of paper clips."

He gazed down at her thoughtfully.

"A working bike?" he asked.

"Well, no."

She woke up still squinting against the sunlight that had flashed off his glasses. He had been wearing a stethoscope, she recalled, looped across the back of his neck like a shaving towel. He hadn't worn a stethoscope since the first week he came to work for her father. It was a new-young-doctor thing to do, really, and new was what Sam had been then, in spite of his age, because he'd had to spend so long working his way through school. But he never would have given her such a stern and judging look when they were first acquainted.

Or would he?

Maybe he'd been that way from the start. Maybe Adrian had it right: what annoys you most, later on, is the very thing that attracted you to begin with.

For her trip to the beach she bought a suitcase —just a cheap one from the dime store, big enough to hold her straw tote. Belle was driving her over early Saturday morning. Noah was still home when Belle honked out front (he'd be leaving for camp around noon), and Delia gave him a quick goodbye hug, which he put up with. To Joel she said, "Don't forget to feed Vernon."

"Who's Vernon?"

She couldn't think why he asked, for a moment. Then she said, "Oh! I meant George." Silly of her: George and Vernon were not at all alike. She said, "George the *cat*!" as if it were Joel who had been confused. "Well, so long," she told him, and she rushed out the door, her suitcase knocking against her shins.

Belle wore enormous sunglasses, the upside-down kind with the earpieces hitched at the bottom. "I have the world's worst hangover," she told Delia right off. "I never want to see another drop of champagne as long as I live."

"You had champagne?"

"Did I ever. A whole entire bottle, because last night Horace proposed."

"Oh, Belle!"

"But he couldn't drink any himself because he's allergic," Belle said. "Just sat there watching *me* glug it down, following every swallow with those hound-dog eyes of his. Yes, that's the way we do things, we two. Still, it made a nice gesture. Champagne, a dozen roses, and a diamond ring: the works." She lifted her left hand from the wheel to display a tiny, winking glint. Then she pulled into the street. "Near as I can recall, I must have accepted. Think of it: Belle Lamb. Sounds like a noise in a comic book: *Blam!*" She was keeping her face expressionless behind the dark glasses, but there was something complacent and well-fed in the curve of her lips. "I guess now I'll have to go through with it," she said.

"Don't you want to go through with it?"

"Oh, well. Sure." She turned onto 380. "I do care about him. Or love him, I guess. At least, if he bangs his head climbing into my car I get this sort of clutch to my stomach. You reckon we could call that love?"

Delia was still considering this question as Belle went on. "But I can't help noticing, Dee: most folks marry just because they decide they've reached that stage. I mean, even if they don't have any particular person picked out yet.

*Then* they pick someone out. It's like their marriages are arranged, same as in those foreign countries—except that here, the bride and groom are the ones who do the arranging."

Delia laughed. She said, "Well, now I don't know *what* to say. Am I supposed to congratulate you, or not?"

"Oh, well, sure," Belle said. "Congratulate me, I guess." And her left hand rose swaybacked from the wheel for a moment so she could admire her diamond.

The Mermaid's Chambers was a peeling turquoise motel on the wrong side of the highway, between a T-shirt shop and a liquor store. But Belle had got her a very good discount, and Delia wasn't planning to spend much time in her room anyhow.

Each morning, she crossed the highway carrying her tote and a motel bedspread, along with a Styrofoam cup of coffee. She rented an umbrella on the beach and settled herself amid a crowd that thickened as the day progressed—squealing children, impossibly beautiful teenagers, parents in assorted weights and ages, and stringy white grandparents. First she sat drinking her coffee as she stared out at the horizon, and then, when she had finished, she pulled a book from her tote and started reading.

Here in Ocean City she was back to romances,

an average of one a day. They seemed overblown and slushy after her library books, and she read them almost without thinking about them, paying more heed to the yellow warmth soaking through her umbrella, the cries of gulls and children, the sunburned feet scrunching past her in the sand. One day, she started a book about a bride who was kidnapped by her fiancé's brother, and she realized partway through that this was what she'd been reading on *last* year's vacation. She checked the title: yes, *Captive of Clarion Castle*. She gazed toward the ocean. A mother was holding her diapered baby just above reach of the surf, and the radios all around were playing "Under the Boardwalk," and Delia fancied she caught sight of her own self strolling south alongside the festoons of sea foam.

Toward noon she would stand up and head toward the boardwalk for lunch. She ate in one or another rinky-dink café—a sandwich shop, a pizza joint—blinking away the purple spangles that swarmed across her vision in the sudden dimness. Then she returned to her umbrella and napped awhile, after which she read a bit more. Later she took a walk down the beach, just a short walk because her ankle still sent out a little blade of tenderness every time she put any weight on it. And then she went for her one swim of the day.

She spent forever submerging, like someone

removing a strip of adhesive tape by painful degrees. Arms lifted fastidiously, stomach sucked in with a gasp, she advanced at a gingerly, crabwise angle so as to present the narrowest surface to the breakers. Finally, though, she was in, and not a hair on her head was dampened if she'd played her cards right. She floated far out with a smug sense of achievement, sending a lofty, amused glance shoreward whenever the swell she bobbed on crashed against the shrieking throngs in the shallows. And she always waited for the most docile wave to carry her back to land—although sometimes she misjudged and found herself knocked off her feet and churning underwater like a load of laundry.

Then she staggered onto the beach, streaming droplets and wringing out the skirt of her suit. By that time all her sunblock would have been washed off, and her face grew steadily pinker and more freckled over the course of her vacation. Her first act when she returned to her room at the end of every day was to check the mirror, and every day a more highly colored person gazed back at her. When she peeled off her swimsuit, a second suit of fish-white skin lay beneath it. In the shower her feet developed scarlet smatterings across the tops.

She lounged on the bed in Sam's beach robe and toweled her hair dry. Filed her nails. Watched the news. Later, when the moldy-smelling, air-conditioned air began to chill her, she dressed and went out to dinner—a different restaurant each night. Her Sundays at the Bay Arms stood her in good stead, and she dined alone serenely, making her way through three full courses as she surveyed the nearby tables. Then she sat on the boardwalk awhile, if she could find an empty bench. The racket of video games and rock music pummeled her from behind; in front stretched the empty black ocean, fringing itself white beneath a partly erased disk of moon.

She was back in her room by nine most nights. In bed by ten. She turned off the air conditioner and slept under just a sheet, lightly sweating in the warm air that drifted through her window.

One day was cloudy, with scattered, spitting rain, and she stayed inside and watched TV. Talk shows, mostly: a whole new world. People would say anything on television, she found. Family members who hadn't spoken in years spoke at length for the camera. Women wept in public. By the time Delia turned the set off her face ached, as if she'd attended too many social events. She went out for a walk and bought a new book to read, not a romance but something more serious and believable, about poor people living in Maine. For her walk she wore her Miss Grinstead cardigan, which clung gently to her arms and made her feel like a cherished child.

Twice she sent postcards to Noah at camp. *Nice weather, nice waves,* she wrote. That sort of thing. She bought a card for Joel too but couldn't decide what to say. In the end, she wrote Belle instead. *This was a really good idea. Thank you for setting things up for me.* Belle's friend Mineola, a dyed brunette in pedal pushers and stiletto heels, always greeted her amiably but otherwise left her alone, which suited Delia just fine.

Occasionally some jolt to the senses—a whiff of coconut oil, the grit of sand in her swimsuit seams—brought to mind the old family beach trips. She was returning her umbrella to the rental stall one afternoon when a child cried, "Ma, make Jenny carry something too!" which swept her back into that packing-up moment toward sunset each day when children beg to stay a little bit longer and grown-ups ask who's got the rafts, where's the green bucket, will somebody grab the thermos? She remembered the bickering, and the sting of carelessly kicked-up sand against burned skin, and the weighty, soft-boned weariness. She recalled each less-than-perfect detail, and yet still she would have given anything to find herself in one of those moments.

Whose sneakers are these? Someone's forgetting their sneakers! Don't come to me tomorrow whining about your sneakers!

She bought a postcard showing a dolphin, and

she wrote on it, *Dear Sam and kids, Just taking a little holiday, thinking about you all.* Then it occurred to her that they might assume she was referring to this whole past year, not a mere two weeks in Ocean City; and she wasn't certain how to clarify her meaning. She tore the card in half and threw it away.

On her last night, she was supposed to meet Ellie at The Sailor's Dream. She regretted having agreed to it. Carrying on a conversation struck her all at once as a lot of work. However, canceling would have been work too, so she showed up at the appointed hour in front of the restaurant. Ellie was already standing under the awning. She wore a white halter dress shot with threads of silver, the kind of thing you'd expect to see on cruise ships, and she carried a little white purse shaped like a scallop shell. Men kept glancing over at her as they passed. "Why, Delia! *Look* at you!" she called. "Aren't you all healthy and rosy!" Delia had forgotten how good it felt to have somebody know her by name and act glad to see her coming.

The Sailor's Dream had the padded-leather atmosphere of an English gentlemen's club, but with some differences. The carpet, for instance, gave off the same mushroom smell as the one in Delia's motel room. And all the waiters were deeply tanned.

"So tell me," Ellie said as soon as they were

seated. "Have you been having a good time?"

"A lovely time," Delia told her.

"Was this your first vacation by yourself?"

"Oh, yes," Delia said. "Or rather . . ."

She wasn't sure whether traveling alone to Bay Borough qualified as a vacation or not. (And if it did, when had her vacation ended and her real life begun?) She met Ellie's eyes, which were fixed on her expectantly.

"Doesn't it feel funny going swimming on your own?" Ellie asked.

"Funny? No."

"And what about eating? Have you been eating in your room all this time?"

"Goodness, no! I ate out."

"I *hate* to eat out alone," Ellie said. "You don't know how I admire you for that."

They had to stop talking to give their orders —crab imperial for Delia, large green salad hold the dressing for Ellie—but as soon as the waiter moved away, Ellie said, "Did you practice beforehand? Before you left your, ah, previous place of residence?"

"Practice?"

"Did you *use* to eat out alone?"

Delia began to see what Ellie was up to here: she was hoping to gather some tips on how to manage single life. For next she said, "I never did, myself. I never even walked down a street alone, hardly! Always had some escort at my elbow. I was awfully popular as a girl. Now I wish I'd been a little less popular. You know how long ago I first thought of leaving Joel? Three months after we were married."

"Three months!"

"But I kept thinking, *What would I do on my own, though?* Everyone would stare at me, wonder what was wrong with me."

She leaned even closer to Delia. Lowered her voice. "Dee," she said.

"Yes?"

"Did you *have* to leave?"

Delia drew back slightly.

"Like, were you in just . . . an impossible position? Had to get out? Couldn't have survived another minute?"

"Well, no," Delia said.

"I don't want to pry! I'm not asking for secrets. All I want to know is, how desperate does a person need to get before she's certain she should go?"

"Desperate? Oh, well, I wouldn't say . . . well, I'm *still* not certain, really."

"You're not?"

"I mean, it wasn't an actual decision," Delia told her.

"Take me, let's say," Ellie said. "Do you think I made a mistake? There you are in that house with my husband; do you think I was overreacting to leave him?"

"I'm not married to him, though. There's a difference."

"But you must know what he's like, by now. You know how persnickety he is and how . . . right all the time and always criticizing."

"Joel, criticizing?" Delia asked. "Belle Flint says he worships you! He's trying to keep the house exactly like you left it—hasn't anyone told you?"

"Oh, yes, *after* I left it," Ellie said. "But while I was there it was, 'Why can't you do it this way, Ellie?' and, 'Why can't you do it that way, Ellie?' and these big cold silent glowers if I didn't."

"Is that so," Delia said.

And just then she saw Sam standing in front of the fridge, delivering one of his lectures on the proper approach to uncooked poultry. Sam was so phobic about food poisoning you'd think they lived in some banana republic, while Joel never mentioned it. No, Joel's concerns were more endearing, she thought—his household maps and his chore charts. They so plainly arose from a need for some sense of stability. All he was really after was *sureness*.

Or could the same be said for Sam?

Their food arrived, and the waiter flourished a pepper mill as big as a newel post. He asked, "Would either of you like—?"

"No, no, go away," Ellie said, waving a hand. As soon as they were alone again, she turned

back to Delia. "Three months after our wedding," she said, "Joel went to a conference in
Richmond. I said to myself, 'Free!' I felt like
dancing through the house. I almost *flew* through
the house. I played this kind of game with myself,
went through all his drawers and packed his
clothes in boxes. Packed what hung in his closet
too. Pretended I lived by myself, with no one
peering over my shoulder. He wasn't due home
till Wednesday, and I planned to put everything
back Tuesday night so he'd never guess what I'd
done. Except he came home early. Tuesday
noon. 'Ellie?' he said. 'What *is* this?' 'Oh,' I told
him, 'it's just I wanted to picture what it would
feel like to have more drawer space.' That's how
women get their reputations for ditsiness. The
real reason wasn't ditsy in the least, but who's
going to tell him the real reason?"

She hadn't touched her salad. Delia plucked
a piece of crab cartilage from her tongue and set
it on the side of her plate.

"In a way, the whole marriage was kind of like
the stages of mourning," Ellie said. "Denial, anger . . . well, it *was* mourning. I'd go to parties
and look around; I'd wonder, did all the other
women feel the same as me? If not, how did they
avoid it? And if so, then maybe I was just a
crybaby. Maybe it was some usual state of affairs
that everybody else gracefully put up with."

Finally she speared a lettuce leaf. She nibbled

it off her fork with just her front teeth, rabbitlike, all the while fixing Delia with her hopeful blue gaze.

"That reminds me of Melinda Hawser," Delia told her. "This woman I met at Belle's last Thanksgiving. The way she talked, I figured she'd be divorced by Christmas! But I run into her uptown from time to time and she's still as married as ever. Looks perfectly fine."

"Exactly," Ellie said. "So you can't help thinking, *Wouldn't I have been fine too? Shouldn't I have stuck it out?* And you get to remembering the good things. The way he loved to watch me put on my face for a party so I always felt I was doing something bewitching; or after the baby was born, when we weren't allowed to have sex for six weeks and so we just kissed, the most wonderful kisses . . ." Now the blue eyes were swimming with tears. "Oh, Delia," she said. "I *did* make a mistake. Didn't I?"

Delia looked tactfully toward a brass lamp. She said, "It's not as if you couldn't *un*make it. Jump in the car and drive back home."

"Never," Ellie said, and she dabbed beneath each eye with her napkin. "I would never give him the satisfaction," she said.

And what would have become of Delia if Ellie had answered otherwise?

Belle told Delia she hadn't missed a thing in Bay Borough, not a blessed thing. "Dead as a tomb," she said, driving languidly, one-handed. "Little fracas in town council—Zeke Pomfret wants to drop the baseball game from Bay Day this year, switch to horseshoes or something, and Bill Frick wants to keep it. But no surprises *there*, right? And Vanessa swears she's known about me and Horace all along, but I don't believe her. And we've set the wedding date: December eighteenth."

"Oh, Christmastime!" Delia said.

"I wanted an excuse to wear red velvet," Belle told her.

They left the glitter of the beaches behind and rode through plainer, simpler terrain. Delia watched shabby cottages slide by, then staid old farmhouses, then an abandoned produce stand that was hardly more than a heap of rotting gray lumber. She would never have guessed, the first time she traveled this road, that she could find such scenery appealing.

At the Millers' house, the front lawn was mowed too short and crisply edged, and each shrub stood in a circle of fresh hardwood chips. Evidently Joel had found himself with an abundance of spare time. Inside, the cat cold-shouldered her and then trailed her footsteps in a guilt-provoking way as Delia walked through the empty rooms. The house was tidy but somehow desolate, with subtle signs of bachelorhood like a huge wet dish towel instead of a proper washrag hanging over the kitchen faucet, and a thin film of grease coating the stove knobs and cupboard handles (those out-of-the-way places men never think to clean). On her bureau, a note read: *Delia—I've gone to pick up Noah. Don't fix supper; we'll all grab a bite out someplace. J.* Also, she had mail: a handwritten invitation on stiff cream paper. *Driscoll Spence Avery and Susan Felson Grinstead request your presence at their wedding, 11 a.m. Monday, September 27, in the Grinstead living room. R.S.V.P.*

What a lot could be deciphered from a couple of dozen words! For starters, the writing was Susie's (blue ink, running steeply downhill) and no parents' names were mentioned—certain proof that she was proceeding on her own. Sam must have acquiesced, though, because the wedding would take place at the house. The date was harder to figure. Why September? Why a Monday morning? And had Susie found a job or had she not?

Delia wished she could phone and ask, but she felt she didn't have the right. She would have to respond by mail, like any other guest.

Of course she planned to attend.

She looked up and met her own face in the bureau mirror—her eyes wide and stricken, her freckles standing out sharply.

When they told her that her firstborn was a girl, she had been overjoyed. Secretly, she had wished for a girl. She had planned how she would dress her in little smocked dresses; but Susie, it turned out, insisted on jeans as soon as she could talk. She had planned how they would share womanly activities (sewing, baking pies, experimenting with skin-care products), but Susie preferred sports. And instead of a big white wedding, with Susie swathed in antique lace and both her parents beaming as they jointly (in the modern manner) gave her away, here Delia stood in an Eastern Shore ranch house, wondering what sort of ceremony her daughter was inviting her to.

Noah seemed to have grown two inches while he was at camp, and the macramé bracelets he wore around both wrists pointed up the new brownness and squareness of his hands. Also, he'd developed a habit of saying, "Are you inputting that?" in a way that already seemed to be exasperating Joel. They sat in a booth at Rick-Rack's, Joel and Noah on one side and Delia on the other, and she could observe Joel's wince even if Noah couldn't.

"Take my word for it," Joel told him finally. "I have indeed managed to grasp your meaning, but I would certainly not choose to convey that fact in computer jargon."

"Huh? So anyhow," Noah said, "at camp they made us do fifty push-ups every morning. Fifty, are you inputting that? I guess they wanted to kill us off and keep our fees for nothing. So me and Ronald went to the infirmary—"

"Ronald and I," Joel said.

"Right, and tried to get a health excuse. But the dumbhead nurse wouldn't write one. She goes, like—"

"She said."

"She said, like—"

Their food came—burgers for Noah and Joel, pork barbecue sandwich for Delia. "Thanks, Teensy," Noah said.

"Sure thing," Teensy said cheerfully.

"Mrs. Rackley to *you*," his father told him.

Noah glanced across at Delia. Delia merely smiled at him.

"Daddy's been asking where you got to these last couple of weeks," Teensy said to Delia.

"I went to Ocean City."

"Yes, I told him so, but he couldn't seem to keep it in mind. He said, 'She never even mentioned it! Just walked on out and left!' His memory's a whole lot worse lately."

"Oh, I'm sorry to hear that," Delia said.

"He says things are coming at him too fast for him to take in. And Rick tells him, just trying to be nice, tells him, 'Oh, I know exactly what you—' but Daddy says, 'Don't you poke your black self into this!' and I said, *'Daddy!'*—"

Teensy broke off, glancing at Joel. "Well," she said. "I guess I better get back to work."

She slid her hands down her apron front and hurried away.

"Remarkable," Joel said.

He seemed to have no inkling that it was his impassive gaze that had sent her rushing off.

"Maybe Mr. Bragg should go live in Senior City," Noah said.

"I don't think he can afford it," Delia told him.

"Maybe they have scholarships. Or grants or something, are you inputting that?"

Joel rolled his eyes.

"So anyhow," Noah said, picking up his burger. "Next thing, me and Ronald worked out that we'd pretend we were injured. Only we couldn't do it both at once, because it would look kind of fishy."

"You went about it all wrong," Joel told him. "Nothing good ever comes of resorting to subterfuge."

"To what?"

"Subterfuge."

"What's that?"

Joel stared across the table at Delia. His eyebrows were raised so high that his forehead resembled corduroy.

"He means something underhanded," Delia told Noah. "Something sneaky."

"Oh."

"He means you should have protested the rule

openly. Or so I assume." She expected Joel to
elaborate, but he was still gaping. "Is that what
you meant?" she asked him.

"He doesn't know what 'subterfuge' is!" Joel
said.

She took her sandwich apart and started
spooning in coleslaw.

"He never heard the word 'subterfuge.' Can
you believe it?"

She wouldn't answer. Noah said, "It's no big
deal. Geez."

"No big deal!" Joel echoed. "Don't they teach
kids anything in school these days? 'Subterfuge'
is not all that arcane, for God's sake."

Delia watched Noah decide not to ask what
"arcane" meant.

"Sometimes I think the language is just shrink-
ing down to the size of a wizened little pellet,"
Joel told her. "Taken over by rubbish words,
while the real words disappear. The other day,
I discovered our cafeteria supervisor didn't know
what cutlery was."

"Cutlery?" she asked.

"It seems the word has dropped out of use."

" 'Cutlery' has dropped out of use?"

"That's the only explanation I can think of. I
told him we were ordering a new supply of cutlery, and he said, 'What's that?' "

"Oh, fiddlesticks," Delia said. "*You* know
what cutlery is," she told Noah.

He nodded, although he didn't risk demonstrating.

"See there? It hasn't dropped out of use! Teensy," Delia called, "could we have more cutlery, please?"

"Coming right up," Teensy said, and behind the counter they heard the rattle of knives and forks.

Delia looked triumphantly at Joel.

"Oh. Well . . . ," he said.

Noah grinned. "Way to go, Dee," he told her. And eventually even Joel started smiling.

Delia smiled too, and put her sandwich back together and gave it a pat. Underneath her breath she was making a humming sound—a thin, sweet, toneless hum, not much different from purring.

# 18

Binky's baby was born on Labor Day—very fitting, Nat said. He telephoned that same afternoon; he spilled the news in a swelling voice that seemed about to break. "Eight pounds, eleven ounces," he crowed. "James Nathaniel Moffat."

"James!" Delia said. "It's a boy?"

"It's a boy. Can you believe it?" He gave one of his bearded chuckles. "I'm not sure I'll know what to *do* with a boy."

"You'll do fine," Delia said. "Noah's off on a picnic right now, but he'll be thrilled when I tell him. How's Binky?"

"Couldn't be better. She just *sailed* through this, and so did James. Wait till you see him, Delia. He's got the roundest face, little pocket watch of a face, and lots of blondish hair, but Binky says . . ."

To listen to him, you would never have guessed he had been through this experience four times.

Delia had overstated when she said Noah would be thrilled. Oh, he was interested, in a mild sort of way—wanted to know who the baby looked like, and what the board of directors had said. But when Wednesday morning rolled around, he asked if he couldn't put off his regular visit. School had just reopened, and he wanted to try out for the wrestling team. Delia said, "How about we look in on the baby for just a second, and then I drop you at tryouts afterward?"

"Can't we do it tomorrow?"

"Tomorrow I have tutoring, Noah, and the day after is the Grade Mothers' Tea, and if you wait too long your grandpa's going to think you don't care. I'll phone ahead and tell him you can stay just a minute."

"Well, okay," Noah said halfheartedly.

When she picked him up at school, he was trying to elbow Jack Newell off the sidewalk, and she had to tap her horn to catch his attention. He disentangled himself, jerked open the passenger door, and fell into the car. "Hi," she told him, but he just slid down in his seat and jammed his Phillies cap on his head. Then, out on the highway, he said, "I've got to stop doing this."

"Doing what?"

"I can't spend all my time visiting people! Mom, and Grandpa . . . I'm in the eighth grade now! I've got important activities!"

He cracked froggily on "activities," and Delia shot him a glance. His voice was about to start changing, she realized. Oh, Lord, here she was with yet another adolescent.

But all she said was, "Maybe you could switch your visits to weekends."

"Weekends I hang out with my friends! I'd miss all the fun!"

"Well, *I* don't know, Noah," she said. "Talk it over with Nat and your mom."

"And could you please drive something under ninety miles an hour? I'm not going to *live* to talk it over, riding with a maniac."

"Sorry," she said. She slowed. "Take a peek at what I found for the baby," she told him. "It's on the back seat."

He glanced back, but he didn't reach for it. "Why don't you just *tell* me what it is," he said.

"A little bitty pair of athletic shoes, not any bigger than thimbles."

"Huh."

In the old days, nothing could have stopped him from peeking at that gift.

The day was cool and cloudy, with a forecast of rain, but all they encountered during their drive was a stray drop or two on the windshield. Noah listened to a radio station where the singers screamed insults, while Delia played calmer songs in her mind—a technique she had learned with her own children. She was just starting "Let It Be" when they turned in at Senior City.

"You've got to be kidding," Noah said.

Next to the double front doors stood a four-foot-tall wooden cutout of a stork, sporting a pale-blue waistcoat and carrying a pale-blue bundle. Pale-blue balloons floated from the portico. The lobby bulletin board (which ordinarily bore cards of thanks from convalescents and sign-up sheets for bus trips to the shopping outlets in York) was plastered with color snapshots of an infant just minutes old. Three women wearing the regulation jaunty neck scarves stood peering at the photos and discussing the significance of hand size. One woman said large hands in infancy meant great height in adulthood, but another said that held true only for puppies.

In the elevator they found Pooky, taking one of her never-ending rides. Today, though, she seemed fully aware that she had reached Floor One, and she said, punching Three for them, "If you hurry you'll be in time for the burping."

"Oh, have you seen him?" Delia asked as they rose.

"Seen him twice. I was one of those in the lobby yesterday when they brought him home from the hospital. I hope that gift is not shoes."

"Well, sort of," Delia said.

"So far he's got Swedish leather clogs, inch-long flip-flops, and eentsy little motorcycle boots. And that's not even counting all we've knitted."

The elevator stopped with a lilt, and the door slid open. "I would come with you," Pooky called after them, "but I've got to get back to my apartment and finish childproofing."

It was Nat who answered when they rang the

doorbell. "There you are!" he said. "Come in, come in!" He was using his cane today, but he walked rapidly and bouncily as he led them toward the bedroom. "James is just having a snack," he called over his shoulder.

"Should we wait out here?" Delia asked.

"No, no, everyone's decent. Bink, sweetheart, it's Noah and Delia."

Binky was sitting against the headboard of the bed, dressed but in her stocking feet. The receiving blanket draped over her bosom covered the baby's face, so all they could see was a fiery little ear and a fuzzy head. "Oh, look at him!" Delia whispered. It always seemed the bottom dropped out of her chest when she saw a new baby.

Noah, though, looked everywhere but. He stuck his hands in his back pockets and studied a distant corner of the bedroom till Binky, winking at Delia, asked, "Want to hold him, Noah?"

"Me?"

She removed the baby from her breast, at the same time adroitly rearranging the blanket. The baby's eyes were closed, and he made nostalgic little smacking movements with his lips, which were rosebud-shaped, tightly pursed. He did have big hands, with long, translucent fingers knotted just under his chin. "Here," Binky said, holding him out to Noah. "Just support the back of his head, like this."

Noah received him in an awkward, jumbled clump.

"He seems to be a very easy baby," Binky said as she buttoned up. "Most of the day he's slept, which is miraculous considering all the callers we've had. Your mother phoned, Noah; wasn't that nice? That was so nice. No word from the other three yet, but I hope—"

"Oh, forget it, just forget it, hon," Nat told her. "Who cares about them!" He gave an angry shake of his head, as he often did when his daughters were mentioned. "Let's go sit in the living room."

They followed him—Noah still carrying James, feeling his way with his feet—and settled amid an uncharacteristic clutter of slippers and afghans and gift boxes. Already the apartment had that rainy, sweet, baby-powder smell.

Binky unwrapped the athletic shoes and laughed and passed them to Nat, and then, at Delia's request, she brought out the baby's motorcycle boots. A present from her sons, she said; they claimed to be disgusted with her, but Peter had cut classes to deliver these in person. Then Nat reported on their ride to the hospital ("I said, 'Binky,' I said, 'didn't I say from the start we should have gone to Floor Four?' "), and Binky rehashed the birth, which all in all, she said, had been a cinch compared to her first two. ("I shouldn't discuss this in mixed company," she said, "but ever since Peter was born, I just never have known when I needed to tinkle. The best I can do is go every couple of hours, just in case.")

Noah looked downright queasy by now, so Delia stood up to collect the baby—an excuse to feel, for an instant, the limp, crumpled weight of that little body—and return him to Binky. "We have to get Noah to his tryouts," she told Binky. "Is there anything I can do for you? Grocery shopping? Errands?"

"Oh, no. Nat's taking wonderful care of me," Binky said.

Nat, Delia happened to know, felt the ache of his flashbacks most keenly when he was driving, but she couldn't point that out when he was looking so proud of himself.

Joel seemed very nervous about the Grade Mothers' Tea. He must be wishing for Ellie, Delia thought—for Ellie's clever, theme-party style of entertaining. But when she proposed phoning Ellie and asking for suggestions, he said, "Why should we do that? We're surely capable of a simple tea, for God's sake."

"Yes, but maybe—"

"All we need from Ellie is her recipe for lemon squares," he said.

"Lemon squares. I'll ask."

"The ones with the crispy glaze on top. Also her cucumber sandwiches."

"Well, *I* can make a cucumber sandwich," Delia snapped.

"Oh. Of course."

After that he let the subject drop—forced himself to drop it, no doubt. On Friday afternoon, though, he paced circles around her as she set up the party-sized percolator on the dining room buffet. "This group will be nothing but women," he told her.

"Well, so I gathered: grade mothers."

"There is a grade father, but he's away on business. It's one hundred percent women."

She went to draw the water for tea. He followed. "You do plan to help with the conversation, don't you?" he asked.

She hadn't expected to. She had envisioned herself biding her time in the kitchen, like those discreet lady housekeepers in nineteenth-century novels. She had been looking forward to it, in fact. She said, "Oh, um . . ."

"I can't do it alone, Delia."

"Well, I'll try."

But no help was needed, she found. Fourteen women showed up—two for each homeroom, minus the traveling father and a mother who couldn't get off work. All of them were acquainted, most since childhood, and they slid easily into topics so well established that they seemed to be speaking in code. "What did Jessie finally decide?"

"Oh, just what we figured all along."

"Darn!"

"Yes, but who can say—maybe this will turn out like the Sanderson girl."

"Well, that's a thought."

Delia wore her navy knit, on the assumption that teas were dressy, but the guests wore slacks or even jeans, and one had on a sweatshirt reading COMPOST HAPPENS. They all seemed unduly curious about her. They kept coming up to ask, "So how do you *like* it here? How is Noah handling all this? Has he adjusted?" When she answered, the voices nearby would trail off and others would edge closer. "Golly," one said, "Mr. Miller must be awfully glad to have you. And you help with the tutoring too! You tutor the Brewsters' youngest! Mr. Miller's always complaining he can't find enough math tutors."

Now she knew how new girls must feel on their first day at school. But she responded politely, keeping a smile on her face, holding the teapot before her like a ticket of admission. She liked Bay Borough very much, thank you, and Noah was getting on well, and she had probably learned more from her pupils than they had learned from her. The usual remarks. She could have made them in her sleep. Meanwhile Joel stood talking with two women at the other end of the room, nodding pensively and from time to time wrinkling his brow. He no longer seemed nervous. And when she approached with a plate of cookies, he said, "You're doing a fine job, Delia."

"Thank you," she said, smiling.

"It may be the best tea we've given."

"Oh! Well, the lemon squares were Ellie's, remember; Ellie was kind enough to—"

Then one of the women asked Joel what had been planned for the Fall Bazaar, and Delia escaped to the kitchen.

She straightened things up, wiped counters, put a few items in the dishwasher. The cat had taken refuge under the table, and she hauled him forth to cuddle him and scratch behind his ears. For a while she watched the minute hand of the wall clock visibly jerk forward: five-eighteen to five-nineteen to five-twenty. Time for the guests to recall that they should get home and fix supper. In fact, she could detect a certain shift in the blur of voices—the rising notes of leave-taking.

"Didn't I have a purse?"

"Has anyone seen my keys?"

And then, "Where's *Delia*? I should say good-bye to Delia."

She had to drop George and make another appearance, see them all to the door. ("It was good meeting you, too. I'd be happy to give out the recipe.") Then she returned to the dining room, and Joel unplugged the percolator while that woman who always has to stay longest (there was one at every party) fussily separated the clean spoons from the dirty ones. "Please," Delia told her, "just let them be. I've got a system." How quickly the old formulas came back to her: *I've got a system. Don't give these a thought. It won't be a bit of trouble.*

The woman was reluctant to leave and stood awhile gazing into her purse, as if searching for instructions on where to go next. She had triplets, Delia had overheard—all boys, all just starting to drive. Easy to understand why she wasn't rushing home. Finally she said, "Well, thanks, you two. This was a real treat." And darting a smile in Joel's direction, she told Delia, "Isn't he helpful! Why, if I asked *my* husband to clear, he'd think I was joking. He would just act . . . bemused and go off with his pals."

Joel waited till she was gone before he snorted. " 'Bemused'!" he echoed. "Discouraging, isn't it?"

Delia wasn't sure what he was objecting to. (At least, she thought, he hadn't seemed to notice the woman's apparent belief that they were a couple.) She carried a stack of cups to the kitchen and began fitting them into the dishwasher.

"You realize what's going to happen," Joel said. He set the percolator on the counter. "Bit by bit, more and more people will say 'bemused' in place of 'amused,' thinking it's just the twenty-dollar version, the same way they think 'simplistic' is a twenty-dollar 'simple.' And soon enough that usage will start showing up in dictionaries, without so much as a 'non-standard' next to it."

"Maybe she really did mean 'bemused,' " Delia said. "Maybe she meant her husband was puzzled; he was perplexed that she'd asked him to help."

"No, no. Nice try, Delia, but no, she meant 'amused,' all right. Everything's changing," Joel said. "It's getting so we're hardly speaking English anymore."

She looked over at him. He was winding the cord around the percolator, although it hadn't been emptied yet or washed. "Yes, I've noticed that's what bothers you, most times," she told him.

"Hmm?"

"Most times it's not grammatical errors— other than the obvious, like 'me and him.' It's the *new* things, the changes. 'Input' and 'I'm like' and 'warm fuzzies.' "

Joel shuddered. Too late, Delia recalled that he had never to her knowledge mentioned "warm fuzzies"—that it came from Ellie's interview. She hurried on. "But think," she said. "Probably half your own vocabulary was new not so long ago. Well, 'twenty-dollar,' for instance! These terms pop up for good reason.

'Glitch.' 'Groupie.' 'Nickel-and-diming.' 'Time-shifting.' "

"What's time-shifting?" Joel asked.

"When you record a TV program to view later. Mr. Pomfret used to say that, and I thought, *Oh, how . . . economical!* Don't you sometimes *wish* for new words? Like a word for, a word for . . ."

"Freckles," Joel said.

"Freckles?"

"Those freckles that are smaller than ordinary freckles," he said. "And paler. Like gold dust."

"And also, um, tomatoes," Delia said, too quickly. "Yes, tomatoes. You have the true kind and then you have the other kind, the supermarket kind, the same color as the gums of false teeth, and those should be given a whole separate name."

"And then," Joel told her, "that different sort of surface people take on when you really begin to see them."

She had nothing to say to that.

"They get so noticeable," Joel said. "It seems you can feel every vein and pulse underneath their skin. You think, *All at once she's become* . . . but what word would you use? Something like 'textured,' but textured to the vision, instead."

His eyes seemed a softer hue of brown now, and that long, notched mouth had grown shapelier, more tender.

"Goodness!" she said, spinning toward the door. "Is that Noah?"

Although Noah had gone to Ellie's and was not due home till bedtime. And anyhow, would be dropped off at the front of the house, not the back.

Sometimes when Delia said to herself, *Only x number of days till Susie's wedding,* she felt a clammy sense of dread. *This is going to be so embarrassing. How will I face them? It's not a situation I've been taught to handle.* But other times she thought, *Pshaw, what's so hard about a wedding? We'll have all those other people there as buffers. I can just breeze in, breeze out. Nothing to it.*

For a while she had an idea that Susie might ask her to come early, as much as several days early, to help with preparations. At least that way she wouldn't feel like a mere guest. She pounced hopefully on the mail every morning, cleared her throat before answering the phone, delayed notifying Joel of her plans till she knew how long she'd be gone. But Susie didn't ask.

And sometimes she considered not attending. What purpose would she serve? They wouldn't even miss her. A day or two after the wedding, one of them might say, "Hey! You know who didn't show up? Delia! I just now remembered."

And still other times, she fantasized that they

could hardly wait to see her. "Delia!" they would
cry, "Mom!" they would cry, running out onto
the porch, letting the door slam behind them,
flinging their arms around her.

No, cancel that. More likely they would ask,
"What do you think *you're* doing here? Did you
imagine you could waltz back in just as if nothing
had happened?"

She should remember to bring her invitation,
in case there was any question.

She broached the subject to Joel at Sunday
breakfast, having waited till the very last day for
word from Susie. Sunday was a good time anyhow, because Noah was there, wolfing down
buckwheat pancakes; the conversation couldn't
get too probing. She said, "Joel, I don't know
if I mentioned or not"—knowing full well she
had not—"that I'll need to take the day off
tomorrow."

"Oh?" he said. He lowered his newspaper.

"I have to go to Baltimore."

"Baltimore," he said.

"Geez, Delia!" Noah said. "I promised my
wrestling coach you'd give a bunch of us a ride
to the meet tomorrow."

"Well, I can't," she said.

"Well, geez! *Now* what'll we do?"

"Your coach will think of something," Joel
told him. "If you wanted to volunteer Delia's
services, you should have asked her first." But

he was keeping his eyes on Delia's face as he spoke. "Is this a, some kind of emergency?" he asked her.

"No, no, just a wedding."

"Ah."

"But it's one I'd very much like to attend, a family wedding, you know, and so I thought if you didn't mind . . ."

"Of course; not at all," Joel said. "Could I drive you to the bus station?"

"Oh, thanks, but I'm going by car," Delia said. "Baltimore's on Mr. Lamb's sales route, it turns out."

Joel probably had no idea who Mr. Lamb was, but he nodded slowly, eyes still fixed on her face.

"So!" she said. "Now, I assume I'll be back by evening. Maybe suppertime, but I can't be sure; I'm returning by bus; so I've left a chicken salad in the fridge. There's a tub of Rick-Rack's coleslaw next to it, biscuits in the bread drawer . . . But I bet I'll be back by then, anyhow."

"Should I meet your bus?"

"No; Belle's doing that. I'll call her when I get into Salisbury."

"You could call me instead."

"No, really, I have no idea when . . . it might be late at night or something. It could even be the next day; who knows?"

"The next day!" he said.

"If the reception runs very long."

"But you *are* coming back," he said.

"Well, of course."

Now Noah was watching her too. He looked up from his pancakes and opened his mouth, but then he didn't speak.

Toward noon she set out on a walk, planning to end at the Bay Arms for lunch whenever her ankle grew tired. It had rained in the morning, but now the sun was shining, and the air felt so thick and warm that she regretted wearing her sweater. She pulled it off and swung it loosely from one hand. Everywhere she looked, it seemed, she saw people she knew. Mrs. Lincoln waved to her from the steps of the A.M.E. church, and T. J. Renfro, roaring past on his Harley, called out, "What say, Teach!" and on Carroll Street she ran into Vanessa and Greggie, poking along in matching yellow slickers. "Delia! I was just about to phone you," Vanessa said. "Want to ride with me to Salisbury tomorrow?"

"Oh, I'm sorry, I can't," Delia said. "I have to go to Baltimore."

"What's in Baltimore?"

"Well," Delia said, "my daughter's getting married."

She'd told Belle this too, but nothing more, and now all at once she felt an urgent need to pour it all out. "She's marrying her childhood sweetheart and I'm so worried how to behave at the wedding but I really want to be there; her father thinks she's rushing things since she's only twenty-two years old and I say—"

"Twenty-two! How old were you when you had her: twelve?"

"Nineteen," Delia said. "I married right out of high school, practically."

Vanessa nodded, unsurprised. Well, most of the girls in Bay Borough married right out of high school, Delia supposed. And had babies at nineteen or so. And ended up mislaying their husbands somewhere along the line. Vanessa's only question was, "What'd you buy for a wedding gift?"

"I thought I'd wait to see what they needed."

"That's always smart," Vanessa said. "Greggie! Let the bug go where it wants to. That's what I did with my girlfriend," she told Delia. "I thought I'd get her a hand-held mixer but then I thought no, why not wait, and I'm so glad I did because the first time I went to visit her I saw she didn't have one single piece of Tupperware in her whole entire kitchen."

Vanessa's face, above the slicker, glowed with a fine film of sweat, and her eyes seemed very pure and clear, the whites almost blue-white. Delia suddenly felt like hugging her. She said, "Oh, I'd have loved to ride to Salisbury with you!"

"Well, another time," Vanessa said. "There's

this place there we buy our barley in bulk, to make Grandma's gripe water recipe."

"Gripe water?" Delia asked.

"It's for babies. Soothes the colic and the afternoon frets and the nighttime willies."

Delia wished they made gripe water for grown-ups.

She dreamed she was in Bethany, walking down the beach. Ahead she saw a highway, a sort of narrowing and darkening of the sand until it turned to asphalt, and there sat her old Plymouth, baking in the sun. Sam encircled her upper arm to guide her toward it. He settled her inside. He shut the door gently after her and leaned through the open window to remind her to drive carefully. She woke and stared at the motes of darkness swarming above her bed.

From Noah's room she heard a repetitive dry cough, beginning sharply each time as if he'd tried first to hold it in—one of those infuriating night coughs that won't quit. For half an hour or so, she lay debating whether to get up and bring him the lozenges from the medicine cabinet. Possibly he would stop coughing on his own. Or possibly he was asleep, in which case she hated to wake him. But the cough continued, pausing and then resuming just when she thought it was finished. And then she heard the creak of a floorboard, so she knew he wasn't asleep.

She rose and went to open her door. "Noah?" she whispered.

Instantaneously, almost, Joel was standing in front of her. She couldn't see him so much as feel him, as the blind are said to feel—a tall, dense, solid shape giving off warmth, his moon-pale pajamas only gradually emerging from the dark of the windowless hall.

"Yes, Delia?" he whispered.

He had misunderstood, she realized. "Noah" and "Joel" sounded so much alike. The same thing often happened when she called one of them to the phone. She said, "I thought I heard Noah."

"I was just going to see to him," he said.

"Oh."

"I'll bring him some of those cough drops."

"All right."

But neither one of them moved.

Then he stepped forward and took her head between his hands, and she raised her face and closed her eyes and felt herself drawn toward him and enfolded, surrounded, with his lips pressing her lips and his palms covering her ears so all she could hear was the rush of her own blood.

That, and Noah's sudden cough.

They broke apart. Delia stepped back into her room and reached for her door with trembling hands and shut herself inside.

## 19

Mr. Lamb's car was a dull-green Maverick with
one orange fender and a coat-hanger antenna.
Inside, several scale-model windows filled the
back seat—wood-framed, double-sashed, none
more than twelve inches tall. Little girls from the
neighborhood were always begging to play with
them. The bottom of his trunk was paved with
panes of clear plastic, so that when Delia leaned
in with her suitcase, she had an impression of
bending over a gleaming body of water. Mr.
Lamb told her the plastic was pretty near inde-
structible. "Slide your suitcase right on top," he
told her. "It won't do the least bit of harm. That's
where our product beats anything else on the
market. When I go to a house that has pets? I
like to lay a square of Rue-Ray on the floor and
let a dog or cat march straight across, gritching
with its toenails."

Rue-Ray, Delia knew, took its name from the
married couple who owned the company, Ruth
Ann and Raymond Swann. They lived above
their workshop on Union Street, and Mr. Lamb
was their one and only salesman. She had
learned all this from Belle, but still she felt like

laughing at the sound of those two slurred, slippery *R*'s.

It also struck her as comical that Mr. Lamb turned out to be so talkative. Before they reached Highway 50, even, he had gone from storm windows (their noise-reduction powers) to the wedding gift he planned for Belle (a complete set of Rue-Rays, fully installed) to his philosophy of salesmanship. "The important thing to remember," he said, veering around a tractor, "is that people like to proceed through a process. A regular set of steps for every activity. For instance, the waitress wants to give you your bill before you hand her your credit card. The mechanic wants to tell all about your fuel pump before you say to go ahead and fix it. So I ask my customers, I ask, 'You notice any drafts? Northern rooms any colder than southern?' *I* know they've noticed drafts. I can hear their durn windows rattle as I'm speaking. But if I let folks kind of like describe the symptoms first— say how the baby's room is so cold at night she has to wear one of those blanket sleepers with the fold-over flaps for the hands—why, they get this sense a certain order has been followed, understand? Then I'm more apt to make the sale."

Unfortunately, he was one of those drivers who feel the need to look at the person they're talking to. He kept his muddy, deep-socketed eyes fixed on Delia, his scrawny neck twisted in his collar, while Delia glued her own eyes to the road as if to make up for it. She watched a column of cypress trees approach, then a long-dead motel as low to the ground and sprawling as a deserted chicken shed, then a strip of fog-filled woods where entire clouds seemed trapped in a web of branches. Only a few leaves here and there had developed a faint tinge of orange, and she could imagine that it was still summer—that it was last summer, even, and she had not lost the year in between.

"Many people don't realize that salesmen consider such things," Mr. Lamb was saying. "But salesmen are a very considering bunch, you'll find. I say it comes from traveling by car so much. Belle had an idea we should travel by car for our honeymoon, but I told her I just didn't know if I'd focus on her right, driving along with my own thoughts like I do."

Delia said, "Hmm." Then, because she felt she wasn't holding up her end of the conversation, she added, "*I* honeymooned by car."

"You did?"

She had startled herself; she very nearly turned to see who had volunteered this information. "I don't recall that it interfered with our focus, though," she said.

He glanced at her, and she gave an artificial cough. Probably he thought she'd meant something risqué. "Of course, my husband was not so attuned to driving as you must be," she said.

"Ah," Mr. Lamb murmured. "No, not many people are, I suppose."

Sam's car at the time had had a bench seat, and Delia had sat pressed against his side. He had driven left-handed, with his right hand resting in her lap, his fingers loosely clasping her nylon-clad knee, their steady warmth sending a flush straight through her. She coughed again and gazed out her window.

The passing houses looked arbitrarily plunked down, like Monopoly-board houses. The smaller the house, it seemed, the more birdbaths and plaster deer in the yard, the tidier the flower beds, the larger the dish antenna out back. A brown pond slid by, choked with grappling tree trunks. Then more woods. In Delia's girlhood, the very word "woods" had had an improper ring to it. "So-and-so went to the woods with So-and-so" was the most scandalous thing you could say, and even now the sight of winding, leafy paths conjured up an image of . . . Well.

Goodness, what was *wrong* with her?

She forced her thoughts back to Mr. Lamb. He seemed to be talking about dogs. He said that after he and Belle were married they might just get themselves one, and then he went into a discourse on the various breeds. Golden retrievers were sweet-natured but sort of dumb, he said, and Labs had that tendency to whap a person's knickknacks with their tails all the time, and as for German shepherds, why . . .

Gradually the scenery began to have a different feel to it. Around Easton she started noticing bookstores and European-car dealers, neither of which existed in Bay Borough, and by the time they hit Grasonville, the road had widened to six lanes that whizzed past gigantic condominiums, flashy gift shops, marinas bristling with masts.

Mr. Lamb settled finally on a collie. He said he might name it Pinocchio if it had one of those long, thin noses. They crossed the Kent Narrows bridge, high above the grassy marshland. Delia could remember when crossing the Kent Narrows could use up the better part of an hour— long enough to get out of your car and stretch your legs and buy a watermelon, if you wanted —but that was in the days of that cranky old drawbridge. Now they were beyond the narrows in no time flat and speeding through a jungle of factory outlet stores, strip malls, raw new housing developments with MODELS NOW OPEN! DESIGNER TOUCHES! And then here came the lovely, fragile twin spans of the Bay Bridge, shimmering in the distance like something out of a dream, while Mr. Lamb decided that he might let Pinocchio have one little batch of puppies before they got her fixed.

The countryside seemed so green, so lush,

after the scoured pallor of the Eastern Shore. Delia was surprised when they turned onto Highway 97—a road she'd never heard of—but then she relaxed in the glide of brand-new pavement not yet bordered with commercial claptrap.

She might have been away for decades.

Mr. Lamb said Belle was scared of dogs but he thought it was all in her head. Where else could it be? Delia wondered. Not that he gave her a chance to ask. He said women just got these notions sometimes. Delia smiled to herself. It amused her to see how quickly he had come to take his happiness for granted.

On the Baltimore–Washington Parkway, the lanes were so crowded that she gathered herself inward, as if that would help their car slip through more easily. She looked ahead and saw the Baltimore skyline—smokestacks, a spaghetti of ramps and overpasses, monster storage tanks. They began to pass gray-windowed factories and corrugated-metal warehouses. Everything seemed so industrial—even the new ballpark, with its geometric strutwork and its skeletons of lights.

"Mr. Lamb, ah, Horace," she said, "I don't know where you're headed, but if you'll drop me at the train station, I can grab a taxi."

"Oh, Belle told me to drive you direct to the door."

"But it's only . . ." She checked her watch.

"Not quite ten," she said, "and I don't have to be there till eleven."

"No, no, you just sit tight. Belle would never forgive me," he said.

She would have put up more of an argument, but she was afraid her voice would shake. All at once she felt so nervous. She wished she'd worn a different dress. In spite of the gloomy weather, it was warmer than she had expected, and her forest-green was too heavy. It was also too . . . Miss Grinsteadish, she realized. Luckily, though, she had brought other clothes. (She had debated which was worse: wearing the wrong thing or lugging a suitcase to a wedding, and like the most insecure schoolgirl, she had opted for the suitcase.) Maybe once she reached the house she could duck into a vacant room and change.

Mr. Lamb was asking her a question. Which street to take. She said, "Up Charles," using as few words as possible. She didn't seem to have enough air in her lungs.

How intimate this city seemed! How quaint and huddled to itself! After all those superhighways, Charles Street threaded between tall buildings like the narrowest little river in a ravine.

She opened her bag and searched for Susie's invitation. Yes, there it was, safe and sound.

Mr. Lamb was admiring the Johns Hopkins campus now. He said he had a cousin who had gone there for one semester. "Oh, really?" Delia murmured. He said he himself had not had the opportunity of a college education, although he felt he would have put it to good use. Delia wished he would stop talking. He was so irrelevant, so extraneous. She kept swallowing, but there was something in her throat that wouldn't go away.

When she told him to turn left he had to ask her to repeat herself. "Hah?" he asked, like a deaf old man. Like an irritating, deaf old man.

At a red light on Roland Avenue, a jogger ran toward them, a young woman with her long dark hair in a topknot and the fingers of her right hand delicately clasping two fingers of her left hand. A man in a tweed hacking jacket crossed with a tiny chihuahua. ("Now, there is a dog you couldn't pay me to put up with," Mr. Lamb said. "Might as well own a mosquito.") The air had a greenish, fluorescent quality, as if a storm were brewing.

She showed him where to turn next, which house to park in front of. (Was this how their house looked to strangers: so brown, so hunched, so forbidding?) She said, "I can get my things myself, if you'll just pop the trunk." But no, he had to unfold from the car, walk around to the rear, take forever hauling forth her suitcase. "Thanks! Bye!" she said, but even then she wasn't free to go. He kept on standing there, swaying slightly on his long, scuffed shoes and gazing at the house.

"We could easily manage the round one," he told her.

"Pardon?"

"The round little window up top there, what is it, over a stairs? Rue-Ray makes round windows all the time."

"Oh, good," she said, and she shook his hand, just to get him to leave. But an odd thing happened. Holding on to his bunched-twig fingers, meeting his bucktoothed, wistful smile, she unaccountably began to miss him. She felt like climbing back into the car with him and riding along for the rest of his trip.

Four vehicles stood in the driveway: Sam's Buick, a beat-up purple van, Eliza's Volvo, and a little red sports car. The mulberry tree had already started to scatter its chewed-looking leaves, and she had to step around acorns on the front walk. Evidently no one had thought to sweep.

The shutters had been repaired. The replacement louvers were a different color, though—a paler, flatter brown, as if they'd been given just a primer coat and then forgotten. There was a new sisal mat at the top of the porch steps, and a foil-wrapped pot of yellow chrysanthemums next to the door.

Knock, or walk in?

She knocked. (The doorbell would have been too much, somehow.) No answer. She knocked harder. Finally she turned the knob and stuck her head in. "Hello?"

For a house that was hosting a wedding in less than forty minutes, it didn't seem very welcoming. The front hall was empty, and so was the dining room, although (as Delia found when she advanced) the dining-room table was spread with a white tablecloth. She set down her suitcase, intending to continue into the kitchen, but just then Eliza walked through the kitchen door with a mug of something hot. She was concentrating so hard on the mug that it took her a second to see Delia. Then she said, "Oh!" and stopped short.

"I know I'm early," Delia told her.

"Oh, Delia! Thank heaven you're here!"

"What's wrong?" Delia asked. She was alarmed, of course, but also grateful to find herself in demand.

"Susie's changed her mind," Eliza called over her shoulder. She was proceeding toward the stairs.

Delia grabbed her suitcase and followed. "Changed her mind about marrying?" she asked.

"That's what she claims."

"When did this happen?"

"This morning," Eliza tossed back, starting

upward. She wore a new dress, a magenta A-line Delia couldn't imagine her buying, and patent-leather shoes whose heels rang against the stair treads. "Last night she slept in her old room," she was saying, "and this morning when we got here I asked Sam, 'Where's Susie? Isn't she up yet?' and he said—"

Delia felt disoriented. Susie's *old* room? Where was her new room? And who were "we" and what place had they got there from?

There wasn't a sign of Sam. Not a sign.

They had reached the second floor now, and Eliza, holding the mug in both hands, was sidling through the partly open door of Susie's bedroom. "Look who I brought with me!" she said. Delia set her suitcase down and walked in after her.

The room itself was what she noticed first. Frilly and flowered and stuffed with chintz since the days when it had been Linda's, it was a hollow cube now, unsoftened by curtains or rugs, furnished only with a foldaway cot and an ugly, round-cornered bureau from the attic. Susie sat cross-legged in a welter of blankets, wearing striped pajamas. Surrounding her—seated on the cot as well but all dressed up, even overdressed—were Linda, Linda's twins, and a pudgy young woman Delia could almost name but not quite. They raised a flank of alerted faces when Delia entered, but Delia looked only at Susie. Susie said, "Mom?"

"Hello, dear heart."

She bent over Susie and hugged her, absorbing that unique Susie smell that was something like dill weed. Still holding on to her, she settled on the cot beside her.

"Mom, I don't want to get married," Susie said.

"Then don't," Delia told her.

"Delia Grinstead!" Linda shrilled. "We're trying to talk some sense into her, do you mind?"

Linda was wearing bifocals—a new development. The twins had grown several inches, and from their dresses—stiff, mint-colored lace that hardly touched their skinny frames—Delia suspected they might be bridesmaids. Everyone looked so detailed, so eerily distinct: she couldn't explain it. Her eyes kept returning to Susie, craving the sight of her uncombed hair and her sweetly round chin and her cushiony lower lip.

The other young woman wore mint lace too. Driscoll's sister, that's who she was. Spencer? Spence. Driscoll Spence Avery's sister, Spence Driscoll Avery. "This exact same thing happened with my cousin," Spence was saying. "You all remember my cousin Lydia. She cried the whole way down the aisle of St. David's, and now she's happy as a clam and her husband is a bigwig in D.C."

"What kills me," Susie told Delia ("kills be," was how it came out, as if earlier she had been crying), "is we just signed a two-year lease on this fancy-shmancy apartment near the harbor. I've been phoning the realtor ever since last night, but all I get is his answering machine. I don't want to say why I'm calling, because then he might not call back. I figure if I could just reason with him . . . I left three different messages; I told him it was urgent; I said could he please get back to me immediately? But he didn't! It's after ten and he hasn't phoned and I'm stuck with that damned apartment forever!"

She was wailing now. Eliza said, "Oh, dear, oh, dear . . . have some tea, why don't you," and Linda said, "Well, for God's sake, Susie, the realtor is the least of it!"

But Delia told Susie, "I'll take care of it. You just give me his number, and I'll keep calling till I reach him."

"Would you?" Susie asked. She jumped up, trailing blankets, and went over to the bureau. "Wait a minute, I'll find his . . . Here. Mr. Bright, his name is. Tell him I apologize and I know I said we wanted it but to please, please let me out of this if he has a shred of human decency."

"You may have to forfeit your deposit," Delia said, examining the business card Susie handed her.

"Delia! Honest to God!" Linda cried. "Could we address the issue here?"

"Well, I'm not getting married, Aunt Linda,"

Susie told her, "so why waste time discussing it? Has anyone seen my jeans?"

She was roaming the room now, rummaging under the cot, scooping up a T-shirt. How shiny the floor was! Delia couldn't help noticing. Then she recalled the refinishers from last year's beach trip, and she felt all the more like an outsider. She set her handbag primly on her knees, trying to take up less space. But Linda noticed her anyway. She said, "Tell her, Delia."

"Tell her what?"

"Tell her all brides go through this."

Did they? Delia hadn't. Before her own wedding, her one concern had been that Sam would die before she got to be his wife. *Groom Slain on Wedding Eve,* the papers would read, or *Tragic Accident En Route to Nuptials,* and Delia would miss her chance for perfect happiness.

She had never doubted for a moment that it *would* be perfect.

Susie was dressing now, nonchalantly facing the wall while she peeled off her pajama top and hooked a gray-seamed bra. (Accustomed to locker rooms, she evidently thought nothing of changing in public.) Her back was a beautiful butterscotch color, as sturdy as a tree trunk. She pulled her T-shirt over her head, shook her hair loose, sauntered toward a suitcase on the floor, and bent to study its contents. Everybody watched. Finally Eliza, still holding the mug, said, "Susie has a very nice wedding dress. *Don't* you, Susie. Show your mother your wedding dress."

"It's a dopey dress," Susie said, but she turned and crossed the room to fling open the closet door. White chiffon exploded forth. Both twins rose, as if pulled by strings, and floated toward the closet with their lips parted. Susie slammed the door shut again. A filmy white triangle poked through on the hinge side.

"And your veil? Show her your veil," Eliza urged.

Obediently, Susie stomped over to the waste-basket. "*Here's* my veil," she said, and she pulled out several tatters of gauze and a head-band of white silk roses snipped into jagged shreds.

The two aunts sucked in their breaths. Spence said, "Great God Almighty!"

"Allow me to model it for you," Susie said. She clamped the headband around her neck, then let her head flop to one side and half closed her eyes and stuck out her tongue.

"Susan Grinstead!" Linda shrieked.

"So," Susie said calmly, removing the head-piece. "Driscoll and I are sitting downstairs last night, watching a movie. Folks had made this big federal case about how I ought to spend my final unwedded hours in my ancestral home."

"Well, how would it have *looked*?" Linda demanded.

Susie dropped the headband into the waste-basket. "So the two of us are in the study like old times," she said, "and the phone rings. It's this high-school-sounding boy; you can tell the call is taking all his courage. He clears his throat and says, 'Um, yes! Good evening. May I please speak to Courtney, please?' I tell him he has the wrong number. Not ten seconds later: *ring!* Same boy. 'Um, good evening. May I please—' 'You must have misdialed,' I tell him. So we're just getting settled again—Driscoll had rented *Nightmare on Elm Street*; he thinks it's the major motion picture of our time—when sure enough: *ring! ring!* Driscoll says, 'Let me handle this.' He picks up the receiver. 'Yeah?' he says. Listens a minute. Says, 'Tough luck, feller. Courtney doesn't want to have anything to do with you.' And slams the phone down."

"Oh! How mean!" Delia said involuntarily, and Eliza clucked her tongue. Then everyone looked at Driscoll's sister. "Well, sorry, Spence," Delia told her, "but really! That poor boy!"

"Yes, it *was* mean," Spence said complacently. She prinked her skirt out around her. "But that's how guys are, Sooze. What can you do?"

"It is not how guys are," Susie said. "Or if it is, all the more reason not to marry *anyone*. But for sure I'm not marrying Driscoll. And don't you defend him, Spence Avery! There is nothing you can say that will make him look good to me after that."

Thérèse said, "Couldn't he just apologize?"

"Apologize to who? Not to me; I'm not the one whose feelings he hurt. No, I see it all now," Susie said. She was drifting around the room without apparent purpose, wearing her T-shirt and pajama bottoms. She stopped in front of the mirror to yank at a handful of hair; then she continued her travels. "All these things I've been trying not to notice all this time. Like when we get ready to go out and he says, 'How do I look?' and I say, 'Fine,' he just goes, 'Thanks,' and never mentions how *I* look. Or when I'm telling him something that happened, he won't let me tell it my way. He always has to interrupt, to sort of . . . redirect. So I'll say, like, 'This patient of Dad's came into the shop today—' and right away he's, 'Wait a minute, you know who your dad's patients are? Isn't that a violation of confidentiality?' and, 'Now hold on, she asked for this by brand name? Or not,' and, 'What you should have told her is . . .' Till I feel like saying, 'Just shut up! Shut up! Shut up and let me get to the end of this story which I'm sorry now I ever began!' And speaking of my shop—"

*What shop?* Delia would have asked, except she didn't want to sound like Driscoll.

"He has never for one minute supported me on that. Oh, at the start he did because he thought it was just a whim, you know? He figured it would pass. But then when I borrowed the money from Gram—"

Eleanor had lent Susie money? (Eleanor didn't believe in lending money.) Susie must have noticed Delia's bafflement, because she said, "Oh. I've started this kind of like, business. House in a Box, I call it."

"A darling little business!" Linda chimed in.

"Got a mention in *Baltimore* magazine," Eliza said, "two and one-quarter inches long."

"I'd moved to an apartment," Susie told Delia, "after that bust-up with Dad. Me and Driscoll found a place on St. Paul Street. Well, I couldn't have afforded anything by myself. And I was looking for a job, but first I wanted to settle in, you know? Buy supplies for the kitchen and all. We had some furniture from home but no incidental stuff, skillets and stuff; didn't own so much as a spatula. So there I was, running around the stores, spending a fortune I didn't have, finding one thing one place and another thing another place. . . . I said, 'Wouldn't it be great if they sold a kitchen in a *box*? Kind of a one-stop purchase?' And that's what started me thinking. So now I've got this little showroom out past the fairgrounds; well, it's only about three feet square, but—"

"It's darling!" Linda said.

"And I sell these boxes: Kitchen in a Box,

Bathroom in a Box . . . just things I buy in bulk and combine in a kit and deliver, you know? I've tacked an ad on every campus bulletin board for miles around. I'm open seven days a week and I'm slaving away like a dog; that's why I set the wedding for a Monday. Didn't want to miss the weekend shoppers. As it is, I'm closed till Friday, which I hate. But Driscoll acts like this is some kind of hobby. When he heard about Gram's loan he was, 'Oh, you wouldn't want to get in over your head, hon.' He was, 'Wouldn't want to bite off more than you can chew, now, hon.' So discouraging and dampening; he doesn't think I'm up to this. Doesn't credit me with the brains to buy a simple shower curtain for college kids and a few damn rings to hang it with."

"Now, Susie, that is just not fair," Spence told her staunchly. "He's only trying to protect you."

"Plus he leaves spat-out fruit pits all over the apartment," Susie said.

Eliza suddenly set the mug on the bureau, as if this were the last straw.

"So I stopped *Nightmare on Elm Street*," Susie said, "and I gave him back his ring and sent him packing. And then I phoned the realtor, but I guess it was too late at night. And I'm sorry you all came for nothing, but I said to Dad, I said, 'Which is more trouble: calling off the wedding or suing for divorce?' "

"Where *is* Sam, anyhow?" Eliza wondered.

Delia was glad she hadn't had to ask that herself.

"He went to dress for the wedding," Susie said.

"But you did tell him—"

"I did tell him I'd changed my mind, but he just shut his eyes a minute and then he said he had to go dress for the wedding."

Yes, that was Sam, all right.

Delia stood up. She said, "I should get busy."

"Doing what?" Linda demanded.

"I have to phone the realtor."

She started for the door (the nearest phone was in Eliza's room), but Linda said, "Delia, my stars! Are you just going to accept this?"

"What else can I do?" she asked. "Drag her by the hair to the altar?"

"You could reason with her, for God's sake!"

"This is not a now-or-never proposition," Delia told her. (Really she was telling Susie, who stood leaning against the bureau, watching her with interest.) "If Susie isn't sure she wants to marry Driscoll today, she can marry him to-morrow, or next week, or next year. What's the hurry?"

"*She* can say that," Linda told the others. "*She* didn't fork over an arm and a leg for three airline tickets."

Delia latched the door quietly behind her.

At the same time, Sam's door, catty-corner

across the hall, swung open and he stepped forth. He was tugging down his shirt cuffs. He caught sight of her and stopped still. They were separated by the stairwell, with its varnished wooden balustrade, and so she waited where she was. He said, "Why, Delia."

"Hello, Sam."

His suit was that slim, handsome black one they had bought on sale several years ago. His face looked thinner. It was all straight lines— straight gray eyes and an arrow of a nose and a mouth that seemed *too* straight until (she knew) you saw the upward turns at the corners. His glasses happened to be slipping, the way they had a tendency to do, and when he raised a hand to adjust them he appeared to be doubting his eyesight. She said, "Didn't you know I was coming?"

"I knew," he said.

"Well . . . I guess you heard Susie's not going through with the wedding."

"She'll go through with it," he said. He rounded the balustrade—no, not to approach her (though already she had taken her first step forward to meet him), but to start down the stairs. "We'll proceed as planned," he sent back as he descended. "She'll come around."

Delia gazed down at him over the railing. She could clearly see his scalp through the fair hair on top of his head. *If I glimpsed him in a crowd,*

*I'd say he was just another worn-out, aging man,* she thought. But she didn't really believe that.

She made herself turn away and go into Eliza's room.

Here, too, she sensed a difference. The furniture was the same, but there wasn't a single object on the bureau, and only the gaunt, old-fashioned black telephone sat on the nightstand. Had Eliza changed rooms, or what? This one had been hers from the day she was born.

*I knew,* he had said. *We'll proceed as planned,* he had said.

Well, no point dwelling on it. Delia propped the realtor's card on the nightstand, lifted the receiver, and dialed.

"This is Joe Bright," a man announced thinly. "I can't come to the phone right now, but you may leave a message after the beep."

"Mr. Bright, this is Delia Grinstead calling, Susan Grinstead's mother. Could you please get back to me as soon as possible? It's very important. The number is . . ."

As she hung up, she heard the doorbell ring downstairs. "Hello, come in," Sam said, and next she heard one of those drawling, gravelly, Roland Park matron voices. Instantly, she lost all her confidence. She wasn't wearing enough makeup and her dress wasn't dressy enough, and when she looked in Eliza's mirror, her face seemed unformed and childish.

But she might have just imagined that, because when she started down the stairs (planting
her feet just so and holding her head very high),
everyone looked up at her with the most re-
spectful attention. The pastor—a tweedy, shaggy
man—said, "Mrs. Grinstead! What a pleasure!"
and Driscoll's parents broke off their chitchat
with Sam.

"It's a pleasure to see *you*, Dr. Soames," she
said. (Considering she attended church only on
major holidays, she was impressed that she remembered his name.) "Hello, Louise. Hello,
Malcolm."

"Why, hello, Delia," Louise Avery said, as if
they'd last seen each other yesterday. She was a
leathery woman with a lion's mane of gold hair
rearing back off her forehead. Her husband—
older, smaller, crinkly-eyed—said, "I don't
guess you could have brought some sunshine
with you."

"Oh," Delia said, and she glanced past him
toward the door. "Is it raining?" she asked.

"No, no, we're sure it will hold off till later,"
Louise said. "I was telling Malcolm this morning,
I said, 'At least this is one good thing about a
home wedding.' Can you imagine if they'd
planned a big formal church affair? Or something
out on the lawn?"

"No, I certainly . . . can't," Delia said.

She looked over at Sam, but he was fitting Dr.

Soames's rolled umbrella into the umbrella stand, and he didn't meet her eyes.

Maybe they would just have this wedding without the bride, she thought. Was that the plan?

In the living room, all available chairs had been lined up facing the fireplace. That must be where Dr. Soames would stand. In the dining room, Linda and Eliza were setting out platters of pastries. In the kitchen, the twins were gazing enraptured at Driscoll; he was discussing the honeymoon. "I told Sooze we ought to just head to Obrycki's for crabs," he said. "Call *that* our honeymoon, in keeping with the general tone of the wedding. And she said, 'Or why not carry-out?' but in the end we settled for three days at— Oh, Miz Grinstead! Hey there!"

"Hello, Driscoll," Delia said. She was puzzled to see him looking so cheerful. He was dressed in a navy suit with a white rose in the lapel, and his face had a scrubbed, fresh, oblivious look. She said, "Ah, have you . . . talked with Susie this morning?"

"Oh, can't see the bride before the ceremony, Miz Grinstead!" he said, wagging a finger.

"Yes, but just to talk with her—talk on the phone, maybe," Delia said.

"Say! Where's those ushers of mine, Miz Grinstead? Any sign of them yet?"

"Ushers?"

"Ramsay and Carroll!"

"Well, no, I . . . gosh, I hope someone thought to wake them," she said. Neither one of the boys had yet lost the knack of sleeping till noon.

"Maybe you should give them a ring," Driscoll told her.

With her mind on wedding matters, she thought for an instant he meant the kind of ring you wear on your finger. She looked at him blankly. Then Eliza, sailing past with a three-tiered cake stand, said, "Why they need ushers anyhow, with no one but family attending and seats for not more than a dozen . . ."

"It's so these glamorous bridesmaids will have somebody's arm to hang on to," Driscoll said, winking at the twins. Marie-Claire giggled, and Thérèse sent him a solemn, worshipful stare and stood straighter inside her tepee of mint lace.

Delia gave up and left the kitchen. She would go see if Susie had decided to get married after all. Who knows, she might have. (For it was easy to believe, in such company, that she was at this moment adjusting her magically reconstructed veil.) And if so, then Delia would check on the boys, make sure they were awake and dressed.

But the boys were already downstairs, standing by the front door in their suits. They looked astoundingly grown-up—Ramsay square-jawed and almost portly now, Carroll as wiry as ever but taller, with something more carved about his face. With them were Ramsay's girlfriend,

Velma, wearing an upside-down pink hollyhock of a dress that ended just below her crotch, and her little daughter (who? oh, Rosalie) in aqua. Ramsay said, "Hi, Mom," and kissed Delia's cheek, and Carroll allowed her to hug him, and Velma said, "Well, hey! How was your trip?"

"It was fine," Delia said.

So that was the way it would be, evidently. She had been settled into a convenient niche in people's minds: just another of those eccentric wives you see living year-round in an Ocean City condo or raising horses on a farm in Virginia while their husbands continue their workaday routines in Baltimore. Nobody gave it a thought.

She passed through the assembling guests, smiling and murmuring greetings. Sam's uncle Robert squeezed her hand but went on listening to Malcolm Avery rehash a recent golf game. Sam himself was helping his aunt Florence out of a black rubber raincoat that looked capable of standing on its own.

"How do we know when the ceremony starts?" someone asked at Delia's elbow.

It was Eleanor, in a gray silk shirtdress. "Oh, Eleanor!" Delia cried, and she threw her arms around Eleanor's spare figure.

"Hello, dear," Eleanor said, patting her shoulder. "How nice you came for this."

"Of course I came! How could I not?"

"I was wondering about the procession,"

Eleanor said smoothly. "Do they plan any kind of music? Susie has been admirably sensible about the arrangements, but how will we know when the bride walks in?"

"Eleanor, I'm not even sure there's going to *be* a bride," Delia said. "She claims she's reconsidered."

"Ah. Well, you'll want to go see to her, then," Eleanor said, unperturbed. "Run along; I can take care of myself, dear."

"Maybe I *should* go," Delia said, and she fled up the stairs.

Susie was alone now, dressed in jeans and sneakers, lounging on the cot and reading *People* magazine. She glanced up casually when Delia knocked on the doorframe. "Oh, hi," she said. "Are they having conniptions down there?"

"Well, they don't . . . exactly grasp the situation yet," Delia said. "Susie, should I send Driscoll up?"

"Driscoll's here?"

"He's here in his wedding suit, waiting for you to come marry him."

"Well, shoot," Susie said, lowering her magazine. "It's not like I haven't informed him in plain English."

"And his parents are here, and Dr. Soames—"

"Did you talk to the realtor?" Susie asked.

"I left a message."

"Mom. This really, really matters. If I don't

get that lease revoked, it'll be me they come after for the money, do you realize that? I'm the one who actually signed my name. And I didn't want to say this in front of Driscoll's sister, but the fact is, I am dirt poor. I'm in debt for the wedding, even—four hundred twenty-eight dollars, no thanks to that father of mine."

"What did the four hundred twenty-eight dollars go for, exactly?" Delia asked out of curiosity.

"My dress and veil and the bouquet in the fridge. Aunt Eliza's footing the bill for refreshments. *Please* go call Mr. Bright. If he's still not there, tell his machine it's a life-or-death situation."

"Well, all right," Delia said. "And then should I send Driscoll up?"

"He knows where to find me."

Susie went back to her magazine. Delia started to leave, but in the doorway she turned. She said, "How come the house looks so different?"

"Different?"

"All the furniture's gone from your room, and Eliza's room seems . . . unlived-in."

"Well, it is unlived-in," Susie said, flipping a page. "Nobody lives here but Dad anymore."

"What?"

"Didn't you know that?"

"*No,* I didn't know that. What happened?"

"Well," Susie said, "let me see. First Ramsay

and Dad got into a fight about—no, wait. First
*Eliza* and Dad got into a fight. She claimed it
was because he didn't let her know he'd be late
for dinner, but the real truth is, she was making
a play for him, Mom, like you wouldn't believe.
It was pitiful. All us kids told her so, but she
was like, 'Hmm? I don't know what you're talking about,' and meanwhile there was Dad, out
of it as usual, just going about his business and
paying her no mind. So one day she picks a quarrel about a totally nother issue and flounces off
to visit Aunt Linda, and when she comes back
she announces she's leaving for good. Now she
lives on Calvert Street; that's where Linda and
the twins are staying for the wedding. Okay, so
*then* Ramsay and Dad got into a fight, on account
of Dad calling Velma 'Veronica' by accident
which Velma swore he did on purpose, and Ramsay moved to Velma's in a huff; and then Carroll
moved there too because he missed his curfew
one night and Dad was pacing the floor and picturing him dead on the road, he said. . . . And
me: you know about me. I moved out in July,
just before Ramsay."

"Yes, I suppose I . . . ," Delia said
abstractedly.

"So are you going to call the realtor, Mom?"

"Oh. Right," Delia said, and after a brief
pause, she walked out.

In Eliza's old room, she sat on the edge of the

bed, lifted the receiver, and then stared into space.

Imagine Sam pacing the floor. Always before, it had been Delia pacing the floor, and Sam pooh-poohing her and telling her to simmer down. "How can you be so cool about this?" she used to ask him. "What have you got in your veins: ice water?" And it seemed to her that he had given a little smile at that, a gratified, sheepish little smile, as if she had paid him a compliment.

She dialed the realtor's number again. "This is Joe Bright," the machine said. "I can't come to the . . ."

"It's Delia Grinstead again, Mr. Bright. I'd appreciate your calling me at your earliest convenience," she said. And just to oblige Susie, she added, "It's a matter of life and death. Bye."

Downstairs, the voices were a woven mass, as if people had given up on the wedding and settled for a party instead. But when she descended to join them, conversation halted for a moment and people turned expectantly. She smiled at them. She was glad now she'd worn the forest-green, with the skirt that swung so alluringly just above her ankles.

She crossed the hall to the living room, and the others followed. Probably they thought this was a signal of some kind. In fact, Carroll, killingly attractive in his usher's suit, caught up with

her to offer his arm and lead her to a front seat,
and a moment later Eleanor joined her, escorted
by Ramsay. "Put Aunt Florence in a straight
chair," Ramsay muttered to Carroll. "She says
her back is acting up." Delia heard the usual
audience sounds—coughs and rustling skirts.
Driscoll's parents settled on the couch. Dr.
Soames took his place on the hearth, smiling
benignly toward the room at large and extracting
a folded sheet of paper from his breast pocket.

"Bridal jitters all over now?" Eleanor whispered to Delia.

"No, um, not exactly."

Velma's colorless child chose a wing chair so
big for her that her Mary Janes failed to touch
the floor. A young man Delia didn't know—
some relative of Driscoll's, no doubt—deposited
Eliza on the love seat, and Linda plopped next
to her unescorted and eased her feet out of her
pumps. "Is she coming?" she mouthed when she
saw Delia looking at her. Delia merely shrugged
and faced front again.

Now Driscoll was standing beside Dr. Soames,
fidgeting with his boutonniere. And the bridesmaids were clustered at the foot of the stairs,
where the ushers joined them when the very last
guest had been seated.

Sam bent over Delia. She hadn't seen him
coming; she drew back slightly. "Should I put
the record on?" he asked her.

"Record?"

"Is she ready?"

"Oh," she said. "Well, no, I don't believe she is."

He straightened and stared down at her. He said, "Then shouldn't you be doing something?"

"Like what?"

He didn't answer. His lips were very dry and white. Delia smoothed her skirt and sat back to observe the next development.

She had never realized before that worry could be dumped in someone else's lap like a physical object. She should have done it years ago. Why did Sam always get to be the one?

Now he turned toward the record player, which was housed in a walnut cabinet at Delia's elbow. He clicked a button, and a moment later the sound of horns flared out. Delia recognized the theme from *Masterpiece Theatre*. Privately she found the selection a bit too triumphal, and she suspected from the sniff on her right that Eleanor felt the same way. Everybody else, though, sat in a reverent hush as Sam strode from the room. Delia heard his shoes crossing the hall and crisply mounting the stairs. Why, this wedding must have been planned to duplicate her own: the father of the bride escorting the bride down the stairs and through the double doorway to the center of the living room, to a spot directly beneath the gawky brass chandelier.

But suppose the bride did not stand waiting in the upstairs hall?

The footsteps must have continued, but the music drowned them out. Or maybe Sam had stopped at the top of the stairs, just beyond the guests' view, instead of going in to talk with Susie. That was more like him. In any case, the trumpets blatted on while people smiled at one another *(Isn't this so informal and so family,* they were probably thinking), and then the footsteps started down again. But anyone could tell that no bride was keeping pace with that rapid, noisy descent.

Sam marched to a spot directly in front of Dr. Soames. Delia wondered, for an instant, whether he planned to carry on regardless—take the vows in Susie's place. But he moistened his lips and said, "Ladies and gentlemen . . ."

It was Delia who reached over and lifted the phonograph needle. That was the least she could do, she figured, since it was Sam who announced that he was sorry to have to say this, he hated to put people out like this, but the wedding had been postponed a bit.

"Postponed" was optimistic, in Delia's opinion. But people did seem to view it as the most minor readjustment in the couple's schedule. Linda announced crossly that she and the twins were reserved on a noon flight home two days from now, totally nonrefundable, which she damn well hoped Miss Susie would bear in mind. Dr. Soames, leafing through a pocket diary, muttered something about meetings, visits, Building Fund . . . but later in the week looked all right, he said; looked quite promising, in fact.

Even Driscoll's mother, who seemed more distressed than anyone, turned out to be thinking mainly of a reception she was giving after the honeymoon. "Will they be married by Saturday night, do you think?" she asked Delia. "Could you just, maybe, feel Susie out a little? We've got fifty-three of our closest friends coming; you too if you're still in town."

"Maybe Driscoll will know more when they've finished talking," Delia said. "I'll have him get in touch with you the minute he comes downstairs."

For Driscoll had at long last gone up to speak with Susie. He should have done that at the start, if you asked Delia.

The rain that had been threatening all day was falling now, and people scurried to their cars once they were out the front door. First Dr. Soames left, and then Sam's aunt and uncle with Eleanor, and Driscoll's sister with the unnamed usher, and finally Driscoll's parents. Then Eliza said, "Well! I thought that little sports car of Spence's had boxed me in for life!" and she swept out, with Linda and the twins in tow. But Ramsay and Carroll stayed on, dogging Delia's heels as she carried platters of food to the kitchen, which meant that Velma and Rosalie had to stay as well. They made themselves scarce, though, watching TV in the study. Meanwhile Sam set the living-room furniture in order, and Carroll told Delia the entire plot of a movie he and Ramsay had seen. This man, he said, had been stuck in some kind of time warp where he had to keep reliving the same one day over and over. Delia thought that with all the topics they could have been discussing, Carroll had made a mighty peculiar choice, but she just said, "Mmhmm. Mmhmm," as she flitted around the kitchen, swathing various platters in plastic wrap. Carroll followed so closely that she couldn't reverse direction without advance notice, and Ramsay wasn't far behind.

But then Sam brought in the tablecloth, bunched in a clumsy cylindrical shape, and the atmosphere changed. Carroll stumbled in his recitation. Ramsay got very busy shutting cupboard doors. Both of them seemed to be watching Delia even while they were looking away.

"Tablecloth," Sam said. He passed it to her.

Delia said, "Oh! Good! Thanks!" Then she said, "I'll just take it down to the . . . ," and she wheeled and walked through the pantry and down the basement stairs.

Not that that tablecloth had the slightest need of laundering.

At the bottom of the stairs the cat was waiting, gazing up at her intently. Vernon always escaped to the basement when there were guests. She said, "Vernon! Have you missed me?" and she bent to cup his round, soft head. "I missed you too, little one," she whispered. He was purring in that exaggerated way cats have when they want to put humans at ease.

Footsteps crossed the pantry and started down the stairs. Delia rose and went over to the washing machine. Vernon vanished into thin air. The machine was full of damp laundry, but she stuffed in the tablecloth anyhow and recklessly poured detergent on top.

Behind her, Sam cleared his throat. She turned. "Oh! Hello, Sam," she said.

"Hi."

She busied herself with the washing machine, selecting the proper cycle and rotating the dial with a zippery sound. Water started rushing; pipes clanked overhead. Outside the dust-filmed window, ivy leaves bobbed beneath the falling raindrops.

"As soon as Driscoll comes down," she said, turning again to Sam, "I'm going to call a cab, but I figured I'll wait till then so I can say good-bye to Susie."

"A cab to where?" Sam asked.

"To the bus station."

"Oh," Sam said. Then he said, "It would be silly to call a cab, with all these cars at hand. Or rather, I don't mean silly, but . . . I could drive you. Or Ramsay could, if you prefer. Ramsay's been using the Plymouth, you know."

"Oh, has he?" Delia asked. "How has it been running, anyway?"

"All right."

"No more electrical problems?"

He just looked at her.

"Well, thanks," she said. "I probably *will* ask for a lift, if it isn't too much trouble."

She left unanswered the question of who would drive her.

They went back up the stairs, Delia preceding Sam and moving with self-conscious gracefulness. The kitchen was empty now. The dining-room table had a naked look; Sam had not thought to replace the candelabra after removing the tablecloth. The hall was empty too, but they paused there a minute, gazing toward the silence overhead.

"I don't think he's going to change her mind," Delia said.

"It's only wedding-day nerves."

"I think she's serious. I think she really means this."

"You remember how she was when she was little," Sam said. "She used to get these fixations, remember? Like when she wanted to wear her cowboy pajamas to kindergarten. You said no and she came to breakfast in her underwear, but you pretended not to notice and by schooltime she'd put on a skirt."

"A skirt and her pajama tops, which I'd covered partway with a bandanna to hide the snaps," Delia said. "We compromised. There's a difference."

She was touched, though. She wasn't sure why. Maybe it was because she herself figured so prominently in his story, as if he had taken notes on what she'd done and then attempted, years later, to do the same.

She stayed in the hall a moment longer, in case he wanted to tell her anything more, but evidently he didn't. He turned away and made for the living room. Delia first smoothed her dress and adjusted her belt (not wanting to appear to chase him), and then she followed.

In the study, the lamps were unlit, and everyone sat in pewter-gray light watching TV— Velma and the boys on the couch, Rosalie on the floor between her mother's feet. They turned as Sam and Delia entered. "What's for lunch?" Carroll asked.

Delia said, "Lunch!"

"We're starving."

She checked the time. It was after one. She glanced toward Sam for some cue (the kitchen wasn't hers anymore; the household wasn't hers to feed), but he didn't help her. Then footsteps sounded overhead.

"Driscoll," Sam said.

Rosalie continued gaping at a soap opera, but the rest of them went out to the hall—Velma and the boys rising in an elaborately bored, stretching way, everyone moving slowly so as not to seem overeager. They gathered at the bottom of the stairs and watched Driscoll descend.

He looked distraught. His hair was raked and ropy, and his tie was wrenched askew. When he reached the bottom step he shook his head.

"No wedding?" Delia asked him.

"Well, I wouldn't say *no* wedding."

"What, then?"

"She says she hates me and I'm not a good person and now she sees she never loved me anyway."

"So, no wedding," Delia mused aloud.

"But if I want to change her mind, she says, I know what I should do."

"What should you do?"

"I don't know," Driscoll said.

Sam snorted and moved off toward the living room.

"Send flowers?" Velma suggested. "Send a singing telegram?"

"I don't know, I tell you. I said, 'Couldn't you give me a hint?' She said, 'It'll come to you. And if it doesn't,' she said, 'it's a sign we shouldn't get married.' "

"Send a Mylar balloon with a message printed on?" Velma pursued.

"Saying what, though?" Driscoll asked.

"Driscoll," Delia said, "I believe your mother wants to talk with you."

"Oh. Okay," he said dully.

He stood thinking a moment. Then he gave his shoulders a shake and let himself out the front door—no raincoat, no umbrella, nothing. The rain was falling so hard it was bouncing off the porch railing.

"Hire a skywriter!" Velma said after he'd gone.

"Mom," Carroll said, "could we just eat?"

"I'll fix something right away," she told him.

Might as well. Nobody else was going to do it.

Delia prepared a tray for Susie and brought it up to her room. She found her asleep on top of the covers—not all that surprising. Susie was the kind of person who retreated into sleep like a drug, losing whole days at times of emotional crisis. Oh, the *otherness* of Delia's children never failed to entrance her! She considered it a sort of bonus gift—a means of experiencing, up close, an entirely opposite way of being.

"Susie, honey," she said. Susie opened her

eyes. "I thought you'd want something to eat," Delia told her.

"Thanks," Susie said, and she struggled blearily to a sitting position.

Delia placed the tray in Susie's lap. "It's all your favorites. Ginger cheesecake, Jewish-grandmother cookies . . ."

"Great, Mom," Susie said, shaking out her napkin.

"Lemon chiffon tartlets, chocolate mousse cups . . ."

Susie looked down at the tray.

"I had to use the wedding food," Delia explained. "There weren't a lot of groceries in the kitchen."

"Oh," Susie said. She said, "So is that . . . what everyone's eating?"

"Well, yes."

"They're eating up my wedding food?"

"Well . . . would you rather they didn't?"

"No, no!" Susie said too breezily. She picked up a tartlet.

Delia felt confused. She said, "Did you want us to save them? If you were planning on, um, rescheduling in the near future, why, then I suppose—"

"No, I said! It's fine."

"Well, what *are* your plans? I'm not trying to pressure you or anything, but Driscoll did mention . . . I'm just asking so I can make travel arrangements."

In the midst of taking a bite, Susie looked over at her.

"On account of my job and all," Delia explained.

"Oh, just *go,* if you're so set on it!" Susie burst out.

"That's not what I—"

"I'm amazed you came at all! You and your stupid job and your man friend and your new family!"

"Why, Susie—"

"Gallivanting off down the beach and leaving Dad just wandering the house like the ghost of someone, and your children . . . orphaned, and me setting up a whole wedding on my own without my mother!"

Delia stared at her.

"What did he *do,* Mom?" Susie demanded. "Was it him? Was it us? What was so terrible? What made you run out on us?"

"Sweetheart, no one did anything," Delia said. "It wasn't that clear-cut. I never meant to hurt you; I didn't even mean to leave you! I just got . . . unintentionally separated from you, and then it seemed I never found a way to get back again."

She knew how lame that sounded. Susie listened in silence, gazing over her tartlet, and now that letter she'd sent—the forced gaiety of all those exclamation points, the careful carelessness of *See ya!* and *Luv*—made Delia want to weep. "Honeybun," she said, "if I'd known you wanted help with the wedding, I would have done anything! Anything."

But all Susie said was, "Could you please phone the realtor again?"

"Yes, of course," Delia said, sighing, and she bent and kissed Susie's forehead before she left.

By a process of inaction, of procrastination (much like the one that had stranded her so far from home in the first place), Delia stayed on through the afternoon, waiting for Susie to come downstairs. But time passed, and when she went back up to check, she found Susie asleep again, the tray nearly untouched on the floor beside the cot.

Sam was in his office, presumably—doing what, she had no idea, since she hadn't seen any patients arrive. The others sat in the study watching TV, and she settled on the couch next to Velma and pretended to watch too. The good thing about TV was that everyone talked around it in an unthinking, natural way; they forgot that she was listening. She learned that Carroll had gone out three times with a girl from Holland; that Ramsay's history professor had a grudge against him; that Velma had promised Rosalie a beauty-parlor manicure if she would quit biting her cuticles. It reminded Delia of her car-pool days, when she'd been privy to all the latest gossip because children don't seem to realize that drivers have ears.

Nobody mentioned Susie.

Sam came to stand in the doorway, and when she looked over at him he asked if she would like him to go get some groceries for supper. She felt absurdly pleased. She said, "Yes, why not," and then everyone started requesting specific dishes—her tarragon chicken, her ziti salad. She went out to the kitchen and made up a grocery list. She waited for Sam to invite her along when he left, but he didn't.

Eliza phoned—her second call in two hours. "Now, where is Driscoll in all this?" she asked. "Don't tell me he's just letting her be."

"It does seem that way," Delia said. She was talking on the kitchen extension, so she didn't have to lower her voice. "I don't know *what* to think," she said. "Susie's fast asleep and Driscoll's disappeared and the rest of us are just sitting here, wondering what next."

"Mark my words," Eliza said, "they'll be married before sundown tomorrow. That's what I told Linda. I said, 'You won't even have to switch your airline reservations.' How about *you*? You're not leaving yet, are you?"

"I haven't decided."

"You can't," Eliza said. "You'd only have to turn around and come back."

"You may be right," Delia said.

The real reason she couldn't leave was Susie —her sad little face above the tartlet. But she didn't tell Eliza that.

As soon as they said goodbye she called Joel, but the telephone rang and rang. They had probably gone out for supper, ignoring what she'd left for them. They were probably at Rick-Rack's. She knew what they would order, even, and the tune of their conversation—Noah's exuberant spurts of words and Joel's neutral answers. His palms cradling her head. His mouth firm but not insistent. His body tensed as if, with every move, he had been gauging her response.

*After the baby,* Ellie said, *we just kissed, the most wonderful kisses . . .*

Delia hung up.

When Sam came back from the grocery store, she asked him (with her head in the fridge, tossing the question over her shoulder) whether he would mind if she stayed till tomorrow.

"Why would I mind?" he said.

It wasn't a very satisfying answer. But before she could go into it further, Ramsay and Carroll trooped through—off to the video shop, they said, to rent that time-warp movie again—and Sam left the room. Delia fixed supper by herself. Everything came back to her: those weird little nipples on the cabinet knobs, the squeak of the exhaust fan above the stove. But here she was, in Miss Grinstead's forest-green dress and old-maid shoes with the strap across the instep.

Susie did appear in time for supper. She sat at the table swaddled in a blanket, looking like a little girl awakened from her nap. But she didn't refer to the wedding, and nobody else brought it up. Then afterward they all watched the movie—even Sam, his glasses glinting in the dark. Although really it was Susie they were watching. Any time Susie made a moderately humorous comment, her brothers fell all over themselves laughing, and Velma gave a hissing titter, and Rosalie sent her a deadpan, penetrating stare.

At the end of the movie Ramsay and Velma collected Rosalie and said good night, but Carroll announced that he might as well sleep over. Delia went upstairs with him to put sheets on his bed. While she was plumping his pillow she heard Susie come upstairs too, and she knew that left only Sam in the study. She didn't go back down, therefore. Instead, she returned to the linen closet for another set of sheets, and she made up the bed in Eliza's room.

Much later, flat on her back in the dark, she heard Sam's shoes on the stairs. He crossed the hall to his room without so much as a pause, and she heard his door click shut behind him.

It was ridiculous of her to feel so wounded.

# 20

"This sugar caster," Linda told the twins, "was a gift from your great-great-aunt, Mercy Ramsay, when her sister married Isaiah Felson in 1899."

Delia couldn't imagine how Linda knew that. The twins, however, seemed unimpressed. They were busy admiring Carroll, who was shaking the caster upside down over his bowl of cornflakes. It was eleven-thirty in the morning, and he was only now eating breakfast. Linda and the twins had had breakfast earlier, after Eliza dropped them off on her way to work. Sam, presumably, had fixed himself something before he went into his office, and Susie wasn't awake yet. It was going to be one of those days when the tail end of one person's meal ran into the start of another's from morning to night. Delia herself was just sort of munching along with every new shift.

"Mercy Ramsay was a huge concern to her parents because she never married," Linda was saying. "She had a job as a 'typewriter,' was what they called them then, at a law office down near the harbor."

Delia glanced over at her.

Carroll was shoveling in cornflakes now, and Marie-Claire appeared to be warming her hands on the sugar caster—which was not, to tell the truth, very imposing: a chesspiece-shaped urn of dulled and dented plate. Thérèse was setting an index finger here and there on the table to mash stray crystals of sugar and transfer them to her tongue.

Linda said, "In every generation of our family, there's been one girl who never married."

"This generation it'll be Thérèse," Marie-Claire said.

"Will not," Thérèse said.

"Will so."

The phone rang.

"If that's the school, I'm sick," Carroll told Delia.

"Carroll Grinstead! I refuse to fib for you," Delia said. She dumped the cat off her lap and rose to answer. "Hello?"

"Delia?" Noah said.

Delia turned away from the others. "What's wrong?" she asked, as quietly as possible.

"I've got a cold."

"Are you in bed?"

"I'm on the couch. Where'd you *get* to? Why aren't you back yet?"

"Well, I did try to telephone last night, but you were out," Delia said. "How'd you know where to call, anyway?"

"And that's another thing! You didn't leave a

number! I had to phone Belle Flint and she said you'd gone to your family's so I told Information, 'Look for Grinstead,' and the first Grinstead turned out to be this lady and she said, 'Oh, that's my daughter-in-law you want,' and she had me write down the . . . But you said you'd be back yesterday!"

"Or today," Delia reminded him. "I'll probably catch a bus, oh, maybe this afternoon; I'll know more as soon as—"

"Is that the *realtor*?" Susie called from upstairs.

Delia covered the mouthpiece of the receiver. 'No, it's not!" she called back. Then she told Noah, "You just stay on the couch. I'll be home soon. Bye."

When she hung up, she turned to find everyone watching her. "Well!" she said vivaciously. "So!"

From their expressions, you would have thought she'd been caught in some crime.

Then Sam walked in, wearing his white coat. He was taking his lunch break, and here they were, still at breakfast. In fact, Linda had his chair, which she made no move to give up. "If it isn't the good doctor," she said in an acid tone.

Delia said, "Sam, what would you—?" and then she stopped. It wasn't her place, really, to offer him lunch. But he didn't seem to realize that, and he sat in Susie's usual seat and said, "Anything would be fine. Soup."

Soup must be what he lived on, because it was just about the only thing in the cupboard—his special salt-free, fat-free, taste-free brand, with a dancing heart on the label. She opened a tin of soya-milk mushroom and poured it into a saucepan.

Now he was asking Carroll why he wasn't in school. He was going about it all wrong, taking a drilling-in approach that would only raise Carroll's hackles, and Carroll was hunching belligerently over his cereal bowl. Both of them, Delia noticed—in fact, everyone in the room—had become less perceivable to her since yesterday. Already they had lost that slick exterior layer of the unaccustomed.

Sam said that the distant likelihood of a sibling's wedding was not sufficient grounds for playing hooky. "What do *you* know about it?" Carroll asked him. "Some of the kids in my class take off for Orioles games, for Christ's sake."

"Watch your language, young man," Sam said. Delia merely stirred the soup. She pictured Sam shifting in midair like some kind of kite or streamer, like a wind sock changing shape with changes in the wind. From one angle he was gentle and reserved and well-meaning; from another he was finicky and humorless. She remembered all at once that when she had gazed across her desk at him the morning they first met, there had been a split second when his fine-boned face had struck her as *too* fine, too prig-

gish, and she had faltered. But then she had
brushed that impression aside and forgotten it
forever—or at least, until this moment.

"Please, Uncle Sam?" the twins were coaxing.
Marie-Claire said, "Can't he stay home just this
once? For our sakes?"

The front doorbell rang before he could answer. Everybody looked at one another, and the
cat made a dash for the basement. "I'm not
here," Carroll said with his mouth full. Finally
Delia lowered the flame beneath the soup and
went to see who it was.

In the sun-glazed windowpane at the center of
the door, Driscoll Avery stood gazing off to one
side and whistling. Whistling! Goodness. Delia
opened the door and said, "Hello, Driscoll."

"Hey there, Miz G.!" he said, stepping inside.
"Super weather."

It was, in fact. Autumn had moved in overnight, nippy and hard-edged, and Driscoll's
cheeks glowed pink. He wore fall clothes, weekend clothes even though this was a Tuesday. Delia shut the door against the chill. "Come into
the kitchen and have some breakfast," she said.
"Or lunch, or whatever you're on."

"No, thanks. I just need to talk to Susie a
minute."

"Well, I think she must be awake, but she
hasn't come downstairs yet," Delia told him.

"Okay if I go up?"

"Oh, I don't know if she—"

"Please, Miz Grinstead. I believe now I've got it! I know how to get her to marry me."

Delia gave him a skeptical look, but he said, "All right?" and without waiting for her permission, he wheeled and bounded up the stairs.

It took real character not to listen for what happened next.

Back in the kitchen, everyone was waiting. "Well?" Linda demanded.

"That was Driscoll."

"Driscoll!" both twins said.

"He's gone up to speak with Susie."

The twins scooted their chairs away from the table. Linda said, "Stay right where you are."

"Can't we just—?"

"They'll never sort things out with you two making pests of yourselves."

Delia returned to the stove. She stirred the soup until it started dimpling, and then she poured it into a bowl—a bleak gray liquid that reminded her of scrub water. "Taupe soup," she said as she set the bowl before Sam. The phrase tickled her, and she gave a little snicker. Sam glanced at her sharply.

"Thank you, Delia," he said in his deliberate way.

The twins were badgering Linda about their bridesmaid dresses. Could they put them on right now? Could Linda iron their sashes where they'd

wrinkled from before? Delia placed a spoon beside Sam's bowl, and he thanked her all over
again and picked it up. "You go get your books
together," he told Carroll. "A half day of school
is better than none."

"I'm just waiting to hear what Driscoll says,"
Carroll told him.

"Driscoll has nothing to do with this."

"He does if the wedding is on again. And anyhow, I don't *have* my books. They're at Velma's
place. So there."

Sam started spooning soup, ostentatiously
composed.

"I've been in charge of getting my own self to
school all fall," Carroll told him. "How come
the minute I'm under your roof I'm treated like
a two-year-old?"

"Because you're behaving like a two-year-
old," Sam said.

Carroll pushed back from the table. His chair
scraped across the floor, and he very nearly
slammed into Driscoll, who arrived at that moment in the dining-room doorway. "Hi, all,"
Driscoll said.

"Driscoll!" the twins screeched. "What'd she
say?" "Did she say yes?"

They should have known she hadn't. Driscoll
had come back down far too soon, and if that
were not enough, they could have read the bad
news in his face, which was somber and no longer

pink-cheeked, somehow thicker through the jaw. He gave a deep sigh and then turned and —it seemed for an instant—took his leave; but no, he was fetching a chair from the dining room. He dragged it back to the kitchen and placed it next to Carroll and sat down heavily. "She says I've got to do it myself," he said.

"Do what?"

"See, all night long I thought and thought," he said. He seemed to be addressing Delia, who had reclaimed her own seat at the end of the table. "I thought, *What is it Susie wants?* And it came to me: I had to set things straight with that kid who called on the phone. But the only person who might know his name was the girl he was trying to reach—Courtney. So this morning I started dialing every possible variation on you-all's number, looking for Courtney."

"Lord have mercy," Linda said.

"Well, it's simpler than it sounds. Turns out I had to transpose two digits, that was all. About my tenth or so try, I get Courtney's mom, I guess it was, and she tells me Courtney's at school."

"Ah," the twins said together.

"So I say, 'Well, I was supposed to drop off her history notes, so what I'll do, if you don't mind, I'll bring them by her house after school, is that okay? And could I please have that street address again?' "

"Cool," Carroll said.

Even Sam looked mildly interested. He had stopped eating his soup and was watching Driscoll, with his eyebrows raised.

"Lucky for me, the mom fell for it," Driscoll said. "Gave me their address straight off—place right here in the neighborhood." He paused, struck by a thought. "Carroll," he said, "*you* don't know any Courtneys, do you?"

"I know six or seven Courtneys," Carroll said.

"Any on Deepdene Road?"

"Not that I'm aware of."

"Well, anyhow," Driscoll said, "all I have to do now is ask her who her caller was."

"But what if she has no idea who he was?" Delia said.

"She might have *some* idea. If he's been hanging around her a lot, giving her, like, signals or something."

Sam was spooning up soup again, shaking his head.

"So next I go talk to Susie. Ask her to come with me to Courtney's after school. You know I can't do it alone! Strange guy showing up full of questions . . . Except Susie says no."

"No?" Linda echoed.

"No. Sends me straight downstairs again. Says I'll have to manage without her. Bring her the boy in person, was how she put it, if I want her to forgive me."

*If you want to win the princess's hand,* Delia

thought to herself, because the errand did have a certain fairy-tale ring to it. She began to feel slightly sorry for Driscoll, although he himself seemed to be recovering his good spirits. "So now it's up to you, Miz G.," he said almost jauntily.

"Me!"

"Could you come with me to Courtney's after school?"

"Why, Driscoll, I—"

"I'll go!" Thérèse said.

"Me and Thérèse'll go!" Marie-Claire said.

Driscoll didn't seem to hear them. He said, "Miz Grinstead, you can't imagine what I feel like. I feel like I've got this . . . cloud in my chest! You think at first it's some snit she's having, some temporary snit, and you're mad as hell and you figure if you ignore it . . . but then it starts to get to you. You start to feel really, I guess you'd say, sad, but still mad besides and also eventually just, almost, *bored*, I mean so sick of it all, so sick of going over it and over it, sick of your own self, even; and you say to yourself, 'Well, look at it this way: you ought to be glad you're free of her. She always did act kind of irritating,' you say. But then you say, 'If she'd give me one more chance, though! I mean, how did things get so out of hand here? When did they start to go wrong that I didn't even notice?' "

Sam set down his spoon. Linda gave a sudden sigh. Delia said, "Well, I . . . well, why *don't* I come with you? I doubt I'd be much help, but certainly I could try."

"Oh, God, thank you, Miz G.," Driscoll said.

"I don't know if this will work, though," Delia told him.

"It'll work," he said, standing up. "If school lets out, say, two forty-five, three o'clock, and I come pick you up by . . ."

That wasn't what Delia had meant. She'd meant that in her opinion, Susie might reasonably refuse to marry him even after he apologized. But she changed her mind about saying so. She didn't even say goodbye to him, because just as he was leaving, the telephone rang.

This time it was Joel. He said, "Delia?"

"Yes," she said evenly. She glanced toward her family. They were all watching her—everyone but Sam, who seemed to be studying the table.

"Where *are* you?" he asked.

This was such an illogical question that she couldn't think how to answer it. She said, "Um . . ."

*Where are you?* Sam had asked in another phone call, months ago, and she wondered now if he had meant the question in the same way Joel did.

Then Joel, as if recollecting himself, said, "I

came home to have lunch with Noah and he told me you haven't left Baltimore yet. I just thought I should find out if everything's all right."

"Oh, yes. Fine," she said.

She wished the others would resume talking, but they didn't.

"But you do plan to be back, don't you?" Joel asked. "I mean, eventually? Because I see from your closet . . . I wasn't trying to pry but I did just, so to speak, glance in your closet, and I noticed all your clothes are gone."

"They are?" she said.

"I thought you might have left for good."

"Oh, no, it's just . . . things are taking longer to finish than I expected," she told him.

Sam rose and walked out of the room.

From upstairs, Susie called, "Mom? Mom?"

"It's *not the realtor*!" Delia called back.

Joel said, "Pardon?"

"Sorry, Joel, I'd better go," she said. "See you in a while."

She hung up.

"Well, aren't *you* the popular one," Linda said.

Delia gave what she hoped was an offhand laugh and started clearing the table.

It was true, she saw when she went upstairs, that she had brought all her clothes. Well, not really all. Joel would have found enough in her bureau to reassure him, if he'd looked. But what with one thing and another—the iffy season, the dither over a wedding outfit—she had packed as if she'd be gone for days. She pictured Joel standing in front of her closet, his broad forehead creased in perplexity as he surveyed the empty hangers. Abruptly, she closed her suitcase and snapped the latches shut.

Then she crossed the hall to Sam's room. Here she had left plenty behind. How odd that when she was debating what to wear for the ceremony, she hadn't considered her old wardrobe! Or maybe not so odd—all that froufrou and those nursery pastels. She turned away. She went to her bureau and found, in the top drawer, a draggled blue hair bow, safety pins, ticket stubs, everything hazed with talcum powder. A pair of sunglasses missing one lens. A fifty-five-cent hand-lotion coupon. A torn-out photo of a fashion model in a stark, bare sliver of black. She couldn't imagine ever wearing such a style, and she studied the photo for some time before recalling that it was the model who'd caught her eye, not the dress. The sickle-shaped model with the same snooty haircut as Rosemary Bly-Brice.

Footsteps climbed the stairs, and she closed the drawer as stealthily as a thief. She turned and found Sam halting in the doorway. "Oh!" she said, and he said, "I was just—"

They both broke off.

"I thought you were seeing patients," she said.

"No, I'm through for the day."

He put his hands in his trouser pockets. Should she leave? But he was filling the doorway; it would have been awkward.

"Mostly now I keep just morning hours," he said. "I don't have a lot of patients anymore. Seems half of them have died of old age. Mrs. Harper, Mrs. Allingham . . ."

"Mrs. Allingham died?"

"Stroke."

"Oh, dear, I'm going to miss her," Delia said.

Sam very kindly did not point out that she'd lost all touch with Mrs. Allingham sixteen months ago.

His bed was made, but like most men, he seemed unable to grasp the concept of tucking a fold of spread beneath the pillows. Instead, a straight line of fabric slanted dismally toward the headboard. Just for something to do, Delia set about fixing it. She turned down the spread and whacked both pillows into shape.

"I guess you think I've destroyed your father's practice," Sam told her.

"Pardon?"

"I've run it down to a shadow of its former glory, isn't that what you're thinking?"

"It's not your fault if people die of old age," Delia said.

"It's my fault if no one new signs on, though,"

he said. "I lack your father's bedside manner, obviously. I tell people they have plain old indigestion; I don't call it dyspepsia. I've never been the type to flatter and cosset my patients."

Delia felt a familiar twinge of annoyance. *I would hardly consider "dyspepsia" flattery,* she could have said. And, *I don't know why you have to use that bitter, biting tone of voice any time you talk about my father.* She stalked around to the other side of the bed.

But then Sam asked, "What is that limp you've got?"

"Limp?"

"It seems to me you're favoring one foot."

"Oh, that's from a couple of months ago. It's almost healed by now."

"Sit down a minute."

She sat on the edge of the bed, and he came over to kneel in front of her and slip her shoe off. His fingertips moved across the top of her foot with a knowledgeable, deft precision that shot directly to her groin.

In her softest voice, she told him, "Your patients never minded, that *I* was aware of. They always called you a saint."

"They don't anymore," he said. He was gazing out the window while he traced a tendon, as if he expected to hear the injury rather than see it. "The other night Mrs. Maxwell phoned with one of her stomach problems, and I told her, 'If

I let myself think about it, Mrs. Maxwell, I could list quite a few complaints of my own. My eyes burn and my head aches and my knee is acting up,' I said. Which of course offended her. It seems I've lost my tolerance. Or maybe I was never all that tolerant to begin with. I don't have a very . . . wide nature. I'm short on, you might call it, jollity.''

The very word, in connection with Sam, made Delia smile, but he was prodding her ankle now, and he didn't notice. "Does this hurt? This?" he asked.

"A little."

She thought of how Joel had held her foot in exactly this way. But Joel's touch had felt so foreign, so separate from her—not quite real, even, it seemed as she looked back.

"I suppose that's why I married you," Sam was saying. Had she missed something? "You were extremely jolly when we met," he said. "Or more like . . . lighthearted. Now I see that I chose you for all the wrong reasons."

She drew back slightly.

"There you sat on that couch," he said, "next to your two scary sisters. Eliza preaching sea kelp and toxic doses of vitamins; Linda tossing off words like *louche* and *distingué*. But you were so shy and cute and fumbly, smiling down at your little glass eyecup of sherry. You were so wavery around the edges. You I'd be able to handle, I thought, and I never stopped to ask why I needed to believe that."

He dropped her foot and sat back on his heels. "Stand up, please," he told her. She stood. He narrowed his eyes. "It does seem there's a bit of swelling," he said. "I would guess you've torn a ligament. Ligaments can be very slow to mend. How'd you do it?"

She'd done it acting fumbly, acting wavery around the edges, but she didn't want to say so. He was continuing, anyway, with his original train of thought.

"When you left," he said, "the police were sympathetic at first. But then they figured out you'd left of your own accord, and I could see them beginning to wonder. Well, you can't blame them. I was wondering myself. I asked Eliza, when she came back from seeing you: 'Was it me? Did I have any part in it?' Maybe I hadn't phrased it right about that man friend of yours. Or I nagged too much about sunblock, or you hated how my chest hair had grayed. Or the angina; I know the angina business must have gotten tedious."

"What?" she said. "Now, that is just not fair!"

"No, no, I did go overboard for a while. Checking my pulse rate every two minutes. I think I had it in mind I was going to drop dead like my father." He rose, carefully brushing his knees even though they weren't dusty. "But

Eliza said it wasn't any of those things. She said you were suffering from stress. I'm still not sure what she meant."

*Nor am I entirely clear,* he had written, *what "stresses" you are referring to.* Delia wished now she hadn't thrown that letter away. Had its tone, perhaps, been less cold than she had imagined? She reflected on the deletions; she recalled how they had increased near the end and how the commas had fallen away, as if he had been hurtling headlong toward his final sentence. Which he had then crossed out so thoroughly that she hadn't been able to read it.

The phone on the nightstand started ringing, but neither of them reached for it, and eventually it stopped.

"The thing of it is," he said, "you ask yourself enough questions—was it this I did wrong, was it that?—and you get to believing you did it *all* wrong. Your whole damn life. But now that I'm nearing the end of it, I seem to be going too fast to stop and change. I'm just . . . *skidding* to the end of it."

Susie called, "Mom?"

"It's like that old Jackie Gleason show on TV," Sam said. "The one that used to open with a zoom shot across a harbor toward a skyline. Was it Miami? Manhattan? That long glide across the glassy water: my picture exactly of dying. No brakes! No traction! No time to make a U-turn!"

"Mom, telephone!"

Delia didn't take her eyes from Sam's face, but Sam said, "You'd better get that."

Still she didn't move.

"The phone, Delia."

After a moment, she picked up the receiver. "Hello?" she said.

"Delia?"

"Oh, Noah."

Sam's shoulders sagged. He turned toward the window.

"Haven't you even started out yet?" Noah demanded.

"No," she said, with her eyes on Sam. He was setting his forehead against the panes now, looking down into the yard. "I won't know what my arrangements are till afternoon," she told Noah.

"But it's afternoon now, and I'm lonesome!" he said. Sickness, it seemed, had turned him into that open-faced child she'd first known. "I've got no one taking care of me! Grandpa came but he wouldn't stay, and now I've finished the cough drops."

"Well, there's another box in the . . . your grandpa? Came to Bay Borough?"

"For about a nanosecond."

"What did he want?"

"He said he was just riding around, and then he left. I told him I was sick, but what did *he* care? And Dad claims I don't even have a fever and Mom can't come till after work and also something's wrong with the television set."

"Read a book, then," she told him. "I'll be home before long. Either this evening or maybe tomorrow; tell your father, will you?"

He was in the midst of a theatrical groan when she said goodbye.

"Sorry," she told Sam. "That was just—"

But Sam said, "Well, it's obvious you have things to attend to," and he started toward the door.

"Sam?" she said.

He stopped and turned.

"It was just the little boy I'm taking care of," she told him.

"So I gathered," he said, somehow not moving his lips.

"He's sick with a cold."

"And you have to get 'home' to him."

His voice had that pinched, tight, steely quality that always made her shrivel inside, but she forced herself to say, calmly, "Well, it *is* where I happen to live."

"I may not be perfect, Delia, but at least I don't delude myself," Sam said.

"What is that supposed to mean?"

"I don't go around trying to roll the clock back," he said. "Shucking off my kids as soon as they turn difficult and hunting up a whole new, easy, *little* kid instead."

Delia stared at him. "Well, of all the preposterous theories!" she said. "What do you know about it? Maybe he's not easy at all! Maybe he's just as difficult!"

"If that's the case," he said, "you can always shuck him off too."

"I didn't shuck him off!" she shouted. "I just came for Susie's wedding and then I'm going back—and not a moment too soon, might I add. I have no intention of shucking him off!"

Sam studied her impassively. "Did I say you did?" he asked.

And while she was grabbing for words, he left the room.

One of Delia's handicaps was that when she got angry, she got teary, which always made her angrier. So there she was, banging around the kitchen and fighting back tears as she washed the dishes, while Linda followed behind, trying to console her. "There, there," she said. "*We* love you, Dee. Your blood kin loves you. Careful, that's Grandma's last soup bowl. *We'll* stand by you."

"I'm all right," Delia said, dabbing her eyes impatiently with the heel of one hand. She ran water over a sponge. It had a horrible cilantro smell, as if it had soured in the cupboard.

"You shouldn't put up with him," Linda said.

"Give him the boot! Send him packing. This is our house, not Sam's. It's you who ought to be living here."

Delia had to laugh at that. "Really? On what money?" she asked. "If not for Sam, we'd have lost this place long ago. Who do you think pays the property tax? And the maintenance, and the bills for all those improvements?"

"Well, if you call uprooting every last shrub an improvement," Linda sniffed. "*I* call it high-handed! And did you know he's got plans to paint the shutters red?"

"Red?"

"Fire-engine red, is what he told Eliza. Though she says he's sort of petered out on his projects lately. But think of it! Like an old, old man with his hair dyed, that's what red shutters would look like. You notice he only started doing this after his heart attack."

"Chest pains," Delia corrected her mechanically.

Susie wandered in, dressed in her jeans and a navy pullover of Carroll's. "When's lunch?" she asked Delia.

"Lunch! Well . . ."

"A gold digger's what he is," Linda said. "He had his eye on you from the moment Daddy hired him."

"Who did?" Susie asked.

"Sam Grinstead; who do you think? He

schemed to marry your mother before he ever
laid eyes on her."

"He did?"

"Oh, Linda," Delia said. "If you get right
down to it, I schemed to marry him, too. I sat
behind that desk just pining for someone to walk
in and save me."

"Save you from what?" Susie asked.

Delia ignored her. "Look at our own grandmother," she told Linda. "Marrying Isaiah to
escape TB. Look at the woodcutter's honest son,
marrying the princess for her kingdom!"

"Who was T.B.?" Susie demanded. "What
woodcutter? What are you two *talking* about?"

Linda went over to Susie and draped an arm
across her shoulders in a chummy, confiding way
that made Delia feel excluded. "If your mother
had half the sense you do," she told Susie, "she
would kick your father out and get herself a job
and move back to Baltimore."

"I already have a job," Delia said. "I have a
whole life, elsewhere!"

And Bay Borough seemed to float by just then
like a tiny, bright, crowded blue bubble, at this
distance so veiled and misty that she wondered
if she had dreamed it.


"Here's what I'm hoping," Driscoll told Delia.
"When Courtney hears somebody's phoned her,
she'll know right off it's got to be this guy she

gave her number to. I mean, he did call you-all's house three times. So you know he didn't get the number from the phone book; he must have written it down wrong. Don't you think?"

"Well, it's possible, I suppose," Delia said. In fact, it seemed very likely, but she couldn't work up the energy to tell him so. For the past forty-five minutes they'd been standing out here in the cold. From time to time she sent a longing glance over her shoulder at Courtney's white clapboard house, but they had already rung the doorbell and no one had answered. "Driscoll," she said, "has it occurred to you that Courtney might have after-school sports? I mean, Susie used to come home in the dark, some days."

"Then we'll wait here till dark," he said.

Other students were passing—Gilman boys in their shirts and ties, and teenage girls in Bryn Mawr aqua or Roland Park Country School blue. "We should be holding up one of those signs," Delia said, "the way they do at airports."

Driscoll scowled at her.

"Couldn't you have brought Pearce for this instead?" Delia asked him.

"Who's Pearce?"

"Your sister, for heaven's sake!"

"You mean Spence?"

"Spence. Sorry."

She gave a little laugh. He scowled harder.

"Spence is at work," he told her. "But I doubt

she'd have come anyhow. She doesn't think I
ought to get married."

"She doesn't!"

"Well, why is that such a shock?" he asked.
"You're not the only one who's against this."

"Did I say I was against it?"

"You sure act like you are. Dragging your
heels every step of the way, wishing I'd brought
someone else."

"I'm just getting cold, is all," Delia told him.

"For your information, my whole family
claims I'd be better off single."

Delia felt stung. She said, "Well, thanks a
lot!"

"Oh, they like Susie," he said. "But, you
know . . . 'Why get mixed up with those Grinsteads?' my mom is always asking."

"There's nothing wrong with Grinsteads!"

"No, well, but . . ." He followed a knot of
passing schoolgirls with his eyes. "You've got to
admit," he said, "you-all are so . . . you do things
such a different way. Not mingling or taking part,
living to yourselves like you do; and then you
pretend like that's normal. You pretend like
*everything's* normal; you're so cagey and smooth;
you gloss things over; you don't explain."

Delia breathed again. He could have named
flaws much worse, she felt, although she didn't
know exactly what. "Well," she said, "those
sound to me like good qualities, not bad."

"See there?" Driscoll demanded. "That's exactly what I mean!"

"Look who's talking!" Delia said. "Someone who had his wedding canceled and then showed up for it anyway! How's that for glossing over?"

"At least *I* didn't make believe I was nothing but a guest," Driscoll told her. "Walking in at the very last minute like the bride was some passing acquaintance."

"I would have come earlier! But nobody asked me!" she told him.

"See what I mean?" he said.

"What *do* you mean?"

A car drew up at the curb, a station wagon teeming with faces. A girl got out with an armload of books. "Thanks!" she called, and the car honked and pulled away.

"Courtney?" Driscoll asked.

The girl paused on the sidewalk. Delia had known, somehow, that Courtney would be a blonde. She was tall and slim and golden-skinned, and her clothes were just the right degree of unstudied—her blazer expertly tailored but her knee socks falling down. "Yes?" she said.

"My name is Driscoll Avery," Driscoll said, "and a couple of nights ago I believe I answered a phone call that was meant for you."

Courtney tilted her head. Her pageboy swung prettily to one side.

"Some guy called, a wrong number," Driscoll told her, "and now my fiancée is mad because I was, um, maybe a little bit rude. So I need to ask if you know who might have called you."

Courtney looked over at Delia.

"I'm his fiancée's mother," Delia explained. The word "fiancée" brought to her mind someone in a pillbox hat, nothing at all like Susie. She felt herself assuming the flat-faced, wide-eyed expression of a liar. She said, "Driscoll's telling the truth; I swear it. A boy phoned, asking for Courtney, and Driscoll said you didn't want to talk to him."

"You said *that*?" Courtney asked Driscoll. The smile was gone now. "What if it was someone I was dying to hear from?"

"Well, like who?" Driscoll said. "I mean, *was* there someone?"

"There's Michael Garter."

"Did you give Michael Garter your number?"

"No, but it's in the book."

"You think he's the one who called you?"

"Well, maybe. He could have. Well, sure!" She seemed to be warming to the idea. "In a couple of weeks, there's this dance?" she told Delia.

Delia said, "But you didn't actually tell him your number."

"Well, no."

"We were thinking it might be someone you'd told."

"No, but there's this big homecoming dance? And Michael Garter's this guy I know? He's the second-strongest guy in his school."

"But—" Delia began, at the same time that Driscoll said, "Well, great! Let's get moving!"

"But *was* there someone you told?" Delia asked.

"Oh, gosh, guys are always wanting my number. You know? And I give it to them, but, like, I just do it to be nice. I would never actually go out with them."

"Would you give them the *wrong* number?" Delia persisted.

"Well, sure, if they're, like, totally not of interest."

"You'd just transpose a couple of digits, say."

"I might."

"Did you do that recently?"

"Well, maybe to this guy at my Christian fellowship group."

"What's his name?"

"But I think it's more likely Michael Garter," Courtney said.

"But the name of the boy at your fellowship group . . ."

"That's Paul Cates. But he's, like, a dork. You'd know what I meant if you saw him."

"I bet anything it was Michael Garter," Driscoll said soothingly.

Courtney sent him an appreciative look.

"Well, whoever," Delia said, "you just tell

Driscoll all the possibilities, and then he can track down which one it was."

"And maybe I could come along," Courtney said. "I could show you exactly where Michael Garter has football practice."

Anybody with half a brain would look for Paul Cates first. Hoping to convey that, Delia screwed up her eyes at Driscoll. "Huh?" he asked her, and then, "Ah. Does, ah, Paul Cates play football too?"

"Are you serious?" Courtney asked. "Paul Cates? Play football?"

Delia collected herself to go, hitching her handbag strap onto her shoulder. "Good hunting," she told Driscoll.

"What, you're not coming with us?"

"You'll do better by yourselves."

He opened his mouth to argue, but Courtney said, "Nice meeting you!"

Delia waved and walked off.

She was glad to have some time alone. Had family life always been so cram-packed? she wondered. How had she kept her wits about her? But then she remembered she hadn't, at least not in Sam's opinion.

Skimming south on Roland Avenue, she passed Travel Arrangements, the Mercantile Bank, Eddie's Supermarket. She was careful not to look toward the other pedestrians, in case they were people she knew. Suppose they asked where she'd been all these months and what she planned to do next. Or suppose—here was a thought—she met Adrian Bly-Brice.

The funny thing was that she couldn't picture Adrian's face anymore, although she tried.

"Delia," Linda whispered at the front door, "you've got someone waiting for you."

"I do?"

Delia felt herself flush, but Linda said, "An *older* gentleman. Name of Nat?"

"Oh," Delia said.

She followed Linda through the dining room and into the kitchen. Nat was sitting at the table with Susie and the twins, but he rose to his feet when Delia entered. "There she is!" he said.

Away from Senior City, he seemed older. His hair was so white that it glittered, and he was leaning very heavily on his cane. This must be one of his flashback days. She said, "Nat? Is everything all right?"

"Oh, yes," he said, "quite all right. Hello, my dear." He gave her a courtly kiss on the cheek, prickling her with his beard. "I just happened to be tootling around in the car," he said. "Thought I'd offer you a lift back."

"Tootling around . . . Baltimore?"

"Yes, well, hither and yon."

This was puzzling, but she didn't pursue it. "That's nice of you," she said, "but I'm not sure exactly when I'll be leaving." She glanced toward Susie, who was watching her over her coffee mug. "Driscoll is still working on that telephone matter," Delia told her.

The twins nudged each other. Nat said, "Oh, I know all about that! Your sister here has filled me in. So how is it progressing? Have we located the hapless young man?"

"Well, we've narrowed the field some," Delia said. "Nat, is anything wrong at home?"

"Wrong! Why do you keep asking that?" he said. "Can't a man take a little drive on his own these days?"

Linda placed a mug of coffee on the table in front of him, and he lowered himself back onto his chair with a thud. "Thank you, my dear," he said. He set his cane aside. It stood on its four little legs in a perky, independent manner.

"Cream?" Linda asked him. "Sugar?"

"Just black, thanks." He told Delia, "You never mentioned you had a sister. And such a charming daughter! And two gorgeous nieces!"

There was something feverish about his enthusiasm, but none of the others seemed to notice. "She doesn't only got a daughter," Marie-Claire told him. "She's got two boys besides."

"Two boys!" Nat marveled. "Where does she keep them hidden?"

"Well, Carroll's hiding upstairs, on account of this fight with his dad. And Ramsay lives with his tacky girlfriend at a place we don't know the address of."

Nat shot Delia a questioning look. "Yes," she said with a laugh. "You'll have to excuse us, I'm afraid. Nobody here is on speaking terms."

"They seem to *me* to be speaking," he said reasonably.

"Oh, speaking, yes. But . . ."

She gave up and went to pour herself some coffee. Nat resumed quizzing the twins. "And do all of you live in this one big house? All except Ramsay, that is, and his tacky girlfriend?"

"Oh, no, none of us live here! Just only Uncle Sam."

"Uncle Sam! This is government property?"

The twins chortled. Thérèse said, "Silly! Uncle Sam is Aunt Delia's husband."

Delia sensed Nat's glance in her direction, but she didn't turn around, and the twins moved on to the topic of Eliza. "She burns weeds in little bowls," Marie-Claire told him. "She has a bottle called Forbearance, to smell from when she's feeling fed up."

"Where would one buy that, I wonder," Nat said wistfully.

Delia went to the silverware drawer for a spoon and found Susie all at once lounging in front of it, waiting for her, one sneakered foot cocked across the other. Her nonchalant expression didn't fool Delia for a second. "So," Susie said. "Driscoll did get hold of Courtney, sounds like."

"Yes."

"And narrowed down who the boy was, you said."

"Well, Courtney gave him a couple of possibilities."

"So I guess now he's gone to talk to them."

"He's working on it," Delia told her.

She reached toward the drawer, and Susie slid infinitesimally to one side. "Looks to me like you would have gone with him," Susie said.

"Well, you can see I'm right here," Delia snapped.

She supposed that Susie must care for Driscoll; and in that case, well, all right, they should probably get married. How simple-minded Delia had been, to take their breakup seriously! And how sage and mature and practical Susie seemed in comparison! Delia flashed her a radiant smile. Susie examined her warily.

People always talked about a mother's uncanny ability to read her children, but that was nothing compared to how children could read their mothers.

The twins were describing their bridesmaid dresses. "Big floppy bows—"

"Puffy shoulders—"

"Exact same color as Crest fluoride toothpaste."

"They must be stunning," Nat told them. "And when do you plan on wearing them?"

"Maybe tonight," Marie-Claire said, while Susie, overlapping, said, "Tomorrow."

Everyone looked at her. She met Delia's gaze defiantly. "Well, if Driscoll brings me that boy, I mean."

"But he could do that in the next five minutes!" Linda told her. "You could get married this evening, if he hurries."

"Yes, but Dr. Soames can't fit us in till ten a.m. tomorrow."

"He told you that?" Delia asked. "You talked to him? When?"

"Oh, um, just a little while ago."

"But if our flight home is tomorrow at noon," Linda said, "and the drive to the airport takes, let's see . . ."

Nat told Delia, "Sounds as if you won't be riding back with me tonight."

He spoke cheerfully enough, but Delia hadn't lost her suspicion that something was troubling him. She glanced toward the others, who were still discussing schedules, and then she said, "Nat, what brought you here? Really."

"Nothing, I tell you!"

"You just drove two hours for no reason."

"Two and a half, actually," he said. "Little backup on the bridge."

She scrutinized him. "How's the baby?" she asked.

"He's thriving."

"And Binky?"

"Healthy as a brood mare."

"Does she know you're in Baltimore?"

"I called her a few minutes ago. Your sister let me use your phone."

"And Noah has a cold, I hear," she said, still ferreting.

"The merest sniffle," Nat assured her. "I looked in on him this morning while I was driving around. Found him playing Tetris. Hardly on his deathbed, I'd say."

"It's true he didn't sound very sick," Delia said. "Maybe he just needed a day off."

"Yes," Nat said. "We could all do with a day off, from time to time."

Something bumped against the back door, and then Sam walked in bearing two bags of groceries. A long stick of French bread poked forth from one of them. "I found the ginger," he told Linda, "but they were fresh out of shallots."

"Well, never mind; we'll make do with green onions," Linda told him, taking the bags. "Is that okay, Delia?"

"Is what okay?"

"Can you make your Chinese dish using green onions?"

"I always use green onions anyhow," Delia said. "But—"

"Oh, good. Because we're going to be so many, you know, I thought you could fix your . . . Oh, Sam, you haven't met Nat, have you. Nat Moffat, this is Sam Grinstead. I certainly hope you plan to stay for supper, Nat. Delia's Chinese dish feeds an army, believe me."

"I would love to stay for supper," Nat said, to Delia's surprise. He had risen during the introductions, and now he stood holding on to the back of his chair. Sam, who must have had no idea where Nat had materialized from, wore a pleasant, slightly blank expression as they shook hands. "Good to meet you," he said.

"Good to meet *you*," Nat told him. And then he added, darting a mischievous glance at Delia, "I've heard so much about you."

This was lost on Sam, of course. He just smiled politely and asked Linda, "Have I got time for a house call before supper?"

"Ask Delia; she's the cook," Linda said.

Sam turned to Delia. "I promised Mr. Knowles I'd check on him," he said.

"You have plenty of time," she told him.

They spoke without letting their eyes meet, like people in a play, whose words are meant for the audience.

No one had to tell Delia which boy had turned out to be Courtney's caller. She knew it was Paul Cates as soon as she saw him—sweet-faced and naive, with a tousle of rust-colored curls. His jeans were a little too short for him, his sneakers too thin-soled and childish, his plaid wool jacket the kind boys wear in elementary school. He followed Driscoll over to Susie, who was perched on a stool chopping water chestnuts for Delia's Chinese dish. Behind him came Courtney, of all people. She took her place close behind Driscoll and Paul, tucking her hands into the pockets of her blazer and regarding Susie with undisguised curiosity. Susie, who had turned from the counter at their approach, looked only at Driscoll.

"Susie," Driscoll said, "this is Paul Cates." Then he faced Paul Cates and said, "Paul, I'd like to apologize. When you phoned here by accident the other night, I let you think you'd reached Courtney's house, but I was wrong, wrong, wrong."

Paul was beaming. "That's okay," he said.

Formally, Driscoll faced Susie again. "*Now* will you marry me?" he asked.

Susie said, "Well, I guess."

One of the twins said, "Hot dog!" and the other said, "Kiss him! Kiss him, Susie!"

Susie planted a kiss to one side of Driscoll's mouth. She told Paul, "It's nice of you to be so understanding."

"Oh, I don't mind a bit!" he said, and he sent Courtney a shining glance from under his long lashes. Courtney just surveyed him coolly and then turned back to Susie.

"And Courtney, it was nice of you to come along," Susie told her.

"No problem. Me and your brother Carroll met last spring at a party."

"Oh, really?"

"My girlfriend asked him to her birthday party; I put it all together when your fiancé told me your name."

Paul was looking less happy now; so Delia broke in and said, "Can you two stay for dinner? We're having this Chinese dish that's infinitely expandable."

"Well, I *might* could," Courtney said.

Paul said, "I'll just need to phone my mother."

"Right over here," Delia told him, and she cupped his elbow protectively as she led him toward the phone. How cruel and baffling—how tribal, almost—young girls must seem to boys! Somehow she hadn't realized that when she was a young girl herself.

"I propose a toast," Nat said. He raised his coffee mug. "To the bridal couple!"

Driscoll said, "Why, thanks"—not having the dimmest notion, of course, who this old man might be, but adapting with his usual good humor. "Hello, Ma?" Paul said into the phone, and then Carroll appeared from the dining room just as Eliza stepped through the back door; so both of them had to be filled in on the latest developments. Eliza hadn't even heard yet what

Driscoll's magic task was. She kept saying, "Who? He brought who?" with her eyebrows quirked in bewilderment, her pocketbook hugged to her chest, and Courtney was sidling toward Carroll to ask, "Carroll Grinstead? I don't know if you remember me," and the twins were insisting that this time they should wear lipstick to the wedding.

Delia took her cutting board to a less populated area, and she started chopping ginger. Her Chinese dish required eleven different bowls of ingredients, most minced no bigger than matchstick heads, all lined up in a row for rapid frying. So far she had finished only bowl number four. She was thankful to be occupied, though. She chopped rhythmically, mindlessly, letting an ocean of chatter eddy around her. *Tick-tick,* the knife came down on the cutting board. *Tick-tick,* and she slid all her thoughts to one side as she slid the mounds of ginger into a bowl.

With every one of its leaves in place, the table filled the whole dining room. ("This tablecloth came from your grandma's hope chest," Linda told the twins. "The stain is where your aunt Delia set a bowl of curry. *She* doesn't give a damn; she was your grandpa's favorite; she treats these things like Woolworth things.") Twelve place settings marched the length of it—five at each side, one each at head and foot. There had been talk of inviting Eleanor, but Susie didn't want to jinx her entire marriage with thirteen at table; and no one answered the phone when they called Ramsay.

"Courtney, I'll put you in the middle here," Delia said. "Then Paul, you're next to Courtney . . ."

Courtney, however, had obviously made up her mind to sit with Carroll, which left Paul stuck between the twins; not that the twins weren't delighted. And the others remained standing while they continued a discussion they'd started in the living room—something about Mr. Knowles's tingly arm. "Didn't Daddy always say the same thing!" Eliza was exclaiming. "He used to say he wished he had a dictionary of pains. Those symptoms people came up with— 'Pepsi-bubble stomach' and 'whiny argumentative back'!"

"Driscoll, you're beside Linda," Delia said, but Driscoll, feigning engrossment in the conversation, kept his face turned toward Eliza and sneakily drew out the chair beside Susie. Delia gave up. "Oh, just *sit*," she told Nat, and Nat sat down where he was, which happened to be exactly where she'd intended, at her right hand. "Help yourself to some rice," she said, passing him the bowl, and she told the others, "Everything's getting cold!"

Eliza settled at Sam's left, shaking her head

at what Sam was saying. "Who knows, any-how?" he was saying. "Maybe it's all equal: hangnail for one, cancer for another. Everything on the same level, just barely within endurance."

"Sam Grinstead, you don't believe that for a minute!" Linda squawked. "What a bizarre suggestion!"

Delia said, "Paul, will you have some rice and pass it on, please? Everybody! Sit down!"

Very suddenly, the rest of them sat. They seemed to have run out of steam, and there was a pause, during which Paul dropped the serving spoon to the table with a loud clunk. He bared all his teeth in embarrassment and picked it up.

Nat said, "Do any of you know the photographs of C. R. Savage?"

The grown-ups turned courteous, receptive faces in his direction.

"A nineteenth-century fellow," he said. "Used the old wet-plate method, I would suppose. There's a picture I'm reminded of that he took toward the end of his life. Shows his dining room table set for Christmas dinner. Savage himself sitting amongst the empty chairs, waiting for his family. Chair after chair after chair, silverware laid just so, even a baby's high chair, all in readiness. And I can't help thinking, when I look at that photo, *I bet that's as good as it got, that day. From there on out, it was all downhill, I bet.* Actual sons and daughters arrived, and they quarreled over the drumsticks and sniped at their children's table manners and brought up hurtful incidents from fifteen years before; and the baby had this whimper that gave everybody a headache. Only just for that moment," Nat said, and his voice took on a tremor, "just as the shutter was clicking, none of that had happened yet, you see, and the table looked so beautiful, like someone's dream of a table, and old Savage felt so happy and so—what's the word I want, so . . ."

But now his voice failed him completely, and he covered his eyes with one shaking hand and bent his head. "So anticipatory!" he whispered into his plate, while Delia, at a loss, patted his arm. "I'm sorry! I'm sorry!" he said. Everyone sat dumbstruck. Then he said, "Ha!" and straightened, bracing his shoulders. "Postpartum depression, I guess this is," he said. He wiped his eyes with his napkin.

"Nat has a three-week-old baby," Delia explained to the others. "Nat, would you like—"

"Baby?" Linda asked incredulously.

Sam said, "I thought Nat was *your* friend, Linda."

"No, he's mine," Delia said. "He lives on the Eastern Shore and he's just had a baby boy, a lovely boy, you ought to see how—"

"Most irresponsible thing I've ever done in my life," Nat said hoarsely. "What could I have been thinking of? Oh, not that it was anything I

planned, but . . . why did I go along with it? I
believe I thought it was my chance to be a good
father, finally. I know it was, or why else did I
assume it was a girl? All my others were girls,
you see. I must have thought I could do the
whole thing over again, properly this time. But
I'm just as short-tempered with James as I ever
was with my daughters. Just as rigid, just as ex-
acting. Why can't he get on a schedule, why does
he have to cry at such unpredictable hours . . .
Oh, the best thing I could do for that kid is toddle
off to Floor Five."

"Floor Five? Oh," Delia said. "Oh, Nat!
Don't even think it!" she said, patting his arm
all the harder.

She should have realized at his wedding, she
told herself, that someone so elated would have
to end in tears, like an overexcited child allowed
to stay up past his bedtime.

"Yes. Well," Sam said, clearing his throat.
"It's really very common now, this more senior
class of parent. Why, just last week I was reading, where was it I was reading . . ."

"The important thing to remember is, this is
your assignment," Eliza said in ringing tones.
She was all the way up near Sam, and she had
to lean forward, bypassing a row of tactfully
expressionless profiles, to search out Nat's face.
"It's my belief that we're each assigned certain
experiences," she said. "And then at the end of
our lives—"

"*The New England Journal of Medicine!*" Sam announced triumphantly.

Nat asked Delia, "Do you have a place where I might lie down?"

"Yes, of course," she said, and she slid her chair back and handed him his cane. "Excuse us, please," she told the others.

Everyone nodded, abashed. As she and Nat crossed the hall, she could almost feel the furtive exchange of glances behind their backs.

"There's a flight of stairs," she warned Nat. "Can you manage?"

"Oh, yes, if you'll hang on to my other arm. I'm sorry, Delia. I don't know what got into me."

"You're just tired," she told him. "I hope you're not thinking of driving back tonight."

"No, I suppose I shouldn't," he said. On each stair step, his cane gave a tinny rattle, like a handful of jacks being shaken. His elbow within his tweed sleeve was nothing but knob and rope.

"I'm going to make up a bed for you," Delia told him when they reached the second floor, "and then you should call Binky and tell her you're staying over."

"All right," he said meekly. He hobbled through the door she held open and sank into a slipcovered chair.

"This used to be my father's room," Delia said. She went out to the hall closet and came back with an armload of sheets. "There's still a telephone by the bed, see? From the days when he was in practice. Even after he stopped seeing patients, he could pick up his receiver whenever Sam got a call; chime in with a second opinion. He just hated to feel left out of things, you know?"

She was babbling aimlessly as she bustled around the bed, smoothing sheets and tucking in blankets. Nat watched without comment. He might not even have been listening, for when she went to Sam's room to borrow a pair of pajamas, she returned to find him staring at the blue-black windowpanes. "In fact," she said, placing the pajamas on the bureau, "I can't tell you how often I made up his bed just the way I did tonight, while Daddy sat where you're sitting now. He liked for his sheets to be fresh off the line, oh, long after we switched to an automatic dryer. And he would sit in that chair and—"

"It's a time trip," Nat said suddenly.

"Why, yes, I suppose it is, in a way."

But he'd been talking to himself, evidently. "Just a crazy, half-baked scheme to travel backwards," he said as if she hadn't spoken, "and live everything all over again. Unfortunately, Binky's the one who's left with the consequences. Poor Binky!"

"Binky will be fine," Delia said firmly. "Now. That door right there is the bathroom. New toothbrushes on the shelf above the tub. Can I get you anything more?"

"No, thank you."

"A tray of food, maybe? You didn't touch your supper."

"No."

"Well, you be sure to call me if you need me," she said.

Then she bent to press her lips to his forehead, the way she used to do with her father all those nights in the past.

Delia was the next to go to bed. She went at nine-thirty, having struggled to keep her eyes open ever since dinner. "I am *beat*," she told the others. They were all sitting around, still—even Courtney, although Paul had been picked up by his mother at some point. "It seems this morning took place way back in prehistory," Delia told them, and then she climbed the stairs to Eliza's room, so weary that she had to haul her feet behind her like buckets of cement.

Once she was in bed, though, she couldn't get to sleep. She lay staring at the ceiling, idly stroking the curl of warm cat nestled close to her hip. Downstairs, Linda and Sam were squabbling as usual. A Mozart horn concerto was playing. Eliza said, "Why *wouldn't* he, I ask you." Wouldn't who? Delia wondered. Wouldn't do what?

She must have slept then, but it was such a fitful, shallow sleep that she seemed to remain partly conscious throughout, and when she woke again she wasn't surprised to find the house dark and all the voices stilled. She sat up and angled her wristwatch to catch the light from the window. As near as she could make out, it was either eleven o'clock or five till twelve. More likely five till twelve, she decided, judging from the quiet.

She propped her pillow and leaned back against it, yawning. Tears of boredom were already edging the corners of her eyes. It was going to be one of those nights that go on for weeks.

Let's see: if the wedding began at ten tomorrow, she supposed it would be finished by eleven. Well, say noon, to play it safe. She'd reach the bus station by half past, if she could catch a ride with Ramsay. Or with Sam. Sam had offered, after all.

She saw herself riding in the passenger seat, Sam behind the wheel. Like two of those little peg people in a toy car. Husband peg, wife peg, side by side. Facing the road and not looking at each other; for why would they need to, really, having gone beyond the visible surface long ago. No hope of admiring gazes anymore, no chance of unremitting adoration. Nothing left to show but their plain, true, homely, interior selves, which were actually much richer anyhow.

Where was she? Bus station. Catch a bus by one o'clock or so, reach Salisbury by . . .

The tears seemed not exactly tears of boredom

after all. She blotted them on her nightgown sleeve, but more came.

She folded back the covers, mindful of the cat, and slid out of bed and walked barefoot toward the door. The hall was lit only by the one round window, high up. She had to more or less feel her way toward Sam's room.

Luckily, his door was ajar. No sound gave her away as she entered. But she knew, somehow, that he was awake. After all these years, of course she knew, just from that bated quality to the air. She stepped delicately across cool floorboards, then scratchy rug, then cool floorboards once again—terrain she had traveled since the day she first learned to walk. She sat with no perceptible weight upon the side of the bed that used to be hers. He was lying on his back, she saw. She could begin to sift his white face from the flocked half-dark. She whispered, "Sam?"

"Yes," he said.

"You know that letter you wrote me in Bay Borough."

"Yes."

"Well, what was the line you crossed out?"

He stirred beneath the bedclothes. "Oh," he said, "I crossed out so many lines. That letter was a mess."

"I mean the very last line. The one you put so many x's through I couldn't possibly read it."

He didn't answer at first. Then he said, "I forget."

Her impulse was to stand up and leave, but she forced herself to stay. She sat motionless, waiting and waiting.

"I think," he said finally, "that maybe it was . . . well, something like what Driscoll was wondering earlier. Was there anything that would, you know. Would persuade you to come back."

She said, "Oh, Sam. All you had to do was ask."

Then he turned toward her, and Delia slipped under the blankets and he drew her close against him. Although, in fact, he still had not asked. Not in so many words.

Long after they went to sleep, the telephone rang, and Delia resurfaced gradually. This late, it had to be a patient calling. But Sam didn't even change the rhythm of his breathing; so she inched out from under his arm to reach for the phone.

"Hello?" she said.

"Mrs. Grinstead?"

"Yes."

"It's Joe Bright."

A voice as bright as his name, wide awake and chipper at the ungodly hour of—she peered at the alarm clock. One twenty-three.

"Um . . . ," she said.

"The realtor?" he prompted.

"Oh!"

"You called me? You and your daughter? Left a whole bunch of messages?"

"Oh! Yes!" she said, but she was still floundering. "Um . . ."

"I would never phone so late except you did say it was life and death, Mrs. Grinstead, and I only now got in from out of town. Wife's mother died, spur of the moment."

"Oh, I'm sorry to hear that," she said. She sat up straighter. "Um, Mr. Bright, why I called was . . ." She shifted the phone to her other ear. "My daughter has been wanting to know," she said. "Yes . . . will she be allowed to pound nails in the walls?"

There was a silence.

"Just in case they need to hang some pictures, say, or a mirror . . . ," Delia said, trailing off.

"Nails," Mr. Bright said.

"Right."

"She wanted to know if she could pound in nails."

"Right."

"Well," Mr. Bright said. "Sure. I reckon. Long as they spackle the holes upon vacating."

"Oh, they will!" Delia said. "I can promise. Thank you, Mr. Bright. Good night."

There was another silence, and then, "Good night," he said.

Delia replaced the receiver and lay down again. She had assumed Sam was still asleep, but then she heard him give a little whisking sound of amusement. She started smiling. Outside, far downtown, a train blew past. In the house, a floorboard creaked, and a moment later a foggy cough broke from the room where Nat slept.

"It's a time trip," Nat had said.

She thought of her attempt, that afternoon, to picture Adrian. She had begun with his resemblance to her high-school boyfriend, and only now did she realize that the image she had come up with happened to be Sam's, not the boyfriend's. A younger Sam, earnest and hopeful, the day he'd first walked through the door.

It had *all* been a time trip—all this past year and a half. Unlike Nat's, though, hers had been a time trip that worked. What else would you call it when she'd ended up back where she'd started, home with Sam for good? When the people she had left behind had actually traveled further, in some ways?

Now she saw that June beach scene differently. Her three children, she saw, had been staring at the horizon with the alert, tensed stillness of explorers at the ocean's edge, poised to begin their journeys. And Delia, shading her eyes in the distance, had been trying to understand why they were leaving.

Where they were going without her.

How to say goodbye.

(continued)

Gabriel García Márquez, *Of Love and Other Demons* (paper)
Peter Gethers, *The Cat Who Went to Paris*
Martha Grimes, *The End of the Pier*
Martha Grimes, *The Horse You Came In On* (paper)
Martha Grimes, *Rainbow's End* (paper)
Lewis Grizzard, *If I Ever Get Back to Georgia, I'm Gonna Nail My Feet to the Ground*
David Halberstam, *The Fifties* (2 volumes, paper)
Kathryn Harvey, *Stars*
Katharine Hepburn, *Me* (hardcover and paper)
P. D. James, *The Children of Men*
P. D. James, *Original Sin* (paper)
Naomi Judd, *Love Can Build a Bridge* (paper)
Dean Koontz, *Dark Rivers of the Heart* (paper)
Dean Koontz, *Icebound*
Judith Krantz, *Dazzle*
Judith Krantz, *Lovers* (paper)
Judith Krantz, *Scruples Two*
John le Carré, *The Night Manager* (paper)
John le Carré, *Our Game* (paper)
John le Carré, *The Secret Pilgrim*
Robert Ludlum, *The Bourne Ultimatum*
Robert Ludlum, *The Road to Omaha*
Cormac McCarthy, *The Crossing* (paper)
Audrey Meadows with Joe Daley, *Love, Alice* (paper)
James A. Michener, *Mexico* (paper)
James A. Michener, *The Novel*
James A. Michener, *Recessional* (paper)
James A. Michener, *The World Is My Home* (paper)
Sherwin B. Nuland, *How We Die* (paper)
Richard North Patterson, *Degree of Guilt*
Richard North Patterson, *Eyes of a Child* (paper)
Louis Phillips, editor, *The Random House Large Print Treasury of Best-Loved Poems*

(continued)

Maria Riva, *Marlene Dietrich* (2 volumes, paper)
Andy Rooney, *My War* (paper)
Mickey Rooney, *Life Is Too Short*
William Styron, *Darkness Visible*
Margaret Truman, *Murder at the National Cathedral*
Margaret Truman, *Murder at the Pentagon*
Margaret Truman, *Murder on the Potomac* (paper)
Donald Trump with Charles Leerhsen, *Trump:*
    *Surviving at the Top*
Anne Tyler, *Ladder of Years* (paper)
Anne Tyler, *Saint Maybe*
John Updike, *Rabbit at Rest*
Phyllis A. Whitney, *Daughter of the Stars* (paper)
Phyllis A. Whitney, *Star Flight* (paper)
Lois Wyse, *Grandchildren Are So Much Fun*
    *I Should Have Had Them First*

––––––––––

*The New York Times Large Print Crossword Puzzles*
    (paper)
Will Weng, editor, Volumes 1–3
Eugene T. Maleska, editor, Volumes 4–7
Eugene T. Maleska, editor, Omnibus Volume 1